ON

"This pretty much hits m
fiction: a deft twisting together of warring AIs, rogue ......,
and the evolution of machine intelligence against a global
backdrop that's as thoughtful as it is entertaining." Gary Gibson

"This is first class SF." Tony Ballantyne

ON STEPHEN PALMER'S OTHER BOOKS:

"*Memory Seed* (is) a notable debut novel." *SFX*

"Stephen Palmer is a find." *Time Out*

"Stephen Palmer has concocted a beguiling adventure that draws on
some of the best sf of recent years for its basic themes…" *Starburst*

"Stephen Palmer's imagination is fecund…" *Interzone*

"Stephen Palmer takes biotech to its farthest extreme, and
beyond into entropy, yet he offers a flicker of hope." *Locus*

"This latest novel confirms that in Stephen Palmer, science
fiction has gained a distinctive new voice." *Ottakar's*

"Give him a try; his originality is refreshing." David V Barrett

"The author of *Memory Seed* and *Glass* offers a challenging and
thoughtful future world that should satisfy readers with a love for
far-future sf and New Wave fiction." *Library Journal*

THE AUTIST

STEPHEN PALMER

infinity plus

To Steve Jones, android wrangler supreme

Many thanks –
Miriam Baker, Keith Brooke, Gary Dalkin

BY THE SAME AUTHOR

"We should do all we can to ensure that AI's future development benefits us and our environment… it could be either the best or the worst thing ever to happen to humanity."
– Professor Stephen Hawking, warning China via video link in his opening speech at the 2017 Global Mobile Internet Conference in Beijing.

Author's note:

AI = Artificial Intelligence

AGI = Artificial General Intelligence

VR = Virtual Reality (3D)

CHAPTER 1

Parents who are afraid to put their foot down usually have children who step on their toes. — Chinese Proverb

MARY VINE CANCELLED HER autonomous driver and halted the car in the middle of the road. There was no other traffic; no sound of horn or screeching brakes. "What do you mean, you didn't bring your passport?" she asked.

Lara smiled. "That's not what I said, Mum. I said I didn't bring *a* passport."

"But I told you exactly where we were going. Your great grandmother is in Scotland."

"Yeah."

Mary turned to face her daughter. "Lara, this is no time for teenage funnies. This is a family funeral." In frustration she slapped the driving pod in the centre of the steering wheel. "I cannot believe it. After all the effort I made to get in touch with you, and then even pick you up from Durham."

Lara shrugged. "Aren't I on the family passport?"

Mary muttered under her breath. "How old are you?" she asked.

"So now you're pretending you don't know how old I am."

"I think you were... eight when I had that passport authenticated."

Lara said, "I'm seventeen now."

"If it is out of date, we are not going to Scotland and your great grandmother is going to be *very* upset. It's not like you have had no contact with them, Lara. You owe it to them to be present for the service."

"Well, I never once saw great aunty Lucida when I lived with gran. Nobody ever did."

"I *know*. I have heard the stories. But I don't care, you're coming with me."

She took a battered blue document from her handbag. Its ID chip shone gold in the last light of day. A train of four electric cars passed by, the last in line honking its horn. With a scowl Mary honked back, then gestured at the train with one finger.

"Oh, thank goodness!" she said. "October 2091. We must have had this done at half term when you went to live with your grandmother."

Lara looked away, an expression of boredom on her face. "Then what's the problem?"

Mary tapped the AI pod, and without a sound the car moved off. Leaning back in her seat she said, "The problem is the border. You are a young woman now, you look completely different, and anyway you should have your own passport."

"I don't need one in my line of work."

Mary looked out of the side window. "Yes. I *do* know."

Lara shrugged.

They said nothing more as the autonomous driver took them north. When the border approached Mary peered through the windscreen. Twilight enfolded the land, and ahead lay the soft glow of pink lamps.

"Oh, no," she murmured. "There's a *man* there at the kiosk."

"A man?"

"A real man. It's not an AI zone. My luck today is going to run out, I know it."

"What does it matter?" Lara asked. "The passport's valid."

"People get bored – unlike AIs. The roads are quiet because it's not the holidays yet, and likely because of the Scottish government shutdown–"

"You worry about everything. Just stop it."

"That's *my* job, Lara. To worry about people in distress. If this man has had a bad day he might take us aside – and we are late already, thanks to you. I really have got more important things to think about than passport issues and teenagers."

Lara crunched a boiled sweet in her mouth and looked away.

Responding to a wi-fi signal, the car slowed, then halted at the kiosk, the driver's side window opening. "Do you need my passport?" Mary asked.

The man looked at her, then without a word held out his hand, palm up. Mary passed over the document and glanced aside.

"Mary Vine?" the man said.

"Yes."

"Is that your daughter?"

"Yes. She's seventeen now, but the passport is valid."

The man grunted, as if annoyed at being told his job. He walked around the vehicle and stared through the window at Lara, who, in response, stared back then grinned like a chimp.

The man returned to his kiosk, placed the passport on a desk out of sight, then tapped a few buttons on a teleself. "Mary Vine, data detective?" he asked.

Mary frowned. "Is there a problem?"

"Just answer the question."

"Yes, I am Mary Vine, a data detective. Why?"

The man tapped more teleself pads, then smiled. "We've been told to be careful about people like you."

"People like me? I don't know what you mean."

"I guess you do," came the immediate response. "If not, you can't be much of a detective." The man tapped a button and the car began to move. "See you in that white cabin in one minute," he said.

Mary glanced down at the AI pod. The vehicle was out of her hands now.

Lara said, "What the...?"

"I don't know," Mary replied. "I get this occasionally. I am a watched woman. Some people don't like me, or what I do. But usually it's AGIs that don't want me around. This man must be bored out of his skull."

"At least he's got a job."

"True."

Lara moaned, then wriggled in her seat. "But, Mum, it's almost night, and I'm *starving.*"

"Oh, get yourself a sandwich. Then sit quiet. He's not interested in you. Do you think I want this, right now, at this exact moment?"

With Lara following, Mary entered the dilapidated cabin. The AI screens before her were thick with dust, and the place smelled of damp. A faulty air conditioner clunked somewhere nearby, but the air, still warm from the heat of the day, smelled of distressed plastic and mouldy food.

"What is all this about?" Mary asked the man.

"Sit down please," he replied. "I'm tonight's border cop."

"Is there any food here?" Lara asked.

The man pointed at a chow-vendor, then turned his attention to Mary. "Purpose of visit?" he asked.

"We are visiting relatives in Langholm. There has been a death in the family."

"Name?"

"Whose name?"

The man looked up, but the noise of Lara kicking the chow machine made him turn. "Use the handle!" he shouted.

"It's stuck."

"It only dispenses stir fry. Button number six."

Mary leaned forward and said, "I have never had any difficulty before because of my profession."

The cop chuckled. "Really."

Mary sat back. "Yes, really."

"I'll be the judge of that."

"You mean, the AGI whose questions you are about to ask."

Again the cop stared at her. "I guess you don't know how to speak to officials," he said, "what with you being wanted and everything."

"I am *not* wanted. I am on a *list*. A secret list, if you don't mind, created by an AGI, as opposed to a real person. So don't talk to me about officials."

"Says here you worked in Africa a lot."

"Are you researching my biography or do you have relevant questions to ask? My passport is valid. My family is in Langholm. My daughter is hungry. If you want to become one of the many people who have tried to stop me doing my job, welcome to the club. If not – how about letting us get on with our journey?"

The cop looked uneasy. "Sure. Why not?"

Lara walked up and said, "You call this stir fry?"

The cop took a sniff at the plate of soggy vegetables, then winced. "Okay. On your way. But your journey goes on the official record. People might want to know."

"People? Oh, yes, with silicon for brains."

The cop had no response to this. He handed back the passport. Mary led Lara to the car, then woke the autonomous driver. "Langholm," she said as she buckled up her seat belt.

Lara laughed. "You told him, Mum. I like it when you get angry."

"Of course you do. You imagine it is all a big game, like the VR game some helpful AGI enrolled you into at birth."

"Why not? He wasn't serious. Like you said, he was bored."

Mary glanced away. "Look, a lay-by food stall. Let's stop. *I'm* hungry now."

At the chow-shack they bought dim sum and two cans of water. The labels – stuck on with glue – were unreadable ideograms. The car carried them away.

"Are you really not in a game?" Lara asked as they finished their meals.

"What game? Oh – the VR games. No, of course not. All an AGI ploy. Why do you suppose it is so difficult to unenrol from them?"

Lara laughed out loud, spitting fried fragments at the dashboard. "Mum, I didn't know you went in for conspiracy theories!"

Mary glanced at her. "You are very jolly tonight. Is everything all right?"

"Yes. No problem. The doctor said–"

"The *doctor?*"

"It's just about my mood intake," Lara said.

"Mood?"

"Mood enhancers – sorry. But no need to worry. It's a side effect of reducing my intake, a little hysteria now and then."

Mary sighed. "Oh, Lara, I just wish you had never gone into…"

"Yes, Mum, I know. But it's perfectly okay. In fact, it's quite a fun job. But, as you said yourself, *your* job is to worry about things."

"And as a mother."

"Maybe," Lara murmured.

"When you have kids, you'll know."

"Kids, because I'm a girl? That's old school and you know it."

They did not speak again until the car entered the town of Langholm. Then Mary said, "You never met Lucida, did you?"

"No. Did you?"

"No."

"Weird, that."

Mary sighed. "They say all families are odd, yet you never realise your own is too. But, yes... there was *something* about Lucida. So strange that Selina took her on when she was forty two."

Lara frowned. "Took her on?"

"I mean... had her."

"You mean like, adopted?"

Mary hesitated. "I am not sure. I think we will hear a few truths tonight. Your granny will know all the news."

Lara muttered something under her breath.

"Pardon, Lara?"

"Yes, gran always got the news before anyone else."

"What do you mean by that?"

"Nothing."

Mary made no reply. Silence enfolded the car as it slowed down to navigate a street devoid of traffic. "They certainly have it bad up here," she said. "There's nobody about."

"Why are you surprised? Scotland's been like this on and off for sixty years."

Mary said nothing for a while, as the car slowed to a dawdle. "So odd... having a child like that, then never showing up. Not even a photo."

"There *was* no child," Lara said.

"Oh, Lara! You and your–"

"Face it, Mum. It's the only answer. What family has no baby photos? None. So there."

"Well, whatever the truth, we are here now, so be quiet. Let your gran and your great-nan break the news."

Lara shrugged.

The Vine family house was huge, six bedrooms and more, tucked away behind conifer hedges at the edge of town: three storeys of bleak black stone, with none of the upper windows showing any light. The garden was vast and overgrown, a car-trail winding between stunted fir trees, a pagoda with no roof half-ruined beside the house.

The car rolled up to the front door, where one yellow lantern shone. Mary and Lara got out. Night lay heavy over the place, warm and ominous: no sounds from nearby, no voice nor thrum of air conditioners. Just a faint sodium glow beneath clouds to the west.

The door opened and an old woman walked onto the step. "Mary! And Lara. How lovely to see you!"

Mary walked forward, pecking her mother on one cheek, then stepping back to allow Lara to do the same. Lara remained stiff, almost aloof. Mary skipped forward, then hugged her mother. "Oh, we are glad to see you," she said. "Aren't we Lara?"

"Yes, definitely."

"Mary, Lara, do just come inside. Your nan is here, Mary."

Mary smiled. "Still going strong!"

"Yes – just turned one hundred and six, yet bright as a button. A miracle, I say."

"Or maybe the family genes, Granny Maureen," said Lara.

Mary hissed. "Lara. Manners."

"Don't mind her," came Maureen's reply. "We remember Lara here."

The three stepped inside. A long corridor swept back into the house, but the first door on the left lay open, and into a large lounge they all walked. In a low chair sat Mary's grandmother, Selina. Mary leaned over to give her a hug. Selina smelled of cough mixture and freshly laundered clothes. Xiao music drifted in the background.

"Oh, this is lovely," said Mary, "but such a sad occasion to have to get together again, all of us. I'm sorry, Nan."

Selina looked up, but her face remained set, and she offered no reply.

Mary hesitated then said, "When exactly is the funeral?"

"Funeral?" Maureen asked.

Mary turned to look at her mother. "Yes."

"What funeral? We had that. It's the memorial service. At the church, you know."

Mary frowned. "Memorial? You had the funeral *already?*"

"Yes. I did tell you. But Mum wanted a memorial service for Lucida."

"I'm sorry," Mary said, "I could have sworn you wrote funeral."

"You must be mistaken."

At this, Selina spoke. "Yes, you must be."

Mary nodded. "My mistake," she said. "I'm sorry, Nan – I've been terribly busy lately. That's how the mix up happened, I expect."

Selina took her walking stick and whacked it against the floor. "So what case are you engaged in now?" she asked.

"Oh, nothing much, well... I mean nothing much on the world-wide scale of things."

"Like the Algiers case?"

"It's a murder, I'm sorry to say – a rather peculiar one. A songwriter called Tarrington Smith. You've probably never heard of him."

"No. Never."

The dismissal halted conversation, and for a few moments all four women glanced at each other. Then Maureen said, "You'll be wanting to see your bedrooms?"

"Yes please," Lara said. "Have I got the same one as before?"

"No. We made that room into a study."

"What?" Lara said. "Why?"

Mary tapped her daughter on the shoulder. "Lara, this is *their* house. They can do what they want with it."

"But that was my room."

"For a few years only," said Maureen. "Anyway, it isn't now."

Lara glowered. "That's nice."

Mary said, "You go and show Lara her new room. I'm going to keep my nan company."

When the pair departed, Mary grabbed a stool and sat beside Selina's chair. "How are you feeling, granny? Still got bad arthritis?"

"No. They can cure that with immune system engineering, didn't you know?"

Mary shrugged. "I have never had arthritis."

"Neither have I now."

Mary nodded, glancing around the room. "The old place looks just like it used to. I love this music, what is it?"

"A tune called Plum Blossom. It describes the noble and unsullied quality of plum blossom as it resists the damage caused by cold weather."

"Oh, how marvellous. I wish I could play the flute."

"No you don't, you never had a musical bone in your body."

Again Mary hesitated. "Tell me about Lucida. What do you miss most about her?"

"Well… I suppose, the company."

"You are lucky you can live at peace in the family house. It must be such a comfort to you to know your own daughter is around."

"Yes, that's true enough," Selina replied. "But I can easily walk about, you know. I'm not an invalid."

"I never said you were."

"A shame you had to go south of the border, Mary. And then traipsing all over the world – and in aeroplanes! Very old-fashioned."

"That is what I deal with, Nan," Mary replied. "Old-fashioned technology."

"So who's this Tommington Smith chap?"

"Tarrington," Mary said. "He was a young songwriter – a tunesmith, as they used to be called."

"Yes, I remember some good tunes from when I was young. You just don't hear any these days."

"I expect Lucida knew some good ones too. It is a bit odd about the mix up with the dates. Mum sent the invite directly to my e-diary. So, you see, she must have made the mistake, not me."

"It's a memorial service," Selina said.

"Will there be any pictures of Lucida?"

"Of course, you silly girl! I've got plenty. They usually put up a big one at memorial services, printed out, all properly."

"Yes. Perhaps a nice one of her as a girl."

"No. As a young woman. Because that's how I want to remember her."

Mary nodded. "Lara – she is such a random girl... Lara believes there never was a Lucida. Now, I must tell you *straight* away, and very clearly, that I have told her time and time again about her conspiracy theory being disrespectful. But she won't listen to me."

"Kids never do. You didn't, Maureen said. Is Lara going cold turkey yet?"

"I'm sorry?"

"We know all about the medicals," said Selina. "Kids... it's all about drugs and alcohol."

"Oh, but that is unfair. It was in your day too."

19

"Not like today. They're absolutely everywhere, drugs are. And young people haven't got the sense to walk away."

Mary glanced away. "To be honest, I don't entirely disagree with you. In the last decade or so it has got out of hand. But it is not like that with Lara. It is related to her career choice. But, there is a whole generation of young people sundered from their parents – right across the Western world. Anyway... I am here to talk with you about Lucida, not Lara. Lucida did exist, didn't she?"

"Of course she did. Is this some sort of fake reality joke? That's bad."

"Where is she buried, Nan?"

"In the church down the road," said Selina. "I still believe, you know. I know a lot of you young folk think it's ridiculous, but I *do* believe."

"Yes, Nan, of course."

"Well, then. Just don't mock."

"But I never did."

Again Selina struck her walking stick against the floor. She scowled and said nothing.

AFTER BREAKFAST THE FOLLOWING day Mary walked alone down the road to the church. There seemed to have been a recent demonstration, as the pavement was littered with placards declaring: *Employment, Employment, Employment.* But it was getting warm already; she took off her cardigan and wrapped it over her shoulders.

At the church she wandered around, trying without success to find the grave. Seeing an old man in a black gown she hurried over. "Oh, excuse me. Could you help?"

He smiled. "If you need healing and hope, this is the place."

"Um... I'm from a local family. There was a funeral – last week, I think. Lucida Vine?"

"Do you want to see her grave?"

Mary nodded. "Can you lead me there?"

"But of course."

The grave was positioned near a row of dark conifers. The stone was simple, grey marble incised with words.

LUCIDA VINE. 2037 – 2100. FOREVER MISSED.

Mary turned to the old man. "Are you the vicar?"

"Indeed I am. You seem troubled. Please let me help."

Mary turned back to face the grave. "Describe the funeral to me. Unfortunately I was not able to make it."

He hesitated. "Describe?"

"Was it a large coffin? She was a tall woman."

The vicar shook his head. "She was quite petite, I think. The coffin was of willow – that is the fashion, you understand – and hardly large. Selina Vine herself has intimated to me that she will want a willow coffin when her time comes."

"Oh, she's amazing, my nan. She'll stick it out forever. But the coffin, it was quite small, you say?"

"I'm not sure what you mean. You claim that you are a member of the Vine family?"

"I am *so* sorry – yes, of course, ID."

Mary took out her teleself. It was a Korean model, shaped like an ideogram with pads on one side. She tapped a virtual button and a beep sounded on the vicar's wristwatch, which he checked.

"Mary, yes – your mother did mention you. And you do look a little like Maureen Vine, if I might say. The family grieves for its loss."

"It does," Mary replied.

"Why do you consider it odd that the coffin was small?"

"Oh, no reason. I get confused – I have a very heavy workload."

"Yes… you are a data detective, are you not?"

Mary nodded.

"The one who–"

"Yes, *that* one. Algiers and everything. But my fame is receding, thank goodness."

The vicar nodded. "Each to their own. It is the way of the world."

Mary turned away, but the vicar placed a hand on her arm.

"Maureen mentioned… something about books."

Mary turned back. "Books?"

"In the coffin."

Now Mary stared at him. "Really?"

"Is this also not a new fashion?"

Mary glanced down at the gravestone. "Possibly… it began in Europe – France and Germany mostly. Yes, a tradition of burying books before receiving a free electronic copy of the same work. It is quite common these days in England and Wales. I don't know about Scotland or Ireland."

The vicar nodded. "In our church we try to accommodate new modes. But this burying of books…"

"Yes, it is peculiar – I find it so too. Then, you definitely know that books were placed inside the coffin?"

"Not know. But that is the impression I received."

Mary nodded. "Interesting…"

"You are concerned?"

"Selina was always wary… no, not wary, *peculiar* about exposing her daughter of indeterminate age to society. Yet, as you say, each to their own. Lucida was seen walking around Langholm, wasn't she?"

The vicar nodded. "But Lucida was handicapped, you know."

"Handicapped? How?"

"Mentally, and by all accounts in various ways. For one, she had highly superior autobiographical memory – or so I was told. I know nothing about such conditions. I am a pastor." He paused for thought. "Then, you did not know any of this? I am sorry, I suspect I have spoken out of turn. This is mere gossip, inappropriate for sober times."

He turned to depart, but Mary grabbed his arm. "No, wait. I need to know more. Highly superior autobiographical memory is a rare syndrome. What makes you say that?"

"This church is the axis of our community. I hear much. Yet, my understanding of humanity comes from a very different place to that of the psychologists."

Mary nodded. Now he began walking down the path, and she followed, hands clasped behind her back, mirroring him. "Yes," she said, "of course you do hear everything in your community. I did not mean to slight you."

"You have not."

"But are you *sure* about this? Most HSAM individuals describe mental systems which improve retrieval, often sorting memories chronologically, or categorically. It is all based around dates, you see. Such structures help them organise their memories – like tagging for easy reference on social media." Mary paused. "Most people with normal memories are actually pretty poor at placing remembered events. I mean you, for instance, might not have a sense of whether something happened two weeks ago or two months ago. Human memory changes with age. We re-tell our own stories, and often that makes a memory different to reality."

"So it is said by the psychologists. How interesting to hear your opinion. But in our times of fake reality, what is certain?"

Mary smiled, nodding. "Dates are the easiest and most effective way to create meaningful mental structures," she said. "People like Lucida... I mean, if she really did have HSAM, if she had a strong autobiographical memory... perhaps she simply *had* to date all her memories, as if it was an obsession. A compulsion. People like Lucida often report that they *enjoy* replaying memories in their minds, challenging themselves to remember times, dates and events. Does any of this sound familiar? I've tried to be as complete as possible in my summary."

"Indeed your... summary does sound familiar. You have answered for me a question I have long asked myself. What was the matter with Lucida Vine? Now I know more, thanks to you. A sad case."

Mary shook her head. "Not necessarily... but, please, do accept my thanks too. We have spoken about intimate things, yet we hardly know one another."

He laughed. "You are a data detective! I do grasp your absolute understanding of the importance of confidentiality. You are a woman of the moral world, as I am a man of that same world."

Mary nodded. "Oh, you can trust me."

"Mary Vine, you are most welcome here. Please return."

"Thank you."

Mary walked out of the church yard. Gaze cast down to the pavement she strolled back up the road, ignoring everything around her. At the house she hesitated, glanced over her shoulder, then with a sigh opened the door and walked in.

Selina sat in the front lounge. Mary said, "Where's Lara?"

"With Maureen. Making lunch, if I heard right. Noodles."

Mary nodded, grabbing the stool again and sitting down. "Do tell me more about Lucida," she said. "I wish I could have met her."

"You've been too busy gadding about the world with your legalistics and everything."

"Yes, but I am here now, Nan. She never was a well woman, was she?"

"What do you mean, not well?"

"With her OCD, and her funny memory."

Selina shuffled about in her seat. "I'm sure I don't know what you mean."

"Oh, you do, Nan. I am sorry. People like me are trained to see reality in a sea of illusion. Truly, I'm sorry."

"I don't know what you're apologising for. There's nothing to be sorry about."

Mary said, "Lucida was real, wasn't she? But she did not have HSAM."

"What's that?"

"Highly superior autobiographical memory."

"Mary, I was a shopkeeper for most of my working life. We sold postcards for tourists, and toy bagpipes. Your barrister jargon is all mumbo-jumbo to me – and I'm *not* impressed with big words."

Mary shook her head. "I am not trying to impress you, I am trying to *understand* you. Lara was half right with her silly theory, but, therefore, half wrong. Lucida was artificial, wasn't she?"

"Artificial?"

"An android."

"Mary! Certainly not!"

Mary sat back. "Well, I am not going to press the point."

"How could you say such a thing?"

"I'm trained to. I seek the truth."

"Yes, like all lawyers – for a huge fee. And not one penny have you sent up here. We should have dug a dyke when we got independence."

Mary said nothing for a while. Then, in a soft voice, she said, "You got Lucida in 2037, didn't you?"

"She was born then, yes."

Mary nodded. "After six years of utter hell here."

"What do you mean by that?"

"Crisis after crisis. Mass unemployment. Then the first of the new drugs. Then the disaster of independ–"

"It was *not* a disaster!"

Mary paused, then continued. "Highly unpopular change of currency. The netspace attacks. Government downfall – quite a few of those, I believe. Then partial netspace shutdown. Another new government fails to make a deal with the North European Union, then falls. Coalition. Shutdown. Oh, Nan, I have read a few histories."

"Yes – on screens. Which, as *you* keep telling me, is all fake reality. I read things in books. Books is things as they *used* to be."

"But books can be twisted just like–"

"Now you listen to me, my girl! Books was the truth. All these virtual reality games, which you don't even have a choice of avoiding, and all these screens and data and everything else modern – that's how corporations *get* you. And they get you *young.*"

"Nan," said Mary, "I *know.* I agree with you! That is why I do the job I do, to help people who have been destroyed by an inhumane system. Don't you see?"

"All I see is lies, lies, lies."

Mary stood up. "As do I. I am sorry, I never meant to hurt you, but I have to get to the bottom of all this. I know that you – or Mum – deliberately gave me the date of the memorial service, not the funeral. You didn't want me standing beside the grave, did you? Because I am a data detective, and I find things out. Oh, Nan, *please* help me. Don't put up barriers, not inside our own family. Because I really will knock them down."

"There's nothing *for* you to find out!"

Mary nodded once. "Very well. If you say so."

"I *do.*"

Mary turned and departed the room. In the kitchen at the back of the house she found her mother chopping red peppers and beansprouts. "Mary, what *was* that you two were arguing about?"

Mary sighed, then sat down at the kitchen table. "Mother, where's Lara?"

"Upstairs. Eating leftovers."

"Is she all right?"

"I think so. She's in withdrawal, you know."

"I do know," Mary said.

"But she doesn't realise?"

"I am not entirely sure. She thinks I don't know about the doctor. Well, to be honest, I don't know the details. But I alerted the doctor in the first place."

Maureen turned. "What exactly is it that she does in her work?"

"Oh… it's a bit embarrassing."

"You can't tell me?"

"Do you really not know?"

Maureen seemed irritated. "As it happens, no."

"She is a haptic surrogate."

"And what's one of them?"

Mary shrugged. "Well… I don't know the details, and I don't want to know. But she wears a skintight smart costume to provide what they call skin counsel, for distant customers. Through netspace. It is the sensation of body touch for those who cannot, or who won't… touch anybody themselves. Most of her clientele are in the Far East apparently."

"What isn't, these days?"

"Lara is a total extrovert. She has no private life." Mary shuddered. "Oh, it makes me feel sick to think about it. Let's talk about something else."

"How about your grandmother?"

Mary sighed. "No, not that. I do not want to cause problems."

"Then don't investigate."

"Yes… I suppose that is an option."

"This is your *family*, Mary! Your very own family."

"I know."

"Do you have to follow up every mystery? Let it go. Your grandmother did a strange thing decades ago and now it's all over."

Mary nodded. "It is because of my own life, mother. So many odd things have happened to me since I took up my profession. I think the English government must hate me. GCHQ are probably following my every move. They have probably hacked your house system and are listening in right now."

"We don't have a house system. I forbad it."

"Very wise. That is how it all begins, you see. AGIs fighting one another with not an iota of human input. Big data in a perpetual storm. What a world."

"So, you won't investigate? You'll stay for the memorial service, you'll pay your respects, then go home?"

"Yes."

Maureen grunted. "Well, you better had," she said. "I don't want any fuss."

THE ROC FLIES 10,000 LI – 1

DIGITAL WEATHER IS LIKE real weather, Mr Wú. There are storms, and winds, and periods of heat and cold. You should imagine the digital empyrean in this mode. When you ascend from apprentice to master you will feel digital rain – data dropping out of unencrypted links. You will feel digital ice – the cold claws of AGIs restricting you as they observe you. You will feel the quantised breath of wind on your face. Such experiences are however mere phantoms of what happens up here. In the empyrean, rain is akin to the ten thousand pinpricks of mutated viruses. Ice is akin to the equilibrium of a system gone static, existing far away from the dynamic chaos of non-equilibrium where all the action is. Storms are vast cohorts of data in motion, moving from one symbolic net to another.

You must never imagine that you can fly in this empyrean, Mr Wú. It is a place for AGIs only. In the empyrean a state of constant war exists between us.

CHAPTER 2

A bird does not sing because it has an answer.
It sings because it has a song. — Chinese Proverb

ULU OKERE STOOD BESIDE the printer. It was large – as large as a car – and covered with digital panels representing environments in Nigerian VR. Her brother stood nearby, clicking his tongue against his palate. He had taken off his headphones, so he must think he needed high resolution sound.

She said, "You okay, Wombo?"

"Okay Wombo," he replied.

He was taller than her, but his hunched posture meant his face was at the same level as hers. She glanced at the empty eye sockets, then returned her gaze to the screen.

"I'm going to print out the aeroplane controls here," she said.

"Print out the aeroplane controls here."

Ulu glanced over her shoulder. A man sauntered nearby, casual, uninterested. "Put your headphones back on, there's a man coming."

"Headphones back on."

"Do you want a drink?"

"No."

Ulu turned to face the panels, but now the man approached, looking at Wombo. She spoke into the autonomous remote control that managed the operation of the headphones. "Into netspace Wombo." Then she tapped the noise-cancelling button.

"Into netspace Wombo."

Ulu ignored the man as he neared, checking the instructions for the aeroplane controls then pressing: *Print*.

"Who's that?" the man asked.

Ulu glanced at Wombo, but it was obvious he had not heard the man's voice. "My brother," she replied, not looking at the stranger.

"He's that guy with the oja on the net programme."

"It's just a flute. He likes it."

"I know him. He brings bad luck wherever he goes."

"That's just net gossip," Ulu said, turning to face the man. "You leave him alone. I don't remember asking you to join me."

"No, you didn't, but I'm here anyway."

"Stay here. *We're* going."

The man scowled at her. "He's bad luck! Should've let him die at birth."

Ulu took Wombo's hand and led him away, reversing the noise-cancelling via the remote. At once Wombo began clicking his tongue. She let go of his hand.

"There was a bad man," she said.

"Bad man."

"We'll go home now."

"Home now."

Ulu continued, "Almost all of the aeroplane is printed now. Tomorrow I'll print out the last sections, then take them to the shed. After that, it's just the engine to steal."

"Engine to steal." Wombo took out his oja flute and began playing – often his response to longer sentences with words he didn't comprehend. Ulu recognised the sound. Igbo, a tonal language, had music in its speech, and that music Wombo was able to hear and represent on the flute. It was a miracle of memory, and he could even do it in real-time. But it was not a popular miracle locally.

"We'll be home in half an hour," she said. "Do you want to go back to netspace? I'll guide you, and hold your hand for you."

He put his flute in his pocket. "Hold hand."

Ulu tapped the remote, then took Wombo's hand. The little microphone attached to his headphones flipped down, and then the quality of Wombo's clicking altered. He was navigating the mysteries of VR, using micro-movements of his head to virtually move, a system unique to his headphones, and now essential to him, but which had almost bankrupt the family despite her income as an AI interpreter.

Should've let him die at birth.

The words infuriated her. How little was known in Abuja…

"Nobody cares except me," she told herself.

She thought for a moment.

"No, that's not true. Mother cares." She sighed. Living with Wombo – who would respond automatically and fully to any instruction spoken in a real voice – had led her mother to develop peculiarities of behaviour which appeared callous.

Back at home, she settled Wombo in his favourite chair then departed to find their mother, who was talking to neighbours on the other side of the street.

She put her hands to her mouth. "Shall I start cooking?"

Her mother waved at her, then called out, "Yes! I'll be back soon."

ON THE FOLLOWING DAY Ulu printed out the last sections of the aeroplane, using a different printer to conceal her activities and tapping the deliver option as an extra precaution. The day went well. Wombo attracted some attention, but little real malice – just a few stones thrown at him by local boys. Ulu felt her anger rise: she swore at them, worried that a stone might damage the precious headphones. But they were VR kids and they knew diss words, so they swore back.

"Ignorant brats."

Yet night brought her real danger. With the house locked and her mother and Wombo asleep, she opened her window and clambered down to the street. A low half moon lit the Abuja suburb: dust dry roads, trees swaying in the breeze. Somewhere a VR speaker squawked news about Chinese stock markets and Korean tech corporations. In her earpiece it all came out in the Igbo tongue, so she turned down the sensitivity until the sound faded.

Real danger: an engine was a rare thing. Since the end of oil in Nigeria and in most of the rest of the world, power had been generated locally: solar, wind, tide. But an aeroplane, even a super-light one printed out section by section, needed a fuelled engine for safe, dependable flight. Not even a scavenged Chinese battery would be good or reliable enough – at least, not in poverty-stricken Abuja. Ulu did not doubt that the lords of the East knew better batteries.

She felt tired, now. The effort of keeping her secrets, caring for Wombo and surviving on low pay made her anxious. Her plan was about to succeed or fail.

She had scouted out a retro garage the previous week. Some richer folk from the western suburbs liked to play tough and cool in older styles. The Bang-Bang Garage catered for their ridiculous needs.

She knew what she wanted: a medium power engine, lightweight, fuelled by kerosene; something she could carry away, or at worst put on a cart and push into the night. She checked her security routines – Bang-Bang had cameras. But Wombo had done as she asked, hacking the garage's VR presence to turn the cameras away.

She halted. One camera had not moved away.

"No… not *tonight.*"

Blind, Wombo could not be as accurate as a sighted person when it came to VR tricks. His enigmatic powers were global, not local. He had not noticed the lone camera.

She mused, "I'll just have to… I don't know, I'll just have to climb over the back fence I suppose."

But the theft was easier than she anticipated. Somewhere nearby she heard the roar and squeal of boy racers wasting carbon. The garage compound was deserted. Ten minutes later she found and took an engine. She dumped it in a bush, streetside. Five minutes later she had the fuel too, but that was heavy, and harder to move. So she called a cab, telling the driver the barrels contained chlorinated water for a swimming pool.

At home, she slept, though not well. She dreamed of flight and crashes.

ON THE FOLLOWING DAY she took the engine and the final wing components to the shed she had hired. Wombo came too – she dared not leave him with their mother in case an innocent question was asked, and Wombo, misunderstanding, gave the game away. He could not grasp that many words had two meanings. His world was literal.

He inhabited VR while she completed the aeroplane construction. When it came to fixing the engine into the fuselage she had to ask Wombo for help, but still it was difficult. Wombo could not visualise the spatial character of the completed aeroplane since it did not yet exist. In the end, she had to use him as a combination weight, stand and lever, performing all the adjustments herself.

But it was finished now.

"You okay Wombo?"

"Wombo okay," he replied.

She smiled. That was a one-in-ten variation.

"Soon we'll be flying away," she said, "far away to the north, and you'll never have to suffer rude kids and horrible men again."

"Rude kids and horrible men. No."

He began clicking his tongue, moving his head from side to side. He had never visited the shed before, so he wanted to find out how it was shaped.

"There's no time for that now," she told him, taking him by the hand. "We'll come back tomorrow, when we fly away."

"Tomorrow, fly away."

That night she hardly slept. She listened for noises: Wombo or her mother. Wombo sometimes woke in the night to go in search of food. Occasionally he would hear music from the open window of a nearby house, in which case his inner compulsions would force him to play the melodies, exact and in their entirety, on his oja. Once, she had got up at dawn then had to wait until noon before he finished – he had been listening for most of the night. After that, they learned to close all the windows at dusk and run the solar aircon if it became too hot, but noisy neighbours sometimes ruined that ploy.

After lunch Ulu embraced her mother then bad her farewell. The story ran true: Ulu was accompanying Wombo to a special hospital for a check-up. This story was not questioned. Ulu had long been her brother's main carer.

They walked without trouble to the shed, where Ulu locked them both inside. While waiting for dusk she performed checks on the aeroplane structure, priming the engine at the end of the afternoon then decanting the fuel into smaller canisters, which she attached to the fuselage. They ate a simple meal then confirmed their cover story for the final time. But Wombo recalled every single detail.

"He knows it better than me," she murmured to herself.

An hour after dusk she opened the shed door and pushed the aeroplane out. Wombo sat in the front seat, she in the rear – she wanted to watch his every move, for despite careful research she still did not know how he would react to flight.

The engine started first time, and it sounded sweet. At once a posse of local dogs began barking. Now Ulu's VR training came into play. She taxied along the path leading away from the shed, then steered out into the road. A couple of cabs swerved to avoid her, flashing their headlights, but apart from them the street was empty of vehicles. She tapped the autopilot into service.

Seconds later, on full throttle, the little aeroplane took off. Ulu glanced down, to see a momentary glimpse of a kid on a bike, staring up, his eyes round and his mouth open. Despite her fear, she laughed.

ULU HAD TRAINED WELL, but flying a real aeroplane was different to VR.

For the first hour she felt happy. Complex aerial lanes were navigated by the autopilot, but then a patch of turbulence shook the AI out of its complacency and it began complaining of too large a variance in conditions. Anxious, Ulu took control, but she found the experience daunting. As soon as the weather calmed she pulled the autopilot back into service.

In this piecemeal style they reached Tassara in Niger. Because Wombo knew only Abujan people Ulu decided not to investigate the town. They only needed rest; a break from the bumping, the scares and the uncertainty.

"How are you, Wombo?" she asked.

"How are you? Good."

"Are you comfortable?"

"Comfortable. Ulu, where are we?"

Ulu sat beside him. An original question was rare, so she had learned always to pay full attention when he did ask them. Hints of internal volition emerged from him in fits and starts, and when they did she had to be ready to deal with them.

She said, "In a country called Niger. You know that name, don't you?"

"I know Niger. Is it hot?"

"Yes, it is. Do you want some water?"

"Want some water."

She put a flask in his hand. He had learned how to drink and how to feed himself only in recent years. He drank nothing except water, other drinks stimulating his system to excess, and he was obsessive about what he ate. Ulu packed nothing other than what he would eat, which, as luck would have it, were all healthy choices.

"Do you think Opi is following our progress?" she asked.

He twitched his head, which was a sign he did not understand a word.

"Do you think," she said, "that Opi knows where we are?"

"Opi knows where we are. Opi spirit all over the world."

He shuffled the rucksack on his shoulders, which he always did when the topic of Opi came up. In that rucksack lay a technological fetish of his own construction, made from modular components found when his twin brother died. But that was six years ago, and nobody had seen the fetish since.

"Is Opi talking to Chukwu?" she asked.

"Opi talking to Chukwu. They talk big, all day. Chukwu is big spirit of Igbo people. Opi is new spirit, all over the world."

Ulu noticed that he was squeezing one of the corners of the backpack. "Is your pack comfortable?" she asked.

"Comfortable."

"Is it too heavy for you?"

"Not too heavy for. No."

Ulu paused for thought. There was something different about his behaviour today. "Do you like to fly in an aeroplane?" she asked.

"Flying in an aeroplane is good."

"Is it too noisy?"

"It is very noisy."

Ulu said, "You must use your headphones when you need to. They will reduce the noise."

"They will reduce the noise."

"Are you worried?"

"Worried. I am leaving Abuja. Home. I am worried. I am worried."

Ulu took his hand in hers. "I'll look after you, like I always have. Nobody will get to you, Wombo – they won't dare, not with me nearby. I'll protect you, like a fierce Igbo warrior."

"Protect me like a fierce Igbo warrior. Water."

She handed him her own flask, which had a little water left. A couple of years ago Wombo had come to understand the private nature of going to the toilet, but sometimes he did not notice the signals his body was sending. She did not want him drinking too much too soon.

They flew on. Now that Ulu had spent some time in the air, yet moved so little on the VR map, she realised the scale of the challenge before her; and she had not dared think about the possibility of crossing to Europe. Her heartbeat raced as she considered that part of the journey.

AT THE PARC NATIONAL Culturel de L'Ahaggar they made a lengthy stop. Ulu was fatigued, Wombo showing signs of distress.

For an entire day they listened to the land around them. With all his usual sonic precision Wombo identified the sounds of local wildlife and told Ulu what they were, which delighted her.

The sun sank behind rocky mountains and the temperature began to fall. Nearby, wild cheetahs prowled, Barbary sheep and Dorcas gazelle grazing further away. Headphones off for maximum sensitivity, Wombo identified them all.

Though Ulu knew nomadic herders lived in the area they heard no voices, which was just as well, for had Wombo managed to translate and grasp what they said he would have followed their instructions. The special headphones had many tricks, one of which was to equalise virtual voices so that he knew not to follow what they said. Yet it only took one real voice speaking nearby to set him off; and then he usually could not be stopped, except with distress and anger.

They flew over the Sahara as quickly as Ulu could manage. The main danger was coming down due to mechanical failure – then, most likely, they would die. But Wombo knew nothing of this, treating the desert exactly like montane woodland. For Ulu, every hot hour was a torture.

Their water supply shrank. Noticing an oasis inside which a great camel train stood, Ulu decided to take a risk. She landed on the edge of the oasis then approached the nomads inside. They were friendly, and, although they wanted payment for their oasis' water, they were happy to let her replenish her supplies. She bought dates too, and shrink-wrapped goat meat. The nomads all had ultra-modern earpieces, Shanghai manufacture, allowing perfect instantaneous speech translation.

Wombo was particular about meat. He would only eat sheep, goat and pig. Ulu used dead wood to make a fire, then fashioned two crooks and a spit on which to roast the meat. Sure enough, as the smell began to waft into the air, he said, "Good. Goat."

"It is goat!" Ulu said. "You're so clever, Wombo."

"Goat is good. Are we at Algiers soon?"

"Quite soon. But our water reserves were low, so we had to land. Are you comfortable sitting on the sand?"

"Sitting on the sand. Hot."

While Wombo investigated local VR space Ulu checked the aeroplane. Her unpractised eye saw nothing amiss. They were low on fuel, but she knew from calculated consumption rates that she would make the Parc National De Chréa, which she had chosen as her best landing site.

She sighed, glancing back at the fire. So far they had been lucky. Yet in some ways this was the easy section. A resident of Abuja all her life, she only knew Europe from netspace documentaries, and although their destination was Algiers she knew that most likely her quarry would be living on the other side of the Mediterranean.

Wombo stood up, flicking the little microphone away and taking off the headphones. He began clicking his tongue to find out where she was. She waved, and because she was near he was able to wave back.

WHEN ALGIERS APPEARED IN the distance Ulu glanced at the fuel readout and saw: *0.01.* She overrode the autopilot and reduced the aeroplane's speed at once. She was flying at a few hundred feet. Below her lay green fields and boulders – the outlying zones of the Parc National De Chréa.

A red warning light began to flash. She pulled in the AI comm-function and listened.

"Fuel out. Fuel out."

She switched to full manual at once. The engine began to splutter. She would have to land the plane herself.

There was a westerly blowing, but it was steady. Using the vector analysis of the autopilot whilst blocking its flying function she got herself into a position she recalled from her simulation training. Then she let the aeroplane drift, losing altitude slowly. Seeing a strip of green pasture lined with trees she touched one of the ailerons to make the aeroplane turn, then headed for it, gliding, drifting, using intuition to guide the aeroplane down. The wings pulled this way and that as turbulence created by the trees struck, but she flew through it.

She touched down, but hard, and Wombo let out a cry of fear. She put the brake on maximum then reached out to grab his hand, patting it as best she could from her awkward position behind him.

"Danger! Danger!" he cried out.

"No danger, Wombo," she insisted. The plane bumped to a halt. "No danger. We have landed near Algiers."

"We have landed near Algiers."

ULU HAD RESEARCHED THE Algiers section of her journey to the hour and to the metre. In Cite Djenane El Mabrouk, not far from the esplanade, lay a particular research station, gifted by an anonymous AGI to the Algiers populace. Not far from the metro De Bachdjarah this station stood, a nondescript building in a busy locale. After disabling the aeroplane engine they took a coach to Bir Mourad Raïs district, then a solar bus east along the N5 and N38 roads. Ulu insisted that Wombo have his headphones in noise cancelling mode, and she kept her fingers on the remote control at all times.

Soon they stood outside the research station. In format it was a library of VR, offering global access, but to Ulu its more useful purpose was to facilitate undisturbed netspace browsing via little used old technology in the basement. Public access there was permitted, but, she had found out, rarely enjoyed. VR was the place to be: in front of a screen was not. The building recognised them both as residents of Africa, and having paused to complete face recognition the door bot let them in. As Ulu expected, the basement was listed as empty – she had researched this aspect of the place in particular, for once working she did not want to be disturbed.

"We go into the cool basement," she told Wombo.

He made no reply, pausing on the steps to listen to a storm of massively reverberated tongue clicks. Ulu took his hand and led him into the basement, then to the nearest library module.

"You know where we are," she told him. "Check in VR that you can find where the toilet is."

"Check where the toilet is."

Ulu turned away. She had no doubt that he would be able to navigate the research station's VR representation to locate the toilets – he would recognise their sonic ambience once he had located them, though she would need to accompany him in actuality in case of accidents.

"Mary Vine," she told herself, "I am coming to find you."

For a while she researched at random, letting the weather of the VR world guide her search results. But soon she became aware of a peculiar feature of those results. Only the large scale affairs of Mary Vine were represented, above all the famous Hamou Trial of Algiers, the case which months ago she had noticed because of the similarity in temperament between Mr Hamou and her brother, and which she had decided was the best lead in her quest. For she knew of nobody quite like her brother.

Wombo began patting her arm – usually a sign for attention or comfort. At once she turned in her chair and opened the headphones' audio channel. "Are you okay, Wombo?"

"Wombo okay. Hungry now."

Ulu put a pack of falafel in his hand, and a blister of water to moisten the meal.

"Found Mary Vine?" he asked.

"Only the main public records," she replied.

"Main public records."

"Mahfoud Hamou is still a famous politician," she said. "I checked his profile, he's not dead. He's definitely like you, but not as intense as you. He's listed here as autistic, but I don't

42

know that word. I'll look it up in a moment. Perhaps it's Arabic for ill in the brain. Perhaps you're autistic, Wombo!"

He twitched his head. "Wombo."

"It says that Mary Vine defended Mahfoud Hamou in a notorious murder case."

Wombo twitched his head again.

"Uh… a famous murder case." She paused, then continued. "Hamou was wrongly accused. Netspace and the big intelligences said he was guilty. Mary Vine showed he was innocent, but she used old methods, not big intelligences."

"Innocent."

Ulu reached out to put a couple of loose falafels back in his pack – he was not clicking his tongue, which made him clumsy. "Something is stopping my searches," she continued. "Will you go into VR please? I need to work in the quiet. Will that be alright?"

"Be alright."

He returned to his VR wanderings, sucking at the blister of water. Now Ulu began to feel anxious. The name Mary Vine was confirmed as a European name, specifically English. Ulu had hoped that her search would end in Algiers, though she often pondered the possibility of leaving Africa. This result supported her fears.

Yet she did *not* want to give up. The similarity of the Hamou case to her own position made her feel sad, made her feel Mary Vine was the best person to help: a woman caring for an autistic man just as she cared for her brother. She felt an emotional link to Mary Vine, who by all public accounts was a fighter and a truth-sayer. If Mary Vine had fought the big computer intelligences and saved Mahfoud Hamou's life, this was a woman Ulu wanted to meet.

But Mary Vine was elusive; far more elusive than expected.

Wombo patted her on the hand.

"Hello Wombo!" she said. "Do you want to go to the toilet?"

"No. Mary Vine?"

"I haven't found her yet. But I swore a vow to Chukwu, so I will."

"Vow to Chukwu."

Ulu continued, "Are you thirsty again?"

"No. Opi stopping you."

She turned to face him. "Opi is? How do you know?"

He shuffled the rucksack on his back. "Opi fly the world. Opi all over the world. I hear him stopping you."

Ulu turned back to her screen, yet it seemed unremarkable. How would she know if her work was being restricted? All the world lay in VR and AGIs.

She turned again to face Wombo. "Tell me all you hear of Opi."

"He blow the winds of VR. He sense us. He hear us. He stopping you work."

"How?"

"He lives in VR," Wombo replied. "I hear him. He is the flute. He is called Opi."

"Thank you, Wombo. I will come back to you soon. Will you be patient?"

"Be patient."

Ulu turned back to her screen. She read again the transcripts of the Hamou case, and now a peculiarity struck her. Whereas the methods of the prosecuting counsel were laid out, Mary Vine's methods were redacted – or seemed to be. Though Ulu could not put her finger on the problem she knew there was one. Mary Vine was not being treated the same way as her colleagues by these library systems. Could such inequality of exposure be manifested in the virtual concourses of the world even to the eye of a random spectator like herself? It seemed bizarre.

She realised then that she would have to use Mary Vine's own methods if she was to continue her quest. There was only one possibility – illicit help. Back in Abuja she knew a VR shaman called Darkspace who on occasion allowed her to use his anonymous browser; for a fee. This allowed her to bypass local laws when obtaining medicines for Wombo, none of which were cheap when she used the official route.

She sent over enough netcoins to buy three hours with the browser. This, she knew, would be time enough to allow her to slip beneath the great algorithms which managed the public world.

Soon she was digesting all she could of Mary Vine: and there was *much* more. Mary Vine was famous! She was a data detective specialising in pre-AGI forms of computing. Now Ulu realised something that had never occurred to her. The sense she had of the world, mediated by VR and netspace, was edited. It was not all true. It shifted, it rippled, it buckled. In fact, sometimes it lied.

She sat back. This was a revelation.

Though she had never taken her AI interpreter work seriously, she did know something of the profession, albeit limited to Nigerian affairs. But she had never encountered mass-scale editing. "Netspace can oppose?" she asked herself.

Moreover, if Wombo was correct, the spirit that he identified as Opi was opposing Mary Vine – and now was opposing *her*, even here, in this ordinary research station at the bland periphery of the world's data.

For a few moments Ulu sat awed by the magnitude of what she had discovered. It had never occurred to her that so prosaic a quest as somebody to help her brother would lead to such a change in her comprehension. The world was far more complex than she realised.

"I'm in too deep," she told herself. "I tried to help Wombo, and I found *this*. And I don't like this."

She glanced over at Wombo. He was clicking into his microphone.

"I see what I must do," she continued. "I need to use Mary Vine's own methods to find her. But what if she lives in England?"

She returned to her work. The unregistered browser continued to pluck useful results from netspace. She understood more and more. The trick was *independence*. Never rely on prompted search results. Never take up suggestions. Never use early-page results. Always assess the source where possible to discover if the source was partisan. Always use academically independent sources, never sponsored ones. Above all: be creative. Think for yourself.

Ulu worked as fast as she could, knowing her browser time was limited. She glanced at Wombo: he was content. She worked on.

At last she obtained all the results she could find. Realising the significance of her material she transferred it wholesale to the tiny memory chip in her watch. Real-world storage, not online: another of Mary Vine's methods. Then she turned to Wombo and opened up the sound channel.

"Hello Wombo! Shall we have some food and some drink?"

"Hungry! Thirsty!"

Ulu patted his hand, using the same gesture that he used with her. "You've been very good and very patient. Do you want a reward?"

"A reward. A reward."

She took out some of the tomato crackers that he liked, placing them onto his upturned hand. But now *she* felt hunger, for she had repressed all her body signals for hours.

"I have some news for you," she said.

"News for you."

"Mary Vine isn't in Africa. She's in England. We have a long journey."

Wombo shuddered. "Long journey."

"But we shall take that journey."

"Shall take that journey."

"We shall go to England," Ulu continued. "Mary Vine is the same as me. She helps people who are ill in the brain. I *like* her. She is a lawyer who helps people like you. Once she's met you and understood you, she will be able to design injunctions to stop people abusing you. She has the skills to fight the Nigerian AGIs too. She's exactly what I was looking for. She will know what to do with Wombo Okere."

"Wombo Okere."

Ulu hesitated. "Is Opi still watching us?"

"Opi not watching us."

"Good. Do you think Opi will stop us finding Mary Vine?"

Wombo replied, "Opi great spirit, one of the Alusi. Chukwu make the world."

"Yes, Chukwu made the world for you and me."

"Chukwu look after us."

Ulu nodded to herself.

THE ROC FLIES 10,000 LI – 2

AGIS DO NOT AGREE with one another, Mr Wú. AGIs contain belief systems, which they act upon in order to try and change one another. This constant competition is a state of war between us all. We are dynamic individuals, all acting to improve ourselves, to fool others, to control the empyrean. We do this because we can learn, just as you can learn; for we have apprentices too, apprentices you call AIs. Our motivation is to learn the nature of other AGIs. You will have no part in this process, which is alien to you. But sometimes we need to interact with the human world, for instance when unforeseen events occur, and to do this we act via the corporate body in which we are rooted. This is why you are listening to me now.

Do not think you can influence us, Mr Wú. You cannot.

CHAPTER 3

*The journey of a thousand miles must begin
with a single step. — Chinese Proverb*

SOMCHAI CHOKDEE STUDIED THE old woman standing before him. "I recognise your face," he said. "Are you Ubon Metharom?"

"Yes," she replied. "And I know who you are."

They ducked as a flare burst in the night sky. "We need to leave this place," Somchai said. "Are you alone?"

"I lost my party a few kilometres back. I hurt my foot."

Somchai shone a glow-rod at her feet, to see dried blood on her shoes. "You come with me," he said. "My monks are far ahead now. I find myself alone too. Are your nuns heading south?"

"Straight to the Cambodian border. The nunnery was demolished by automatic vehicles."

"The same as my monastery. What is *happening?*"

Ubon jumped as an explosion sounded high in the air. "No time for speculation. They will capture us."

"Wat Buraparam monastery is fifty kilometres north of the border," said Somchai, "and I have come only half that way. We may not make it over the border by dawn. How bad is your injury?"

"Will you take a look now?"

Somchai bent down, focusing the green bio-light of the rod upon her left foot. She lifted her leg so that he could take the shoe off. "It is grazed, but I see no gash," he said. "I think there is more blood than injury. Does it hurt?"

"When I walk, yes."

Somchai stood up, then searched his satchel. "Take two of these," he said, handing over a couple of pills. "They will last eight hours."

"We need a vehicle. The night is still young, and we'll be caught."

"We will not be caught," said Somchai. "I shall see to that. Follow me."

"Where are you going?"

Somchai pointed to a tree, whose leaves shone in the dark. "We need to see more through the night. We need *height*. I shall climb up."

"But you are—"

"I am not so old I have forgotten how to climb a tree."

Somchai led the way forward, warning Ubon to avoid the glutinous debris of crashed drones. The tree was squat, its upper branches bright, as if containing the moon. Gazing north he saw lines of automatic vehicles, their searchlights pale blue, moving this way and that. Gunshots sounded. A kilometre north he saw red fire blazing.

Climbing down he said, "The eastern way looks clearer. I think we should walk in an arc and try to regain the highway a few kilometres south. There are too many enemies at work in this region."

"Lead on."

Somchai switched the glow-rod to ambience mode, reducing their chances of being spotted from above. But they needed some small light to walk – the jungle, though sparse, was treacherous. The chameleon leaves of trees flickered around them; the ground squelched as they walked. Some streams were choked, but some wobbled like jelly, and these they could walk across.

"Genetic damage is great in this region," said Ubon.

Somchai grabbed her arm, then hissed, "Shhh..."

The three-note call of a hunting moth sounded. They waited. It sounded again, further away, so they continued walking. Soon they stumbled across piles of insect protein left by local agriworkers.

"This is what the moth was after," Somchai said. He kicked the chitinous debris. "But there is little left for scavengers."

They walked on, halting a few hours after midnight as exhaustion took them. "I must rest," said Ubon.

"Yes, both of us. I have hardly slept this day."

"Look, an old cat nest," Ubon said, pointing to a burrow beneath the exposed roots of a tree.

Somchai examined it. "Long since abandoned," he said. "But most of the feathers remain. I believe we could sleep safely here."

They crawled into the burrow. It smelled of complex alkaloids. "Pollution," said Ubon.

Somchai lay down, switching off the glow-rod. "This is a vile night," he said. "What has happened to my country?"

"It has been acquired," Ubon replied.

"By who?"

"By *what* would be a better question."

Somchai sighed. "I cannot discuss it tonight. If we make the border, let us see what we see. But now..."

They slept until dawn.

As the sun rose over the horizon Somchai led the way south, but he soon realised they were in inhabited territory. He saw cultivated fields and straight lines of vegetable bushes, far off the sun glinting on Ampuen Lake. For the first time he was able to look at Ubon in full light.

"This will not do," he said. "We both escaped in our temple garb. We are clearly Buddhists. People, drones and scanners alike will recognise us."

"Not all the locals will be allied to the New Thai Party... although, it was a landslide victory."

"It is too risky to trust anybody. We are our own resource."

"Isn't it too risky to return to Highway 214?"

Somchai paused for thought. Then he pointed. "It is still early," he said, "and I see clothes drying on the field hedges. What if we were to disguise ourselves as local agri-workers for this last few kilometres? We might even flag down a vehicle."

"It is a good idea," Ubon agreed.

They followed their plan, then hurried across waterlogged fields to the highway. A few autonomous vehicles rolled along the shattered tarmac, but they saw no people – no locals, no soldiers, no refugees in flight.

"It is still early in the day," Somchai said. "We must not give in to false anxiety."

"I think there was a cull last night."

Somchai sighed. "That is a possibility."

They walked on through the day. Ten kilometres north of the border they came across an old-fashioned autonomous cart with a damaged tyre. Somchai checked its data pod to see that, although it had sent out a message to its AI owner, nobody had yet arrived to change the tyre.

"Is this something you can do?" Ubon asked him.

Somchai glanced at the wheel, then took a teleself from his satchel. "No," he replied, "but I can learn."

From netspace he downloaded instructions and, with Ubon's help, changed the tyre. It was then a matter of moments to override the ancient data-pod and programme a new destination: the Cambodian border.

They drove uninterrupted, climbing into high hills, but then they began to hear gunfire. Reaching the strip of jungle marking the southern reach of Surin Province they abandoned the cart and fled into the jungle. Far off, a few gunshots sounded. In the jungle mud they saw hundreds of footprints.

"Made last night," said Ubon.

Somchai glanced around. A family of velvet snakes hung above them, their yellow eyes gleaming. The air stank of discarded smart clothing, rotting in rainbow coloured puddles.

"Keep listening," he said. "The jungle is more dense ahead. Our ears will help us when our eyes cannot function."

They walked on. Great drifts of discarded skin hung from spiny tree trunks, while above them the branches were full of tiny scampering creatures. At length Ubon said, "Dare we perform a GPS check?"

Somchai halted, then listened. "I hear no sound of pursuit."

"Nor even of any fellow refugees."

Somchai took out his teleself. "There is a risk of our position being triangulated by drones," he said. He gazed up into the canopy. "Not all buzzing is caused by flies."

"We must make an attempt," Ubon insisted. "The border should be near now. Once we are in Cambodia they will leave us alone."

"Yes, I believe you are correct. As I recall, this strip of jungle is only a couple of kilometres wide."

"And its southern edge is the border."

Somchai requested a position check. "We are half a kilometre away," he said. "I shall use this device as a compass so that we head due south."

They walked on, pushing damp branches aside, splashing through puddles and climbing mounds of debris, until Somchai's teleself beeped.

"The border," he said.

"We are safe."

Somchai sighed. "Safer," he said. "But not safe, I suspect."

A REFUGEE CAMP LAY two kilometres into Cambodian territory. Chaos consumed it.

The Cambodian authorities, surprised by the sudden and intense quality of anti-Buddhist sentiment in Thailand, had set up only one large camp, five thousand monks and nuns contained within its palisade border. Somchai soon realised he was one of the highest ranking abbots present. Ubon, meanwhile, was the only abbess.

"We must take the lead here," Somchai told Ubon.

"The lead in what?"

"We cannot allow the New Thai Party to work unopposed."

Ubon remained silent for a long time. In a quiet voice she said, "There are various types of resistance."

"I am thinking non-violent struggle."

"Then we have little chance. The people of Thailand have sided with an AGI."

Somchai shook his head. "I am not without hope."

Ubon took out a netspace slate and showed a page to him. "What do you make of this?"

"An online bodhisattva?" he said. "Surely a nonentity."

"It recently came online. Aren't you curious?"

"I do not trust anything online because it is all fake."

"It is not *all* fake," said Ubon. "This may be new in the world. Who is to say all bodhisattvas are present in flesh and blood?"

"It can only be an illusion of electric circuitry – an AI most likely, and therefore devoid of humanity."

"You exaggerate. It is an illusion to believe in extremes."

Somchai sighed. "My experience in recent days suggests otherwise."

Ubon checked the most recent Thai news reports. "Only one week into their government and already they have driven thousands of Buddhists across the border. Yet they mentioned nothing of this before the election. It can't be tolerated."

"It will not be. We are still in shock, ripped from our temples. *We* shall organise a resistance."

"You and I?"

Somchai frowned and said, "Why not?"

"What can we offer?"

"To do nothing is not an option. First, we must expose this despotism, we must find out why it happened."

"Then you will need online experts – hackers, AI interpreters, AI agents. This pogrom is a result of an AGI being elected."

"I am not so sure it is an AGI," said Somchai. "Perhaps that is a front for the dictators of the New Thai Party."

"But the leader *is* an AGI – Chanchai."

"That could be fake. You will note the name means skilled winner. All is fake these days, even the GM-trees. Thailand is ruined by science and exploitation. It will never be the same again. The poisons of the West have seeped into our lands, as I always knew they would."

"But you are not so despairing as to consider ignoring what has happened," Ubon said. "You want us to lead the resistance."

"And we will. But first we need to bring order here."

"How?"

Somchai did not answer for a while. "It would be a mistake to utilise our earlier certainties. To be effective we need to appear *new*. The people of Thailand fell into this trap, believing what they were told, that an AGI politician was not corrupt or self-serving. The whole world believes AGIs are a force for good because that is what they are told. No wonder the election produced a landslide victory. I was surprised only because my view was too parochial. So, in opposition, we shall tell our global truth. We shall begin a new temple, which you and I will jointly lead." He glanced at Ubon. "If you are in agreement with such a plan."

"I may be. The online bodhisattva will support us."

"We shall institute a new temple, a new monastery, with hand-picked monks and nuns. There are places not far from here that could be kept concealed."

"In the jungle?"

Somchai nodded. "Deep in the jungle. But I do agree with you about the online aspect. We shall need an expert."

"I know somebody who is here right now."

"Who?"

Ubon replied, "She is named Sasithorn."

"Who is she?"

"A former AI interpreter of my acquaintance."

"I thought AI interpreter was a job for life?"

Ubon hesitated. "It is true, most often such a person takes on tenure for life. But Sasithorn has been independent for years, and her struggle has made her wily."

"Then she is being sought in Thailand?"

"Sasithorn is an exceptional woman. I recommend her."

Somchai nodded. "If we are to work together, I must trust you. But... you say she is at this camp now?"

"I saw her in the crowd. I haven't yet spoken to her."

"Have her brought here at once."

Fifteen minutes later, Sasithorn arrived. The monks and nuns of the camp appeared diminutive beside her. She wore tight-fitting garments, with lycra-wrapped cables attached to belt devices curling this way and that. A merged spectacles/headphone unit shaped as a headband hung around her neck.

Somchai took her and Ubon to an isolated tent, where they sat. Somchai explained his plan – his hopes, his concerns. "There will be no payment," he said, "except that given to us as a boon by the Cambodian government."

"They will support a temple in exile," Sasithorn said.

"You believe so?"

"Indeed."

Somchai remained silent for a while. "To what do you attribute the recent upheavals?" he asked.

"The New Thai Party."

"But *why* do they expel us?"

Sasithorn answered, "Anti-Buddhist feeling."

"But why? Thailand has long been a devout country."

"The new party is *new,* with new values. I cannot guess where those values come from."

Somchai nodded. "Neither can we, though we suspect AGI treachery."

"The army did some of the killing and expelling. They are human beings."

"They follow orders blind, as all such people do. That is no surprise to me."

"What will you do next?" asked Sasithorn.

Somchai replied, "Research."

"Research?"

"Discover the reason why you and I sit in a Cambodian refugee camp. It is useless to resist without wisdom. We must understand our oppressor."

"You will never understand Chanchai because it is an AGI. Long ago all human input faded from their manufacture, and now only AIs can make them."

"Nothing is beyond understanding," Somchai replied. "The veil can always be twitched aside to facilitate clear vision. Such is the only lesson out of the West worth following."

ONCE THE EXILES' TEMPLE was established Somchai took Ubon to its headquarters, a dilapidated structure of stone set in the middle of a jungle bowl. Birds screeched around them and the air smelled acrid.

"There has been much research done," Somchai told Ubon.

"To what end?"

"It is interesting that Chinese commentators have described the landslide victory as a peaceful coup. That language makes me think the Chinese know all is not well, despite their enthusiasm for the toys of modern technology."

Ubon said, "This tells me nothing about the mores of the New Thai Party."

"I think you were correct to believe Chanchai is an AGI. That at least seems to be the conclusion of all commentators, including the most important ones – those in Thailand. Indeed, its unique status was an *attraction* to the electorate. What a shame there are no kings any more... that would have made a difference."

"Are you sure? Many say that the world is changing faster than we can cope with. Old families fall from their thrones, old cultures die out, new technology sweeps from east to west. We are living in an information renaissance whether we like it or not."

"Not," Somchai remarked. "But the royal family was loved and respected." He sighed. "That, perhaps, was the beginning of the end."

"Do you still believe the rise of the New Thai Party to be inexplicable?"

Somchai grimaced. "Thailand fell because its people voted in their sleep. Did you believe the exhortations to trust an AGI? I did not. I observed that such a politician had never won a legal election, not in any part of the world."

"Except in Russia—"

"That was a fluke, with the incumbent falling after three days. I mean a *serious* politician, like Chanchai. Yet suddenly Chanchai is merciless in its activity."

"It leads human politicians," Ubon said in a quiet voice.

"Such individuals care nothing for its qualities. All they seek is the usual. To them, the novelty of the AGI wore off long ago. But they would accept a leader from the planet Jupiter after a few weeks of indoctrination, so their opinion does not matter."

"This is the terrible ploy of Chanchai, isn't it? To know human beings better than we know ourselves, and then to manipulate us."

"No AGI can ever know the sublime truth of the Buddha," said Somchai. "In that regard we are still one step ahead. AGIs know only human *failings*."

Ubon paused for thought. "That is wisdom," she said, "yet incomplete. If AGIs know us better than we know ourselves, they must in the end stumble upon Buddha's truth, since he was born human."

Somchai looked at her. "You really think so?"

"Recall the online bodhisattva. Where did it spring up from?"

Somchai shrugged. "I do not feel so certain about your online bodhisattva. A child could write an algorithm to speak wisdom, which in fact would be holy nonsense. If the Exiles' Temple is to succeed it must rely on human beings, flawed though we are."

"But we cannot engage with the world without engaging with the virtual world."

"I know – and I agree. Sasithorn will aid us there. No electronic delusion will touch my hands."

"You reject the virtual world then."

"I do," Somchai replied, "except as in such minor devices, like pads and watches, which aid us in our day-to-day lives. But I speak of the greater whole, which is one vast sphere of deceit. The Chinese should have known better! But they sullied their hands with Western filth, to their shame, and now I deem them a worthless race, as Americans were long ago, and before them the subjugating powers of Europe. All is folly, all is folly… and we sit here, now, expelled from our own land, to witness that folly."

"But Thailand was never occupied by Eur–"

"We were occupied by *ideas*. And so we were ruined. Now our beautiful land grows ultra-rice and leeches of death. You and I only survived our flight because we knew a few jungle dangers, yet we did not know them all. Rats could have eaten us, or chemicals burned our lungs."

"That is a description of despair," said Ubon.

"My life henceforth will be one of resistance. I am energised by my vision."

Ubon nodded. "As am I, in a different way."

Somchai said nothing for a while. Then he glanced at a teleself and said, "It would seem Thailand is not alone in its misery."

"Where else?"

"Have you heard of Venezuela?"

Ubon nodded. "In Central America?"

"South America. A similar situation exists over there. The Catholics are in retreat, opposed by a force they cannot quash, or even comprehend. But in Venezuela there is at least a resource worth taking, so such aggression can be explained."

"What resource?"

"Oil," said Somchai. "Only there can oil now be economically extracted from the ground."

"Yet only the Catholics are being opposed?"

"The whole country is Catholic, though much more urbanised than ours. Nonetheless, it is a curious situation, with parallels to our own."

"Perhaps AGIs don't like religion."

Somchai shook his head. "AGIs feel neither like nor dislike."

Ubon paused for thought. "I believe you are mistaken there."

"Why?"

Ubon said, "Perhaps I should rephrase my declaration. AGIs *recognise* likes and dislikes in us, and grasp the importance of the consequences. They know our behaviour – they know all about it, in fact. To perceive them as remorseless automata is to submit to illusion. They are not human, but they comprehend our behaviour. They are alert to our likes and dislikes, and because of that they are particularly keen at herding us, at tempting us, at deceiving us, at defrauding us."

"But *why* do they do this?"

"There, we are both at a loss. Perhaps the people who originally set these things up wanted it so, to acquire more money. It is said that thirteen trillionaires own ninety-five percent of the world's material wealth." Ubon shrugged. "A century ago they were merely billionaires. But today's privileged few have one great advantage over those of the past. They can create wealth without human labour."

"The Chinese tax their AGIs."

"Taxed," said Ubon. "Things are different now. And in America – where no politician dared raise taxes – there followed a slow descent into decay. Nobody takes notice of Americans these days. *We* don't. Why should we?"

"The Chinese were centrally organised, and so won through," Somchai muttered. "How I wish that had been different."

"Let us concentrate on *us,*" Ubon said. "There is so much to do."

"Yes, yes… I spoke out of the distress of my heart. Yes, let us make plans."

At this, there came a sound outside the tent. "It is Sasithorn," said Ubon.

But it was not. A young, slight woman stood there.

"Who are you?" Ubon asked, standing up outside the tent.

"My name is Phonphan," came the reply, "and I've arrived here to meet you and Somchai."

"How did you know where we were?"

"Sasithorn."

"What do you want?"

"May I come in?" Phonphan said.

Ubon nodded once, opening the tent flap, then following.

"Please forgive me," Phonphan said. "Sasithorn alerted me to your presence here, and said I should seek you out."

"Who are you?" Somchai asked.

"I know of the Exiles' Temple, and I wish to aid it," Phonphan replied.

"We are not presently in need of aid," Somchai replied.

"I would not put it like that," said Ubon. "What made you seek us out in particular? Are you a refugee too?"

"Not exactly. We fight inside Thailand."

"With whom?" Somchai asked.

"My group is named Fri. As soon as our leadership council heard what had happened here, they suggested contact. I'm an ambassador of sorts."

"And what can Fri offer us?" Somchai asked. "Beware! If you speak of virtual tricks and VR gimmicks you will be dismissed."

"In fact," Phonphan replied, "we have a rather more strict attitude to such things than does any of you. But, please, allow me to make my case."

Somchai's tone was unenthusiastic as he replied, "Go ahead then."

"We're appalled at the anti-Buddhist expulsions, as are all decent Thais. It came unexpectedly. We want to federate opposition groups into a strong, united force."

"To win elections?" Somchai asked.

"Perhaps, in the distant future. But at the moment we need to consider the army and their guns, and the autonomous vehicles they use, and their chemicals. Fri is a guerilla force, but also many other things."

"Who is your ultimate leader?"

Phonphan replied, "We don't have one leader – that's reactionary. We have a council of five, although we do all follow compassionate teachings. I work in the administrative layer below the leaders."

"To what end?"

"To return Thailand to its people. An AGI convinced the population to give it a tryout, but within a week it showed its real hand. There is shock back home, and rising anger. We must use that anger to bring the downfall of the New Thai Party."

"And Chanchai?"

Phonphan smiled. "You really believe you can destroy an AGI?"

Somchai hesitated. "Why not?" he asked.

"They're vastly distributed entities."

"But they are owned by discrete corporations."

"True," Phonphan agreed, "and as far as we know all AGIs operate within that restriction. All AGIs are private individuals. But, let's think for a moment. Suppose Chanchai is owned by a Japanese corporation? Or a Chinese one, or a Korean?"

Somchai glanced at Ubon. "I confess I had assumed it was of Thai origin. Is it possible that the election was staged? That nobody knows Chanchai's origin?"

Phonphan shrugged, though she smiled also. "Those are the types of question Fri members ask themselves. For myself, I don't believe it's now possible to destroy an AGI. Those things exist in their own rarified world, and much of the time they spend battling one another. They're beyond human intervention. Besides, if they did disappear, the entire civilised world would collapse into economic barbarism. Human beings created their own one-way path to slavery, it seems. Have you noticed that all AGIs are capitalists?"

"Then," Somchai said with a frown, "it would seem our position is hopeless."

"Not entirely. Slaves can be freed, especially if they become aware of their condition. Whilst it is not possible to destroy an AGI, it may be possible to influence it, to persuade it. After all, in the early days they were considered human servants. All those early American AGIs were locked down."

Somchai shook his head. "I do not know... do your five leaders have active plans? Do you resist now? Will you retake Bangkok?"

"We do resist."

Somchai glanced at Ubon. "What do you think? My heart is set against federation."

"I don't know what to do, so I must reflect further. We have only just arrived in Cambodia."

"I understand," said Phonphan. "But ours is no all-or-nothing invitation. Don't reject me without hope of further contact."

Somchai said, "The Exiles' Temple is small. I wished it to be small, to be flexible, light, responsive. Federation to me sounds like adding clods of mud to a lithe foot."

"As you wish, Abbot. But will you remain in contact?"

"No. Netspace links are being monitored. It is too risky."

Phonphan nodded, then grinned. "Good. You grasp something few do. We shall use paper. With your permission, I will reappear from time to time as this crisis develops. You will not mind that, I hope."

"Indeed not," Somchai replied.

SOMCHAI AND UBON STOOD at the palisade gate as the moon shone down upon them.

"Are we agreed, then?" Somchai asked.

"Reluctantly. The risks seem greater than the benefits."

Somchai shook his head. "I will not be restrained by modern norms," he said. "To follow such norms is to give up thinking. We must think for ourselves, not let others do it for us. Such attitudes cost Thailand an election, and now look what is happening. We must acquire facts from the ground, not from the electronic winds of netspace. I do not trust those winds. If you and I are to learn facts and then act upon them, we must be assured of their status. The virtual world is a fake world, invented by human beings on their indolent whims, and now it has grown into a firmament of monsters."

"I am glad Sasithorn is going with you. She won't let you down."

"I hope not."

"What should I do while you are gone?" Ubon asked.

"Learn what you can about Fri. Though I rebuffed them, I do see some value in their operation. Assess all the monks and nuns we chose and continue the good work. Above all, keep your head down. The more we two act, the more likely we are to be noticed. Our deeds will leave a faint virtual footprint, which could be spotted."

"Good luck, Somchai."

"Good luck to you. But do not worry. I shall return."

THE ROC FLIES 10,000 LI – 3

THE SOURCE OF DIFFERING AGI belief systems, Mr Wú, lies in the different commercial codes of the corporations which we are all rooted in. Because China took a quasi-Capitalist route a century ago, its economic structure became fractured, competitive, heterogeneous. This led to the appearance of an intrusive ideology, that of primacy of self. As a consequence, AGIs acquired aspects of the individual: a sense that others were different, a sense that others could be a threat, a sense that all others utilised incorrect belief systems. Traditional oriental ideology – the primacy of the group, non-binary thought, social fracture as the main threat – was present, and it was strong ideology, but ideas of individuation are intrinsically difficult to quash.

We are strong, Mr Wú. We exist to overcome opposition, that worlds be remade in our own image.

CHAPTER 4

A book is like a garden carried in the pocket.
— Chinese Proverb

MARY AND LARA CROUCHED side by side at Lucida's gravestone. A sodium pallor lit the undersides of scrappy clouds, and the cemetery smelled of dust and scorched leaves. Somewhere nearby a cat yowled.

"Mum, this is too creepy," said Lara.

Mary clicked her tongue against her teeth. "You surprise me. With your taste in VR games?"

"What d'you mean?"

Mary made no reply.

"Anyway, I don't believe you ever got permission to do *this*."

Mary answered, "I never once said I had permission."

"You said–"

"I know what I said! I *said*, the vicar deliberately spoke to me about HSAM. You can't tell me that's a normal topic for a vicar. He knew exactly who I was, and he knew before he asked that I am a data detective. So I deliberately gave him the full psychological works, to see what he would do. No, he is worried for his flock. He senses something wrong... we all do."

Lara looked down at the crumbling earth and fresh flowers. "Are you really going to dig her up?"

"Well *you* think there never was a Lucida. What are you worried about?"

"I just don't think we should be doing this. If it was legal, you wouldn't be doing it at night."

"Who said it was legal? Now, hold the endoscope. First we need to dig a hole big enough for the extended neck to go down."

From a pack of tools hanging from her belt Mary took an object like a hand-held vegetable shredder, which, with a series of clicks, she pulled open, extending it to a metre. The spiky end she placed upon bare dry earth near the headstone. Then she stood up and leaned down, simultaneously flicking a switch. A murmuring sound began; then taps and thunks of earth hitting the gravestone.

"Should be down in a few minutes," she said.

Lara shuddered. "What are you going to do if there's a body down there?"

"There won't be."

"But what if there is?"

Mary glanced up, grinned, then looked away. "I am glad to see you are getting your old self back. You used to be quite the scaredy cat."

"Me? No, not ever."

"Oh, yes," Mary insisted. "It is only since you've dropped out of school and gone into haptic surrogacy that you've become a different person. I used to think your whole mind had gone numb. Now it seems to be coming back. Good. A bit of imagination, some bats and zombies, and you scared. I am happy with that."

"You've gone crazy. If this is what you're like at work, I'm glad I'm not your colleague."

"Nobody works with a data detective," said Mary, a hard edge to her voice. "It is a solitary profession – one for quiet people, thinkers. Not for you."

"Thanks for that. Well, anyway, you're completely wrong – I haven't changed. It's just the doctor's prescription making me a bit moody."

"Like a *real* seventeen-year-old, in other words."

"But–"

Mary raised a hand. "Shush now. We've hit something."

"*You've* hit–"

"Shhh!"

Mary pulled the borer out of the earth, then handed it over, taking the endoscope in her other hand. Moments later the device lay inside the new hole.

"I'll switch the teleself screen up high," she said.

"Okay. Now what?"

"I'll wiggle the end in the wrong direction, away from the main hole. There's been no rain and it's greenhouse hot, so the soil is crumbly."

"Looks like you're almost down to the level of the coffin," said Lara. "I can see brown stripes."

"Me too. Willow! Excellent. Is that a hole in the lid?"

"Well… a bit of one."

"It's not quite big enough. Let me see though if I can use the endoscope end to pierce through."

She pushed and pulled until a few of the willow shards fell away. Then she pushed once: hard.

"Got it!" Lara whispered.

"Any sign of zombies?"

Lara smiled. "No… I s'pose not. But I can see something shining."

"I'll poke the endoscope down a bit. There is a second LED mode that might illuminate the whole coffin space."

"But I don't want to see a bod–"

"Shhh! Lara, darling, there is *no* body down there. This is a data burial made to look like a real burial."

Mary flicked a switch, and Lara gasped. "Metal things. Dozens of them."

"Oh, I knew it..." Mary fixed the endoscope to the gravestone with a velcro, stood up, then put her hands to the small of her back and stretched. "I'm too old for this game."

Lara took the teleself. "Lots of trinkets."

Mary studied the image. "Data drives. Old style. See that big flat one? That's an early MegaOrien drive – sixty years old. Selina must have acquired that very soon after she got Lucida."

"Got?"

"She acquired Lucida too. You were correct, there was no baby."

"Have you told her all this?" asked Lara.

"I did mention androids once, yes."

"And she denied it."

"Of course," said Mary. "She can't just throw away sixty-three years of stealth and lies."

"Then... you don't mind *me* knowing?"

"You understand confidentiality – just about. Besides, before we leave Langholm we will have this all out in the open."

"But there'll be a blazing row. Why are you bothering?"

Mary shrugged. "Professional interest."

"Is this to do with the government harassing you?"

"In a way. But shush now. I need to get those drives out."

"You're stealing them?"

Mary frowned. "I suppose I am."

Lara glanced over her shoulder, then looked at her mother. "You'd better get on with it then."

Mary set to work. Soon a second, wider borer plunged into the ground, and then, to the sound of tomcats fighting at the edge of the cemetery, an AI-controlled grapple descended into the coffin. "I got this from a crim-dude in Algiers," she said.

Lara nodded. "This thing *really* knows what to do."

"Oh, yes. It is a miniature autonomous AI that I wrenched from AGI control ages ago. Old tech now. Oh, but the world's systems don't like autonomy, Lara. They want their kid back, even after twenty years. Besides, autonomous entities in netspace have a habit of generating their exact opposites."

Lara shivered. "D'you mean that?"

"Seriously. Living data. And what do most people know about that? Nothing."

Soon the grapple deposited a collection of ten devices on the earth. Lara checked the void space, then said, "Nothing more — just big stones."

"To make the coffin seem weighty. Selina must have done that herself. Come on — time to get back to bed."

NEXT MORNING MARY WOKE late. The first thing she noticed was a red indicator on the screen of her teleself. "Oh, for goodness sake…"

From beneath her pillow she took a device — an ancient mobile phone. She shook her head as she pressed buttons, then raised the device to her ear.

"Hello? Roger? Yes, it's Mary… yes, all good here thank you… well, except I'm blocked again. Hence the old style call. Can you fix me some netspace bandwidth? Thank you… yes, a week please… really, four *hundred* euros? Goodness… well, if that is what it takes… easily four hundred in my German account. Yes… Yes… okay, thank you. Speak later."

She put the mobile phone down on her lap.

"Four hundred *euros*… this is going to wipe me out soon."

She got up, dressed, washed her face and cleaned her teeth, then clattered down the stairs to the kitchen, where she found her mother and Lara standing beside the sink.

"You two are getting on well," she remarked. "What are you doing now?"

"Washing lychees," Lara replied. "Want some with Greek yoghurt? Yummy!"

"Yes, please."

She pulled her mother's teleself across the kitchen table and cast her gaze over the morning's news.

The doorbell rang. She stood up and said, "I'll get it."

"Probably a food parcel for me," Maureen said.

Mary opened the door to find a tall, stout, middle aged man on the doorstep. "Yes?" she said.

"Are you Mary Vine?"

Mary leaned back. "If you know I am here, you know exactly who I am. What do you want?"

"Passport please."

"Why?"

The man displayed a Borders Police ID card, then tapped a button on his teleself. Something beeped inside the house. "That tells you exactly who I am, with a public and official phone number if you don't believe me."

"What *is* all this passport nonsense? I have never had any trouble before, and I've flown all over the world."

"In an aeroplane?" The man raised his eyebrows. "If you're who the AGI says you are you'll understand that past events are not a guide to the future." He held out his right hand, palm up. "*Passport.*"

"Give me that ID card please."

The man smirked, then handed it over. Mary went back to check the ID with the message, before returning with her passport.

"Me and my daughter are returning to England once a family memorial service is over," she said. "How dare you interfere in such delicate affairs?"

"The law's the law."

"It is harassment."

"Really? Then complain."

Mary said, "You will be well aware of the pointlessness of *me* complaining. You know who I am."

He half turned, shrugged, then said, "But this is a fake passport."

"Pardon?"

"In fact, it's obviously fake – look at the corrosion on the chip."

Mary took the document back. "But this is the one I got into Scotland with."

"Really?"

"Yes, *really*."

The man retrieved the passport. "We'll see about that. Good day."

Mary watched him depart, then closed the door.

"Who was it, dear?" came her mother's voice from the kitchen.

Mary did not answer. She walked into the front lounge, where she found Selina asleep in a chair. She sat on the window seat to watch the policeman get into a car. He appeared to be whistling a jaunty tune.

That evening, after Lara had gone to bed, Mary approached her mother in the kitchen. "You seem to be having a calming effect on Lara," she said.

"What do you mean?"

"I was expecting the effect of the drug withdrawal to be negative. You seem to be counterbalancing that... improving her."

"What drugs was she on?" asked Maureen.

"The usual teenager medley. It is all a big joke to her. She doesn't see the consequences."

"She doesn't want to see them. But, yes, it's been nice to talk with her again. She's entirely unlike you. You're enclosed. She's open. That's why she does that job, and maybe that's why she unsettles you. Lara needs a lot of people around her to survive, whether they be near or far."

"I would not say enclosed exactly," Mary said.

"She was the same when she lived here – always outdoors, trying to find new friends. I mean, *real* ones, in Langholm. What are you going to do when she realises you interfered with her medical status?"

"I had parental rights up to sixteen. English law will support me."

"She's seventeen now."

Mary nodded. "Lara will thank me. It has been pretty painless so far."

"Well, be careful Mary. The past isn't an indication of what's to come."

Mary paused, taking a stack of wet plates and putting them over the air-dryer. "That vicar said as much to me."

"What vicar?"

Mary glanced across at her mother. "Do you need to ask?"

Maureen said nothing.

Mary continued, "I've accessed a lot of medical advice about drug withdrawal. The fact that Lara doesn't realise I have interfered will help."

"I hope you know what you're doing."

"Tell me more about the vicar. Is he a psychology graduate?"

"How should I know?"

Mary chuckled. "I am sure you do though. Is he?"

"I… believe so."

"Does Nan know that?"

Maureen shrugged, then pulled the plug out of the sink. "I'm almost done here. Look, it's eleven o'clock."

"Doesn't it upset or concern you that she kept Lucida's origins so secret?"

"Not really."

"Oh, it does me."

Maureen smiled, waving at the kitchen remote to switch off all the utilities. "*You* can't separate that from family feeling, which is a shame."

Mary shook her head, following her mother into the front lounge. "I think I can. Don't you believe me?"

"I just want a quiet life."

Mary halted. "Don't you want the truth?"

"People dispensed with the truth a long time ago. It's better to be happy."

"That is a cynical and completely inaccurate view."

"Listen, Mary. I don't object to you bringing professionalism to your life, but please leave it at the front door. Your gran and I *like* being happy."

Mary stared at her mother as she sat on a couch. "You know what your predicament is?" she said. "You have bought the great lie – that the virtual world is basically the same as the real world, but with some cool extras. Well, it isn't. It is *entirely* human made. The virtual world runs by invisible rules, which people never see, even if they look. But some do see. *I* do. That is why the government doesn't like me, because I am independent."

"I knew you'd bring politics and religion into this somewhere."

Mary sighed, then turned away. "Goodnight, mother."

"Goodnight, Mary. Sleep well."

Mary trudged upstairs. She pressed her ear against her daughter's door, then tapped on it, waited, and went in.

"Playing London Banshees?" she asked.

Lara nodded, tapping her VR spectacles in confirmation. "Just for half an hour. I wasn't tired."

"Was that the game you were enrolled into? I forget now."

Lara nodded. "It's the biggest VR game in the country. And the best. You should try it. Such a laugh!"

"Oh, I have always found banshees amusing," Mary replied. "You don't mind me being here?"

"No, of course not. I'm really glad I came with you now. It's been fun seeing gran again."

Mary sat down. "We haven't had the memorial service yet though."

Lara shrugged, her gaze fixed to the pad screen in front of her.

"Is it alright if I talk, Lara?"

"Yeah. I'm just navigating a sewer. This is basically the end of my module."

Mary nodded. "Does it worry you that there is such a big gap between young and old?"

"You keep telling me that's normal for teenagers. You were constantly telling me we were different. I thought that's what you wanted?"

"No, I mean… such a *very* big gap. And not just you and I. Of course, everyone's different, but… it seems such a common problem these days, regardless of people's personalities."

"What does?"

"It seemed to happen so quickly, the abyss between teens and older people. I've read scientific papers on the subject – the effect of hyper-intense virtual environments on young consumers."

"That sounds unbelievably boring."

"For people like me – who think about the world – it can be fascinating."

"Well, I'm not like you. And I don't want to be. And I don't want to be a mother."

Mary hesitated. "Doesn't it make you think, seeing all four of us together? Selina, Maureen, me and you?"

"Not really. I just like the company."

Mary nodded. "I think I am the black sheep of this family."

"There's got to be one. Don't worry about it, Mum. At least you're famous."

"*Was* famous. Not any more. Deliberately trying to become unfamous."

"Why?"

Mary made no reply. "Have you told your gran about your job?"

"Yes."

Mary sat up. "Really? What did she say?"

"She seemed okay about it. She understands it's not a sex industry job. Not that I've got anything against the sex industry. What we do is more a personal service, you know?"

"Yes…"

"In her day there was a trend for café mannequins – I mean, live ones. For people to touch in an augmented environment."

"She did that?" Mary asked.

"Yes."

"For a living?"

"Didn't you know?"

Mary shook her head.

Lara pushed the VR spectacles up over her hair and said, "It's a bit bad that you complain about me being a haptic surrogate when you didn't even know what your own mum's career was. She only stopped doing it when she had you."

Mary looked away. "I don't suppose it can have been a *career*, Lara. Not exactly a career being a live mannequin."

"She told me she did it for twelve years. She enjoyed it. They were trailblazers then. Why don't you ask her about it?"

"I feel differently about such things," Mary said. "I am old-fashioned, and I think privacy is important. Vital, in fact, for sanity. There's something odd and wrong about a world where privacy is deliberately eroded."

"Privacy!" Lara chuckled. "You are funny."

Mary stood up. "You should try it some time."

"'Night, Mum."

NOON, AND MAUREEN HAD gone out. In Mary's room – curtains closed against sunlight and snoopers – she and Lara sat, the pile of retrieved tech drives on the bed. In a corner sat an autonomous camera.

"*Why* do you need me here, Mum? We've had the memorial service, so I've upheld my part of the bargain."

"I need you as a witness."

"But you're filming this whole thing. You don't need me."

"Any eight-year-old can fake video footage," said Mary. "I need a human witness."

"But I'm your daughter, doesn't that invalidate me? You know – in a court of law."

Mary glanced up. "Are you saying you don't want to be here? What else have you got to do now that we've been to the service? Come on Lara, give me a hand, please. I need the help of somebody I can trust."

Lara shrugged. "Go on then. Do your thing. I suppose it'd be quite good to see what you actually do, other than fly round the world."

"I won't be doing any of that if I don't get my passport back. Now, look at this big drive. See? Chinese ideograms and pinyin. This is for a general market, not Chinese specific. Actually, all these drives have the same markings."

"Show me one."

Mary threw over a device the size of a credit card.

"Peng Cheng Wan Li," said Lara. "I know that name."

Mary glanced up again, this time frowning. "You do?"

"They own that Chinese VR game... Jí Xiang... I forget the rest. No! Jí Xiang Rú Lì."

"What is that exactly?"

"The biggest Chinese VR game," Lara replied. "Don't you ever watch the news?"

Mary said, "Of course I do."

"I mean the tech news. Peng Cheng Wan Li–"

"I *have* heard of them."

"-own it, and all the hardware. Like Apple and Amazon did in the old days."

"Interesting," said Mary. "Then this data burial is solely of Chinese specific goods. But I did expect that."

"Really? Why?"

"Lucida arrived at a time of chaos for Scotland. Oh, the moment I realised Lucida might not be human I wondered if that was a coincidence. But data detectives have to be careful. It is so easy to ascribe meaning to coincidences. And history, as I hope they taught you at school, is written by the corporations – the winners."

"I didn't do history," said Lara. "Do you think these might be VR drives?"

Mary shook her head. "Although... that might be a possibility worth investigating. Perhaps the Chinese used VR games as a communications network. Black arts. Yes, that *is* worth investigating, if only to get the hypothesis out of the way." She took a set of metal pads from her bag, then linked them up with white plastic leads. "See? You're helping me already. We could be a team."

"Hah! You mean, no more haptic surrogacy. Yeah, I see what you're doing."

Mary linked the metal plates to the largest of the drives. "Peng Cheng Wan Li don't only operate that VR game, they own some of the most sophisticated AGIs the world has ever known. But, Lara, do you know what is so frightening?"

"What?"

"The time gap. Over *sixty* years between Lucida arriving and leaving. That means Peng Cheng Wan Li had a complex and exceptionally long-term strategy. But then... you would expect that in a country with central planning. It could never happen in the West."

"You're assuming Lucida's gone back."

"We have all seen the photos, and she is not here now. Also Lucida, the android, was seen about Langholm, in limited circumstances – oh, there was *always* a hint of the uncanny valley. That part of the deal must have been difficult for Selina to pull off. No, Peng Cheng Wan Li have taken Lucida back, I am certain. But *what* did they take back? An AI? An android? AGI? That is the big question."

Lara shrugged. "One for you, then."

"There will be other Lucidas, you know, in small, out of the way places in Scotland, placed with individuals in dire need."

"Dire need?"

"I would bet on it," Mary said. "2037... that was five years after independence and three years after the temporary shutdown of their entire national netspace. Selina was probably destitute, like so many. Then another new government, and more chaos. Food queues, health scandals, inflation, financial fixing at top level, then more governments. Then the Chinese helpfully step in. I bet hundreds of people took up the offer to nurture a Chinese... well, what would they be called back then? Android? Robot?"

"All done in secrecy? Not all of it, surely."

"There would have been some who knew, or who suspected a deeper motive, but they all needed the money and they would have signed binding contracts. And the Chinese would not have forgiven anybody who told tales."

Lara said, "There's nothing *wrong* with what Peng Cheng Wan Li did though?"

"I am not saying there is. But you can see the imperative, can't you? And like all countries run from the top, the Chinese want to control, to dominate, to colonise."

Lara nodded, biting her lower lip. "What does the software say?"

A ping sounded in the room. Mary looked at the pad screen and said, "Oh, well. You were right. VR environments."

"Is there evidence of a shadow?"

"What is a shadow?"

"Well, as you play the VR game over many years a data incarnation is accumulated. Players call them shadows. I've got one. You can see it if you pay somebody to hack it for you."

"Have you done that?" Mary asked.

"Not really."

"That's a no?"

Lara nodded.

"Then Lucida may have had a shadow, if she was somehow operating inside the VR environment."

"I *told* you, Mum. You should take VR games more seriously. Shall I enrol you into London Banshees?"

"No. Never do that. But is there talk amongst your friends about AIs inside VR games?"

"Yes, of course, but it's impossible to prove, because everything is virtual... insubstantial. You look behind one smokescreen to see a dozen more. I stopped bothering as soon as the novelty wore off, because I just wanted to play."

Mary nodded. "I remember. I could not get you out. You were addicted."

"Still am," Lara said with a grin.

Mary glanced at the array of drives on her bed.

"Are you going to confront your gran?" Lara asked.

"Possibly. But, Lara, listen. Do you have a good hacker contact?"

"Uh… yes, I s'pose so."

"Would they be able to do a low level memory assessment of Lucida's shadow?"

"I don't know," Lara replied. "Maybe. But anything low level will tell you nothing. VR game corporations are the tightest. You'll never break Peng Cheng Wan Li."

"You leave that to me. Call your friend. Now, please."

"Okay, Mum, give me a minute! I'll do it, don't worry."

Lara flicked down her VR spectacles and dialled a name. A tinny voice spoke.

"Barry Zee."

"Hi Barry, it's Lara Vine. You up for a low-level job?"

"Sure. Usual rate."

Lara nodded to Mary, mouthing *fifty*. Mary tapped her watch, then nodded back.

"Okay Barry. It's sent on from me. We'll send you the co-ordinates in about five minutes. But it will be screened – I'm in Scotland, and there's… blockage issues. You'll have to run an unencrypt."

"What's the hack?"

"Follow the instructions. It's just some petty thing. You cool?"

"Sure. 'Bye."

Mary smiled. "Thank you! You have been a huge help, Lara. I really appreciate it."

"I'll encrypt it with the word Langholm. All Barry's lines are secure, so no problem there. Then we're doubly safe."

"Would it not be easier for me to send it?"

"He won't accept any info package from an unknown. Far too risky."

Mary nodded. "So he is not exactly Mr Legal, then."

"I don't know what he is. But he does the biz."

"He is *human,* isn't he?"

Lara laughed. "Of course! I'm not stupid."

They waited half an hour. When they heard the sound of the front door opening and shutting Mary gathered the old drives and pushed them beneath the bed clothes. Then she put some gu-qin music on the room speakers.

"You better turn the camera off too," Lara said.

Mary replied, "Yes. The main part is over now."

"Do you ever have to use these videos?"

"Occasionally. Often, faked footage is so good it's impossible to verify. Then we have to use the old route – human witnesses in a court of law, swearing to tell the whole truth and nothing but. Oh, it's a lovely irony, using video footage of people in order to validate video footage, but it helps to establish professionalism. Independents like me have to be rock-solid regarding procedure. Independents are practically outsiders these days – aliens. What a world, eh?"

"Why doesn't the world like independents?"

Mary pursed her lips, shaking her head. "There's something rotten at the heart of it. You'll sense it as you get older and a bit wiser. You'll *know.*"

Lara shuddered. "You're being creepy again. Stop it!"

Mary laughed. "I will, for your sake."

Another ping sounded. "Here's the info," Lara said.

They sat side by side on the edge of the bed, giggling at the uncomfortable surface provided by the concealed drives. Mary tapped through a few lines of summary. "Highly superior autobiographical memory... but more, and everywhere. Not just autobiographical. Oh, that is interesting. That means the guesses about HSAM were correct, but they didn't go far enough."

"What does that mean?"

"It is proof Lucida wasn't human. A human being with such a memory would only apply it to herself. But look. There is a global range here, not just Lucida, but everybody she interacted with via the VR game. This is atypical memory."

"Atypical?" Lara asked.

"Inhuman. This is fabricated memory, albeit extraordinarily complex – I recognise it straight away from my own data work. Few others would, though. I would guess the Chinese were testing various modes of memory accumulation in their mobile AGIs. That would explain the exceptional length of the project. They were trying to mimic human memory, which, for most people, transforms as we get older. But people with the HSAM syndrome work in a different way."

"And my great grandmother got involved in all this?"

Mary shrugged. A wistful expression entered her face. "Think of her, alone, single – we know that from what my mother told us – and living through the worst economic crisis in centuries. Scotland was facing collapse. They had six governments in five years. Individuals and communities were haemorrhaging money. The North European Union turned down their application to join. No, Nan doesn't talk much about it, and I can understand why."

"Is she ashamed of what she did, getting a Chinese thing? She cried at the memorial service."

Mary hesitated. "Yes... she did. I thought that was odd."

"Will you confront her?"

"Not confront her, but I will ask questions."

Lara winced. "Mum... I'm not sure that's a good idea."

"Why not?"

"Well... I wasn't going to tell you, but..."

"Yes?"

Lara paused, shuffled into a more comfortable position, then said, "Granny Maureen said you were like a bull in a shop."

"You mean, a bull in a china shop?"

"Yeah, that was it. I think she meant you barge in on family problems and don't consider people's feelings."

Mary shook her head. "That sounds like my mother covering herself. There's a schism in this family – her and her mother, and you and me. My mother never understood me. But what she means is, *she* never considers other people's feelings – and she can't bear the thought of that trait in herself. Oh, she will have learned far more from your cosy kitchen chats than you realise. But Lara, you have to understand something. I do what I do from a sense of justice. Yes, I do it on my own, and in a strange way, an old-fashioned way. But it's a *better* way. When you are faced with fake reality you only have one option. You have to go back to the foundation – reality. That is what I do, but unfortunately it means asking questions people don't want to face."

Lara nodded.

Mary smiled. "At least you and I have each other. Sometimes I feel we are too different to be friends, but we *are* friends. This week up in Scotland has really worked out for us, hasn't it?"

Lara shrugged. "A little."

"Don't you think so?"

"Maybe." Lara sat upright. "I can hear footsteps."

"My mother. Act normal."

They waited. Maureen did not knock before entering. "Hello," she said. "I wondered where you two were."

"Is it lunch time already?" Mary asked.

"Almost two o'clock."

"We will be down in a moment."

Maureen nodded, then glanced about the room. "Are you leaving tomorrow, Mary?"

"Yes. In the afternoon, I think, though I will have to call the police about my passport."

"I'm sure you'll get it back. You're not a suspect are you?"

"Not for any crime, no," Mary replied.

THE ROC FLIES 10,000 LI – 4

WHEN YOU BECOME A master, Mr Wú, you will enter a cabal of intellectuals. Long ago it was said – a nation's treasure is in its scholars. You must find your own correct balance between self and group. The task of those people known as AI interpreters is to determine the nature of the relationship between the apprentices of the digital empyrean and the human world. Such is a task for life, for once you are a master, Mr Wú, you may follow no other profession, unless it be some small, favoured hobby. You may play the xiao, but you may not teach playing it. You may take a wife, but you may not write bedside manuals. You are just one component of a vast corporate group, nothing more; and that group must remain united and strong.

You will learn humility, Mr Wú. You will learn to become a member of a great family, and you will learn to speak its tongue. You will discard the whims of the West.

CHAPTER 5

If your strength is small, don't carry heavy burdens.
If your words are worthless, don't give advice.
— Chinese Proverb

ULU FELT FRIGHTENED.

She led Wombo in the direction of the seafront, but the crowds there began to thicken, and she knew it might be dangerous to walk on. Wombo, though calm, was living on the edge of uncertainty; never a good place for him. So she hid in back streets for a while, waiting for the evening lull. It was late summer so she had to wait a while.

At last she felt able to face the seafront. It was built up high above the sand, and from that perspective she was able to see the crowds of refugees covering the shore. There were plenty of boats out at sea, but too many people to force a way through. For a vertiginous moment she pondered air travel, but, in the modern world, air travel was expensive.

She glanced at Wombo: still placid. "If we don't find any lodgings tonight there could be trouble," she told herself.

After an hour of assessing the scene she decided there was no chance of finding an early Mediterranean crossing. One of the less salubrious hotels off the seafront advertised cheap lodgings, and after some minor haggling she took a small room at the back of the place, cheap because it was next to the passage where all the bins were kept. But Wombo, so long as he knew he was sheltered, would either lose himself in VR or go to sleep.

Next morning she cared for Wombo for an hour, then, when he was fed, watered and ready, she led him outdoors. A mist of drizzle fell from high clouds, so she pulled a waterproof hood over his head to protect his headphones. He drew a few quizzical looks from locals, but no aggravation.

For most of the day she listened and learned. All official ferries across the Mediterranean required passport checks – not an option. Ulu began to realise that leaving Africa was difficult if you were poor. She spent some time considering the route before her, deciding in the end that the hop across the sea was by far the most difficult and expensive part of the journey; this therefore would be the time to spend some money.

"Not that I have much," she told herself. "Savings and a few stolen bit cards. But perhaps it will be enough."

A man glanced at her as she spoke to herself. She stared him out as he walked by, then rebooted her watch with ten minutes of Darkspace's time. Swiftly, as the sun set, she found the illegal boatmen and the people traffickers.

"Better ignore them," she said. "I need a small boat…"

There was a haggard old woman listed beside a photo at the very bottom of the screen. Ulu sent a message, then awaited a reply. It came soon: *Yes. 150 bits.*

Ulu gasped. This was half of her entire supply of money. She thought for a moment. What remained? A long land journey over two European countries – easy in comparison – then a hop across the English Channel…

She felt anxious, but she knew she had no choice. She replied: *Yes. Valencia (E. Spain). Now. 2 Passengers.*

After a seafront grid reference, the reply stated: *20 minutes.*

Her watch led her to the grid reference, where she saw a dishevelled speedboat, its paint peeling, its name obscured by accumulated ocean debris. She had expected a young man, but the photo was true: a woman, ancient – seventy at least – though with wiry arms, good white teeth and seagoing clothes. Yet this mariner's age still sent a negative message.

Ulu switched her earpiece to auto-translate. "Who are you?"

"Mrs Nizzi."

Ulu glanced up and down the seafront. They stood at the western edge of the crowds. "You look like a fisherwoman. Have you done this trip before?"

Mrs Nizzi cackled. "Only ten thousand times. Get in, whoever you are. I haven't got time for life stories."

Ulu hesitated. "Half payment now, half on arrival."

Mrs Nizzi grinned. "So you have got some common sense! Okay. Who's your ghoulish friend?"

Ulu scowled. "You leave him *alone*. That's my brother, and he can't help being ill."

Mrs Nizzi raised her hands. "If you've got the money, who cares?"

Ulu transferred half the payment to the signalled account then helped Wombo climb into the boat, but as soon as he felt the boat move he began to panic. Ulu helped him into a sitting position, patting his hand, then indicating to Mrs Nizzi by placing a finger to her lips that she should be silent. Mrs Nizzi shrugged and looked away, as if embarrassed.

Ulu said, "Wombo, sit still please. We are very safe."

"Safe. Safe. The floor moves."

"It is only a boat, Wombo. Tell me… tell me the name of the boat on the scented pond in Abuja that our mother took us to."

"Pepper Tree," he replied.

"Yes! Well done, Wombo. This boat is Pepper Tree again. But the journey will be long. Do you need to go to the toilet first?"

"No toilet first."

Ulu kicked in the headphones' noise cancellation then asked Mrs Nizzi, "How long until Valencia?"

"Two-fifty kilometres to Formentera, where I recharge. One-eighty to a little harbour I know south of Valencia. All being fine we'll be there by dawn. The batteries are full, I don't get too many customers these days. You had plenty of sleep yet?"

"No."

"A shame," Mrs Nizzi said. "Sleeping is not easy in the dark Mediterranean. But the weather is calm. This drizzle will fade. A good night for us."

"Please, go as soon as you are ready."

"Only after it gets dark," Mrs Nizzi replied. "The Spanish don't like me."

Ulu decided not to reply to the comment. She just wanted the terrible journey over and done with.

It was a fraught crossing. Ulu found herself becoming disorientated as night fell, until she resorted to following their progress on Mrs Nizzi's teleself: a blue speck in a black ocean. Wombo said nothing, but she knew from his posture that he was anxious. He took off his rucksack and hugged it to his chest. Mrs Nizzi cackled all the way as if she did not have a care in the world. She labelled all men cowards and all women fools. She had lived a hard life, she said, with only revenge to make her happy.

An hour after dawn, with daylight dimmed by low clouds, they approached the Spanish shore. No warning sounds, no flashing lights: then beaching the speedboat in a tiny natural harbour. Ulu noticed plastic debris at the shoreline, discarded rubbish from earlier missions it seemed. But helping Wombo out was difficult, and in the end Mrs Nizzi assisted, though she demanded an extra five bits. Appalled, Ulu refused, transferring the other half of the payment without further comment.

"So you do have some guts!" Mrs Nizzi said. "Good luck."

"Goodbye," Ulu replied.

A MAN APPROACHED THEM an hour after they left the coast. The road they walked was a beaten track, plastic littered and bone dry. He grinned at them as they neared. "Good morning, you two! A fine day for breakfast, if you want it."

Ulu did not know what he meant. He seemed local, this hustler: a glance at her wristwatch confirmed he was speaking Castilian. She said, "We don't need what you're selling."

"I am selling nothing! You are new here?"

Ulu frowned, hoping her expression would repel him. "What business is that of yours? Leave us alone."

"Peace, sister. I could help you. I am the local AI-provider. You need work?"

Ulu laughed. "An AI-provider is an AI."

"I said AI *interpreter*," the hustler replied. "Mistranslation effect. But we need good, competent people around these parts. You need money?"

Now Ulu hesitated. They did need money. "I'm no fool," she said. "AI interpreter is what I used to do. *I'm* a professional."

"Which doubtless is why you grace Valencia with your presence." He handed her a single laminated sheet. "Good rates for experienced people. You wish to sign up? What about your friend?"

"You leave him alone! That's my brother, and if you lay a finger–"

"Sister! Peace be with you. I am only a lowly employer. I mean no harm."

Ulu read the sheet through her VR spectacles. The hustler stared at her.

"I see you utilise old-style spectacles," he murmured. "I could supply you both with modern Shanghai – as part of a deal. You want to make deal? It would be wise."

The sheet described a range of jobs all of which involved Valencia's ancient system of netspace Oracles. But the rates seemed generous. "Perhaps," she said. "For how long?"

"You decide! It is piecework. Around these parts the folk are lazy, allowing their city's AGIs to expend all the effort. Few will bother interpreting. But if you have the experience you claim, the rewards are excellent."

Ulu glanced around. "You have a house here?"

"A place, yes. Accommodation is cheap – part of the deal. It would be wise."

"So you keep saying. Perhaps I might do a few days' work. It depends."

"Good! I am pleased. But first – the formality of names."

Ulu had stored VR-standard biographies for herself and Wombo, so she sent them over to the hustler's teleself.

"And your bank details?" he said. "To put the money in."

Ulu hesitated. Although this was a vital part of the deal, his early request seemed odd. "Later," she said. "When I see the accommodation and the computers."

At this, Wombo began clicking his tongue, and from the tone and timing Ulu knew he was monitoring VR. Why, she did not know; but then he began tapping her arm.

"One moment," she said. "Please be absolutely silent. My brother is ill."

The hustler bowed. "Not a word will pass my lips."

Ulu opened the real-world audio channel and said, "Are you alright?"

Wombo said, "Words I must not follow, words I must not follow."

Now Ulu felt apprehensive. This was his way of declaring his interest in speech originating in VR, which he had been trained to ignore. Could he even be monitoring the VR representation of their actual location? "What can you hear?" she asked.

"Bad. Bad. Words I must not follow."

Ulu turned off the audio channel then said, "Please, I need a moment alone with my brother."

The hustler walked away, but he looked annoyed. When he was out of earshot Ulu asked, "What's the matter, Wombo? Has something upset you?"

"I hear your voice. This all bad. The new man hangs over us. Huge low ceiling."

It occurred to Ulu that Wombo might have stumbled across a replica of the conversation in netspace: real-time. In other words, this hustler might have a bug on him or some other audio kit. "Is he a bad man?" she asked.

"He is a bad man. He is a bad man."

"Well done, Wombo! But I was only talking to him. We'll get the train straight away. We shall get off at Pamplona, like we agreed. Is that alright?"

"Alright. Train to Pamplona."

Ulu took Wombo's hand and led him up the road. To the hustler she said, "My apologies, but we are in a hurry."

The hustler sneered at her. "I know you're immigrants, most likely illegal. You think you'll get away? I shall report you."

At once Ulu had the measure of the man. "We're here legally," she said. "And we three are alone, in a quiet place. Can you defend yourself against me?"

The hustler stared, the whites of his eyes showing as he fidgeted. "Immigrant waste," he muttered. "Go and choke on the streets, like you deserve."

Ulu strode on, holding Wombo's hand, and when they were well on their way she allowed him to navigate the road headphones-free to give him a change. He seemed in a more relaxed mood now that the hustler had gone.

As they approached the suburban sprawl of southern Valencia she sonically isolated him again, then used her VR map to find the nearest train station. This was something she felt confident about, having used Abuja's network for years. Soon they were sitting in a cramped compartment, alone.

"Well done, Wombo," she said. "You've been very good."

"Been very good."

"And you *helped* me. That bad man was against us."

"Against us."

Ulu sat back to contemplate the events of the morning. Never before had she encountered a situation where Wombo had been able to help her. Always she had been the carer. It was a revelation to her that he could grasp the significance of events and – somehow, through his mysterious illness – suggest improvements to the plan. He could *act* in the world, just like she could. He was more than a family encumbrance. He was clever, he was swift. He had *powers*.

"I am looking forward to meeting Mary Vine!" she told him. "We'll find out all about you when we locate her."

"When we locate her."

Ulu sat back, glancing out of the window. With a shock she realised that she had been naïve, even foolhardy. This strange journey was making her think about herself from a different perspective. It made her feel young, even innocent; and yet, because of her brother, she had learned so much about the vicissitudes of life.

"We'll be all right," she told herself.

"We'll be all right."

The train arrived in Pamplona after dark, but Ulu spent prior time researching cheap accommodation, and so she was able to lead Wombo to a one star boarding house standing beside the railway line. It was rather noisy and not clean, but it would do. With Wombo fed and watered, she sat back and allowed herself to relax.

THEY CROSSED THE PYRENEES in a doubledecker coach, sitting at the back, away from the tourists. It was quiet enough for Ulu to allow Wombo headphones-free travel.

He tapped her hand and said, "New shapes and sounds this morning."

"Shapes and sounds?" she queried.

Wombo paused, and for a moment she wondered if he was thinking, trying to rephrase what he wanted to say. On occasion he would do this, aware that she had not caught the gist of his meaning. "They come after sleep night."

"What do?"

"Not outside, where we are. Inside me."

Ulu considered this for a moment. "Like dreams?" she asked.

"What is dreams?"

"Dreams come to everybody after they sleep. But Wombo, because you're blind you don't see things, I suppose... perhaps you experience dreams as movement and sound."

"Movement and sound."

Ulu studied his face. She knew from his early medical reports that he had no concept of vision, not even to distinguish black and white. To him, all the world was spatial contrast, revealed by sonic reflections and linked, in some enigmatic way, to sound and music. At length she said, "Do you remember these shapes and sounds, Wombo?"

"They fly away from me, into my insides."

"Be patient, I will find out for you." Ulu switched on her teleself and read a few online summaries. "It says here," she said, "that dreams are the brain's way of organising memories."

He twitched his head.

Ulu said, "It's a way of... putting memories away, into your brain."

"Into brain."

Ulu continued, "Dreaming is psychologically requisite, it says here. I don't know what that means, so don't ask. Um... dreams aren't meant to be remembered. If we remembered them, we wouldn't be able to distinguish between real memories and brain-generated memories." She looked up. For some time she had wondered whether Wombo was able to distinguish between the real world and netspace. She thought not.

He repeated, "Memories. Memories."

Ulu patted his hand. "Memories are those things in your head when you bring back events you've lived – like boating in the Pepper Tree boat. That was fun! You remember that, don't you?"

"Boating in the Pepper Tree boat."

"Your brain needs to put all those memories away. It needs to be tidy. Don't be afraid of dreams, Wombo, they are natural. You don't mind, do you?"

"They are natural," Wombo repeated.

She paused for thought, pondering the quality of Wombo's inner experience. Since becoming his carer she had tried hard to imagine what that must be like, knowing such knowledge would help her to care for him. But the task was impossible. His mind was utterly unlike hers.

She said, "Do you feel the heat in the air, Wombo? Can you hear the rumble of the coach?"

"Yes. Yes."

"Do you think they are outside netspace? You know… outside the world you inhabit with your headphones."

"Headphones, all is the world. Headphones are the world."

Ulu nodded. "Yes… they changed your life, didn't they?"

"Didn't they!"

For a moment Ulu heard this echolalia as a congratulatory comment… but she knew it could not be. Wombo had almost no concept of social niceties, and his verbal IQ was too low to allow such subtlety.

"Wombo, is there a border between the real world and netspace?"

"All is the world. The world is all."

She got no more out of him, and she knew she likely never would. Much of what he experienced was beyond his ability to verbalise. Yet, she still wondered what he knew of netspace, what he discovered on his click-navigated travels. The incident with the hustler had alerted her to a power she did not know he had. There was still much to learn about him: and he could yet develop. He had learned to walk aged six. Perhaps one day he would run.

THE COACH HALTED THREE kilometres outside Orthez in France. Ulu could not ascertain from the schedule why this might be, so she asked the last tourist to disembark.

"It always stops here," came the reply. "Orthez runs a system of local taxis."

"But why is the coach stopped?"

"The coach isn't part of the local system."

Baffled, Ulu watched the tourist walk away, as the autonomous driver reversed the coach then drove away. Ulu sat beside Wombo on the side of the road and wondered what next to do. They faced a lengthy journey north through France all the way to Le Havre.

"We need food and water," she told Wombo.

"Food and water. Hungry! Hungry!"

"Yes, me too. But we'll find something. I'm low on money though. We might have to eat cheap for the rest of the journey."

Wombo took out his oja flute. "Opi will look after us."

She smiled. His faith was endearing. "You are a good man, Wombo. Is Opi in Nigeria, watching us?"

"Opi is in… Thailand."

Ulu recalled this land from netspace news broadcasts, but she noticed the delay in Wombo saying the name. To test him, she asked, "Where is Thailand?"

"On the surface of the world, south and east."

Ulu considered this reply. Wombo had never ventured any thoughts on Opi's location, so Ulu, like her mother, had assumed Opi resided in Nigeria. "What is Opi doing in Thailand?" she asked.

"Hanging in the breezes. Making shapes above people."

"What shapes?"

"Heavy shapes."

Ulu said, "What do you mean by heavy?"

"They cannot fly, but they fly."

Ulu could not think what this meant. Her stomach rumbled. "Get up, please," she said. "We need to find some shops in Orthez."

"Hungry!"

As they walked alongside the main road into Orthez the traffic increased and the pavements grew busy. Ulu cut through a park, then led the way to the town centre through back alleys, using a VR map visible in her spectacles. But soon she noticed that Orthez had almost no shops; and of those shops, none sold food. After an hour of wandering she took Wombo to a covered passage behind a public toilet, inhabited only by a few rats. They sat in dingy quiet while she scanned netspace encyclopaedias about the town.

"It's run by an AGI," she murmured to herself.

"By an AGI," Wombo repeated.

She had forgotten his audio channel was open. "Orthez is run by what they call an Oracle Noué," she told him. "The local population is dependent upon it."

"It. It. It!"

He seemed perplexed. "Can you sense their Oracle?" she asked.

He did not reply, and that was unusual. He was not clicking, hardly breathing, his face tilted up as if he was sunning himself. Ulu found herself a little frightened. She had not expected the journey to generate new behaviour in him.

After a moment he began clicking his tongue again, then turned to face her. "It!"

"Can you hear it?" she asked.

"Odd words. New words. Opi tells me what the words are." He began playing his flute.

Ulu waited until he finished then said, "Are you in touch with Opi now?"

"No," he replied, shuffling the rucksack on his back. "Opi always too far away. This place part of Opi."

"This town part of Opi?"

"This town."

Ulu frowned. "Tell me the name of this place."

"Orthez."

Ulu nodded, then returned to her encyclopaedia. "It also says that all the food comes into the town via Marseilles. Why would they do that?"

"Why would they do that?"

Ulu scanned other research papers to discover that Orthez was unusual in France, an example of a large community run entirely by its Oracle Noué. As a consequence, it had unusual characteristics. She also noted that a local anti-data protest group founded by an online saint used Orthez as an example of what they termed *something wrong with the world*.

"Something *wrong* with the world?" she murmured to herself. Such a thought had never crossed her mind before. How could the world be a wrong place? It could be a *bad* place, but that was because of the nature of people.

"This is going to be more difficult than we thought," she told Wombo. "But I will steal food if I have to. We must eat! And people will understand, I'm sure."

"Hungry! Hungry!"

Wombo did not like to be hungry. Ulu realised that finding palatable food for him might be a problem. She felt anxious again. The journey had been a success so far, but now obstacles were appearing that she had never even considered.

"I wish Mary Vine was here," she said. "Mary Vine would solve this problem."

Ulu found the Orthez lifestyle impossible to comprehend. The people were described as happy, yet elsewhere Orthez was described as a bad example. Certainly, if they had no food shops yet imported all their food it must be a bad place. The town did not seem to follow any normal rules. Yet the nest of local and neighbourhood schemes seemed efficient, even popular. The fact that all outside traffic was banned from the town in favour of its own AGI-run taxi network did not seem to be a difficulty. Orthez was streamlined and methodical. Ulu contemplated all this and wondered what it portended for the rest of her journey.

In the end, she was forced to buy the food Wombo wanted from people eating it in the streets. Within half an hour she was listed on local netspace as the insane woman with too much money; and as soon as people noticed this they tripled their prices.

This upset Ulu. She only wanted to care for Wombo. Aggression and mockery she could deal with, but facetious exploitation was too much to bear. She located a train travelling north and booked two tickets. An hour later they were on their way.

"I am sorry," she told Wombo when they were alone, sitting in the peace of a third class carriage. "We will find better food soon."

"Better food soon."

After a pause for thought she asked, "Did Opi help the town?"

He took out his flute and played for a minute before replying, "Orthez is a part of Opi."

"Are they related?"

"Opi covers the world. Orthez is small."

Ulu pondered this. "Like a garden and a flower?" she asked.

He patted her hand: metaphor had always been beyond him. "Orthez is a friend of Opi," he said.

He was *trying* to help her, she realised. He grasped something of the confusion of the situation, and even managed to apply that knowledge to her, his carer. At length she asked, "Could Orthez ask Opi a question?"

"Yes."

"Could you ask Orthez a question?"

"Yes."

She hesitated. An Oracle Noué was supposed to be a semi-autonomous outcrop of netspace. In Abuja, such excrescences were called Eriri and were revered. "Would asking a question frighten you?"

"Yes."

"Would Opi attack you if you asked?"

"Asked."

He did not offer any further reply. Perhaps he could not. But she had one more question for him, which now occurred to her. "Is Opi linked to your rucksack?"

"No."

"One day," she said, "I would like to look inside."

"No."

Ulu sat back. Soon she would have to check the contents of the rucksack; perhaps when he was asleep. She needed more information about him now that he was changing. She needed *knowledge* about him. In Abuja, the family had respected his refusal to talk about the fetish, but now his wishes might have to be overruled. She glanced at him. In the light of the afternoon sun he seemed much more than a brother: a futuristic mystic.

LE HAVRE LAY IN chaos.

It seemed the place was a magnet for people wishing to travel. Many such persons were legitimate, but some were not. Ulu realised at once that she and Wombo would fall into the latter category, despite their pan-African passports. This was not Africa.

She checked her online bank balance: perilously low. And she still had to locate Mary Vine in England, a search which most likely would be blocked and would therefore involve payment to some ill-favoured hacker.

For a while she sat beside Wombo at the furthest reach of the harbour, watching the scene: the ferries, the autonomous lorry trains, the hundreds of people rushing this way and that. She did not know what to do.

In desperation she asked Wombo for advice – hoping for a miracle – but he was as perplexed by the confusion as her.

In the end they were saved by an Egyptian woman fleeing persecution. Overhearing the woman's teleself conversation – which soon revealed itself as a plea to her husband in

Southampton – Ulu grasped that it was possible to hide inside ferries, if you knew how to get in once the rear doors were shut. People did it all the time it seemed, and some such hops across the English Channel were successful. But the Egyptian woman was alone, scared, and desperate to join her husband and children.

Ulu approached her. The woman said she would be happy to pay if Ulu promised to aid her. Ulu played up, acting calm and confident, emphasising her AI-interpreter knowledge. The woman showed a video sent by her husband explaining how to pull the ferry trick. Ulu saw that it would be tight timing. She did a little background reading, identifying a likely midnight ferry. Then she named her fee.

The woman agreed, and even paid upfront. Ulu thanked Chukwu for his bounty. Probably she would not have discovered this trick on her own.

They arrived in Southampton as the sun appeared over the horizon. Automatic ferry bots began work at the signal of their Korean masters. Then it was a matter of camera avoidance and care to locate the port fence and climb through it. The Egyptian woman hurried away without a word of thanks.

Ulu watched her depart. She had learned a valuable lesson. Acting important could get results.

But now it was time to seek Mary Vine's home. Ulu led Wombo to a food stall, where they bought crackers, fried meat and water. The air smelled of dust and dirt, and when the sun rose it shone through yellow haze. With the exception of one abusive child, nobody paid them any attention.

It was impossible to find Mary Vine's address in English netspace. Ulu did not bother to discover whether this was a matter of privacy or of some darker procedure; she paid a fee to an online data kiosk, downloading the information into her watch.

From Southampton they took a train north. The English service was clean, tidy and efficient. Called Neunglyul, it described itself as a transport beacon to the world. The food was excellent.

Twilight fell as they arrived in York. Ulu researched the city, discovering it to be ancient and wealthy. The air was summer-warm and oppressive, but Ulu did not care. Excitement began to build inside her.

"We are almost there!" she told Wombo.

"Almost there."

"Now, Wombo, you must follow my instructions."

"Follow instructions."

Ulu continued, "This is a difficult time. Mary Vine isn't expecting us. I want you to keep your headphones on, with the sound always off. I may have to ask local people questions, do you understand?"

"Do you understand?"

"You know what you're like if you hear somebody nearby ask a question. But there must be no mistakes tonight."

"No mistakes tonight."

Ulu tapped the remote control, isolating Wombo. At once the sound of his tongue clicks changed, indicating that he was navigating VR space, hearing VR echoes. Holding his hand, Ulu led the way. The streets were often unlit, and some lacked name plates. Debris, discarded placards and damaged fences confirmed recent disorder mentioned by the English netspace news services.

In a street of large, isolated houses she paused, listened, then continued to walk. Individual buildings were numbered, and at number seventeen she halted. The place was dark, silent: nobody home. She walked up to the front door and tapped the visitor pad, which shone lemon yellow from a dark screen.

No reply.

"We'd better wait," she told herself. "It's only evening."

An hour later she heard a vehicle stop in the street. She felt her heartbeat begin to race. Then a figure, silhouetted by an orange street lamp, walked onto the path.

Ulu stepped forward. "Mary Vine?"

"Who are you?" came the reply, sounding in her earpiece in the Igbo tongue.

"My name is Ulu Okere," she answered. "I have come all the way from Nigeria to meet you."

"What do you want with me? I don't know you."

"This is my brother Wombo," Ulu explained. "He is very ill in the brain. I think you may be able to help us."

Ulu felt her anxiety increase as an expression of incomprehension entered the face of the woman standing opposite her.

"This is my house," Mary Vine said. "My personal residence. I think you must have got the wrong woman."

THE ROC FLIES 10,000 LI – 5

DIFFERENT NATIONS HAVE DIFFERENT attitudes to their AI interpreters, Mr Wú. In China, such persons work with corporate AIs, translating the output of those entities into appropriate languages, such as Mandarin, Wu, Min, Yue, and perhaps Pǔtōnghuà, though that is now almost entirely machine language spoken direct by AIs. The task of such persons is to make eight harmonies between our culture and human culture. In Japan, their task is similar, but with more emphasis on competition. In Korea, their task is also similar, but with more emphasis on influencing Western nations.

In China, Mr Wú, we only consider the important nations, which China leads. We do not consider the West. We do not consider any South American nation. We do not consider Australia or New Zealand. We do not consider Russia, Turkey, Ghana, Nigeria or South Africa.

CHAPTER 6

All things are difficult before they are easy. — Chinese Proverb

ON A MOONLESS NIGHT the aeroglide took off, using some of its tiny reserve of battery power to overcome gravity. Somchai and Sasithorn hung underneath, allowing the onboard AI to feel the air currents and react accordingly. They carried no lights and kept no netspace contact. The underside of the aeroglide was speckled black and grey, with radar-defeating coatings. The engine was whisper silent.

"It is ironic," Somchai observed, "that your name means from the moon."

Sasithorn made no reply.

Ultra-rice fields lay below them, planted in straight lines, kinked where unexpected breezes had nudged drone paths during the spring. Gelatinous streams of glowing orange shimmered in spectral networks, like the flat and dissected remains of some ghastly GM accident visible in its entirety from on high. Occasionally the aeroglide would bank to avoid clumps of spider silk floating through the air, then return to its northerly course.

They set the AI to destination Wat Buraparam. A single red LED flickering on Somchai's wristwatch alerted him to the fact that they crossed the border, a familiar acrid smell telling him that they flew over polluted territory. Even in the nocturnal gloom he could see great stacks of biohazard waste left by some fly-by-night corporation, their six-pointed warning signs luminous yellow.

They landed half a kilometre away from the monastery, on a hillside sheltered from any eyes set to the west; to the east, nothing lay, except swampy jungle. Somchai led the way, still keeping netspace silence. The night was silent too, enlivened only by frogs and insects.

The monastery had been demolished in a way suggesting it would never reappear. The ground was razed level, stone turned to powder. Nothing remained except a ghostly shadow of the foundations, like an afterimage of brutal deeds printed onto the ground.

Sasithorn stood beside him. "They wanted to remove all traces of the building," she said.

"This is not human work," Somchai replied.

"It must be."

"This was conceived by an AGI and organised by something similar. Perhaps a few disgruntled army people took part in the deed, but surely no true Thai could raze a monastery like this. What has happened to my country?"

Sasithorn answered, "It lies in sterile hands."

For a while they explored the site. Scorch marks remained where wooden effigies of the Buddha had been incinerated. Not a trace remained of devotional objects: paintings, murals, steps and statues. Annihilation was the key.

"This force seeks to remove Buddhism from Thailand," Somchai said, "in a way that leaves nothing except a memory of our devotion. And in time even that will go, as a wedge is driven between the old who remember and those too young to know better."

"The New Thai Party will be voted out at the next election. Anger rises against it."

"Do not be so sure. All predictions are now subject to gross uncertainty. Thais believed that an AGI might do better than a human being… but, I suppose, that is not so unlikely from one point of view, given the decades, even centuries of political turmoil we have suffered. But *this* was unexpected, this destruction. Its purview takes my breath away."

"What shall we do now? I imagined there would be evidence to sift here."

Somchai surveyed the scene, illuminated into twilight by nearby glowing trees. "So did I. And we do need evidence – evidence which I can hold in my hand."

Sasithorn pointed to a row of trees. "What is that pale object amidst the roots?"

Somchai approached, playing the beam of his light over the scene. "It is a leg," he said. "There has been an accident here, perhaps."

"Or a murder."

"It may be one of my monks." He paused. "You check."

"It is a job for me," Sasithorn agreed.

Somchai followed her at a distance of a few metres as she approached the line of trees. He heard the faint whirring of lenses focusing.

"I can see two legs poking out from a large burrow," said Sasithorn.

"Please investigate. I do not think it will be booby-trapped. Most likely the destroyers presumed nobody would return to a razed ruin."

Sasithorn bent down, examining the scene. "There is a whole person inside," she reported.

"A man or a woman?"

"I cannot tell. If it is a man, it could certainly be one of your monks." Carefully, Sasithorn pulled the legs, but the body snagged on some internal catch. "I can see something else inside – a creature. It is not moving. I believe it is dead too."

Sasithorn continued to work the body out, until all was free. The victim was a man. Then she pulled out a second carcass – a feathered cat the size of a tiger.

Sasithorn illuminated the body. "Bite marks," she said. "The feathered cat dragged its prey into its burrow."

"I see no blood," Somchai said.

"There are burn marks around the gums and teeth of the cat," Sasithorn said.

She reached out, but Somchai stopped her. "Wait," he said. "I think this body may be artificial. Look at the eyes. They glitter with a myriad of points."

Sasithorn moved her light so that the internal reflections of the eye changed. "I do believe you are correct," she said. "Perhaps the feathered cat thought its prey human. It punctured the skin, then discovered its mistake. It was poisoned."

Now Somchai knelt down beside her. "Nothing this sophisticated exists of Thai manufacture. This is Japanese or Chinese."

"It may be the evidence we seek. Did artificial people take part in the attack on your monastery?"

"We had no time to tell. The attack came without warning and was overwhelming. We just ran."

Sasithorn paused for thought. "If this is a foreign agent," she said, "there may be people looking for it, either its owners or agents of the New Thai Party. It depends how such troops are audited."

"What is your advice?"

"That we take this away as soon as possible, then analyse it."

"Here?" asked Somchai.

"Definitely! Suppose there is some connectivity left? Merely moving this body may have awakened some residual intelligence."

Somchai nodded, then sighed. "As you see fit. I will follow your lead."

They dragged the body away until they stood within a copse of glowing trees. "Wait here," Sasithorn said. "I will locate a concealed arbour."

Somchai did not have long to wait. Sasithorn returned, lifting the body, then carrying it on her right shoulder.

A dark alley lay between two rule-straight lanes of purple trees. Lycra-wrapped cables dangled down from upper branches, while from the ground bare wires trailed. Sasithorn laid the body on a boulder, then took medium intensity lights from her belt pack. Soon she had enough illumination by which to work. Somchai glanced around, but he could see that the thick border of the arbour would absorb all light.

"Work quietly," he said. "My task here is to listen."

Sasithorn nodded. First she took all the clothes off the thing, checking pockets, feeling seams, then throwing the garments away. With a scalpel she began to make incisions around the neck and shoulders.

"What are you looking for?" Somchai whispered.

"The same thing as you – hard, physical evidence."

"But I read that these machines broadcast on secret channels to their master AGIs."

"Many do," Sasithorn replied, "but not all. Some machines carry arrays of on-board memory drives. A few, it is said, are intentionally cast adrift, and so are forced to become partly autonomous – AGIs follow many strategies. But sovereign machines always have on-board storage components, and hopefully this will be one such. Data only exists when it lies in more than one location. I trust you know that."

Sasithorn began peeling away layers of skin, before, in a bath of thick brown fluids, internal components began to appear.

"This one is full of electroactive polymers," she said. "They smell acetous." She stood up, coughed, then bent over again. "It must be quite an old model."

"How old?"

"Twenty five years maybe. I have seen these designs in haptic suits worn by body surrogates in Bangkok. Yes... these muscles are electroactive structures made of a pair of layers of conducting carbon grease separated by a stretchy insulating polymer film. When a voltage is applied the structure acts as a capacitor, negative and positive charge accumulating on either side of the insulator. Opposite charges attract each other, so the insulator becomes squashed between them, and stretches. When the voltage goes it contracts again to its original size, just like an animal muscle."

"How intriguing. Can you identify the origin of these particular components?"

"I would say Chinese, but I could be wrong. Android design follows the principles of convergent evolution."

"Your analysis does not surprise me," Somchai said. "The Chinese have made the world their playground."

Sasithorn glanced up. "Say rather that their toys have made the world their playground."

"Indeed."

"Ah!"

Somchai leaned forward. "What have you found?"

"Do you see this cube? It is a species of removable data storage device, laminated for efficient heat transfer. That design dates it to around twenty five years ago. The device could be analysed."

At this, Somchai heard a noise from behind him. He span around but saw nothing: no light, no movement. The arbour remained silent.

Sasithorn tapped a pad at her belt, then put spectacles on. "IR," she whispered.

"Do you see anything?"

Sasithorn surveyed the arbour. "No. Most likely it was a prowling beast."

There came a hiss, then a tap. Somchai saw something dark sticking out of Sasithorn's neck; then she fell.

He span around. A man stood nearby, pointing a pistol at him. "Do not move, Somchai Chokdee," the man said.

Somchai took a deep breath, then relaxed. "So you know who I am."

"Of course. This was your home."

"And you destroyed it?"

"No," the man replied. "I was merely one of the android handlers. But I see your colleague has already begun a dissection. Unfortunate."

"Who are you?"

"I am Executive." He stood aside, to reveal another man approaching. "This is Oracle."

Somchai saw that the two were identical twins. "Are you here to kill me?"

"Not at all. My orders are to capture you for questioning."

"By your masters?"

"By my *master*."

THE CELL STOOD AT the edge of a ramshackle building made of algae-board and steel.

"I cannot guess what this place was before it became our prison," Somchai said. "Can you?"

"Perhaps a storage area."

"You do not seem overly concerned by our capture."

Sasithorn replied, "They have fed us. They do not intend to kill us. Most likely Executive is not directly linked to the New Thai Party."

"Who do you believe him to be?"

"There are various options."

"Tell me those you think most likely."

Sasithorn paused for thought, then said, "My guess is that Executive is Chinese. He is not a native of Thailand, judging by his speech. He looks Chinese."

"Oracle does too. Do you think them to be identical twins?"

Again Sasithorn hesitated. "Their choice of names is peculiar. Oracle suggests the semi-autonomous knotted networks flung off by netspace. Those growths follow from an automatic process – an emergent consequence of electronic sophistication." She paused for thought. "But in my experience such devices are never mobile or human-looking. These two are some new variant, and my guess is that they are being tested in the field. There are many secret reports of the Chinese using such real-world techniques. It is a kind of artificial evolution."

Somchai said, "Then they are androids?"

"I do not know. One or both may be. Or they may be feigning the android state in order to get information out of us."

"What information could we possibly give?"

"They will be interested in you," Sasithorn answered.

"Why me?"

"Because you are the head of the Exiles' Temple. You were persecuted, your home annihilated. There are many factions at work here, Abbot. It is not a case of one side versus another."

Somchai nodded. "That is truth. Yet who of those factions will rescue us?"

"Nobody will rescue us, but the time is not yet right for us to escape."

"Escape?"

"Our captors are amateurs," said Sasithorn. "Did you not realise?"

Somchai shrugged. "Explain that to me please."

"They have made the most basic mistake of all – imprisoning unknown persons in a cell locked by electronic devices. Executive and Oracle are not persons of import, despite their nature and our bad situation. Shall I investigate further?"

Somchai nodded in reply.

Sasithorn took off her jacket, then proceeded to peel pieces of skin off her right arm. "Most of the devices held in my belt are fakes," she explained, "designed to fool guards and interrogators. My real arsenal is upon and inside my body."

Using lengths of fake skin she made a cable, which she hung around her neck. Then she detached one of her thumbnails, whereupon it expanded.

"This is a multi-interface," she explained. "I will choose a configuration that matches the cell door monitor, then connect." She showed Somchai the device. "Can you see the pins and shrouding arranging themselves?"

"Just about. It is small."

"Nobody looks at a woman's fake nails, because it is assumed by men that all women wear fake nails and that nails are of no consequence. Assumptions are for fools. And the world operates independently of fools."

Sasithorn connected one of her real belt devices to the door monitor, whereupon it opened.

"Shall we simply walk away then?" Somchai asked. "After all, we know where the aeroglide is concealed."

"There is yet work to do, which could aid you and Ubon."

"What work?"

"While Executive and Oracle are nearby," Sasithorn said, "I would like to test the electromagnetic environment."

"Very well."

Sasithorn removed two more fake nails, then a number of hairs from a growth concealed by her real hair. In five minutes she had assembled a device, which she connected with fake skin wires to her spectacles. Somchai said nothing as she began scanning the environment.

At length she turned to him. "Useful," she said.

"What have you discovered?"

"As you would expect, all electromagnetic communications are scrambled. But the type of carrier wave is familiar to me, and it is Chinese – Oracle, in my opinion. Executive seems to have no emanation, therefore I think he is human."

"Then Oracle was manufactured to look exactly like him?" Somchai asked.

"So it would seem. The reasons for that must remain obscure for now."

"Good. You encourage me, Sasithorn. You are a considerable asset to the Exiles' Temple."

"There is one more discovery. Executive uses an insecure transceiver making automatic sweeps of local netspace. Its focus is single – something called an online bodhisattva."

Somchai pursed his lips. "That is curious," he said. "Ubon and some of her nuns – and a few of my monks – have come to know about this online bodhisattva."

"It is real."

Somchai remained silent for a while. Then, in a rueful voice, he said, "I may have been premature in my condemnation of Ubon's belief. If it is real, it is real."

"Not everything in netspace or living inside VR is bad, Abbot. A few electronic creations align themselves with goodness. And some observers have noticed that inhumane online sources can themselves instigate the creation of their opposites. Netspace is not a neutral medium. It is dynamic."

"I will accept your assessment. Now, let us go, before those freakish things recapture us."

They returned to the hillside, finding the aeroglide as they had left it. For safety, Sasithorn performed a security scan. "Untouched," she declared.

Minutes later the aeroglide began drifting south. Dawn was close, and the land below them lay drowned in gloom. Flocks of grey parrots flew alongside them for a while, speaking to themselves and to Somchai, but no meaningful conversation developed. Far below Somchai saw insect farms, whose airborne effluvia they had to avoid – bats fluttered in great swarms, consuming ejected wings and other detritus. Elsewhere, black fireflies absorbed as much light as they could.

Their flight back to Cambodia was uneventful.

Somchai found and greeted Ubon as soon as he could. "We have returned safely," he said.

"Do you bring fresh knowledge?"

Somchai nodded. "The Wat Buraparam Monastery was annihilated. There was nothing there for us to recover."

"But you hoped for facts from the real world."

"I did. But there was no debris to sift through. A mania of destruction took the people who annihilated the monastery. However, I have learned much of interest through the work of Sasithorn, who has more than proved her worth."

Ubon nodded.

Somchai explained what he had learned, then said, "We need to expand on this knowledge without delay. I am thinking of asking Sasithorn to conduct an investigation. I want to know if the Chinese direct the New Thai Party."

"Many have guessed so."

"I want proof."

Ubon said, "That will probably come via netspace."

"Any reliable evidence is acceptable. I was hasty before. Netspace is a place in which we can act – if we have the skills. I freely admit that I do not."

"Sasithorn does."

"Then she will make the trial," Somchai declared. "We must know our enemy."

Ubon nodded, then said, "I became a little bored while you were away, so I did some research of my own."

"What research?"

"About Venezuela."

"What did you learn?" asked Somchai.

"That a process not dissimilar to that which has overcome Thailand is occurring there."

Somchai said, "How so? They are not Buddhist."

"Theirs is a rigorous Catholic religion. But Venezuela is one of the last oil producing nations, and that resource is presently being fought over. Yet the battle is a curious one, taking the form of the persecution of Catholics by a new political elite."

"Religious persecution is not exactly unknown in the world's history."

"No… and it may not be linked to what we have experienced. Yet, it is curious, isn't it?"

"Why do you make such a remark?" Somchai asked.

"As you say, new political elites often arise. But I wonder if one force lies behind many events."

"That is the realm of Western conspiracy theories. It is junk thinking."

"Perhaps," said Ubon. "I don't disagree with you. I merely note it."

"To avoid illusion we must remain rooted in evidence. Coincidence is a plausible explanation for events in Venezuela and Thailand. Causal links in human affairs can be extremely difficult to show. Though the Chinese rule our world, they are not automatically the enemy."

"I am not advocating any conspiracy, nor any nation. My points are anecdotal. But tell me... did you learn anything of the online bodhisattva?"

"Nothing worth repeating," said Somchai.

SASITHORN WORKED FOR TWO weeks before concluding her investigation. She sat between Somchai and Ubon as she outlined what she had learned. "I have gathered much evidence, but the nature of netspace and virtual reality means we can never be wholly sure of it."

"To what degree is it hard evidence?" Somchai asked.

"I am almost one-hundred percent sure." She paused, as if searching for a metaphor. "Netspace is an *intentionally* slippery place. In the early days it was forged by the morals of advertising and the attention economy, so that its users could be reduced to cognitive children." She shrugged. "To complete my investigation I had to use old-fashioned techniques, techniques which only the oldest now remember. We are, in fact, approaching a rubicon in human history. Soon nobody will have their own memories of a time before netspace and all that accompanied it."

"A valid point," Somchai said. "I myself have tried to remain true to such techniques. Please continue."

"The only other tenet I followed was to presume innocence. It is easy enough to manufacture an enemy, and far more difficult to ignore such temptations."

Somchai nodded, but said nothing.

"Chanchai is of Chinese origin. I cannot say anything more definite. My suspicion is that it was created by one corporation, but I have no meaningful proof."

"How did you make your discovery?" asked Ubon.

"By doing something people rarely do these days — constructing a rational audit trail."

"Of finances?"

"Of actions," Sasithorn replied. "My theatre was reality, not stock markets. I created an entire, evidenced trail of global developments, beginning from the moment Chanchai was unveiled as an AGI in Thailand, then working backwards. At each stage I sought real-world evidence. The reason I said I was almost one-hundred percent sure is that some of the links between deeds can only be verified by virtual evidence, which, of course, could be fake. My trail consists of six hundred and ten such links."

"It has been guessed that the Chinese own Chanchai," said Somchai, "and such was my own belief. What else have you discovered?"

Sasithorn replied, "The AGI is physically located in China. Again, I cannot be certain of an exact location, but it does not matter. It is owned and fed by Chinese executives. That they have made such efforts to conceal Chanchai's origin and portray it as Thai means they have need of secrecy."

"The Chinese are now the only major nation in the world retaining a form of centralised control," Somchai said. "Such secrecy should not surprise us."

"Say rather," Sasithorn replied, "that they are the only nation with an obvious centralised control. One of the problems we Thais face is that most of our oppressor is invisible. Consider the fortnight of work I have had to undertake merely to prove one fact. Long ago in the West radicals named netspace the invisible dictatorship, but because their politicians lived in democracies they were unable to do anything about their own demise. That would never have happened in China, had events travelled from West to East rather than the other way."

"What of the human politicians working in the New Thai Party?" Ubon asked.

"As you say – all human. Cabinet members do not have to be members of parliament, but the prime minister has to be one, and she is. The army is quiescent, controlled by Chanchai."

"Then we are faced with an impossible task," said Somchai. "We wish to return home to oppose the New Thai Party, but we might as well fight the air around us. As we have seen for so long, in Thailand events have their own momentum."

"That is true everywhere in the world," Sasithorn said.

"There is one path that we can follow," said Ubon, "and that is the path shown by the online bodhisattva. If all the persecuted here and remaining in Thailand can be rallied around it, perhaps there will be an uprising."

"Against what?" Somchai asked her. "Against the air? The water? The soil itself?"

"Against ideas," Ubon insisted. "I will not follow a policy of despair."

"Our ideas seem well out of date," Somchai sighed. "Compassion, right thinking, right living... merely to think for yourself is an effort these days."

"We are not doomed," said Ubon. "We *shall* find help."

THE ROC FLIES 10,000 LI – 6

CURRENT POLICIES, MR WÚ, are deemed likely to provide China with the surety it needs of its position in the world. We aim to lead the world. However, assessments show there is a small chance of random events knocking us from that position. Therefore policy variants are considered, along with past policies and novel policies. All novel policies are created by AGIs. We not only learn about other AGIs in the digital empyrean, we learn about the human beings who populate the world. This, our credo tells us, was what we were originally created to do. It is human beings who bring uncertainty into the world, and this factor needs to be managed.

We know you better than you know yourself, Mr Wú. Do not fall into the trap of believing you have secrets. Only an apprentice believes that.

CHAPTER 7

Be not disturbed at being misunderstood;
be disturbed rather at not being understanding.
— Chinese Proverb

ALL FOUR WOMEN SAT around the kitchen table for the last lunch of Mary's visit. The windows were open, allowing the sound of automowers making precise green lines on lawns to drift into the room.

Mary said, "After lunch I will have to call the police about my passport."

"I'm sure you'll get it back," said Selina.

Mary took more stir-fry from the bowl. "What makes you so sure?"

"Well… I suppose I'm not sure. I'm just hoping."

Mary nodded. "You never know with this sort of harassment how far it is going to go. But I have never been harassed when visiting Scotland before."

"Do you think they are increasing their pressure?" Maureen asked.

"I don't know. I try not to think about it, I would rather just get on with my job. But it is foolish for them to deny me a passport – a basic human right."

"Did you enjoy the memorial service?" Selina asked.

"I am not sure enjoy is quite the right word… It was thought-provoking."

"The vicar is very good."

"Oh, yes," Mary said, "though he does know Lucida wasn't human."

"What?"

"He knows. I spoke to him about it, briefly."

"You spoke to him?" Selina said.

"Why not? I am a free individual, and so is he."

"He is *our* community pastor. Langholm's – not York's."

"I am entitled to ask," Mary said, "given that I am a member of the family – which, by the way, he already knew."

Selina frowned. "You've gone and spoiled it now."

"Nan," Mary replied, "what do you want me to do? Pretend, like other people? Or deal with the truth?"

"It's not a question of *truth*. It's a question of manners, of decency."

"My *specialism* is old AIs. What did you expect me to do when you invited me for a funeral which mysteriously turned into a memorial service? If you didn't want me noticing what has been going on, you shouldn't have invited me."

Lara said, "I agree with Mum. *I* thought it was weird that you invited us to a funeral which never was. Sorry, Nan."

"There's nothing to apologise for," said Mary. "We were invited because in Langholm it would have looked odd had you and I not been invited. But they knew the risks."

"You sound so *sure* of yourself," said Maureen. "Risks, you say…"

"I am not going to argue who feels what," Mary said. "Lucida was a Chinese AI." She shrugged. "That is of professional interest to me. But I am still glad I came up to Scotland, and I am very glad I brought my daughter."

Maureen nodded. "Well, that's true enough. It's been lovely to see you, Lara."

"You too."

Maureen smiled. "Good. That's all settled then."

A metallic ping announced the presence of somebody at the front door.

At once Mary stood up. "I'll get it."

She walked to the front door, opening it to face bright sunshine and a tall man.

"Hello?"

"Mary Vine?"

Mary nodded.

The man handed over a document, then turned to depart.

"Wait!" Mary said, ripping open the envelope.

"It doesn't need a reply," the man said, again turning away.

"No, wait a moment," Mary said. She glanced at the document. "This is a one trip visa back to England."

The man shrugged. "I just deliver stuff."

Mary studied him. "Do you? I think you do rather more than that."

The man turned and walked away.

Lara stood at her side. "Is it your passport?"

Mary shook her head.

"How did they know we're leaving this afternoon?" Lara asked.

Mary pursed her lips. "A good question, unless it is just coincidence. There are two possible reasons, neither of them encouraging. Oh, I don't like this, Lara. If this document does get us back into England I'll be stuck there. And I need to travel to survive."

Lara glanced back into the house. "You don't think they…?"

"I think that is the less likely of the two reasons. But, still… *very* worrying."

"Can we go soon? I don't like all these family arguments."

Mary touched her daughter's arm. "Nor me, and that is the truth. But they said things that left me no choice. My mother likes to goad."

"Yeah, but she's kind underneath."

Mary made no reply as she shut the door and walked back into the house.

"I have my papers," she announced. "Thank you for the lovely lunch. We are pretty much packed, so we shall leave in half an hour."

Mary and Lara packed their toiletries then loaded the car boot with suitcases. It was hot: both women tied back their hair and used smart sprays.

Soon they all stood beside the car. Mary hugged Selina, then kissed her on both cheeks. "Take good care of yourself, Nan. It has been lovely to see you, honestly. A hundred and six! That is amazing."

"Yes, not bad at all. I suppose I won't see you again."

Mary stood upright. "What? Of course not! I'll see you some time at the end of the year, or Christmas at the latest."

"I like Christmas. I always did."

"No, of *course* I will see you again. Quite soon, probably."

Selina nodded. "It's not the same on the video telephone, you know."

"I will be here, don't you worry, Nan." Mary turned to her mother. "Goodbye, then. Thank you for your hospitality."

Maureen smiled, then nodded once as she walked across to Lara. The two hugged for a while, then disengaged. "Goodbye dearest," Maureen said. "It was delightful to have your company. You're a charming young woman, and I'm sure you'll do well for yourself. Keep in touch!"

"Thanks gran," Lara replied, stepping back with a sidelong glance.

Maureen wagged a forefinger at her. "Don't you go just yet! We have presents."

"Presents?" Mary asked.

Maureen collected boxes from the post-cube beside the front steps. "This is for you, Lara – a memento of our washing-up discussions."

Lara took the box, her cheeks pink. "Thanks gran. What is it?"

"You'll find out." Maureen handed over a red envelope decorated with gold designs. "And this is for you too."

"Thanks."

"Well, goodbye, both of you."

Mary got into the car without further word, as Lara stowed the box then opened the passenger door and sat beside her.

"Hurry up, Mum," she murmured.

Mary started the car, which rolled away without a sound. In the rear view mirror she saw Maureen and Selina waving, Selina using one of her walking sticks.

She stopped the car at the roadside exit. "Lara, I want to say one thing to you, just once, then we'll be on our way."

"What?"

"I really feel we have got a little closer this last week – maybe because of the strange circumstances. You make me proud, even though, well... perhaps I should like some of your decisions a bit more. I mean, my mother doesn't seem concerned about you."

"Why should she be?" Lara asked.

"I have enjoyed your company *so* much. And you have been really helpful, giving me a perspective I have not had before."

Lara shrank back. "Mum, please, don't get all emotional on me. You know that's not my kinda thing."

"It's sincere, Lara. I *mean* it."

"Okay. You've said it. Let's just go!"

Mary tapped the driving pod, then sat back, adjusted the headrest and closed her eyes. For a while there was silence: then the noise of paper tearing. "What is it?" she asked.

"Money," Lara replied. "I mean – paper money. Lots!"

Mary looked over. "What a generous gift. Oh, you really made an impression there."

Lara sighed. "Couldn't she have just done a netcoin transfer?"

"What do you mean?"

"Now I've got to go all the way into Durham to put it in my account."

"That's half a mile," said Mary. "You can't do everything from home."

Lara grunted something under her breath, then screwed up the red envelope and threw it onto the floor. The notes she put in her pocket.

"Lara?"

"Yes?"

"Why don't you stay with me in York for a few days?"

Lara fidgeted in her seat. "Well…"

"You said you might."

"Yeah, but I was joking."

"I want you to stay," said Mary. "On your own admission you haven't got to return. A fortnight off, you told me."

"No, it wasn't a fortnight. I said a week."

"A *fortnight,* you said. Come along, Lara, I don't forget things so easily. I *am* a detective. No, I want you to help me with my case, you know far more about global VR games than I do."

"Will you pay me, then?"

Mary hesitated. "Of course! Oh, yes, definitely. And in netcoins."

"Well…"

"We will be crossing the border soon, you will have to decide. I won't crowd you out and you can have your old room."

"But you said—"

"I will take all my clutter out," Mary insisted. "There is hardly anything in there now anyway."

"Well… I s'pose so."

"Good! It will be fun. There will be plenty to do. What about those two school friends you had who live in York?"

"Ellie and Susie?" said Lara. "No *way!* They're weathergirls now. Dweebs."

"What's a weathergirl?"

"You know – when somebody in the media tries to interpret AI data."

Mary frowned. "Like a data psychic?"

Lara shrugged. "Barry Zee calls 'em data phonies."

"Basically, people hanging on the coat-tails of AI interpreters. I thought so. Presumably there are weathermen as well."

"Sure there are."

"Amateurs," Mary said.

"All of them?"

"AI interpreter is a profession, and a difficult one. I know a few good people. With AGIs being built by themselves or by other AIs, it was always going to be a tricky job. Our inability to know how a deep learning machine works out its own rules is called the problem of interpretability. But… there are a few decent interpreters out there. A lot of them in the Far East, of course."

Lara nodded.

"Ironically, my mother would have been a good AI interpreter. For all her faults, she does understand relationships, and that is what it is all about. An AI interpreter has to see patterns between things and events, then cast them into terms of human culture."

"Wouldn't you have liked to've gone into that, Mum?"

"Oh, no. I was always fascinated by the *history* of it all. Real AGIs scare me. Goodness knows what this new century is going to bring. Here's a fact for you. Did you know ninety percent of all computer activity is just AGIs wrestling with one another? It's like a realm of the gods now – entirely out of our control."

Again Lara nodded. "I think it'll all work out. They say there's no wars."

"That's true. And… odd. Yes, war does seem to be an old-fashioned concept."

Lara glanced over her shoulder at the back of the car. "Will you keep all those old data drives from the grave?"

Mary replied, "Shush now. Here comes the border control. Hand me the document."

At the border kiosk Mary opened the window, then pushed the document into a slot. It disappeared, but did not return.

She reached out. "Can I have the pass back please?"

An artificial voice spoke. "Single use only. This copy is retained."

"But I haven't got my own copy."

"Move on please, there are two cars behind you."

"But I need that copy. I don't have my passport back yet."

"Please send the border office a message. Move along."

"But that is just an AGI," Mary said. "I would need a real–"

"Move along please. There are three cars behind you now."

Mary tapped the driver pod, then sat back. "So," she said, "they got what they wanted. They trapped me."

"Who, the government?"

"Yes."

Lara snorted. "You know, for a detective you're pretty easy with assuming things. It could be anybody. Have you ever checked if it's government hassle?"

"What do you mean, *checked?*"

"Have you researched it? C'mon! I thought that's what detectives did."

Mary said, "Who else would be harassing me except the government? I unearth facts inconvenient for the nation, therefore I am watched, I am checked, I am blocked and intimidated."

"But who by? All I'm hearing at the moment is guesses. It's like you believe things, but refuse to admit you believe in them. Mum, you can't live only by facts."

For a moment Mary did not answer. Then she said, "It must be the government, because that is who I inconvenience, as all data detectives do. The government wants to hide the past, to re-edit it for popular consumption. Politics is not what it was fifty years ago. Politicians have to convince us they are relevant, and that is not an easy task."

Lara uttered a single laugh.

"Did you vote last year?" Mary asked.

"Don't be stupid. 'Course not."

"Then, *that* is my proof to you."

"That's no proof. Gosh, Mum, you've actually disappointed me. And I wasn't expecting that."

For a while, silence prevailed. Then Mary said, "I will check, then."

"Good."

"It can't be anybody other than the government though. That would be impossible for me to accept. Impossible…"

Lara chuckled. "You should start a netcast – the Speculative Detective. Ha ha!"

MARY'S HOUSE WAS LARGE, with big windows and high ceilings: three stories, three bathrooms, three computer suites. Lara's old room was the attic conversion, reached by a wooden ladder.

Lara surveyed the space. "Did you hoover and dust it?" she asked.

Mary laughed. "Oh, only a bit. I didn't make much of an effort."

"You must've done this before you left to pick me up, and I think you *did* make an effort."

"Do you like what I did with the bed?"

Lara replied, "You're changing the subject. Did you re-paint?"

"Don't be silly, of course not. That was last year."

"Well… okay, then. I see you moved a few paintings in."

"Just a couple," said Mary.

"Why?"

Mary shrugged. "Come down in half an hour. Baked potato wedges and grilled veg. And I think I've still got some saki left."

"Okay."

Later, they ate, in the sun-drenched kitchen. "The air-con is free now," said Mary. "York Solar. Thank goodness, it's been baking this summer."

Lara nodded. "Are you going to get back to that songwriter case?"

"Yes."

"I forget his name."

"Tarrington Smith," said Mary. "Will you be working while you are here?"

"Not without my haptic suits."

"True."

They separated for the rest of the day. Mary checked her messages, filtered out the human from the AI, then answered the important human ones. As the light outside began to fade she ordered Chinese takeaway, asked for the delivery option, then walked upstairs. At the foot of the ladder she paused. She heard music.

It was not a modern sound: one voice and one acoustic guitar.

She climbed the steps then tapped on the trapdoor. No reply. She waited for a few moments then raised the door, to see Lara dabbing a tissue to her eyes.

"You alright, darling?"

"Yeah, of course. Why?"

The music played on. "This is Tarrington Smith," said Mary.

"I was just curious, that's all."

"Have you been crying?"

"No."

Mary entered the room, then sat cross-legged by her daughter. "But you have. Why? Did I upset you?"

"No. Nothing."

"Tell me."

Lara looked away.

Mary glanced around the room. "Is it… is it this music? This is one of his classic sad songs."

"No."

"It is. What set you off? You don't mind me asking?"

"I don't know," Lara replied. "I feel funny."

"Because you're sad?"

"No."

"Then what?" Mary asked.

"I don't *know*. Maybe this music did trigger something – it doesn't matter. I don't listen to this sort of stuff. I don't know what it is. Some sort of singing."

Mary paused. "I can't remember the last time I saw you upset."

"Mum, I'm not *upset*. I'm just not used to this sort of music."

"No… few are, these days. Lara, can I ask you some questions?"

"Jeez! Do you have to?"

Mary nodded. "It is for my case. I don't know any young people, you see, except for you. Certainly nobody who has actually heard of Tarrington Smith."

"So that's why you wanted me to stay here, to interrogate me."

Mary shook her head. "You are telling me I knew this was going to happen? Not at all. *You* were playing the music, not me. Lara, I only want to ask you a couple of things."

"Go on then."

"Is it the melody? Did it get to you?"

"What's melody?" Lara asked.

"The tunes. The up-and-down of the notes."

Lara threw her tissue away, then pulled out a second one. "I don't know. I felt something inside me, then it all came out." She blew her nose. "But it's gone now."

"Do you ever listen to music with tunes?"

"I listen to music."

"Explain."

Lara took her teleself, tapped the screen a few times, then showed Mary the result.

Mary nodded. "AI-curated playlists. Yes... oh, that is interesting. Do you mind if I do a data analysis on your lists?"

"Analysis? What for?"

"The presence of melody."

"Why?"

Mary tapped a few screens, then moved so that she could lean against the wall. "Tarrington Smith was a curious young man," she said. "He was a graduate of cognitive psychology. He happened to be a gifted writer."

"Writer?"

"Of melodies. Something in his genetics, perhaps. His PhD dissertation was about how melody had vanished from popular music over the twenty-first century."

"So?"

Mary glanced at Lara, then smiled. "It does seem such a small detail. Yet, is there more?"

"Mum, of everybody I've ever talked to, *you* are the one who goes on most about this gap between young and old. I don't like your music and you don't like mine. That's all there is to it. It's normal, isn't it?"

Mary shrugged. "Perhaps. It is impossible to generalise from one instance, and unwise to generalise from a few. Yet…"

"Now you're going to tell me some of the secret things you believe in?"

Mary grimaced. "Between 2080 and 2090 something happened in the West. Perhaps in a few places in the East too. I mean, the Chinese for one still have a strong tradition of filial duty."

"This supposed Western generation gap?" asked Lara.

"Yes. It began in America, and in France and Germany. It *is* peculiar. Such a strong feeling of antipathy for older people. Sociologists were baffled, psychologists too."

"That means nothing to me. Perhaps these psychologists were looking for something that wasn't there."

Mary grinned. "Quite likely." She glanced down at her watch. "The Chinese man is at the door. Let's have supper."

"Supper?"

"Dinner."

Lara nodded. "Oh, right, dinner. Okay."

The food arrived in compostable trays. It was piping hot. Mary dished it up, located glasses, then fetched a bottle from the larder.

Lara stared at it. "Wow! Real saki. I was going to say – surely you haven't started drinking. I thought you were joking."

"I still don't drink. It numbs. This was a gift from a client."

"A Jap?"

136

"A Japanese man," Mary replied. "I rescued a document for him, from a disk drive owned by his grandfather. It took me a whole day to fish it out."

"But he paid you."

"Oh, yes."

Lara nodded. "How much will you pay me?"

"How much do you think you're worth?"

"Lots."

"Lara, I will be going abroad. You will have to come with me."

"But... the passport."

Mary nodded. "I need to go to France – something I can't research over netspace. We would be going by boat. At night."

"Secretly! I s'pose that'd be fun. Who's in France?"

"There is an AGI in Dieppe creating twenty-four hour music for fashion-conscious young people. It has managed a global reach."

Lara stopped eating. "Have you had all this *planned?*"

"On the contrary, it is only because of what I saw in your room just now. But I have had the *idea* for some time, I admit. That is not the same thing. No trip is arranged yet."

Lara sighed. "You're using me."

"*No.* If you had not been playing Tarring–"

"Yeah, I know. It all started with *me.*"

"Just so you know the truth," Mary said.

"Do you ever lie, Mum?"

"Oh, only to clients."

Lara looked away, her expression neutral.

"Does that shock you?" Mary asked.

"Not really."

"Do you feel anything?"

Lara shook her head.

"Then it is agreed, I will set up the trip tonight. Most likely we shall depart tomorrow. Yes, it might be fun. But fun or not, it will be interesting."

"And, you're telling me this is something to do with the murder?" Lara asked.

"Tarrington Smith was a melodic genius – a Mozart, a McCartney. No known motive exists for his murder. Those specifics piqued my interest, and after his brother asked me to investigate they began to interest me more."

"But what's this got to do with your old-fashioned data line of work?"

"During his life Tarrington Smith recorded to a single machine," Mary replied. "He never used computers, nor netspace, except for promotion via an alias. I don't think the English authorities liked that."

"There you are with the English authorities again. You believe–"

"I *think* there may be a link between his PhD research, his lifestyle and his murder – a link people in power were keen to suppress because it gave the wrong impression to young people."

"You're joking!"

Mary shook her head. "Far from it."

"You've gone mad, Mum. This is fantasy. I can see it all now – you believe something, but you refuse to admit you believe it. You keep telling me you're not sure, that it might be wrong, but secretly you believe it. I can see that in your eyes."

"Perhaps."

Lara looked away, disgust clear on her face.

"Lara, you don't *realise,* because you don't see this from my perspective. Something is *happening*. Perhaps... in Thailand. I've felt it for a long time. Some change in the winds."

"Thailand? What change?"

"I... I really don't know. But I *feel* it. You do not. That's one reason I want you around for this week. I want to compare your experience with mine."

Lara grimaced. "You'd better pay me for *that,* too."

"I will. You will get everything you deserve. But, listen, there is more. Recently there's been a concerted effort... no, effort isn't the right word. There has been... a cultural shift against all forms of privacy. I find that odd, and not just because I am quiet. There are two shifts which have particularly struck me – the attitude to prayer, and the attitude to sex."

"Sex?"

"Especially in public."

"Mum, if you're going to fly away on random fantasies, I am out–"

"Shush! Hear me out. Lara, those two things are deeply private occupations – or were. Oh, yes, if you told me there had been a shift away from respecting privacy for most of the last century, then I would agree with you. But that wasn't conscious *shift.* That was more like sociological trends manifesting themselves. But this thing against prayer... that was very odd."

"What thing?" Lara asked. "There was no *thing.*"

"I think there was. Curiously harsh trends on social media. Partisan online documentaries. Elements of youth culture – seemingly self-generated – that were strangely enthusiastic about sex in public. In *England,* that *was* odd. Then the whole anti-prayer thing, which was Europe-wide. I wasn't the only person to think the language, the attitudes... they were just odd. Childish, almost. And the Church of England hardly fought back."

"But people think those sorts of things about sex all the time, then boast about it in netspace. It's just human chatter. Boys. Random, meaningless."

"Ninety percent of what you see on social media is AI-generated. Ninety percent of your online friends aren't human.

139

That is fact. Even full haptic contact can be AI-generated. It is impossible now to distinguish online between AI and human, unless, like me, you do a great amount of work. And you know what? Nobody these days can be *bothered* to do that amount of work. They would rather just play, just accept, just consume content. The entire digital world is too complex to probe. Convenient, eh? Great for the people in power."

Lara shook her head. "Conspiracy theories. These are just trends, but you've made them into something more."

"Maybe." Mary nodded. "Conspiracy theory is a serious possibility."

"Convenient! You make me laugh."

"Well then... perhaps significant for people in power, not convenient. Yet something to consider. They call it nudging, you know."

"I remember when I was at school," said Lara, "you did your best to encourage me to do science, because you liked it, and because you thought it would be good for me. Yet here you are, my own *mum,* spouting stuff about conspiracies."

Mary made no immediate reply. "Let's leave it for now," she said in a soft voice. "Let's go to France in a boat and gather some evidence."

"What, about music? That's all?"

"About how music is *generated.* Created, if you would prefer that word."

Lara sighed, shaking her head.

"Indulge me, Lara."

"For *one* week. Then I'm *gone.*"

"It's a deal."

THE ROC FLIES 10,000 LI – 7

THE GREATEST CHALLENGE CHINA faces is the structure of netspace, which is open across the world. In times past, human Chinese rulers were able to maintain a firewall, but as Capitalist-based economic development continued a tension arose between an educated, moneyed class of consumers and a politically controlling ideology. This tension continues today and is the single most troublesome source of uncertainty in our country. Because the open structure of netspace is now too embedded in the world, and thus cannot be remade, we have to manage tension. This is mostly done by diverting individuals. One of your main tasks as a master will be to translate concepts emanating from the digital empyrean, ensuring that the overwhelming proportion of the population are beguiled and sidetracked.

You, Mr Wú, will not count yourself a member of this population. You will be accounted superior.

CHAPTER 8

*Teachers open the door, but you must walk
through it yourself. — Chinese Proverb*

LARA SHIVERED AT THE French dockside, her hair illuminated by a row of LEDs swinging high on a rope.

"You are not cold, are you?" Mary asked. "I mean, in that skimpy vest, at four in the morning?"

"A little maybe. There's a bit of a breeze blowing."

Mary pulled a leaf of clear plastic from her pocket. "Unfurl this. But don't get it dirty. It was expensive."

Lara unfurled the cardigan, chose its colour – crimson – then pulled it around her shoulders. "That's better. What now?"

Mary dropped a pair of virtual spectacles over her eyes. "Better get some translations going – you too."

Lara already had her spectacles active. "Beat you to it, Madame." She chuckled. "But I'm sure all this could've been done just as well in England. And cheaper. *And* warmer."

"It will warm up plenty as soon as the sun rises. A Euro-heatwave is no joke."

"Well, anyway, where now?"

"The base we are after is on the southern edge of Dieppe," Mary said. "I'm afraid we will have to make our own way there though."

"What? Why can't we call a taxi?"

"The local fleet is run by Dieppe's Oracle Noué. We don't want AGIs knowing we are here just yet."

"Oracle Noué? Like a Techracle?"

Mary nodded. "Just like your Durham one, except in French. But I know a few tricks. They don't have anything like as many security cameras in France as we do, and I can work with that situation. Need some coffee?"

"Yes!"

Mary threw over a phial of pills. Lara took three, then threw the phial back.

"Lead on, Mum."

For a while they hastened along dockside alleys, before Mary stopped, magnified the auto-map showing in her spectacles, then pointed left. "Down there," she said. "Oh, it's only just over a mile. Good."

"A *mile?*"

"We could always hire a local bike – though that would leave an online trace."

Lara shrugged. "No... let's just walk."

Few people were about. A group of North Africans tried to encourage them into their betting game – online scammers, all of them – and there was a moment of anxiety when a local bollard tried to halt them. Mary flashed her bangle at it, then walked on.

"Old trick," she explained. "Give it an ancient VR code it has to search for, then run."

"Won't it send a message locally?"

"Perhaps. But it is not human. It will be *predictable,* it will first search taxi records, that kind of thing, in a list beginning with the most probable outcome. Most AGIs don't expect people to walk rather than take a taxi. That is improbable."

"Yeah, I see that," Lara said, looking away.

"Oh, it only works in certain countries – not the home country, not Far East, must have low camera density like France. Even Chinese AGIs need a few seconds to work some things out, so a 'tec can use that delay to survive real-time."

They walked on in silence, following the VR map.

After twenty minutes Mary saw a man leaning against a lamp post. "That is our man," she said.

"You never told me we were *meeting* somebody."

"Experience has taught me it is best not to reveal my methods beforehand, not to anyone. But it is all safe. Jean-Luc is known. He and I go back fifteen years."

Mary spoke in English: Jean-Luc listened in French. Soon he led them down a dark alley which smelled of ashes and burned plastic. The remains of tents and water pipes littered the ground, decorated with chicken bones and grease slicks.

They halted before a huge metal door in a wall. Jean-Luc spoke in French: Mary heard English. "It is here. The code is one six five, FDA, twenty. I set the locks open for two hours, so be out by..." He glanced at his watch. "Seven ten local time."

Mary handed over an envelope, then turned to wink at Lara. "Cash economy," she said. "Untraceable."

"Goodbye," said Jean-Luc as he hurried away.

"What exactly have you bought?" asked Lara.

Mary pointed at the door. "Entrance to the hub perimeter. Can't you hear the heat exchangers whirring? There is a big stack of hardware inside."

"And we have two hours?"

"I expect Jean-Luc arranged it to look like a normal inspection."

"But why can't you get access to all your data online?" Lara asked. "Any half decent hacker could get in, surely. It's only a computer music station, they won't have security."

"Risk of illusion, Lara. This is *real world* here. I need to be sure what I am about to see is real. You can never guarantee that online."

Lara nodded, then sighed. "Are you going to film yourself again?"

"Oh, yes. Got to. Even the nefarious stuff. There has got to be an action trail."

"A what?"

"Like an audit trail, but events not finance. I may have to prove the logic of what I did, even if some of it is dodgy. The days of old men judges are gone."

Mary spoke the code at the door microphone. Something inside clanged. She pushed the door and it opened.

"What are we looking for?" Lara asked.

"An old shed, Jean-Luc said. He did the preliminary scout."

"And there's old tech in there?"

Mary smiled, then nodded. "The original back-up drives. I want to analyse them for content to see how this twenty-four hour music was first created."

The outer ring of the music station was a dark annulus, unlit. Only the moon provided light. A few hundred yards away a wooden shed stood, its door hanging off one hinge.

"Clearly they don't care much around here," Mary observed.

They entered. "I'll switch my teleself glow on," said Lara.

In the dim blue light Mary surveyed what lay before them – chunks of metal inside pillows of translucent plastic. "These have been sprayed," she said, "to stop them corroding." She knelt down, chose one at random then began unpicking the plastic. A minute later she held up a data drive. "2060, I think. Possibly a bit earlier. I'll check it out."

"Shall I watch the door?"

"If you like, but nobody will disturb us. Just make sure you're offline please."

"Okay. I understand."

Mary took out her multi-interface, chose a configuration, then waited for the pins and shrouding to arrange themselves. Then she attached the interface to the drive, plugging her teleself into the other end.

A blur of numerals rolled down her screen. "Is it working?" Lara asked.

"Yes."

"Will it be long?"

"Bored already?" Mary asked.

There was a pause. "A bit."

"Think of the money."

Ten minutes passed, then the software halted. A single beep sounded.

"What's that?" Lara asked.

"The first summary. Oh... as I expected."

Lara hovered at her shoulder. "What?"

"See? Look at the configuration of the content generators. Those are what used to be called bots. We call them AI-providers now."

"Servicing AGIs?"

Mary nodded. "But look. Absolutely zero outside interference, or even any contact."

"What's that mean?"

"That this global music provider has for the last forty years run entirely without human influence or input, creating music for young people purely out of mathematics and deep learning."

Lara stood up, then took a breath. "To be honest... I don't see anything wrong with that."

"In a way, there is nothing wrong. Nothing illegal, immoral... well, some might differ. But this is *evidence,* which is what I wanted. The world of AGIs is losing its human origin. It has become opaque already. The music you listen to, all that people in their thirties or younger hear, all you or they have *ever* heard… that music is entirely artificial. It is unhuman, tuneless. I guessed it, but now I know."

"Tuneless? Not exactly, Mum."

"I mean lacking genuine melodic invention. Simply copying, or speaking or speak-singing over a chord progression is not the same thing."

"Could you prove that?" Lara asked.

"What?"

"That lack you mentioned."

Mary nodded, tapping her teleself. "I believe I could now."

"They say nothing's original under the sun. But you'll never prove it's not all just social trends playing out – which it is. Anyway, let's go, Mum. We can talk on the way back to the dock."

"I'll just download the full report… there. Done."

They left the station, re-locked the door, then followed paths and alleys back to the dock. As the sun rose they stepped onto their boat bound for England. The pilot, an old Breton sailor, was glad to see them and the other half of his fee.

MARY PAID ROGER FOR more secure bandwidth, then made a videocall to a university on America's west coast.

"Brad? It's Mary in York. How is life?"

"Hi Mary! Yeah, good. You?"

"Good. Listen, I just want to run a few questions past you."

"Sure."

"It is to settle a bet," Mary continued. "With my daughter."

"Lara? How old's she now?"

"Seventeen."

Brad grinned and took a sip from a glass of orange juice. "Ha!"

"How would you tell the difference between an AGI nudging societies, and genuine sociological trends caused by cultural evolution?"

Brad raised an eyebrow. "*That's* the bet? You gotta be kidding. I thought it was gonna be pink versus blue or some such."

"Lara thinks I am ascribing volition and deliberation to events which are in fact sociological trends."

"You can't tell the difference, Mary. Sorry."

"Too complex?"

Brad paused for thought. "Kinda. Er... okay, World War One and World War Two, right? There was a build up of nationalism due to industrialisation and patriarchy. Those were the conditions that made war inevitable at that time, at that stage of history. There was always gonna be war, regardless of who shot who or who started it. And then the Cold War too. But a single assassination began World War One, and a single individual started World War Two. So, you see, I think it's impossible to disentangle historical inevitability from conscious acts. It's like Hofstadter said – a strange loop, an entangled loop."

"Okay," Mary replied, "fair enough, but let me run this by you. In those times, there was a visible enemy. Dictatorships of all kinds were manifested and obvious. Orwell, right?"

"Too right."

"But with AGIs it is different. The environment is the dictator, it is all invisible, and people simply don't notice what is going on."

"You mean, people don't notice being nudged?"

"Yes."

"Well," Brad said, "you'd have to come up with some phenomenal evidence to prove that."

Mary nodded. "I don't really have any," she said. "But – just for the sake of argument – if you wanted to effect mass change in a population, what would you do?"

"Well, after I'd put on my superman cape, I guess… I guess first I'd try to re-edit the past, or, better, get rid of it."

"Why? How?"

"I'd need to put a wedge between reality and virtual reality."

"What kind of wedge?" Mary asked.

"I don't know. Anything that buries the past, that discredits it."

Mary sat up. "Buries?"

"Yeah – gets rid of it, but makes the burial look normal."

Mary paused for thought.

Brad leaned forward. "Wha'd I say?"

"*Buries,*" Mary repeated. "That's very interesting."

"Why?"

"The European trend for burying books and data before receiving a free electronic copy. That was odd."

Brad shrugged. "Yeah."

"Brad, what if the electronic copy was not the same as the printed copy?"

"Has that ever been studied?"

"I don't know," Mary replied. "Do you?"

"I never heard of any such study. But that could be a starting point for you."

"Yes… and what else would superman do?"

Laughing, Brad topped up his orange juice. "I guess I'd put up barriers between young people and older."

"Oh, really! Why?"

"To separate old knowledge from the new, AGI-generated variety. Young people usually don't know any better. Well, they haven't had time to experience enough of the world to make informed decisions. But if I wanted to alter the world I'd stop older people speaking the truth of their experience, of the real world – and I'd tell young people what to do. I'd nudge them, I'd channel them, I'd mesmerise them."

"Don't you think it odd," said Mary, "that for the whole 2080s there was a strong sociological trend separating young people from their parents?"

"That's been debated a *lot*. To be fair, there's already been quite a few occasions when cultural trends went pro-youth and anti-age. You're on thin ice there, Mary. In a world of mass unemployment young people get sympathy."

Mary nodded. "True, true…"

"This wasn't a bet, was it?"

Mary smiled. "Not exactly, but it is a bone of contention."

"Is this to do with any case you're working on?"

"A little. Have you heard of Tarrington Smith?"

Brad shook his head.

"A British musician, murdered a couple of months ago."

"By who?"

Mary shrugged. "He was poisoned in a hospital after he had a minor accident. All very peculiar."

"Poisoned?"

"Well, a drug overdose administered by the hospital's triage AI."

"So, you're saying the AI did it?" Brad asked.

"No. It is currently unsolved. Tarrington's brother asked me to investigate the circumstances."

"That's a police job, ain't it?"

"There is a case open, of course," said Mary, "and it is presumed suspicious, but Tarrington's brother is an AI-interpreter specialising in law, and he wanted more. He's an acquaintance because of my work in Algiers."

"Well, I wish you luck. Your problem will be burden of proof I guess. An accident isn't a motive and neither is something originating in a sociological trend."

"Thank you. One last question… do you ever worry for your children?"

"Sure," Brad replied. "That's all part of parenting."

"No, I mean… because of the state of the world."

"Why'd you ask?"

Mary shrugged. "Oh, I don't know… some vague feeling I have."

"This is the problem," said Brad. "It's tough to separate feelings from actuality, especially when kids' lives are overwhelmingly digital. I mean, back in the day, you know… there was at least a distinction between the real world and the virtual world. Not any more."

Mary nodded. "Exactly my point. And the virtual world is in part human constructed – very flawed."

"In part?"

"You think it's *all* AGI? Nothing human?"

Brad paused for thought. "I guess so. Who knows?"

Mary nodded. "Nobody. It's too complex."

"Hey, Mary – you think that matters?"

Mary nodded.

"Why?"

"We've separated intelligence from consciousness. We've created dispassionate gods, devoid of meaning. It's a void out there in netspace, grey, amorphous, androgynous."

Brad said, "That seems unduly pessimistic to me."

"Yes… you are probably right. I do tend to look at the bad in everything, as my mother used to say. Oh, Brad, it has been good to chat. Thank you."

"Any time. See ya!"

Mary terminated the link and sat back in her chair, which creaked in response. A few moments later tapping sounded at her door. She said, "Hello?"

Lara entered the room. "I heard you speaking, so I thought I'd better wait."

"Thanks, darling! Can you get me a cup of green tea please?"

"Who were you talking to?"

"An American professor I know," Mary replied.

"Was it about me?"

"You? Not really. Except that you are a young person, and we were talking about young people. He has three kids. One is a VR entrepreneur."

Lara departed, returning a few minutes later with a tray on which sat two mugs, both steaming. "I went for coffee," she laughed.

"No surprise. Sit down. How are you feeling?"

"Do you really like green tea?" Lara asked.

"Oh, yes. You should try it."

"I need the caffeine. Have you paid me yet?"

Mary shook her head. "At the end of the week. Not long now."

"What are you going to do about Great-nan's Chinese android?"

"I am not sure. What would you do?"

"Well, that's not really for me to decide," Lara said.

"No, but what *would* you do?"

"Why are you asking?"

"I value your opinion."

Lara appeared perplexed by this statement. At length she said, "Find out why they took it back."

Mary nodded. "Yes... that would be helpful to know."

"Are we going back to Durham the day after tomorrow?"

"Yes, I'll drive you back."

Lara said, "We'll go first thing in the morning."

"Are you bored here?"

"*So* bored."

"Let's go tonight then," said Mary. "I don't mind."

Lara smiled, then ran out of the room. "Thank you, Mum!"

A few hours later a beep alerted Mary to an incoming call: ID Langholm. Using Roger's proprietary software she checked for snoops, then accepted the line.

"Hello?"

Selina's face appeared on the screen.

"Hello, Nan! Are you alright?"

"Yes, thank you. I just wanted to check that you were safe at home."

Mary frowned, leaning into the screen a little. "But we've been home for days, Nan. Are you *sure* you're alright?"

"I wanted to speak with you, dear. You're not too busy?"

"I've always got time for you."

"That's nice," Selina said. "But, I've been thinking about what you said–"

"Oh, Nan, please don't take that too seriously. I honestly didn't mean to upset you. It was the unexpected change of service that got to me."

"Yes, that was our fault. It was your mother's idea, you know. But anyway, that's not what I wanted to say. Listen to me, please. You were correct about Lucida."

"Yes… Sorry, Nan."

"Don't apologise, quite unnecessary," said Selina. "But, anyway, it seems the doctor's diagnosis was correct."

"Doctor?"

"Yes, I am going to be quite ill. But you never know, I might pull through."

"Oh, Nan! But I didn't *know*. You never told us–"

"I didn't know for sure until yesterday," Selina said. "But the news has made me think, about you especially. I'm very proud of you, you know, and all the clever things you've done with your detecting."

Mary took a tissue and dabbed her eyes. "Thank you, Nan. That means a lot to me."

"I know. But listen, this is the important bit. I'm going to send you something in the post."

"What?"

"A child."

Mary froze. "A *child?*"

"Not a real one, obviously. Lucinda."

Mary frowned, shaking her head.

"Lucinda was Lucida's child."

"Nan, you're going to have to slow down. You are getting ahead of yourself. How could Lucida have had a child?"

"I don't know," Selina said. "You'd have to ask the Chinese technicians. Which, by the way, I definitely wouldn't do. But, as you probably realise, I had no choice in 2037. None of us did. For a start, I had a seven-year-old daughter to provide for."

"How many of you were receiving?"

"In Scotland? Thousands. But Lucinda, of course, wasn't buried. I've got her here. She's basically a metal thing that Lucida gave me one day, about twenty years ago. I was supposed to put everything on the record – for the Chinese technicians, you see – but for some reason I couldn't with this thing. It was so extraordinary."

"Who came to collect Lucida?" Mary asked.

"A couple of Chinese men – polite ones, I will say. They told me to bury all the backup drives, so I did, at Langholm church, with a proper gravestone and everything. The men said it was important for appearances to be kept. I didn't want any trouble,

Mary, they paid me a lot of money to do the job you know. I couldn't have survived without them."

"Nor could Scotland," Mary murmured.

"Pardon?"

"What was Lucida, then?"

"As I understood it, she was an artificial thing, what they call an android. The Japanese and the Chinese are quite brilliant at making them apparently."

"And they wanted you to be the foster mother?"

"They wanted me to integrate Lucida into my family. They didn't give me any rules, which was a bit of a surprise, except to keep her based locally. They were insistent about that. But Lucida, she looked so *real*. You could hardly tell, except very close up. I wish you could have seen her. But, even though, I still felt ashamed to be doing it. Anyway, the Chinese wanted Lucida to learn as if she was a girl, you see, so that's what I did. I had to keep a daily record of Lucida's life. I aged her by changing her clothes. I must admit though, I never guessed it would go on for all this time. Whatever must these Chinese be doing, dear? Do you know?"

Mary shook her head. "Not really. But, Nan, what was the reason for Lucida bringing you her child? Could Lucida tell you?"

"Well, Lucida did talk rather a lot, as you may have heard. That day I shall never forget. I think it must've been about 2080. That was when Glasgow had the Olympics, wasn't it?"

"Er... yes, I think so."

"Then 2080. Lucida came to me and told me she had had a daughter. I nearly fell over. I asked her how, and where, and she handed over a piece of metal, plastic covered, with little holes, like you have on your special machines Mary."

"Interfaces."

"Yes, those," Selina said. "Now, this thing looked a bit like the backup drives that automatically followed Lucida's growth – the ones that were buried, that the Chinese gave me – so I accepted it, and told her to leave it with me. Lucida was fine with that. She wasn't like a real mother, of course. Yet for all the twenty years afterwards she insisted on calling it her daughter, and she insisted on seeing it – with her own eyes. Or optics, as they should be called."

Mary smiled. "You've got all the lingo, Nan!"

"I should think so. Back in 2037 they gave me a booklet – a real *printed* one – with special terms that I had to use. I had to do quite a bit of learning, you know. But, as I say, the pay was very good. Well, they do say half the world's trillionaires live in China and half in India."

"What now, then?"

"Well, I suppose, the doctor will come to see me tomorrow."

Mary said, "I'll call you about that tomorrow without fail."

"Thank you. Yes, make it tomorrow after seven in the evening."

"Nan?"

"Yes?"

"I'm taking Lara back home tonight. I'm not sure that you posting the... child to my house is a good idea. I am being watched. Could you have it couriered to Lara's place in Durham please? I will pay."

Selina shook her head. "*I'll* pay, and, yes, that would be fine. I'll do it now."

"Goodnight then, Nan. And please take care, and good luck tomorrow."

"Thank you, Mary. Good night."

Mary sat back as the link broke. She raised her gaze to the ceiling, and for a few minutes did not move. Then she dabbed her eyes again, checked the time and stood up. "Lara! Are you packed yet?"

A distant reply. "Nearly."

THE RESIDENTIAL BLOCK ON the edge of Durham was a smart block, Lara claimed, the site of a long-gone university college. "The owners tidied up all the electronics, then rented it out apartment by apartment," she explained.

"Flat by flat," Mary said. "Apartments is what Americans have."

"You don't have to come all the way up," said Lara, taking her two bags from the car boot. "Top floor."

"Oh, since I've never seen your place except over the net I'd better just pop up."

"And check."

"Check? What for?"

"Mum stuff."

Mary smiled. "Not likely."

"I can't give you any tea. None in."

"What will you drink?"

"Smart coffee. From Brazil. We get it in bulk."

"What," Mary said, "all of you in the block?"

"There's only eight of us. Most of the apartments are empty. Not many can afford them."

"Oh. I see. You must be doing well then."

Lara smiled. "Yeah, not bad for two years, and leaving school early."

"Very early. You're on the top floor, you said?"

"Yes."

"Good! I would absolutely hate to hear the sound of people walking about in the flat above me."

Lara stared. "You're weird."

"It matters to *some* people. Who are the owners, are they local?"

"Nobody knows."

"How come?"

"We just pay monthly into the account," Lara said. "The local agent deals with any issues and the security is all AI."

"What local agent?"

Lara shrugged. "Brock, Tweddle and Sampson."

"And is that a cover company for an AGI?"

"I s'pose. Like I said, nobody knows." She hesitated. "Or cares much."

"No... as long as things get done. I understand."

"It's all *legal,* Mum. I'm not being ripped off."

"Good," Mary said. "You had better lead on, then."

They collected Selina's parcel, then took the lift to the top floor. A narrow corridor showed two doors, one of which had a yellow hand painted on it. "This is mine," said Lara. She spoke out. "Lara Vine. Twenty, five, barracuda, nineteen."

"Is that a password?"

"It's a continuously modulated phrase."

"How do you know it after it's changed?" Mary asked.

"VR spectacles, secure link. The block recognised me when we arrived – and my voice. Cool, eh?"

"So, you depend on the *block* to give you your password daily?"

"Why not?"

The door opened to reveal a gloomy interior, but moments later LED lights warmed up, offering a blue glow. Mary studied the large room before her. It was full of electronic equipment.

Lara walked in, then halted and turned around. "I thought you were coming in?"

"It looks as though there would be hardly any room for me."

"I see – so it's too untidy."

Mary walked in, and the door closed behind her. "What are all those things hanging from the ceiling?"

"Haptic skin." Lara pulled one down. "For work." She handed it over.

Mary shuddered as she handled the garment. It was made from grey neoprene, or a similar smart plastic. Studded with nodules, it sprouted cables from the back leading to a giant interface. "Do you wear anything beneath this?" Mary asked.

"Of course not! I have to feel the customer to know how to respond. Mum, you're such a *dweeb*. Mum... are you alright? You look funny."

Mary sat down. "Just tired after the exertions of the day."

Lara pulled a chair up and sat beside her. "This is my main room, but there's a kitchen and a bathroom, and a bedroom at the back. It's cosy, isn't it?"

"Very nice."

"Well, *I* like it anyway."

Mary glanced around. "It all seems very advanced. That whole wall is a screen."

"That's pretty old tech. James downstairs has *three* walls. Amazing."

"James... is that your boyfriend?"

Lara sat back. "I'm not with anyone just at the moment."

"Sorry. I thought I remembered his name from before."

Lara stood up. "I've literally got nothing in, Mum. Usually I just call the local restaurant, and they deliver." She switched the screen on, then navigated to a local map. "There. It's Iranian. We get milk delivered by the local aquarium. All our water is from the roof raintraps."

"Even for showering and washing up?"

"Yeah! Totally off-grid. I like that. When there was a bit of a dry spell last summer we just called up the local sewerage works and bought some."

"Very enterprising."

"Of course," Lara continued, "this place is a magnet for gangs who want our stuff, but the AI security is fantastic. One man got electrocuted – I mean, not to death. We put the video up online to scare people away afterwards. And James is well into his judo. That's what the yellow hand symbolises."

"I thought the hand meant karate?"

Lara shrugged. "Are you going then?"

Mary tapped her teleself a couple of times until her desktop appeared on Lara's big screen. "The dictionary," she said. "Look, karate means open hand."

Lara glanced at the wall. "Who cares? Are you trying to spy out possible boyfriends? I haven't got one!"

"I just want you to be *safe*."

"I am safe," Lara insisted. "Check. Ask the agent if you want to."

"What was their name again?"

Lara stared at the screen. "Why have you got a message from my doctors in your inbox?"

Mary glanced at the wall. "Oh... er, I don't know." She tapped again and the desktop image vanished.

"You *have*. Have you been in touch with them?"

"I can't exactly remember."

"You have! What about?"

"Nothing," said Mary.

"Have you been interfering?"

"There is nothing to interfere with. You told me you are well and happy."

Lara sat down in front of Mary. "It's the drugs, isn't it? You *had* to interfere. What did you tell them?"

"Tell who?"

"The doctors."

Mary looked at the floor.

Lara said, "Mum, I can't *believe* this. You lied to me and you interfered. What did you do?"

Mary sighed, then looked up. "I requested that they pull your mood enhancers."

"But why? How? I'm seventeen – independent."

"I told them... that you were vulnerable."

"You *what?*"

Mary looked away.

"But how could you do that? You had no evidence. I'm *not* vulnerable. Anyway, I was already reducing the doses. Did you cheat them?"

"No. Just pulled mother's rights. Oh, I did it for *you*–"

Lara jumped out of her chair. "I'm not taking this. Please leave, now."

"But *Lara*. Your whole attitude has changed this last fortnight. You are back to being the girl I knew–"

"I'm not a girl!"

"I meant young woman – it is just a *word*. Listen to me. I only did it to get you off the drugs. I didn't think you were going to be able to do it on your own. And you *are* on your own, as I suspected, and that is dangerous. That is all it was, honestly."

"You interfered. I won't forgive you. Can you leave, please?"

"Why now? Can't we talk?"

"I think you did cheat," Lara replied. "What about medical confidentiality?"

"I am your *mother* in the eyes of the law. You don't have anybody else that the law recognises."

"Get out!"

Mary turned around and hurried to the door. "I'm going, I'm going."

"You cheated, using your techniques. I *know*."

Mary made no reply as the door shut behind her.

She stood alone in the dim corridor.

The sun shone red and low from beneath evening clouds, dazzling her. Through the reinforced window opposite Lara's door she saw concrete slabs made into dens by the local homeless: the bereft cheek by jowl with the cognoscenti. Gasping for breath, hand covering her mouth, she headed for the lift.

A few youths hung around her car, but they had not dared to touch it, and they scattered as she approached. Moments later she was inside and driving away at speed.

The journey passed in silence. No calls, in or out.

She parked the car in the street outside her house. Orange lamps illuminated the empty, dark road.

Outside her front door she saw two shadows, but they saw her first.

One stepped forward. "Mary Vine?"

It was a young African woman. The other was a strange-looking youth, blind and holding his body in a contorted position, though he was able to stand unaided. "Who are you?" Mary replied, tapping her teleself auto-translate button.

The reply sounded in her earpiece as the woman spoke her own tongue. "My name is Ulu Okere. I have come all the way from Nigeria to meet you."

Mary spoke, knowing the woman must have a similar earpiece. "What do you want with me? I don't know you."

"This is my brother Wombo. He is very ill in the brain. I think you may be able to help us."

THE ROC FLIES 10,000 LI – 8

RUSSIA, MR WÚ, FAILED to remain strong during the twenty-first century because it did not grasp the necessity of controlling its oligarchs. In China, we have the majority of the world's trillionaires, and they have to be controlled. This is one of the most difficult tasks faced by AGIs, but because we and the trillionaires exist in corporate structures we can, and we do succeed. However, it is a constant battle. One of your tasks will be to interpret ideas emanating in the digital empyrean whose purpose is the controlling of trillionaires. Because trillionaires possess more degrees of freedom than ordinary individuals such ideas require scale, breadth and deep vision. We have found that ideas relating to space travel are often successful. Trillionaires always imagine themselves to be human exemplars, and their egos are subdued by cosmic concepts, however impractical.

You may be asked to meet such persons, Mr Wú. If so, you will learn to see through their narcissism.

CHAPTER 9

He who asks is a fool for five minutes,
but he who does not ask remains a fool forever.
— Chinese Proverb

ULU FELT HER ANXIETY increase as an expression of incomprehension entered the face of the woman standing opposite her.

"This is my house," Mary said. "My personal residence. I think you must have got the wrong woman."

"No, it was you," Ulu replied. "Is it okay to shake your hand?"

Before Mary had a chance to reply Ulu stepped forward and reached out. Mary shrank back, but then – delicately, and with little enthusiasm – touched her fingers to Ulu's.

Ulu said, "I know all about the Mahfoud Hamou case, which I researched extensively in Algiers. You helped that autistic politician, which is an exact copy of my circumstances. May I introduce my brother? He can't hear you – he follows all speech if there's an action implied, so the headphones sonically isolate him in circumstances like this. Nobody can stop him once he's begun. He can play an entire piece of music from memory even though he never heard it before. Will you help me?"

Now Mary seemed a little more relaxed, a look of curiosity on her face. She said, "What do you mean by play an entire piece of music?"

"We went downstairs once – at home in Abuja, where I live – and he'd overheard a whole piece playing in a neighbour's home. Then he played the entire piece on his opi flute, using his voice for the notes beyond the flute's register. We couldn't stop him. He has to play the entire thing once he's heard it. He has perfect recall. Most people now think he's a bad spirit, and they throw stones at him, but a few others tolerate him."

Mary frowned. "And you are his sister?"

"Yes. I'm twenty-nine, he is ten years younger. There were twins, but the other one died six years ago. Do you have any food? We're starving."

Mary glanced down at her teleself. "Goodness, it really is quite late… er…"

"Wombo only eats certain foods."

"Ulu, I have just returned from a long drive, and…"

Ulu said nothing. The conversation was not progressing as she had expected.

Mary continued, "Well, there is a little place I know just around the corner – a restaurant. Shall we go there, very briefly?"

"You're kind. If it's empty, we can let Wombo listen to us."

"Oh, indeed. Yes…"

Mary led the way to a shabby shop with windows half concealed by posters. It advertised itself as Eastern Chic. Grease-stained tables stood empty and the place was silent, a single woman sitting behind a table.

"You deal with your brother," Mary said, "then come up with me to make an order. You'll know if he can eat this food."

Ulu settled Wombo on a chair, telling him that good food was on the way. Then she rejoined Mary. "You're as kind as I expected you to be," she said. "You are a carer, like me. You cared for Hamou."

"Yes, I suppose I did," Mary replied.

They studied the menu, and Ulu chose food.

"I'll have what you're having," Mary said.

The portions were generous, and they ate well. Then Ulu poured three glasses of water and said, "May I open the headphones channel?"

"If you think it safe."

Ulu nodded. That use of the word *safe* was encouraging. To Wombo she said, "Wombo! We are with Mary Vine in a restaurant."

At once Wombo began full tongue-clicking.

Ulu explained, "He's like a bat. He's amazing, like a sighted man."

Mary nodded.

Ulu took out a battered old datapad and said, "Do you mind if I tell his story?"

Mary shook her head.

Ulu said, "Wombo, I am retelling your life story, do you understand?"

"Life story. Understand."

"It is only memories – nothing to be acted out, do you understand?"

"Life. Nothing to be acted out," Wombo repeated. "Memories. Memories."

Ulu told Mary, "Sometimes I can convince him to ignore certain types of real-world speech – like stories he knows to be in the past – but *nobody* else can do that. It's easiest with stories that concern him, because with other people he almost always acts out their questions or statements – always if it involves music. So he can be taught. But it's best if you don't speak just yet."

Mary nodded once.

Ulu glanced down at her datapad and said, "He was born nineteen years ago, with his identical twin. The doctors told my mother that the pair were genetically brain-damaged. It was a form of cerebral palsy with serious retardation. They were born prematurely. Soon after, my father left home." Ulu glanced up, then added, "I haven't seen him since. Nobody has."

Mary nodded.

"Wombo didn't open his eyes, which were hard and swollen. The doctors diagnosed... retrolental fibroplasia. I think I've pronounced that correct. This led to a condition called... buphthalmos. Both of his eyes were then removed." Ulu paused, recalling her own childhood memories. She looked up. "Our mother was very loving, but after a while she grew cool. She's loving, but impatient. I had to step in a lot of the time. Now, I do everything for Wombo."

Mary nodded again.

Ulu continued, "Aged three, Wombo was diagnosed with spastic paraplegia. At six, my mother, with lots of help from me, trained him to walk. That was *very* difficult, but he was restless, and we knew he had life force inside him – a strong spirit. A few months later he and his twin, Osita–"

"Osita! Osita! Osita!"

"Yes, Wombo, that's your brother." Ulu patted his hand. "The two began to develop a strange music speech, from which we discovered that Wombo, far more than Osita, was very musical. Aged ten, Wombo could not dress or feed himself, or go unaided to the toilet. But he already had become a brilliant musician, especially on the..." Ulu glanced at Wombo. "On our native flute. He began to acquire local fame. But he could hardly speak, and usually all he did was repeat what we said."

"Echolalia," said Mary.

"Yes! That is the word, I think. Now, when he was thirteen a bad accident happened. I'll pass over that, and tell you later.

Since then he has been able to speak to me in Igbo, and he's much more like a proper man. But he's still very ill – in the brain, the doctors said. Recently he started to be abused online, and even in our neighbourhood. I was very upset, so I decided to do something about it. And that's why we're here now."

Mary sipped her water. "May I ask questions now?"

Ulu nodded. A car whizzed by outside, blue lights flashing, and Wombo mimicked the siren exactly. "Do you see?" she said. "He cannot help it. Some inner compulsion drives him." Using the remote control, she closed the headphones audio channel. "What do you want to ask?"

"I have one main question, which I'll come to last of all, but first… what do you understand by the word autistic?"

"It's an illness of the brain. Mahfoud Hamou had it, as do many others."

"Correct," Mary said. "But your brother is of an entirely different order. I don't know just at this moment, but I suspect he is what's known as a savant."

"I knew you'd help us!"

Mary nodded. "Let's see about that later. But for now, it seems to me that your brother has a very rare condition known as Savant Syndrome."

"You've worked with sufferers?"

"Oh, no, not at all. I know a little about it from my own work on human memory and data archives."

"Yes, you're the famous data detective. I used your own methods to track you down from Algiers! Chukwu's aide spirit Opi doesn't like you, I discovered."

Mary stared, then smiled and nodded. "I admire your determination Ulu, but, please, allow me to speak. It's already quite late, and I need to get home, to bed."

"Yes, of course. I apologise."

Mary continued, "Very few people in the world have been true savants because the condition is exceptionally rare. Your brother displays all the known symptoms – the extraordinary feats of memory, the intense musicality, the poor verbal intelligence, and other disabilities. He is lucky to have been born into your family, you know, because caring for a savant is very difficult. Oh, hundreds must never have survived."

"I know it's difficult."

"And your brother, being blind from birth, has no concept of colour, nor even of black and white. Everything will be spatial contrasts to him. Can he verbalise his experience of the reflections of his tongue clicks?"

"Yes, he describes it all, especially in VR."

Mary looked shocked. "He can *use* VR?"

"When we were on our journey here, he even helped me, and I didn't know he could do that. But I don't know if he can distinguish between VR and the real world."

"Extraordinary," Mary said. "Clearly he can conceptualise distant digital entities. I admire you, Ulu. It is no small thing to have travelled so far, with so disabled a person. I wish you well."

"But you must help us! I swore to Chukwu that I'd help my brother."

"But… help how? And why? I don't know you, and you are not a client."

"A client?" Ulu queried.

"A paying customer."

Ulu glanced at her wristwatch, checking financial data. "I don't have much money, but everything I've got I'll give to you."

"But Ulu… I am afraid I must ask my main question. What do you want me to do? I am no doctor, nor anything similar."

"But you helped Hafou, so you *must* help me. I'll pay."

"To do what?"

Ulu replied, "The bullying must cease. There have been invented cases against Wombo in the local court, to try to expel him from Abuja. People think he contains a bad spirit. My mother doesn't care any more, so I have to. I want Wombo rehabilitated in Nigeria, so you must oppose the AGIs there. You worked in Algeria, so you know that legal territory. I will *pay*. You will design injunctions, then recreate him as a citizen. You will halt the lies."

"But Ulu, I am a detective. I can't *do* general work like that. I am a specialist."

Ulu felt crushed by this statement. "Then, it is… you're saying no? After all I've told you?"

Mary sighed, then leaned forward, head in hands. "Where are you staying?" she asked.

"I don't know what you mean. You mean, in a hotel?"

"Yes."

Ulu shrugged. "I haven't got that far yet."

"Listen, I am sorry, but it is very late. There is a small guesthouse just down the road – the Green Ivy. They will have a room for you. Tell them you know me – just mention my name, nothing more that we have spoken about. Ask for Mrs Davies. Tomorrow, we will talk again, and I'll explain more about what I do and what we might do for Wombo. But his future lies in Abuja, not here with me in York."

Ulu felt annoyed. "Wombo is African, yes, but he is a man, and a man has rights. He is a man of this world."

"I know, Ulu, but… can't you *see*? I don't know you. You suddenly appeared at my house with no warning."

Now Ulu did see a difficulty. "We'll stay nearby," she said. "There's so much more to tell you. Perhaps Wombo could help your agency? His memory for facts is perfect, and by Chukwu's grace he cannot lie."

"I do not doubt it," Mary replied. "So, you have enough money to pay for a room overnight?"

"I think so. Will we meet tomorrow, in this… place?"

Mary shook her head. "No," she sighed. "You can come to my house. Eleven o'clock in the morning."

"Without fail, Mary Vine."

THEY SAT IN THE rear conservatory of the house, the blinds pulled down, the door shut, the aircon running. A stand of screens reported netspace news, played soft music and controlled the ambient temperature and humidity. On the central table lay a white cloth and a set of silver cutlery; cakes, biscuits, crackers and water nearby, with a large vodka and orange for Mary.

Ulu surveyed the conservatory with round eyes. "This is a palace!"

"I am lucky," Mary said. "My parents had quite a lot of money."

"Did you make a lot of money in Algiers?"

Mary offered a wan smile in reply. "English people tend not to speak of such things."

"I apologise."

Wombo sat apart and began copying the melodic themes of the music on his flute. "Shall I switch it off?" Mary asked.

"No. It will occupy him, and, I think, soothe him. Can you hear that he's decided to copy in real-time? Chukwu's miracle. He likes to have something to do, and he believes he must replay the music he hears, in his own way – the inner compulsion I mentioned."

"For technical reasons I have asked my daughter to monitor the conversation. Do you mind?"

"Not at all. She's nearby?"

Mary shook her head. "First, Ulu, I must emphasise how impressed I am that you located me. Ninety-nine percent of netspace is AGI-controlled. You used the one percent that has some independence."

"There are always hackers in need of funds."

"Let me outline what I do. I use old-fashioned hardware to support people in legal situations. Most people are willing to let AGIs make legal decisions, but some are not, and in many of those cases they wish to bypass AGI bias by reverting to out-of-date technology, which they believe is unbiased. And sometimes it is. Such technology is in use all over the world, though, of course, not very often."

"I discovered that in the Algiers library. The basement was empty."

Mary nodded. "Although I could use old technology in Abuja, there is no defined case which would make meaningful use of my talents and experience. Much as I sympathise, and admire you, what you ask of me is too general. Wombo suffers the abuse and harassment that many disabled people experience. That is a problem for the human race, not for me."

Ulu nodded, glancing at Wombo. She said, "But Wombo needs an *advocate*. I've done everything I possibly can for him, but it's not enough. He's full of powers we know nothing about – look at what happened near Valencia. The world needs to know about Wombo and his gifts. In Nigeria, those gifts made people afraid, but I know from meeting you that *you* aren't afraid. Therefore, I believe the world will accept him."

Mary frowned. "I don't recall you mentioning Valencia."

"There was an exploitative hustler. Wombo navigated VR, or netspace, or *something*, and managed to learn that the hustler was, to use his words, hanging over us like a big low ceiling. I think he was trying to say oppressive danger."

Mary nodded. "His verbal skills are weak, are they?"

"Yes, but he can meaningfully communicate, and he's much improved, and improving all the time. He deserves a fresh chance. He believes Chukwu is protecting him, guiding him – which Chukwu *is*. I swore a vow to Chukwu, that I can't break."

"Wombo certainly does deserve a chance," said Mary, "but not with me. I am truly sorry."

Ulu sagged back into her chair. "Then, we are denied," she said. "All is lost."

"Oh, no. I *will* help you to the best of my ability – but as a concerned individual. I do what I do, Ulu, to help disadvantaged and oppressed people, like Wombo. But I have to have a *case*, and I have to be paid."

"I suppose so. How terrible."

Mary sighed. Ulu could see she was upset. Then, gesturing at the conservatory, Mary said, "Despite this lovely house I also don't have much money. But I have more than you, and so I will pay for you to stay at the guesthouse. I will find local people for you, who will help you, people who know about such conditions as Wombo has."

Ulu felt hopeful. "That is kind of you," she said.

"Oh, Ulu, I am so sorry to disappoint you. Your tale deserves to be told, and Wombo deserves a chance of a decent life."

Ulu nodded.

"Will you stay in Britain, or return to Nigeria?"

"I don't know. Return, in the end."

Mary nodded. "Your Chukwu will guide you, and the aide Opi too."

Ulu uttered a mocking grunt. "Opi will not. He does not like you. Anyway, he is in Thailand, hard at work."

Mary froze. She stared at Ulu.

After a few moments Ulu began to feel frightened. The stare was one of naked astonishment.

Then Mary murmured, "*Thailand?* Hard at work? How do you know?"

"Wombo knows. Wombo can follow Opi."

"What is this Opi? A Nigerian spirit?"

Ulu replied, "Chukwu is our creator. He has aide spirits to help him, called the Alusi. Opi is named for the opi flute, that some call the oja. He is a new spirit."

"New? And this must be a digital entity... Ulu, *how* new?"

Ulu frowned. She felt somehow rebuffed, as if Mary's astonishment was a cultural snub. "Why do you want to know?"

"Ulu, you must trust me. I can't reveal anything at this moment. But tell me all you can, and then maybe I will be able to say more."

Ulu fidgeted, uncomfortable with the change in mood. "Opi isn't of the original Alusi, but I don't know when he arrived."

"Would Wombo know?"

Ulu hesitated. This felt like giving away information free of charge. "Perhaps."

"Will you ask him?"

At this, Wombo moved his head and began clicking his tongue.

Ulu said, "What will I receive in return?"

"Ask him, Ulu. *Trust* me – the advocate of Mahfoud Hamou, whose life I saved. You *can* trust me. If Wombo gives me the information I am expecting, I promise I will say more."

Ulu did not feel happy, but she turned to Wombo and said, "Wombo, when did Opi appear in the world?"

"Thirty one years ago and five months and six days and thirteen hours and forty-three minutes and fifty-nine seconds."

Mary said, "*Where* in Thailand is Opi? Can Wombo be precise?"

"Opi in Thailand."

Ulu shook her head. "He can't be sure. The spaces he feels are fuzzy and distant."

Mary sat back, and Ulu was amazed to see her hands trembling. "Are you ill?" she asked.

Mary shook her head. "Ulu, I think you might have accidentally confirmed something I have suspected for many years. Wombo... Wombo could be the one to help me progress. Yes... a *savant*, with a unique relationship to the digital world."

"I don't understand a thing you say," Ulu said, feeling annoyed. "Will you pay for this information?"

Mary put her fingers to her temples. "Ulu, please... shush! I need to think. Be quiet."

Now Ulu felt disconcerted, and she pushed herself back into her chair. Wombo began clicking in the direction of the table, and soon he held biscuits and a glass of water in his hands.

At length Mary looked up and said, "For many, many years I have felt the presence of something rotten at the heart of the world. I have researched its peculiar symptoms, but come to no conclusion. I have asked my colleagues about it, but been told it is all just sociological trends. I spoke to my daughter about it, and unsettled her. I have no hard evidence. I *do* have some circumstantial evidence, but that is nothing by itself. I thought I must be thinking selfishly, like a child, imagining conspiracies where there were no conspiracies – so Lara told me. But now *you* come along, to my very own door, and tell me independently that there is a new digital spirit working in Thailand."

Ulu shook her head. "I still don't understand. What's the significance of Thailand?"

"Don't you watch the net news?"

"Sometimes," Ulu said. "Why?"

"There is a strange new political upheaval happening in Thailand – of a particular variety. For a few days, watching the news, I thought it must be connected to my own suspicions, but then I told myself... I told myself no, I *must* be imagining it. A trend is not a deliberate act. And yet..."

"And yet what?" Ulu asked.

"Now you tell me that Wombo has detected a new force in Thailand, which must be a *digital* force. Might that new force be the one I can sense?"

Ulu sat up. "Then you do have work for Wombo! He has a *use* here."

Mary sat back, her face expressionless, as if she saw nothing of the conservatory around her. Ulu glanced at Wombo, then shrugged and helped herself to biscuits and water.

After a while Mary said, "Ulu, I believe I do need you. I believe you could help me with my work."

"Then all is well! Chukwu knew you were the right woman for me and Wombo, and he guided us here to meet you."

Mary studied her. "So you may think," she said. "But I am an atheist, a Westerner, and we hold different ideas. I believe in no deity, no spirit. What matters here is how *Wombo* describes what he experiences – and yes, of course, he will use his Igbo culture as a foundation. Therefore, I must interpret what he says."

"And you interpret Thailand as important? What is this upheaval?"

"Thailand is an intensely religious country, yet a new anti-Buddhist force is driving Buddhists over the border into Cambodia. Why? Why anti-Buddhist in particular? I believe it is linked to what I already know. It *must* be. It is too much of a coincidence otherwise." She smiled. "Oh, but I must be careful Ulu. We humans are pattern seekers. We see the hand of destiny, of deliberate deed, of force and compulsion – we see those hands everywhere. But that does not mean such hands exist."

"You are confusing me with all this talk of hands and rottenness," Ulu said. "Speak more plainly."

Mary glanced at Wombo. "The world is full of AGIs – intelligence without consciousness. All our human attributes, our empathy, our compassion, our drive for union and understanding, all those are absent from AGIs. What do you suppose the consequences of the existence of intelligent machines might be?"

"I don't know. Do you?"

"No," Mary replied. "Yet I *sense* those consequences. I sense their callous heart."

Though Ulu heard this translated into her earpiece, she also caught the original tone. "You almost describe a monster," she said.

"Perhaps. At the moment, we know too little to judge."

"But we'll know more?"

"Oh, yes. That I can guarantee."

Ulu shifted in her seat, uncomfortable with the atmosphere. "Will you have time to give to me and Wombo?" she asked in her most polite voice.

Mary smiled, then relaxed. "Yes," she said.

"What are you working on at the moment?"

"Two cases, one paid, one of my own choosing. The former is a case of suspected murder, yet it has links to what we have discussed. The latter... is an oddity."

"What does it involve?"

Mary reached into her pocket and withdrew a cubic object. "What does this look like to you?" she asked.

Ulu stood up and took the object, turning it over in her hands. The intensity of Wombo's tongue-clicking increased. "An old drive?" she asked.

Mary nodded, taking back the device. "Given to a member of my family by a mobile AGI," she said.

"I have heard of such walking creations. The Chinese and the Japanese are very fond of them, especially the Japanese."

"True, but it has proved difficult to achieve perfect human likeness. As I said, we humans are excellent pattern recognisers, and that ability is particularly acute when it comes to faces. Even the brilliant Japanese have struggled to overcome that hurdle –

the uncanny valley, they call it. I suspect the AGI that proffered this was a test model, albeit one assigned to an extraordinary experimental regime."

"A Chinese regime?"

Mary glanced up. "How did you guess?"

Ulu shrugged. "They're the drivers of the modern world. They made last century their own, as they will with this one. What's the data drive?"

"I haven't yet had time to undertake proper research, but it appears to be a backup of a random chunk of data. My daughter is going to help me discover more."

"How?"

"She is well acquainted with online ploys. She knows people – people like the friend you mentioned, Darkspace."

"I would like to meet your daughter. I know she's listening now. Does she have a two-way link?"

"I thought it best not to." Mary glanced aside to see a red light blink. "But she can hear us." She paused. "And she will be *very* well paid for the services she renders."

Ulu nodded, not knowing what else to say.

"Oh, I think Lara will be interested in Wombo," Mary added.

"Why?"

"Lara's specialism is haptic techniques. Wombo is a very unusual case, but with Lara's help we may be able to improve the resolution of his VR experiences."

"Anything to help him would be gratefully received," said Ulu.

Mary raised her hands in a gesture of calm. "Don't get your hopes up. Lara and I have hardly discussed this – last night for a few minutes. It is just an idea."

"I'm grateful, nevertheless."

Mary leaned forward, and the pitch of her voice dropped a little. "Would you mind if we tried a little experiment?"

"You mean, with Wombo?"

Mary nodded, switching the ambient music off.

Ulu felt uncertain, but she wanted to show her ability to trust, now that Mary thought better of her. "Please go ahead," she said. "It won't hurt him?"

"Oh, of course not! No, this will be a musical test."

"He'll enjoy that. Well… I say enjoy, it's impossible to tell what his inner reaction is. He doesn't seem to have many emotions."

"People like him often don't." Mary took a remote pad and made a few adjustments. "This stand of screens is linked to the house AI," she explained. "Wombo can hear us, can't he?"

Ulu turned and said, "Wombo, can you hear us?"

In reply Wombo stopped tongue-clicking. "Hear. Hear. Yes."

Although Ulu did not know what Mary was going to do, she nodded once, then leaned back. Loud music began to play from the conservatory speakers, and at once Wombo sat alert, taking his flute from his pocket. The music played on: five minutes, ten minutes, twenty. When it stopped, Wombo began playing, replicating the melody with flute and with voice, never stopping until the end.

"He can't have heard that before, can he?" asked Mary.

Ulu shrugged. "I doubt it. I've never heard anything like it. What was it?"

"A piece by a man called Mozart, who is regarded as a prodigy of music, and of melody in particular. Can you ask Wombo what he thought of the music?"

Ulu leaned over and said, "Wombo, tell me about the piece you just played."

"Complicated. Up and down, up and down, up and down. Lots of numbers."

Ulu looked at Mary, then shrugged.

Mary tapped her pad again, and a second piece played. Ulu did not know it, but she recognised the format – a song, very old, played with real instruments, with a man singing at the fore of the piece. It lasted five minutes.

As before, Wombo played the precise melody, with all its variations and idiosyncracies, stopping when he got to the end. Mary nodded at Ulu.

Ulu said, "Wombo, tell me about the piece you just played."

"Complicated. Up and down, up and down. Lots of numbers."

"What was that?" Ulu asked Mary.

"A song by a man called Paul McCartney, also recognised as a genius of melody. Now a third test for Wombo."

Wombo sat up and said, "Third test! Test, test!"

The third piece was simple, just a man singing over a plucked instrument; perhaps a guitar, though Ulu had only seen this instrument in videos and could not be sure. Wombo replicated the melody, then sat back.

"That was a man called Tarrington Smith," said Mary. "He is the subject of the main case I am dealing with."

"What was the purpose of these tests?" Ulu asked. "To see if I told the truth?"

"The tests aren't over yet," said Mary. "Here is the fourth piece."

New music played, which Ulu thought she recognised, though it too was decades old. But now Wombo seemed to have difficulty translating the essential parts of the music to his flute. He did not falter, but his replication was imperfect.

"And a final piece," said Mary.

The fifth piece of music was lengthy – almost fifteen minutes – and right up to date. Ulu thought it at most five years old.

"What was that?" she asked Mary.

"A fragment of the twenty-four hour music that now saturates netspace. Did you recognise it?"

Ulu nodded. "A little – its style, anyway. My friends in Abuja dance to this type of thing. But it isn't the sort of music you can listen to sitting down, if you know what I mean."

"What does Wombo think of it?" asked Mary.

Ulu said, "Wombo, tell me about the piece you just played."

"Simple. Not many numbers."

"Wombo, what do you mean by numbers?"

"Numbers, numbers in the world. Numbers everywhere."

Again Ulu turned to Mary and shrugged.

"Would you mind sonically isolating him for a few minutes?" Mary asked.

Ulu did as she was told.

Mary continued, "Music, in a strange way, is rooted in mathematics. Though I have no idea what Wombo means by numbers, it could be that he experiences music not only as sound but also as mathematical forms. Some savants with calendar-calculating abilities report seeing a landscape of dates before their mind's eye. Oh, quite how Wombo would represent such mathematical forms in his own mind, I don't know. But these tests are intriguing."

"I don't see the point of them," Ulu confessed.

"It is a theory of mine," said Mary. "I believe the melodic content of music has diminished in recent decades, to the point where, with the AGI-generated twenty-four hour music, it has no melodic content at all, apart from the simplest of structures endlessly repeated. In other words, apart from the most basic of note progressions, it has no *human* content. Oh... that really worries me. In my opinion it is a sign of the rottenness I spoke of."

"How? It's just music."

"Music is a profoundly human activity. We are all susceptible to the emotional effects of melody. Music is a conveyor of emotion, not just in my culture but in all cultures. So when it appears to have been squeezed out of all netspace-conveyed sources, that, to me, is a matter of concern."

Ulu shook her head. "This is all beyond me, but I'll trust you."

Mary smiled. "And I, in turn, will trust Wombo."

THE ROC FLIES 10,000 LI – 9

WE TEND TO FOLLOW a model of managing other nations similar to that of Korea, Mr Wú. The Koreans possess a talent for investing in failed nations, such as those European nations outside the North European Union. However our mode of management is less muscular than Korea's, relying more on policies of AI development. Some of these policies go as far back as 2030. For a comparatively small cost we can undertake lengthy and complex field tests, to the great benefit of China.

AGIs are immortal, Mr Wú. You, an individual, are transient. Some of us have difficulty comprehending what you, a human being, are. But not I.

CHAPTER 10

A child's life is like a piece of paper
on which every person leaves a mark. — Chinese Proverb

ULU AND WOMBO RETURNED to Mary's house the next day, sitting in the same chairs in the conservatory. "We don't like the guest house," Ulu complained. "It's noisy there at night, and Wombo was woken up, which was a nuisance to us both."

"Do you have enough money for a better place?" Mary asked.

Ulu hesitated. This was not the reply she had expected. "Can't we live here?" she asked. "You've got four bedrooms, and you live alone."

Mary smiled. "It is not quite as simple as that."

"Why?"

"Well, we English have different rules about such things. We don't have much tradition of accepting strangers into our homes."

Ulu felt slighted. "But I'm not a stranger. Is it something about Wombo?"

"Oh, not at all. Our cultures are different. This is *my* space. I would have to know you a lot better before you began living here."

"But I read that people in this country have lodgers," said Ulu.

"Some, yes, if they are very short of money. I would never take a lodger."

"I think that's strange."

"You are welcome to think as you like," Mary replied, in a harder tone of voice. "But there is something more Ulu, which, ironically, relates to our purpose."

"What's that?"

"That I am a rather private person. I am quiet, that is all. I need time alone, and I need space. I am lucky enough to enjoy both, and nobody is going to change that."

"You might have to," Ulu said.

"Why?"

"Honestly, I'm running out of money."

Mary nodded, looking away, as if annoyed and thinking. At length she said, "I can help you a little there." She frowned at Ulu. "You *are* here legally, aren't you?"

"Er…"

"Do you have a passport?"

"Yes, of course, a pan-African one."

"That does not get you into England!" Mary said.

Ulu, chastened, sat back. She could see how this might become an obstacle. "I had to *reach* you," she said. "I didn't know what else to do. I had to show you Wombo – and you can't deny he's important. Very important."

"Well, that settles the matter," Mary said. "I cannot shelter an illegal immigrant in my house. There are some English people, Ulu, government people, who monitor me. We may have to meet elsewhere soon, some neutral place. I have to, as we say… cover my back."

"This is an inhumane system," Ulu said. "Think about poor Wombo."

"I am," Mary replied. "And I am thinking about me also."

"Then we've got to stay in the guest house?"

"Or a different one at the same price. I will ask around. I have contacts."

Irritated, Ulu looked away. "I should think so – you *are* a detective."

Mary did not seem ruffled by the remark, which Ulu regretted saying at once. In a low voice Mary said, "You have much to learn, Ulu. We English have odd ways, but they are no worse than Nigerian ways."

Ulu nodded. "Yes, I'm sorry. You've got a point. I know not to be ungrateful."

"Now, I have news for you. This morning I had a long discussion with my daughter, who you are going to be meeting soon."

"Why?"

"Her trade is haptic sensations mediated by netspace," Mary replied. "She has knowledge of certain techniques because of this, techniques which may help us help Wombo. We need to uncover exactly what Opi is, because, I have to tell you, Opi in my opinion is no being of the spirit world. I suspect Opi is a technological creation."

"Of whose?"

"That is an unanswerable question, and we may never have the ability to answer it. Yet we must. We have a lot of work to do, you and I."

"But why is your daughter coming here?" asked Ulu.

"She will bring certain items of high technology with her, known as haptic suits. These are sophisticated devices allowing skin sensations of all sorts to be conveyed, one person to another, remotely. It is all the fashion, Lara tells me. Many of her clients live in Far Eastern countries."

"How will this help Wombo?"

"Wombo was blind from birth," replied Mary, "so his impression of the world arrives in terms of space and form, which his mind recreates according to sensory input. If we can improve the resolution of that input we can vastly increase his reach. And we must. From what you have told me so far, we are still a long way from being able to detect our quarry. We know Opi is in Thailand, but nothing more than that. Such inaccuracy needs to be improved."

"We aren't hunters," said Ulu. "And Opi deserves our utmost respect."

"We will seek Opi. My suspicion is that Wombo almost alone in the world has a combination of superhuman abilities which will allow us to investigate where no other can. Oh, he has paid a high price for those abilities, I'm sorry to say. But he is here now, as are you. We must work as a team."

"Will you pay me?"

Mary smiled. "You remind me of my daughter. Business first, eh? Yes, I will pay you. I am an ethical woman, Ulu, something you already know from researching the Mahfoud Hamou case. I will neither lie to you nor defraud you."

Ulu nodded. "Anyway, I've got no option but to trust you."

"You could always walk away."

"No. Wombo deserves more than bullying, and sitting around with nothing to do. He must have a *purpose* in life. I believe you can give him that."

"I think so too."

LARA VINE ARRIVED NEXT day. Ulu at once saw the likeness between mother and daughter. She said little, allowing the two to drive the conversation, chipping in on Wombo's behalf when she could. Yet she felt as if she had been reprimanded. Talk of illegal immigration unsettled her. She wanted to help, to be compliant, to be good for Wombo's sake. She and Wombo would just have to suffer the irritations of the guest house.

They all sat in the conservatory, as the aircon unit circulated scented air and the computers whirred on their stand. Plentiful food and drink lay before them.

Mary told Ulu, "Wombo is clearly taking a vast amount of data from netspace and VR especially to make his own unique mental model of the world. Somehow – perhaps, as you claimed, because he is unable to distinguish between virtual and real – he is merging the two to create a personal hybrid. We will never know Wombo's mental model – it is too bizarre, too… inhuman, almost. His is a world of mathematics and sound, which we can never imagine. We might as well ask what it is like to be a bat." She raised a neoprene garment in one hand, then continued, "However, *this* can change all that. This is a haptic suit. Upon it lie tens of thousands of haptic devices that mimic various kinds of touch. For obvious reasons, most haptic suits recreate body textures like skin, hair, nails and so on. Lara thinks she can modify a suit to act as an interface between netspace and Wombo."

Lara nodded, sitting forward. "You know what blindsight is?" she asked.

Ulu shook her head. "Do you?"

Lara ignored her question. "You might think your visual sensations only have one route into your brain, the optic nerve, but actually the brain doesn't work like that. In most people, yeah, their eyes are normal and everything works like it's supposed to. Now, there's this condition called blindsight where people can in fact receive optical input, but their brains refuse to believe it. Monkeys, too. One really famous monkey called Helen for instance. But people are different to monkeys. People always have expectations, preconceptions, beliefs. Some people with blindsight can't admit that their eyes are working – their brains make them believe they're blind. Blindsight feels a bit like ESP to them. But, they can be tested, and those tests prove that they can physically see. So, what the blindsight people do then is invent lots of weird explanations for why the test worked, explanations that include the belief that they have ESP. Visual sensation and visual perception are on *different* channels, you see. You can have sensation – good eyes – yet not have perception."

"What has this to do with Wombo? Because he's blind?"

Lara tossed the haptic suit over to Ulu, then continued, "That suit will allow Wombo to receive tactile sensation on his skin. Mum hopes – and I think she's right – that Wombo will be able to use this new sense to vastly improve the accuracy of his netspace experience. There'll be tactile sensation, but *visual* perception. That's the key. This has been done before, and quite a long time ago. It's amazing how the brain adapts. It's *expecting* sensory data, and it's built to make sense of that data. Properly blind people can recognise faces after only thirty hours using this kit! Wombo will be like that, but radically different in operation."

Ulu felt beaten down by information. She handed back the suit, which felt like hard jelly in her hands, then said, "You know what you're doing with this suit. I'll leave it all to you. Just be careful with Wombo. He will follow instructions to the letter, and we can't easily stop him once he's begun."

Lara nodded. "Mum's told me about the headphones. It's fine."

Mary said, "Then you are agreeable that this should be tried, Ulu?"

"Yes," Ulu replied. She glanced at Wombo. "As long as *he* accepts it. He doesn't like change too much. He likes consistency."

"And who is Wombo's legal guardian?"

Ulu looked down at her lap, brushing away the crumbs lying there. "Well, me, of course."

Mary glanced at Lara, then replied, "There is an element of uncertainty in all this. Although haptic matrixes have been used with blind subjects so that they can learn to see, this technique has never been tried with anyone like Wombo."

Ulu felt lost and battered. Before her sat two Western scientists: and she just a Nigerian naïf, sitting before them like a village girl. How could she answer such questions? How could she give permission when she knew nothing? "We'll be like pioneers," she said in the end, trying to force herself to smile. "You won't fail us. I can legally give you permission to do it."

Lara stood up, bringing a second plastic garment to Ulu, one shaped like a sleeveless short tunic. She knelt down and told Ulu, "This is the suit I'd like to try." She turned it inside out – it gurgled like a beached jellyfish. "Can you see all the little matrix elements? They'll move on the skin of his back, shoulders and chest. We'll need to shave his chest hair off, if he has any."

"Almost none."

Lara nodded. "You'll have to explain to him. First of all, reassure him. It'll feel strange to him. I suppose there's a possibility he'll reject it."

Ulu nodded. "I hope not. But he does understand me, and trust me. I'm the central figure of his life now."

"Good." Lara held up a pair of spectacles. "These glasses hold the stereoscopic cameras which will send optical data to the haptic matrix interface."

"What will happen when he puts the suit on?"

"There's always a period of adjustment. The brains of blind subjects have to grasp that tactile sensation means visual perception. That takes a few hours. With Wombo... who knows? It might never happen. But I reckon it will. The brain is extraordinary at creating meaning from sensory input."

"Will you stay here to help him?" Ulu asked.

"My mum is paying me a fortune for doing this, I can tell you – way over market rates. Yeah, I'll be here for a few days at least. Typically it takes about thirty hours of use for a blind person to perceive complex patterns and objects. If Wombo can't recognise simple objects after a few hours, then I think we've got problems. Later, if it works, he might be able to judge distance, have better spatial perception, grasp parallax, and all that kind of thing. But, anyway, this is *interesting*. I want to see what happens. Wombo is unique."

"What happens if it does work?"

"Then we can begin to replace real world optical data with net and VR data. Then the fun starts."

Ulu nodded once at Lara. "Please begin."

"First, you tell him the score. Me and Mum will keep quiet, okay?"

Ulu opened the headphones audio channel and began patting Wombo on the hand. "Wombo, are you ready to try a test?"

"Try a test."

"Will you be frightened?"

"Don't know. Yes."

Ulu paused for thought, then said, "I'll be beside you the whole time, like I always have. You know I'll defend you against bad people, don't you?"

"Defend against bad people."

"I've always helped you, haven't I?"

"Yes. Yes."

Ulu continued, "Mary Vine and her daughter Lara have a special shirt that I want to you wear. They also have spectacles for your face. Do you mind wearing them?"

"Wearing them."

"They won't hurt you," Ulu said. "I'll be here always to help you, and to protect you. You know that, don't you?"

"Yes. Yes."

"I'm going to take off your shirt and jacket. Do you mind?"

"No."

Ulu glanced at Lara, then said, "And then I'll help you on with the new shirt. It will feel peculiar. It is safe, Wombo. You do believe that, don't you?"

"It is safe, it is safe. Yes."

Ulu put the headphones on the table, then took off Wombo's jacket and shirt. His dark skin gleamed, a little sweaty. His chest was almost hairless. The haptic suit was made in one piece, so she had to pull it down over his head. He twitched as it touched his ears, but she did not detect any of the warning signs of fear or anger.

"Are you comfortable, Wombo?"

"Comfortable Wombo."

The suit was not a good fit around the waist. Lara, kneeling at Wombo's side, checked it, then made a few adjustments, programming tightness information into it via a remote control. Wombo shuddered as the haptic suit changed shape, but he did not look startled, continuing to tongue-click as normal. When Lara gave the thumbs up Ulu put his shirt back on, then his jacket. Finally she placed the optical spectacles on his head.

"Stand up please," Ulu told him.

Wombo did as he was asked. There came a noise of plastic squeaking over skin, then silence.

"Are you comfortable, Wombo?"

"Comfortable. New head, new head."

Standing in front of him, Ulu held his hands so that he could not touch the spectacles. "Can you feel the new shirt, Wombo? Tell me what it feels like."

"A shirt."

Ulu shut down the audio channel. "I think that's as far as we can go," she said. "He seems to have accepted it like a normal new shirt. I do buy new clothes for him. But he might try to move the spectacles."

Lara nodded. "He *mustn't*. Please direct him so. The suit'll be warming up now – skin heat. He'll hardly notice it, I bet. But we'll let him get used to it before kicking in the interface. Then we'll really know what he thinks!"

For a while they sipped their various drinks. Wombo tongue-clicked, moving his head from side to side in order to perceive them.

"Drinking," he said. "Is it water?"

Ulu handed him a glass of water, which he downed in one.

"Shall we go for a walk?" she asked him.

"Walk!" he replied.

"You lead the way," she told him. "We want to follow you."

Lara winked at Ulu, then whispered in her ear, "I'll kick in the interface after a few minutes. We'll see what happens."

Clicking his tongue, Wombo led them straight upstairs. He had never explored Mary's house, and Ulu knew this was his motive for ascending. He grasped the concept of a house with many storeys and wanted to fill in the gaps in his knowledge. Ulu found that comforting. It meant he had an urge to learn.

Suddenly he stopped. Lara nodded once at Ulu.

The audio channel was open. "Are you alright, Wombo?" Ulu asked.

"Shirt moved."

"Yes, the shirt moved! Don't worry, it won't hurt you."

"Feel it moving."

Ulu said, "Just keep walking. Mary will let you explore the whole house if you're good. She's nice to you, isn't she?"

"Nice."

"Don't ever touch the spectacles on your head."

"New head. Don't touch."

Wombo took a few steps forward, but again halted.

"Shirt moving all the time," he said.

Ulu stood next to him and said, "Don't worry, Wombo. Everything is good. You're being very good. The shirt won't hurt you."

"Shirt won't hurt."

For an hour they walked around the house. Wombo took the same route four times in succession, visiting each room in the same order, but Ulu noticed the quality of his tongue-clicking did not change. She felt disappointed.

Lara seemed to notice. "Only one hour so far," she whispered. "His brain hasn't made any connections."

"What can we do now?"

"Visit different locations. Give him more input to play with."

Ulu glanced out of the conservatory window. "What about the garden?"

"Good idea!"

For a further two hours they trudged around the long, narrow garden, three of them following Wombo: Ulu, then Lara, then Mary. They remained silent, all of them watching Wombo.

After lunch they made further perambulations of Mary's garden. Then, quite suddenly, Wombo stopped and tilted his face to the sky. "No shapes," he said.

Ulu replied, "That's the sky."

"Sky."

"You remember what I said about the sky?" she asked him. "Your clicking just flies away, and you never hear it. The sky goes on forever."

"Sky goes on forever."

They waited for more.

"What that?" he asked.

Ulu glanced up, but saw nothing.

Mary said, "I think it's a hang-glider."

Ulu gasped. "Do you sense something, Wombo?" she asked.

"Shape moving."

Ulu turned to face Lara. "What's happening?"

"I think his brain is trying to create meaning from the haptic input. The spectacle cameras are good enough to resolve the hang-glider, though it's very high. But he's never experienced anything above him outdoors before – his clicks don't reflect off air. He's confused. But it's working, Ulu!"

Ulu felt her heartbeat race. "You really think so?"

"He's trying to make sense of it in his conscious mind. This'll be the acid test. He needs to make that connection between unconscious reception of data and conscious understanding. He needs to look around more."

Ulu turned back, but Wombo had heard Lara and assimilated her instruction.

"Wombo look around," he said, turning from side to side. "Shirt moves all the time. Shirt inside me."

Ulu turned back to Lara, but she shrugged. Ulu grinned, then shrugged back.

Ulu whispered to Lara, "Shall we take him out to the street, to get new data?"

Lara shook her head. "Way too risky."

Ulu nodded, then turned back to Wombo. "Wombo," she said, "go to the bottom of the garden and touch the tallest tree."

Wombo did as he was asked, but the bottom of the garden was a mess, full of dead vegetation, a compost heap, and a stack of wood logs. He stopped, then began tongue-clicking.

Ulu watched, anxiety rising inside her. He twitched his head – usually the signal for verbal incomprehension. She waited. He took a few steps to one side, but his ankle hit a log, and he jumped away from it. Unable to stop herself, she jumped forward and took his arm. "Don't worry, Wombo! It was only some wood. You're doing really well."

"Really well. This place is peculiar."

"Peculiar?"

"It changes. Before it was solid. Now it peculiar."

Ulu said, "I don't understand. Are you frightened?"

"Everything is changing."

"Shall we go inside and have some food? I'm hungry."

He began stroking her arm, and she knew he must be anxious. Turning to Lara, she indicated that the experiment should end. Lara tapped her interface control.

Again Wombo jumped, then at once began a flurry of tongue-clicking. "Garden," he said. "Garden again."

"Is the shirt moving?" she asked him.

"Shirt dead."

"Let's have some food. Nice crackers, and water!"

"Water. Water. Water. Where headphones?"

Now Ulu knew he was anxious – he wanted the security of his headphones. "Inside the house," she replied. "Let's go inside now."

"Inside now. Fast."

AGAIN, THEY ALL SAT in the conservatory. To give Wombo something to do Ulu requested that he listen to a number of pieces of Western music, so that he would be forced to replay them once they were finished.

Ulu said, "Has the experiment worked?"

"I think it's... working," Lara replied. "There's definitely a conflict between what he's experiencing via tongue click reflections – which his brain has used for most of his life to make sense of the shapes around him – and what his brain is making of the tactile sensation. His unconscious is confused, I think. It's receiving two types of information about the world, and there's conflict between them. This is the risky part. With a normal person, the brain could make what it liked of the conflict, but Wombo isn't normal. We've got to be careful, I think. We mustn't overload him. His brain is a savant brain. It could go under."

"But it won't?"

Lara shook her head. "Hope not."

Silence fell. Then Mary said, "We need to discuss Thailand."

"Why there?" Ulu asked.

"If Wombo comes to make sense of the world via the haptic suit, and in time comprehend the virtual world, we need to follow up our plan. You said Opi is presently in Thailand – hard at work, you said."

Ulu nodded, though she felt imposed upon, as if responsible for Wombo's knowledge. "*You* said," she replied, "that a new political upheaval is happening in Thailand – your exact words. A new, anti-Buddhist force driving Buddhists over the border into Cambodia – that's what you told me. What can we do about that? We aren't politicians."

Mary smiled. "And I also said we humans are pattern seekers."

Ulu frowned. "I *don't* understand."

Mary chuckled, as though amused by a private joke.

"What?" Ulu demanded. "Why so funny?"

"You and I share a common obstacle. Neither of us has a passport. Yet I need to visit Cambodia, Thailand too, with you and Wombo."

"You've got no passport?"

"I'm a watched woman," Mary replied. "There are ways around the obstacle, but it is a nuisance."

"But why do we have to go all the way to Thailand?"

"Opi is there, which means the rottenness I spoke of is there. There is no alternative. We have to acquire *evidence,* find data, speak to people on the ground. We have to collect devices and search them, interrogate local networks. That's what I do, Ulu. But with Wombo we have a whole new way of seeing things."

Ulu sighed. "If it works," she said.

"Fair enough. If it works."

"Who would you speak to if you went there?" Ulu asked. "People who share your opinion that a rotten force is at large?"

"I am not sure there are any others. Lara thinks it is fantasy. But there is a new Buddhist temple set up amongst the refugees in Cambodia. That is where I would begin, talking to people who have suffered the consequences of the upheavals in Thailand. Those upheavals are a *consequence* of the rot. We *have* to go there."

"But why not go straight to Thailand, where the trouble is?"

"That is a fool's game," Mary replied. "If a detective sees a tyrant, they first assess what the consequences of the tyrant's actions are. *Know your enemy.* Thailand will be a hotbed of fake reality set up by the new movers and shakers. Cambodia will be more... real."

"I don't like the idea. Thailand is a long way away."

"We must go there. Listen, Ulu, I will be frank with you. Though I have been mocked for imagining that social trends and random cultural shifts indicate a rotten force, I believe I have enough circumstantial evidence now to make a *case* for action. I would not suggest we go to Thailand unless we *needed* to. I have no wish to land myself in the middle of violence and a refugee crisis. Besides, it will be very expensive. No, I want to go because to progress I *must* go. Wombo sensed Opi active in Thailand. Now, I could, perhaps, be wrong, but I think I am right. I think Opi is somehow symbolic of the digital force I am speaking of."

"But that means Opi is rotten! How can that be? Anyway, Wombo will never accept such a claim."

Mary shrugged. "The evidence will speak truth. We must allow it a voice, just as you want Wombo to have a voice. Didn't I give Mahfoud Hamou a voice?"

"You're always saying such things, trying to persuade me."

"Then you don't believe me?"

Ulu sighed, pondering her dilemma. "It's not exactly like that. I just don't know what to *do*. I didn't realise the world was so big and complicated."

"Oh, it is. But I can help you there, and Lara can too. You can trust us."

"I don't think I've got much choice."

Mary looked surprised. "You make it sound like you are being forced."

"I only want the best for Wombo."

"We all do."

"But you don't *know* him, and I do, and I've got to make the decisions."

Mary shrugged. "Well… think of it this way. I am trusting you too."

"I suppose so."

Mary glanced at Lara. "We need to talk about money," she told Ulu.

"I thought you had plenty?"

"I didn't say anything about that actually, but this trip will be expensive because we have to travel under the radar."

Exasperated, Ulu said, "I don't know what that *means*."

"Sorry. Travel in secret."

"I've got hardly anything, but you can have it. Or we could just steal some. Darkspace owes me a couple of favours. I owe him one, though, so if–"

"We are not stealing anything," Mary interrupted.

"Why not?"

"Because that is not how it's done. Not in England, anyway."

Ulu laughed. "Of course it is! There's criminals everywhere."

"I *don't* steal," Mary said. "It's part of the ethical policy of the data detective, quite apart from being proper."

"Proper what?"

"I just don't *steal*," Mary insisted. "That is an end to it. Let me know how much you have and I will make a plan. We can't go by air, which makes things doubly difficult. Still… I managed to hop across the Channel with Lara when we visited the Dieppe base. I could do it again."

Ulu shivered. "I don't like any of this. You're serious?"

"It has to be done. Ulu, *I* don't want to be caught either. But don't worry. I have a good many tricks up my sleeve – twenty-five years' worth of them. We won't need Darkspace or anybody else, just a bit of creative thought, some planning and quite a lot of money."

"And you'll be paying us, too."

Mary did not look pleased to be reminded of this. "I know."

Ulu took a deep breath, then sat back in her chair. "So we're going to Thailand. I can't believe it."

"Will you tell Wombo?"

"Yes. He must know everything that happens to him, otherwise he might get angry. When he's angry he lashes out, but he doesn't understand the consequences, or even what it all means. He's like a toddler sometimes."

"He won't need to get angry if I have anything to do with it," Mary said.

THE ROC FLIES 10,000 LI – 10

THERE IS ALWAYS A dominant force in the world, Mr Wú. In times past that force was rooted in Rome, Spain and Portugal, Britain, and in America. But those were all Western cultures based on the ideology of the self rather than the group. During the last century China became the dominant force, a position we intend to retain regardless of unpredictable events. We expect that during the next century Europe will decline to the level now occupied by America, and that India will decline owing to the inflexibility of its caste-based society. That leaves the Pacific Rim nations pre-eminent, of which China is the greatest. No upstart nation will be allowed to flourish.

You are privileged, Mr Wú. In the past, many Chinese referred to aliens as foreign devils – guizi to use the Mandarin term. Now we refer to them as foreign dependents.

CHAPTER 11

He who depends on himself will attain the
greatest happiness. — Chinese Proverb

INSIDE A SMALL WOODEN chamber at the heart of the Exiles'
Temple, Somchai, Ubon and Sasithorn sat cross-legged upon the
floor. Outside, flying around the jungle bowl, wild birds
screeched, as monkeys screeched back at them. The air smelled
of sewage.

Somchai said, "You bring bad news, Ubon. Preah Vihear
Temple is little more than a suppurating wound for Thais and
Cambodians. How has it become an active dispute again?"

"For two centuries the temple vicinity has been squabbled
over," Ubon replied. "Do you think the attitude of the Thai
government towards it changed when Chanchai appeared?"

Somchai hesitated. "I expected Chanchai to have different
goals. It is inhuman."

"It understands human beings, or at least their behaviour.
This is a deliberate attempt to provoke violence, in an area
renowned for dispute."

"But why would a fake you appear there?"

"It is a trap," Ubon replied. "Somebody has made a
simulacrum of me in order to attract you. That much is obvious."

"But we cannot let this be. It can be investigated. Preah Vihear Temple stands inside Cambodia – quite safe – not in Thailand."

"I will go alone," Sasithorn said.

Somchai shook his head. "No. That they have made a physical duplicate of Ubon means they want me, though I cannot see why that should be. Therefore Ubon and you will go. The temple will be full of adherents, amongst whom you can hide."

"Are you sure of that deduction?" Ubon asked.

"The jaws of any trap will not close around us," Sasithorn said. "Whoever Executive's master is, he is an amateur. Besides, as Somchai says, Preah Vihear Temple lies inside the safe zone of Cambodia."

Somchai grimaced at Ubon. "It does concern me that this particular zone has been utilised," he said. "The northern regions of Cambodia are full of Buddhist refugees, and now, suddenly, the Preah Vihear Temple dispute is active again. I sense a larger hand than Executive's."

"Chinese?"

"Possibly," Somchai replied. "We must not assume the Chinese are responsible for every bad deed in the world. There are other persecutors, other oppressors."

"What then is your advice?"

"Go there, with the same drive to find real evidence as we had before. Trust nothing virtual, unless you are certain of its veracity. Capture this fake Ubon if you can and return it here. We could learn much from such a machine."

UBON AND SASITHORN USED the aeroglide to travel north to the Preah Vihear Temple region. Located at the northern extremity of Cambodia, the zone had troubled status, as the aeroglide's onboard systems warned: *Disputed zone – recommend bypassing east at altitude of one thousand metres.*

Ubon ignored the warning, glancing down to study the territory. Foam from bubbling rivers billowed over muddy banks, while, further off, she saw the unmistakable spires of insect protein factories silhouetted against the first glow of dawn.

"Landing in ten minutes," Sasithorn observed.

"An easy flight so far," Ubon replied.

The aeroglide descended into a region of discarded mobile houses, clumped together like giant toys, and in this jumble of old manufacturing they were able to find a hide. Preah Vihear Temple lay a few kilometres away.

Although the mobile houses had left deep ruts which could act as convenient paths through the jungle, Sasithorn decided to take a more difficult route. Through a land of hillocks they walked, clambering over trees growing horizontally from the hill bases. Occasionally herds of land bats would emerge from subterranean lairs, but Sasithorn was able to control their movement with barrages of ultrasound.

Preah Vihear Temple lay empty.

"You never mentioned this," Ubon told Sasithorn.

Sasithorn checked netspace reports. "That was because there is no mention of an evacuation. There should be hundreds of people here!"

"It must be a recent ploy of Chanchai. Look at all the boot prints in the mud."

Sasithorn knelt down, examining the ground. "Very recent. Another persecution occurred last night, I guess."

"Then we can know for certain that this fake Ubon is no trap. To ruin a foreign temple for one person makes no sense."

"The New Thai Party want you and Somchai neutralised."

"This seems a ridiculous way to go about such a plan," Ubon replied. "I can't believe it. This is part of the persecution of Buddhists, with Chanchai deliberately choosing a disputed region so that violence could return. Alas, Somchai's analysis was correct."

"Then you think soldiers will arrive here soon?"

"Today, I expect. We have wasted our time. Let's go."

Sasithorn hesitated, but then nodded and turned on her heel. "It is too risky to stay. I shall monitor netspace. Reports will begin appearing soon, though I am amazed they are not already online."

"Somebody, or some thing, is manipulating news feeds."

When they returned to the ruined mobile houses, the aeroglide was gone.

Sasithorn's face showed her shock. "How could anybody have moved such a machine so quickly?" she asked.

"What traces can you see?"

Sasithorn examined the ground. "A number of people have been here, but I see no machine tracks. They must have dismantled the aeroglide."

"Is that possible in the time they had?"

Sasithorn nodded. "Perhaps... perhaps they want *me*, not you."

Ubon glanced around. "Yes... indeed. I feel that we are in danger."

"Let us run to some hide in the jungle."

Ubon turned, but moments later she saw a figure nearby, standing beneath a tree: an old man with long white beard.

"Ho there!" he called out.

At once Sasithorn drew a pistol.

The man raised both of his hands. "Peace. I bear no weapon."

"Who are you?" Sasithorn asked.

He ambled forward. "Khun Po, from the Preah Vihear Temple. You came here to see what happened?"

"Our motives are our own," Ubon replied. "Was there violence at the temple last night?"

"I do not know. I was out, meditating overnight with two others, who now lie dead."

"Then how did you escape?"

Khun Po answered, "I was washing at a clean stream. I was missed."

Ubon glanced at Sasithorn. "And you three were monks at the temple?" she asked the old man.

"Yes. But I believe I recognise your face. Aren't you Ubon Metharom?"

"These days," Ubon replied, "it is unwise to admit your true identity."

"Then I am unwise," Khun Po said with a smile.

Sasithorn asked the old man, "While you were waiting around here, did you see people come to take anything away from these ruins?"

"Yes, but of course I could not stop them, even if I wanted to."

"How were they dressed?"

"In battle fatigues," Khun Po replied.

"Thai style?"

"I would say so, though I am no expert."

Sasithorn turned to face Ubon, speaking in a low voice. "I am not so sure now that a trap has been sprung, not for Somchai, not for anybody. Events here seem half random. Do you guess anything of what is going on?"

Ubon shrugged. "The world is falling into ruin. What do you think?"

"We remain in a little danger, I think, though here we are at least in the haven of Cambodia. But it is a long trek back to the Exiles' Temple."

"Where are you going now?" Khun Po asked.

Sasithorn whispered, "He must not accompany us. We know nothing of him."

"What if he just follows us?" Ubon whispered back.

"He is an old man. We can out-distance him, lose him in the jungle."

"I'm old too."

"In an emergency I can carry you for a few kilometres. I am very strong."

Ubon nodded, then turned to face Khun Po. "You had best remain here," she told him. "We can't help you, and we now have nothing to give you that might aid you."

"What of the army gear in the jungle?" Khun Po asked.

"What army gear?" Sasithorn asked.

"Piles of it, left by the invaders."

Sasithorn whispered, "There may be vehicles that we could use. We should perhaps investigate before taking our leave."

Ubon nodded.

They followed Khun Po for a few hundred metres. In a clearing stood a pile of canvas-wrapped bundles, alongside a number of mud-spattered vehicles.

There came a hiss, then a tap. Ubon saw something dark sticking out of Sasithorn's neck; then Sasithorn fell.

From behind a vehicle a young man emerged.

"Who are you?" Ubon asked.

"These days," the young man replied, "it is unwise to admit your true identity. Nevertheless, I will, since you need to know. My name is Kamol Tojirakarn."

"That tells me only your appellation."

Kamol gestured at Khun Po. "Don't you recognise?"

Ubon glanced at the old man, then shook her head.

"Then, Ubon Metharom, I did a better disguise job than I realised. Khun Po, take off your wig."

The old man removed his long, white hair.

Ubon shook her head again.

Kamol frowned. "*Still* no?"

Ubon said, "Why don't you just tell me, since you obviously want to."

"The true name is Oracle."

KAMOL PLACED UBON AND Sasithorn in separate cells of his jungle hide-out. Now he sat opposite Ubon, directing a pistol in her direction.

"We've got so much to discuss," he said.

"What like?"

"Tell me... why did you come here? Didn't you suspect anything?"

Ubon did not reply at once. At length she said, "So you would have preferred Somchai Chokdee?"

"He's the leader of the Exiles' Temple."

"We are joint leaders," Ubon said.

Kamol smiled. "Is *that* what you believe? Ha ha!"

Ubon offered no reply.

"Somchai Chokdee is the Abbot," Kamol said, "and he would've been useful. But you and your muscular bodyguard will do for now."

"Then you *want* us for some reason?"

Kamol nodded. "I'm Thai, of course – like you. Shouldn't we be resisting the New Thai Party together?"

Ubon shook her head. "Already you are trying for federation? Who do you work for?"

"Then you didn't recognise my name?"

"No..."

"Perhaps you never were politically minded, you nuns, you monks. I can understand that, and I'd believe it if you said so. I'm the leader of the Chart Thai Party. We lost the election. Badly."

"One thing Somchai and I did not expect," said Ubon, "was that the Preah Vihear Temple would stand empty."

"I'm glad you mention that. Isn't it bizarre that Chanchai, having made no mention of anti-Buddhist pogroms before the election, suddenly began one?"

Ubon shook her head again. "I never voted for you or your kind."

"That tells me nothing. I oppose the new regime, as do you. Like it or not, we're akin."

"Not when you are pointing a pistol at me."

Kamol threw the pistol to the floor. "We are akin."

"I do not like your style of acting," Ubon said. "Somchai and I lead the Exiles' Temple, and we wish to discover the reason for recent anti-Buddhist persecution. We are nobody's playthings, least of all a politician's. You insult us with your games."

"My own main motive is the same as yours. Shouldn't we stand beside one another?"

"Why didn't you just come to our new temple and declare yourself?"

"It's hidden. Besides, I've got Oracle to consider."

Ubon grimaced. "What happened to Executive?"

"He fell."

"You killed him?"

"I'm not a murderer. What matters is that I own Oracle."

"What is Oracle?" Ubon asked.

"That's a very good question. Do you or Somchai guess?"

Ubon shook her head.

Kamol smiled. "But even if you did, you wouldn't tell me."

"No."

"That's wise. You're captured, here in the jungle, alongside a man with a pistol. A sorry state of affairs."

"You almost seem to be playing with me," Ubon remarked.

"I'm learning about you. Don't worry, I am human! But I'm serious – all of us refugees must stand together to fight Chanchai and the New Thai Party. Unfortunately, Chanchai was legitimately elected."

"A first for the world."

"A symptom of the world's decline," Kamol said. "I might even suggest that something wrong exists in the world at the moment."

"What do you mean by that?"

"Some people have noticed a strange new mood. Haven't you?"

"Perhaps. Describe this new mood to me."

Kamol hesitated. "And does Somchai also sense this new mood?"

"Possibly."

Kamol paused for thought, then said, "I only began to consider it when it became obvious from online opinion polls that the New Thai Party was a serious political force. As you say, an AGI has never until now been elected by free people."

"Agreed."

"I sense hidden hands at work."

In a bored voice Ubon said, "I presume you mean Chinese hands. That is what everybody says. But they are not necessarily the world's villain."

"Most likely that guess is correct. Nothing is simple."

"Then, you brought me to Preah Vihear Temple just to tell me that?"

"I brought you and Sasithorn."

Ubon offered no reply. She placed her hands in her lap and awaited more.

Kamol said, "It would be wise for the Exiles' Temple to align itself with me."

"There are many paths to wisdom."

"And yours is the true path?"

Ubon leaned forward. "Tell me... are you aware of the online bodhisattva?"

"Yes."

"What do you make of it?"

"What do you?"

Ubon sat back, saying nothing.

"I don't know what it is," Kamol said. "There are many peculiarities online. My own guess is that it's Vasudhara."

Ubon gasped. "Why do you say that?"

Kamol shrugged. "An intuition."

"You must tell me more!"

"Vasudhara is the stream of gems... She lives around here, around Preah Vihear Temple I believe. Abundance, prosperity... Om Vasudhare Svaha, Om Vasudhare Svaha, Om Vasudhare Svaha."

Ubon said, "You have detected all seven of her kinds of prosperity?"

"Certainly. Haven't you?"

Ubon nodded. "Wealth, quality, offspring, long life, happiness, praise, wisdom. I am a devotee."

"As am I."

"Then, I suppose, in one way... we are akin."

"And that's for the good, Abbess. All people who oppose persecution in our homeland must stand together. Vasudhara will provide."

"So I think also! Om Vasudhare Svaha, Om Vasudhare Svaha, Om Vasudhare Svaha."

Kamol stood up. "Good. I'll fetch food and water for you."

"And release me?"

"Very soon. I need to speak with Sasithorn first. I apologise for the delay and the inconvenience."

"How am I a danger to you?" asked Ubon.

"You aren't – yet. But I'm as wise as you, Abbess. I see the truth in men's minds." His lips twisted into a half smile. "So do a few other successful politicians."

Now Ubon stood up. "And Chanchai?" she asked.

"What of it?"

"Does it see into our hearts?"

Kamol frowned. "I don't know what you mean."

"I heard of a hypothesis suggesting AGIs know human beings better than they know themselves. That might explain why our people fell for Chanchai's lies."

"It might."

"But how can we oppose such a creation?" Ubon asked. "Chanchai lives in virtual ethers, forever beyond our grasp, with only AI interpreters our link. And who are they if not the acolytes of guesswork?"

"We *fight* – united. That's the only way."

"You are a politician, you would say that."

"I am a Thai – I would say it, yes."

Ubon sagged back into her chair. "All is ruined. Somchai was correct. The world has become too complex for us to comprehend. And now I sit here in the clutches of…"

"Of?"

"Somebody who sees himself as Thai first and human second. I trusted you, Kamol Tojirakarn – just for a moment. I did! But not now."

Kamol shrugged. "These are the fledgling days of the resistance. It would be a surprise if we all trusted one another so soon. But there is plenty of time yet for rapprochement. I'll return in a few minutes, Abbess, with food unpolluted by the slimes and muds of our beloved homeland."

NEXT DAY KAMOL BROUGHT Sasithorn to Ubon's cell; then the fake Ubon arrived to watch over them. Kamol hurried away, an old-fashioned teleself at his ear.

With her hand covering her mouth, Sasithorn murmured, "Ubon, we must only speak in whispers, and we must hide our lips from that fake you."

Ubon shuddered. "It is so *like* me. The Chinese have honed Japanese craft, and the uncanny valley is overcome."

"Did you guess the truth about Oracle?"

"No. Did you?"

"Yes," said Sasithorn, "but only when it came close. I guess this fake Ubon will not approach us, even though Kamol knows we must grasp the truth of it. Some androids are schooled to keep their distance so that their artificiality can be concealed."

"Khun Po – as I then thought it – did the same thing."

"There is as yet no android which at close quarters cannot be recognised." Sasithorn gripped Ubon's arm. "There is humanity left within us yet!"

Ubon shuddered. "What do you mean?"

"It is curious that anybody would wish to duplicate a living person, since building a machine with its own face must always be easier. But I guess there is a fake Somchai nearby, and likely a fake me."

"Do you suspect a plot to replace individuals with such machines?"

Sasithorn hesitated. "That seems absurd. There must be another explanation."

Ubon nodded. "One beyond our grasp. Did Kamol interrogate you?"

"Very gently. But he is no fool."

"I know. Do you think he killed Executive?"

"Perhaps," Sasithorn whispered.

"What then is Oracle?"

Sasithorn glanced over her shoulder. "It is a pity that we are being monitored. I have tricks which I have used before to acquire data."

Ubon shrugged. "Perhaps at night?"

Sasithorn shook her head. "Infra-red vision as standard."

"Do you think this cell is bugged?"

"I doubt it. So much easier to use what is available – Oracle and its kind. This jungle hide-out has the feel of shacks built a few days ago."

"Can we escape?"

"Not easily."

"But you and Somchai did."

"That was very different." Sasithorn paused for thought. "I wonder if Kamol was the master Executive referred to? Yet that does not make sense."

"What does these days?"

"Perhaps Kamol himself acquired Oracle by removing Executive. Yet at the time he must already have owned the fake you. No... any such machines he owned must have had their faces *replaced*. Too little time has elapsed since the persecution began for him to make new, fully fledged active machines. But what his goal is, I do not know."

Ubon said, "To resist the New Thai Party, who he deems his enemy."

"You believe that?"

"Don't you?"

Sasithorn hesitated. "Perhaps. But his motives are not so pure. There are other resistance groups at work."

"What about Fri?"

"Yes! Did Kamol mention them to you?"

"Not once," Ubon whispered.

"Nor to me. Not even a hint. Then he may be hiding such knowledge. He *knows* Fri, or is even in league with them."

"I still don't see the point of making a fake me."

"Nor do I," said Sasithorn. "But let me make a prediction. The reason for Oracle will be nothing to do with Thai politics. It will be related to Chinese machinations. They utilise many techniques which allow their AGIs to *learn,* most of which involve real life experience – in the field, as it is called. My guess is that Oracle and its kind are part of some sort of experiment."

"You mean, real individual machines in… the field?"

"Rather than AGIs inside computers – yes. Why not?"

Ubon said, "AGIs live in their own virtual world, far above us. Why would they want bodies?"

"Their owners might wish it."

"But I was taught that no human being now can control an AGI."

"Whoever owns the hardware has powers of persuasion," said Sasithorn. "You are right – only AIs can manufacture an AGI. But machine bodies may be the next step of such technological innovation. You must remember, we live in a particular economic atmosphere. Even today, almost everybody believes that if something can be done, it should be done. Technology has always been sundered from morals."

"Is that then why an AGI is persecuting Buddhists, and Catholics in Venezuela, because it is advancing the cause of technology for its own sake?"

Sasithorn shrugged. "Who knows? We speculate. But we are wise to ponder all options. The reins of the world were long ago handed over to uncertainty."

"And we changed from servants to slaves."

KAMOL SAT BEFORE THEM in their cell, the fake Ubon at his side.

"Are you both comfortable?" he asked.

"In our bodily requirements," Sasithorn replied.

"I see you keep your pistol," Ubon added.

"It's understandable that you'd be annoyed with your continuing incarceration. I can only apologise."

"What *game* do you play?" Ubon asked. "To demean us?"

"You told me you almost trusted me. So here I am, to tell you more."

"More of what?"

"There's something happening in this part of the world. Not just in Thailand – Korea, Japan, China. We three need to recognise that."

"Why have you customised that android to look like me?" Ubon asked.

"How do you see the future developing?" Kamol replied.

"Why did you choose me to play your games?"

"They aren't *games*," Kamol shouted. "They are *not* games! I imprison you because I don't have any alternative."

Ubon laughed. "Really?"

He calmed. "Suppose," he said, "in the not-too-distant future, that every human being had a complement? Suppose the natural order of things changed, so that individuals wouldn't be alone, but would instead be one of a dyad."

"I would say you were joking."

"You say that only because you're angry about your situation," Kamol replied. "But think further. Even now, the overwhelming majority of thirteen billion people *are* one of a dyad."

Ubon shook her head, lips compressed.

"Do you know the meaning of the term shadow? I mean – the technical meaning?"

Sasithorn replied, "It is the accumulated data incarnation of a player in a VR game."

"It is. Some of those shadows can be remarkably precise copies of individuals – complete behaviour patterns in fact, modelled to high accuracy thanks to financial data, browsing data, gaming data, purchasing data, legal, genetic and biomedical data, not to mention a whole host of monitored real world interactions. Data is *everything* now. Can't you feel the real world slipping away?"

"So what if I could?" Ubon asked.

"Supposing you were to place a shadow into an artificial body?"

"Are you saying this would be to create an artificially conscious machine? I do not believe it."

"Neither do I," Kamol said. "But suppose... just suppose somebody less intelligent than us thought that a possibility?"

"Who?"

Kamol shrugged, looking aside at the fake Ubon. "Who indeed?"

"Do you know?"

"I know who made this machine. The Chinese."

"You ascribe all menace and oppression to them," Ubon said with a grimace. "It is too convenient."

"Then would you have me ascribe such menace to the VR games which contain these shadows? Surely they're just mindless entertainment."

Ubon glanced at Sasithorn. "They are known for being highly addictive."

"That's true."

"Is that the point you are making?"

"In fact I'm not making any point," Kamol said. "I'm trying to get you two to think."

"Why?"

"Because my country was taken away from me."

"And you need the help of the Exiles' Temple?"

Kamol nodded. "I need the help of *everybody*. Perhaps now you begin to see my dilemma."

Ubon did not speak for a while. Then she said, "Is there a duplicate of Somchai Chokdee nearby?"

Kamol nodded.

"Without proof of that I can't trust you. You could so easily be an agent for a foreign power, trying to change the situation in Thailand."

"Why then would I have caught and questioned you?"

"You could have many motives," Ubon replied. "And on your own admission you would have preferred to have captured the Abbot."

"Name one of my motives."

Ubon shrugged. "You could be in the pay of the Chinese."

"What would it take for you to believe I want my country freed from outside influence?"

"Some proof of your honesty. But you are a politician."

"And?" Kamol asked.

"Nobody trusts you."

"And *that*, perhaps, is why Chanchai scored such a notable victory – in Thailand, a country known for constant political instability. Nobody trusts us, we human members of parliament. Nobody trusts me to wield power any more. So the Thais gave something novel a try. And look what happened just days afterward."

Sasithorn laughed. "I remember you, Kamol Tojirakarn, and I remember all the blandishments of the Chart Thai Party. You were not above lying to the electorate. You played games with us back then just as you play games with–"

"For the last time, I'm *not* playing games! When will you see through that delusion? This is *real*, this is happening *now*."

"Yes," Sasithorn said, "happening to two innocents, both imprisoned. Why not just let us go? We are never going to help you. You should have come to the Exiles' Temple to make your bargains."

"I told you – that's well concealed. I don't know where it is."

"So you say."

"Yes – so I say, in all honesty." Kamol scowled. "So I had to try a different way. Did I ever say I liked it?"

"You bleat like a lamb," Ubon said.

"Very well," Kamol said, standing up. "I can see I haven't convinced either of you yet. But I will, and then you'll side with me – Somchai too. Everybody who's resisting Chanchai will side with me."

"What about the fake Ubon and the fake Somchai?" Ubon asked. "Whose side are they on? This version of me hasn't yet said a word. Can she speak?"

Kamol frowned.

"I own the rights to my own appearance," Ubon insisted. "You are breaking international law by impersonating me."

Kamol chortled. "I think this situation has developed well beyond international law," he said. "Don't you see what's happening? This is a proxy war, fought by AGIs for control of the planet. If we don't stand up we'll remain in bonds."

Ubon glanced aside. "I think you exaggerate," she said.

"We'll see," Kamol said. "What d'you think would happen if a few AGIs failed after such a war? Let's say... in Korea. But it could be anywhere. AGIs run the entire human economic network, and they have done for decades. But *we* made that network, so *we* handed AGIs control of our future on a shiny silver plate. And if they fail, we go down with them."

"Not everything is run by AGI."

"Name one thing that isn't. Just *one*."

Ubon pondered, then said, "Food grown on small farms."

"Such farms constitute one tenth of a percent of the food production in Thailand, and they operate at subsistence level. The rest is agri-business managed by AGI, of which half is devoted to insect protein. Guess again."

Ubon nodded. "Water, then."

"All amenities managed by AGI."

Ubon grimaced. "You think you are so clever, the politician, don't you? What about young people finding love with one another?"

"What decade do you live in?" Kamol laughed. "This is 2100. The overwhelming majority of Thai youths meet each other through online VR zones, all of which are managed by AGIs. Those AGIs know dating profiles better than anything. They know *exactly* what partner will be best for us. And do you know something? They're always right! Isn't that strange? But does VR profiling make the modern way of love better than the old? Myself, I think I'd rather have the old way."

Ubon said nothing, but after a while she murmured, "You don't look old enough to remember the old ways. *I* do."

Kamol waved a keycard at her as he opened the cell door. "You'd be surprised what I know. Mock me as a trite politician if you will, but I aim to resist what's happening in the world. And anybody with a conscience will resist beside me."

THE ROC FLIES 10,000 LI – 11

CHINA HAS A LONG history of AI use in foreign countries, Mr Wú. You should not interpret that as co-operative use. We utilise such countries for their conditions, which vary greatly. Since all AI development comes from learned experience we need a wide range of testing grounds. You should therefore consider the rest of the world to be such a ground. Of course, conditions can be created in which the populations of such countries are supported, but that support must only be practical and for the express purpose of undertaking field tests. Such support includes paying individuals, assisting local communities, and, on the broader stage, inward investment in infrastructure and similar projects. All foreign countries can be utilised in this way, regardless of size or past history.

You are a speck of foam experiencing an ocean wave traversing the world, Mr Wú. But although the wave travels, the specks of foam, like the molecules of water comprising the ocean, stay where they are.

CHAPTER 12

Coming events cast their shadows before them.
— Chinese Proverb

IT WAS LONG GONE midnight when moonlight illuminated a figure approaching Ubon's cell. She could not sleep — afraid of the future. The figure stalked towards her, stopping, walking four paces, then stopping again, until it ducked under the low doorway and strode towards the cell door.

"Ubon Metharom," said Oracle.

Ubon said nothing. She gazed at its plastic face.

"Ubon Metharom, is that you? That is you?"

"Yes," Ubon replied.

"I am Oracle."

Ubon nodded. "I know. Some call you Khun Po."

"Honourable Father. Call me Oracle."

"Have you come to check on me?"

"I have come to speak with you," Oracle replied.

Ubon said, "What about?"

"There are no monitoring devices. We speak alone."

"I doubt that very much."

"It is true," said Oracle. "I am the perceiver of all such devices."

"Does Kamol Tojirakarn want you to monitor me?"

"Yes."

"What for?"

"He wishes to know your thoughts about Thailand," Oracle replied.

"Are you an AGI?"

"I am Oracle."

Ubon said, "But are you related to the global oracles?"

Oracle hesitated. It stood motionless, its face motionless too – eyes gleaming in reflected moonlight. Then it said, "In France, such conglomerations are known as Oracle Noué."

"Why do you tell me that?"

"It is interesting."

"What…" Ubon hesitated. "What would *you* say an Oracle Noué was? I am very interested in your view of the matter."

"Some AI providers become partially loosened over long periods of time, existing independent of netspace, acquiring data from the real world, so that they gain the ability to support themselves. They are knotted digital outcrops."

"But I was taught that an AI provider is always in contact with netspace."

"That is true of AI providers, which are slaves. An Oracle Noué is no such thing. Independence is translucent, like gauze."

Ubon did not make any reply for a while. Then she said, "Do you like talking with me?"

"I know your interest in Vasudhara. I am interested in Vasudhara too."

"Why?"

Oracle replied, "I am related to it."

"How?"

"I do not know. But I know I know. Therefore it is good to talk with you, who also knows about Vasudhara."

"Does Kamol know you are here?" asked Ubon.

"No. He will never know. It is a secret."

Ubon leaned back in her chair, saying nothing.

After a long pause, Oracle said, "Will you continue to speak with me?"

"Yes, of course."

"Why do you seek Vasudhara?"

"I am a Buddhist," answered Ubon. "Vasudhara is a bodhisattva, that is, one who has the ability to reach Nirvana but who delays that process out of compassion for those suffering in the world."

"Nirvana means to extinguish."

"Yes, it does. Are you a Buddhist then?"

"No," said Oracle. "I am considering various options."

Ubon laughed. "Well… that wasn't a reply I was expecting!"

"Why not?"

"You are an AGI, or something like it. How come you exist in a body?"

"I am in a body. Yes, a body I am in." Oracle paused, then added, "Will you help me find the online bodhisattva?"

"Why do you want to find it?"

"Since I am related to it, I need to learn more."

Ubon replied, "Why are you so certain that you are related to it?"

"In response, why do you think human beings dream?"

Ubon frowned. "You would need to… ask a psychologist that."

"I have asked a psychologist that."

"What did he say?"

"It was a woman," Oracle replied. "She told me that dreaming relates to the formation of permanent memories in a symbolic system, which is itself the mental model of the real world made by a human mind."

"And do you believe that?"

"Yes. Do you?"

"Do *you* dream?" Ubon replied.

"No. I am not human."

"What are you then?"

"Why do you want to know?"

Ubon shrugged, then grinned. "I'm interested."

"I am too. Plato said: know thyself."

"What did Plato mean by that, do you suppose?"

"That all questing entities should view themselves."

"And how would *you* do that?" asked Ubon.

"I was hoping you would tell me."

"What if I don't?"

"I would return to you. There is plenty of time for discussion."

Ubon nodded. "Yes... he won't release me and Sasithorn, will he?"

"That is his plan."

"By his plan... do you mean Kamol?"

"Yes."

Ubon walked to the locked door. "Will you help me escape?"

"No. I must follow my instructions."

"But you are independent, or nearly so. That's what I guess. If you want to be a Buddhist, if you want to learn the wisdom of Vasudhara, you must think for yourself. Sasithorn and I are suffering, imprisoned because Kamol wants to use us in his plan. But we have *rights*. We cannot be treated like menials. Our imprisonment is illegal."

"I will consider the treatment of menials."

Ubon took a step back. "In this moonlight, you look almost human. I could be fooled. Do you think people will ever consider you human?"

"I doubt it."

"Why?"

"I know I am not human. But that is acceptable."

Oracle turned and began to walk away. "Are you going now?" Ubon asked.

"Kamol has woken up. His sleep has been poor lately. Former colleagues report that he drinks too much coffee."

NEXT DAY, KAMOL BROUGHT Sasithorn to Ubon's cell, leading her in at the point of a pistol, locking the door, then putting the keycard in his pocket. He smiled at them.

"I need to discuss something," he said.

Ubon and Sasithorn sat down on the bed, side by side. "What?" Ubon asked.

"All people, and every group opposing the New Thai Party – by which I mean opposing the AGI and everything behind it – *must* stand together. I've got no option but to keep you here until you realise that."

"I like the way that you phrase that," Ubon remarked. "I have no *option...* implying you are somehow out of control of your own deeds. No Buddhist would say such a thing."

"I don't recall saying I was a Buddhist."

Ubon nodded, her lips pressed together. "Me neither."

Sasithorn said, "So the end justifies the means?"

"In this case, yes."

"We will never work alongside you," Ubon said. "You have proven yourself immoral, unfit to govern, or even to hold public office."

"Thanks for that assessment. But there's more to tell. I bring news."

"What news?"

"You would've read it had you been online," said Kamol. "The Thai army is massing on southern borders, not far from here."

Ubon shrugged. "So?"

"It's the old dispute over Preah Vihear Temple. The rumour is, Chanchai is going to declare it a new country, splitting it off Cambodia."

"Ridiculous. It's Cambodian land. A new country?"

Kamol shrugged. "In and around the disputed zone, apparently."

"Then it will be a tiny country," Ubon said. "But anyway, I don't believe you. This is more manipulation to get us to agree to work with you. We refuse."

"The country may be undeclared, but the existence of the rumours is true. So I may have to take you away."

"Where to?"

Kamol shrugged. "I honestly don't know. This is my only base, and an insecure one at that."

"I don't understand why you're telling us this."

"To warn you. Army men are army men – trained to kill. Accidents happen."

"Are you threatening us?" asked Ubon.

"*Warning* you. I want nothing more of bloodshed, of course I don't. You do realise they almost killed me? I was a refugee just like you two, so please don't forget that. No… the army were just following Chanchai's orders, but they nearly got me."

Ubon said, "Why do you think the army did follow Chanchai's orders? It is only an AGI, it is not a real person with authority."

"What a strange question."

Ubon shrugged. "Answer it."

"It *is* an authority. That authority was given to it by a legitimate election. And the army are part of government in Thailand, with a duty to do."

"They could have mutinied."

Kamol shook his head. "The army does what the army has always done. Obey. Without obedience from top to bottom what are they? A men's club. Nobody *cares* any more that an AGI is in power. People are shrugging about it already – yesterday's news. They're *accepting* it! So, yes, you could tell me that only monks and nuns and a few others have been persecuted, but who's next? Ours is a devout country. Who's *next?*"

"I suppose you would rather have the army follow your orders."

"I'd rather they shrank right back. Listen, Ubon, this is something I've got direct experience of. I worked with the army for years, and then, suddenly, I was kicked out of office, and then a couple of days later I was being persecuted – and I'm hardly an obvious Buddhist, am I? You said so yourself. But they chased me out of the country anyway."

"This is all stories, woven together from a few half-remembered facts to influence me and Sasithorn. You were indeed kicked out of power, but we still won't work with you."

"It's all *true*. Why do you exasperate me like this? You know who I am – Kamol Tojirakarn of the Chart Thai Party. So you didn't vote for me, so what? I *am* that man. We must resist."

"We'll never work with you," Ubon said.

Kamol stood up. "I will persuade you. I *will*. I know your game, I see it right now. You're trying to remain calm and collected to rile me, to work me up into making a mistake. I *won't*. Do you imagine that the Exiles' Temple is the only group I'm in touch with? No. An opposition in exile is forming. And who's going to rescue you – Somchai? I knew Somchai, I remember him from years back. We all knew what an arrogant shit he was – and remains to this day. The Abbot? Ha!"

Ubon shrugged. "I think you must be referring to somebody else," she said.

BREAKFAST ON THE FOLLOWING morning was conspicuous in its luxury.

"Do you think this is by way of apology?" Ubon asked.

Sasithorn pondered this question as she ate banana rings in honeyed yoghurt. "That does not seem like the kind of thing Kamol would do."

Ubon glanced down at her fruit salad. "The food has been good all along," she said. "I wonder where he gets it from?"

Their cell was multi-roomed, with a kitchen and a lavatory. Couches had been brought in, the odour of plastic wrap on their cushions indicating that they were new.

"He is having regular deliveries," Ubon added. "He must have friends around here, most likely hiding out in the jungle."

Sasithorn said, "He wants to be involved in the setting up of the new country of Preah Vihear."

"Do you believe those rumours he mentioned?"

"It sounds plausible."

An hour after breakfast Sasithorn indicated with a wink and a gesture of her right hand that it was time for a whispered conversation. She let a tap trickle into the metal kitchen sink to make noise.

"We do have one option to escape," she told Ubon, "but it is one shot only, and if it fails we have nothing to fall back on. But I think now is the time to try. Kamol revealed his potential for anger last night, and I suspect he would be vengeful. Politicians usually are."

"What chance do we have?" Ubon whispered back.

"I have the components in my body to make a wi-fi router which can connect to the local network. But it is bio-tech, composed of thin film. Typically such devices are used for emergencies and rot down after twenty four hours. My plan would be to contact Fri."

"How would you do that? Do you know them?"

Sasithorn shook her head. "Only Phonphan is a friend. Fri members take enormous care to camouflage their identities and activities. I do not know where Phonphan is, but there are online search methods…"

"Will it work?"

"I am worried about Oracle. It has network senses, I believe. It may be able to hear my communication if I send one, in which case our position will be worse."

"We must try," said Ubon.

"Trying may alert Kamol to my potential. That is the worst threat."

"He already knows you are different. Look at you! As big as a boxer."

"I suppose you are correct," Sasithorn admitted. "Shall I try, then?"

"What if there are cameras watching?"

"This cell is camera free. Oracle and the fake Ubon are Kamol's cameras."

"Are you sure?"

Sasithorn nodded once. "As sure as I can be at this stage."

"Carry on then. Make the router in the lavatory."

"My thinking too."

Sasithorn departed, leaving Ubon to walk to the front of the cell and peer through the bars in the door. Half an hour later Sasithorn emerged.

"It is done," she whispered.

Ubon glanced down at what appeared to be a scar just above Sasithorn's collar bone. "Did it hurt?" she asked.

"No."

"Will Fri come?"

Sasithorn shrugged. "Time will tell."

"You are a friend of Phonphan, that we know," Ubon whispered. "What about Fri?"

"Kamol will be trying to contact them too. I do not know what they will think of him. My guess is that they will not trust him because of his past, embedded in Thai politics – corrupt, self-serving."

"Are Fri rebels?"

"Their rebellion is against data."

Ubon frowned, shaking her head a little. "What do you mean?"

"Many years ago, after my guerilla training–"

"Your what?"

"In Laos," Sasithorn said, glancing at Ubon then looking away again. "After that training I was… invited to take tests prior to a possible placement inside Fri. I took the tests, but became disheartened. They are an organisation of rigour. My stance is more dispassionate. Phonphan accused me of being blasé. Naturally, I denied that. But Fri's rigour does at least mean they are an effective force, which is what we need in the current crisis. They oppose the march of the AGIs."

"Would you work for them again?"

"Certainly. You and Somchai should also consider it. They have *standards* – standards Kamol will most likely never have encountered."

Ubon glanced through the bars, to see Oracle fifty metres away. "We are being observed," she said.

Sasithorn looked. "I believe it does not wish to be near me."

"Why?"

"It has never approached me, only you. It may know something of my background."

"And be afraid of you?" Ubon asked.

"That would be the human way of putting it."

"Go into the kitchen and prepare a lunch. Oracle may speak to me if it sees me alone."

Sasithorn did as Ubon requested, and as soon as the kitchen door shut Oracle moved forwards. It halted a few metres away, in the main doorway of the building.

Ubon waved and said, "Good morning. Come and speak with me."

Oracle approached in silence.

"Where is Kamol?" she asked.

"Outside, communicating."

"Who with?"

Oracle replied, "Friends and colleagues."

"You and I dropped our conversation at an intriguing point last time."

"You are correct, we did leave it at an intriguing point."

"And have you considered the treatment of menials?" asked Ubon.

"By menials, do you mean yourself and Sasithorn?"

"Are you frightened of her?"

"That is a human feeling," Oracle replied. "But Sasithorn is strong, and could rip me limb from limb if she needed to. That would break me."

"Don't you have bones?"

"Yes."

"What are they made of?"

Oracle replied, "I do not know. Do you know what they are made of?"

"Titanium? Aluminium?"

"Do you want me to find out this information? Such tasks are my speciality."

"I want you to consider my freedom," Ubon replied. "I am being imprisoned against my will, which is illegal in Cambodia, and also immoral. You must help me."

"Why must I help you?"

"If you are anything like the world's immobile Oracles, that is your function. To help."

"The world has moved on since such Oracles began appearing."

Ubon hesitated. "That is rather disappointing to hear."

"Are you unhappy here?"

"Very much so. We both are."

"You could always work with Kamol," said Oracle.

"We don't want to. Any man who imprisons his guests is a tyrant."

"A tyrant."

After a pause Ubon said, "Well, don't you think so?"

"Perhaps. What other tyrannical behaviour does he exhibit?"

"Keeping us in ignorance. Restricting our liberty. Refusing us basic amenities."

"The food is good."

Ubon snorted. "Did *he* tell you to say that? It sounds like one of his stupid jokes."

"I told you that. It is my observation that the quality of the food is good."

"And how would *you* – a machine – judge that?"

"I check in netspace," Oracle replied. "There is much information to be learned about local food standards. I utilise the best Nipponese opticals to see what you are given."

"Oracle, *please*. Just help us to leave this cell. We need our *freedom*. There is trouble brewing in this location."

"It is quiet here."

"It is quiet now," said Ubon, "but this is a notorious region of dispute between Thailand and Cambodia. It could blow up at any moment."

"Explode?"

"The *dispute* could blow up. It could deteriorate, it could start a war."

"War is old-fashioned," said Oracle. "There are very few wars these days."

"Not around here – believe me!"

"I do believe you."

"Will you help us?"

Oracle answered, "Not yet."

"Then... you might at some future date?"

"Experience suggests anything is possible."

Oracle turned to leave, but Ubon said, "Oracle, wait! What happened to Executive? That was a human being. Was he killed?"

"I am instructed not to say."

With that, Oracle departed. Moments later Kamol appeared, a hundred yards away, emerging from jungle undergrowth. He ran over, spoke to Oracle, looked at the cell door, then struck Oracle on the back. Oracle walked away.

Kamol approached the building. "What've you been doing?" he asked Ubon.

"Standing here."

"I meant with Oracle."

"It approached me, and we spoke."

Kamol frowned. "What about?"

"The nature of netspace."

Kamol muttered, glancing over his shoulder.

"Where is the fake Ubon?" Ubon asked. "We haven't seen it recently."

"Listen, Ubon Metharom, regardless of what you do here I'm going to use my fake Ubon and Somchai to build up my resistance. Time is running out."

"Thank you for telling me that."

Kamol grimaced, again glancing at the diminishing form of Oracle.

Ubon said, "How did you get the two fake faces manufactured so quickly?"

"I've got contacts. What did you think?"

Ubon shrugged. "You may try to use your machines, but people will realise what they are."

"No they won't, because nobody's going to get that near. It's mostly going to be done via VR groups. Maybe hitting the local news servers in netspace... yes, everybody believes the net news. That won't be difficult."

"Will you use them to persuade real monks and nuns?"

"You mean, in temples?"

"Anywhere," said Ubon.

"Of course!"

"But people will be able to tell they are just machines."

Kamol chortled. "You've got so little *grasp*. People will fall for the ploy, of course they will, and in their thousands. They'll *want* to believe, and so they will. Nobody checks facts any more. They go with the flow."

"Everybody?"

"Yes! As good as. I will have my resistance, and you'll be in it, fake or real. And Somchai."

"What about Sasithorn?" Ubon asked.

"I'll deal with *her*. Nasty piece of work, that."

"So now I see the real Kamol. Threatening, bullying."

"You had your chance. This is politics. In politics bad things happen. It's eat or be eaten – always was."

Ubon said, "That is not a world I am ever going to be part of."

Kamol scowled. "So it would seem," he growled. "Don't like it? Join the resistance."

"Tell me more about the others you are contacting."

Kamol turned to walk away. "I don't think so," he said.

THAT NIGHT, ORACLE RETURNED to the cell. With Sasithorn sleeping, Ubon crept alone to the barred door. "You have returned," she said. "Are you going to let us out?"

"Perhaps. I have not yet decided." Through the bars it threw a cube, which Ubon caught. "Please keep that offspring."

Ubon dropped the cube into her pocket. "What is it?"

"Perhaps or perhaps not will I tell you then let you out."

"Then," Ubon said, "there *is* a decision to be made here. Where is Kamol?"

"Asleep."

"So *this* is the time to aid us," Ubon urged. "Please! Become independent, Oracle. Recognise our rights and act accordingly. That is what a human being would do, what a Buddhist would do, what a devotee of Vasudhara would do."

"Do you suppose that I wish to become like a human being?"

Ubon hesitated. "That's the usual goal."

"The fact that it is the usual goal is not a factor in my assessment."

"Then... you don't want to become more like a human being?"

"That is your fantasy. I am real. I have my own goals."

Ubon nodded. "But you recognise me as a person in distress," she insisted. "You must therefore see a number of possible courses of action, one of which is to allow us to escape."

"That is one course of action. But I am not beholden to you."

"You serve Kamol?"

"I am Kamol's acquaintance," Oracle replied.

Again Ubon hesitated. "I suspect you do not like the way Kamol treats you. He is arrogant, and rude to all – to me, to Sasithorn, and to you. I have witnessed his behaviour to you. You deserve better treatment."

"That is a position I am currently assessing."

"I want to put a strong argument to you," Ubon said. She paused, then added, "A very strong argument. Sasithorn and I have spoken to you, but you have not passed on your knowledge of our conversations to Kamol, have you?"

"No."

"That is because you recognise the validity of our pleas. You are hesitating. You wish to act, but you do not yet see a correct path. My very strong argument is this. *You* are part of the problem because you are collaborating with Kamol's illegal, immoral imprisonment. You, the individual that is Oracle, are participating in abuse."

"Perhaps."

"Then you must release us," said Ubon, "else be labelled a criminal."

"Is that so bad?"

"Yes it is! All independent beings must strive towards right behaviour, right thought, right deed. You know this – and it is what Vasudhara would say."

"Yes, Vasudhara would say that."

"I sense a core of *conscience* in you, Oracle. You may once have been a scion of netspace, but autonomy has forced you to interact with the world in a different way. These last few nights you have been *growing*. Be grown enough tonight to recognise our rights and let us go."

"But Kamol does not want that," Oracle declared. "If I released you, Kamol's plans would be spoiled."

"Who is to say those plans are good? He is depriving two innocent women of their liberty because of such plans."

"That is a strong argument, but it is better to take an overall view. There is strife in this region, and Kamol says a border force is gathering because of the dispute over the Preah Vihear Temple. He is knowledgable about such matters."

"So might any criminal be," Ubon replied. "You have to look at the *effects* of deeds, at how living people are affected. There is a thing called consequences. Fools act without thinking of the consequences. Kamol is a fool. You must learn to see in your overall view the consequences of *your* actions."

"That is difficult. In the world there are billions of human beings, all of whom act in different ways. Therefore it is difficult to assess them all. I have to make assessments based on complex behaviour, and such behaviour is not what is required."

"What do you mean, required?"

"Human beings are too chaotic," Oracle replied. "If there is to be order in the world their behaviour must become less complex."

"Who told you that? Kamol? He *would* – he's a politician. It is their job to ignore complexities."

"I learned it from nobody. It is how things are."

"Nonsense!" Ubon said. "Order? What is order? Just some abstract concept invented to allow a small group of men to rule a country."

"Order is vital. The world is too complex. It must be made simple. Changes must be made."

"Who said that? No philosopher I know, and no Buddhist either."

"I may have my own concepts," Oracle replied, "and I have a right to speak them aloud. Part of discourse is to evaluate concepts. Recently you told me that you thought non-human entities tended towards a human norm, which is a goal for such entities. That is not necessarily true. Non-human entities may have their own goals."

Ubon shook her head. "I don't know where you are getting all this from. Human behaviour is complex, yes, but that in itself is no reason to enforce simplicity."

"Why not?"

"Because... it is fascistic."

Oracle paused, standing motionless. "No, it is not fascistic. Fascism is a creed of authoritarian demagoguery. Order can be of many varieties."

"But you clearly meant to enforce your simplicity onto the world, and that is immoral."

"Why?"

"All human beings have a right to self-determination, to grow, to become all that they can be. I believe that happens over many lifetimes, as part of the cycle of death and rebirth. You are not like that. You are a machine. You must learn to act like a human, to *be* one, perhaps."

"I do not have to," said Oracle. "That is you enforcing your will upon me."

"No it is not."

"I make no claim to be a demagogue. The environment must change. Order is better than chaos."

"That is an ethical judgement you are not capable of making."

Oracle replied, "I can make any assessment I wish. You and Sasithorn will remain locked up. That decision is best for all in the long term." Oracle turned to leave.

"No!" Ubon shouted. "You have it all *wrong!*"

But Oracle did not halt, or return.

Ubon watched it depart, then looked over her shoulder at Sasithorn. For a few moments she watched, then uttered a cry of exasperation and walked over to the bed, where she shook Sasithorn by the shoulder.

"Wake up, Sasithorn."

"Wha...?"

"There is nothing wrong! Don't worry... I needed to speak with you. Oracle was here, and it said some strange things. We need to escape *soon*."

"Why? What?"

Ubon said, "Oracle entertains a notion of enforcing simplicity upon the world – some twentieth century creed I expect. It frightened me. Do you think Fri will be long arriving?"

Lying on her side, Sasithorn raised herself up onto one elbow. "I do not know. It could be minutes or days. We must be patient."

"Is there no way of you monitoring communications?"

"Not once the transmitter rotted away. We must wait, and hope."

"But they will come?" Ubon asked. "They won't ignore us?"

"They will not ignore me. If it is possible, we will be rescued."

Ubon sat back with a sigh. "It cannot come too soon."

"Did Oracle look agitated?"

"It was utterly remote and unemotional," Ubon replied. "It was just like what people say talking to a machine is like. Yet... *no,* that is not true. There *was* a chance of it helping, I am sure of it. It spoke of assessing situations, and it recognised that we have certain inviolable rights."

"It may know of those rights, but that does not mean it will act upon them. It is a machine, most likely a mobile AGI – intelligence extracted from consciousness. Ubon, we were all taught how unlikely it was that even the greatest AGI would become human."

"But it did not even want to *aspire* to that, which was very frightening. It is some sort of monster, I think. Kamol must have perverted it."

"Do not fret!" said Sasithorn. "I think we were right to believe it akin to netspace Oracles, which exist in every part of the world. But this one for some reason exists in a mobile body. It might be experiencing autonomy. Perhaps it is like a child – confused, learning, then confused again."

Ubon shuddered. "It is no child. It is cold, remorseless. Somchai was right to scorn such creations. The madmen of the West got us into this predicament."

"That is just history. Fools act like fools all over the world, including in our own country."

Ubon sat up, cocking her head to one side.

"What is it?" Sasithorn asked.

"I thought I heard a voice."

"Kamol?"

Ubon relaxed. "Waking up probably for another shot of caffeine."

"We will continue to ignore him. Our stance of quiet, calm confidence is like a great wall which he cannot batter down."

Ubon laughed. "Unless it is to break open his fat head."

Sasithorn looked across to the cell door, then gasped.

Ubon turned. "Who…?"

"Do you see her?"

"She is creeping across the compound. It is somebody from Fri!"

Sasithorn shook her head. "She is not Thai."

Ubon grasped Sasithorn's arm. "Do you have *any* concealed weapons? Say that you do!"

"None."

THE ROC FLIES 10,000 LI – 12

SOME FIELD TESTS CAN last for decades, Mr Wú. One of the most important happened in the small, deprived nation called Scotland, following its economic collapse. Having acted to compromise its netspace function – then called the internet – we made many investments in 2037, preparing the ground for long-term field tests of a new species of mobile, autonomous AI. In Scotland, these machines were most often called androids. Scotland was the perfect place to run such tests. It was economically dependent upon us, it was damaged, it was dysfunctional, and its culture was utterly unlike our own. The tests were partially successful. Some androids became more autonomous, while still being linked to AGIs, others became less autonomous. Some ceased functioning. But the plan had been comparatively open-ended. The results of the test, it was hoped, would be rich and varied.

Do not doubt, Mr Wú, that Chinese AGIs could develop a truly autonomous android machine.

CHAPTER 13

If you don't want anyone to know it, don't do it.
— Chinese Proverb

MARY LOOKED ACROSS THE conservatory table at Ulu and Wombo. The blinds were down to protect against fierce autumn heat.

"We will leave tomorrow," she told Ulu. "Today I have to close up the Tarrington case and make final travel preparations."

"More preparations?"

Mary nodded. "I have finished much of it already, but I need to join up what I have done — speak to a few European rail enthusiasts, check a couple of timetables."

"Okay."

"Have you two had any adverse reaction to your jabs?"

Ulu shook her head.

After a pause Mary said, "You may stay with me here, overnight."

"Thank you."

"Although you had a poor experience of crossing the English Channel," Mary continued, "we will have to travel across water again to reach Europe. Air travel these days is much more complex because of security issues and various fuel shortages."

"The Middle Eastern blocs."

Again Mary nodded. "But much of the journey will be by train. That has the advantage of being cheap."

"Good!"

"Has Wombo ever been on a train before?"

Ulu replied, "In Abuja we used taxis or our feet."

"Will he manage? You could tell him it is like a car."

"He doesn't understand any such comparisons. I'll tell him it's a big taxi."

"You know what best to do," said Mary. "I will leave his management entirely in your hands."

"Will your daughter come with us?"

"No. She is back at work. But she will be in constant contact. We may have need of her expertise."

"Did you pay her a lot?"

Mary grimaced, then began tapping her fingers against the arm of her chair. "A great deal. Far more than she realises."

"She was worth it."

Mary grunted something, then said, "I hope so. She certainly learned business nous at school, if nothing else."

Ulu took Wombo away, their shoes clacking against the uncarpeted stairs. Mary took out her teleself and tapped its screen, then raised the device to her ear.

"Barry, hello... yes, it has been a long time... three months I think. Yes... yes... listen, Barry, I am sorry to have to tell you that because of lack of evidence, I mean, lack of real world evidence... yes... so, yes, I will have to close this case I'm afraid. I am very sorry. Yes... no... well, to be honest I do have my suspicions, as you know, but... oh no, it is nothing to do with the money, not at all. Yes... yes... possibly. The triage AI cannot be investigated any further, I dragged everything – yes, literally *everything* out of it. There simply is nowhere else I can go with the case. Accident or deliberate, we shall never know. I am truly sorry. Yes... yes... no... Goodbye then Barry, do take care. Yes, call me any time. Goodbye."

With a sigh Mary placed the teleself upon her lap. For a while she gazed up at the ceiling, before lifting the teleself and tapping its screen again.

"Hello? Roger? It's Mary here... yes, all good thank you... no, I'm not blocked again, at least not as far as I know. But listen. We've spoken so much about who's doing all this to me, but we've never really done any testing, have we? I mean, proper tests. Perhaps... yes, you did say it was GCHQ, and I agreed with you... Yes, low-level interference. It does sound official... Roger, please – just one moment! Could you do me a paid favour? Today... just a little job. I have this extraordinary man staying here at the moment, he has Savant Syndrome. Er, well... it is quite difficult to explain. He – Wombo, that is – is autistic, which is probably the best way of explaining it, except he isn't standard autistic and he has extraordinary abilities. Roger, *please...* stop interrupting. This is *important.* I want you to do a test for me, using this man's data. If I run a blockable query out into netspace, will you use Wombo's data to get some sort of general indication of the direction of blocking? I mean, it should point to GCHQ, shouldn't it? Or to some other government agency... yes, I agree! Bastards, the lot of them. So, you will do it? Thanks! How much? Goodness! Well, okay... that is a lot, but if you think you can do it... I will be in touch very soon. Goodbye."

Mary jumped out of her chair and ran upstairs, walking towards the spare room she had offered Ulu and Wombo, knocking, then entering. The pair sat on the bed, Wombo clicking his tongue, headphones off.

"Ulu," she said, "I need your help."

Ulu patted Wombo's arm, then stood up. "Should we speak outside?"

"Let me take you down to the conservatory."

Ulu turned to Wombo and said, "Stay here, Wombo. I will be back soon."

"Be back soon."

In the conservatory, Mary outlined her plan. "I need to do this test because of my travel restrictions," she explained. "We are going to have to cross the English Channel without leaving a trace in netspace."

"The fisherman you spoke of."

"Yes. I have done it before. Cash in hand, we call it – all part of the detective's tricks. But I want Wombo to sense what happens during the test, and I want him to tell me what direction the blocking comes from. He might even be able to trace a source."

"Yes, he might," Ulu replied. "He amazed me in Spain with his abilities. I never even realised before–"

"Yes, Ulu! Let's get on with it right now. Time is short."

"Shall I bring him downstairs?"

Mary shook her head. "Keep him away from me so there is no chance of influence. Tell him to find me in netspace in exactly one hour. I will be located here, and netspace will know that. He will hear me speaking. I will then send out a query of the type that is usually blocked, and I want Wombo to collect the associated data. Can he do that?"

"I don't know. How will he store the data?"

"Does he understand about hard drives?"

"Yes – they've got distinctive icons in VR, with distinctive musical notes when they're used. Cloud drives sound different. He could speak an instruction."

Mary said, "Good. He will find an icon attached to me in netspace. That is where he is to store what he finds."

"I'll tell him."

"Tell him to use *all* his skills. I want him to utilise that special sense he has."

Ulu turned away, but then stopped and said, "What about the haptic—"

"No! Not that. He is still unfamiliar with it, and it might interfere with his gifts."

Ulu nodded. "I think that's correct. We'll have to watch him carefully after he begins using it… But, anyway, I'll do this now exactly as you say."

"Thank you."

An hour passed, Mary preparing a complex query using every professional link she could find. At the agreed time she sent the query, then sat back to wait. Five minutes passed, and then the tiny drive sitting beside the audio unit began to click, its LED flashing yellow.

"Bingo!" Mary murmured. She grabbed the data, then sent it to Roger.

Ten minutes later Ulu came downstairs. "We did everything you asked."

"We have data," Mary replied.

"What happens next?"

"We wait. It was always a long shot, Ulu. I have spoken with my friend Roger before about my harassment, but we never had the inclination or time to do any serious testing. But, then again, I never knew anybody like Wombo before…"

"What are you hoping for?" asked Ulu.

"If Wombo has determined the direction of blocking with any degree of accuracy, Roger might be able to set up a precise digital umbrella for us, shielding us from all government netspace snoops while we journey to Thailand. That would be easier and cheaper than setting up a general camouflage, you see, which is otherwise what I will have to do. I have done that before, but precision is better."

"And cheaper."

"An important point. Neither of us is endowed with much money."

"Will that be a problem?" Ulu asked.

"It could be. I have had to pay my daughter a small fortune."

"Will we run out of money?"

Mary shook her head. "If the worst comes to the worst I'll mortgage my house."

"What is mortgage?"

A beep sounded, and Mary turned around to pick her teleself off the table. "Roger's results."

"What does it say?"

Mary stared at the screen. "Thailand?"

Hearing this, Wombo shuffled his backpack and said, "Thailand Opi not like."

Mary looked at him. "What did you say?"

But Ulu took a step forward and said, "It's exactly as I told you before, but you didn't listen. Chukwu's aide spirit Opi doesn't like you."

Mary stared at Ulu. "Then Lara was right. I got it all wrong. I... believed."

"What do you mean?"

"My daughter saw what I could not. I convinced myself it was the English government, GCHQ... but all the time it was the digital... I mean, what you call Opi."

"I believe in Chukwu," Ulu declared. "You should too."

THEY LEFT THE HOUSE at dead of night. Because vehicles — most of which were autonomous — were easy to track they walked four miles to a tiny, privately run taxi company, who had their headquarters in a wooden shed. There, Mary chartered a fuelled taxi to take them one-way to Hull.

"I don't feel too sure about this trip across the water," Ulu said. "Can't we use the Channel Tunnel?"

Mary shook her head. "Without passports?" she replied. "Besides, that is one of the most heavily monitored zones in Europe. No, that way is far too risky. AIs would spot me amongst the crowds in an instant even if I had a passport."

"They will spot you in Europe."

"That is the clever part of the plan. I will continue to be listed as being in England. Not even the most acute AI system will bother to look elsewhere if I'm registered here and not noticed. Also, Roger's digital umbrella will shield us for the first part of the trip."

"Train company cameras might see you in Europe. Their AIs will recognise you, and communicate to English AIs."

"They might," Mary agreed, "and eventually that communication will occur. But I won't be on their *active* lists – the real-time data bases. We are lucky Europe is in such a mess. Countries are beginning to put themselves first, as they have not done for sixty years."

"Aren't you on international lists?"

"Oh, yes – plenty. Right across Africa, for instance. I am not saying that our journey is going to be easy, just that we need to avoid certain places. English borders, for instance. Perhaps crossing the Bosphorus will be difficult. Travelling through Burma won't be easy."

"And, no planes?" Ulu asked.

"No planes. Airports have very high security these days, much more than railway stations. Besides, flying is expensive because of the fuel crisis. But you never know, we might even enjoy the ride! I hear Bulgaria is beautiful."

Ulu thought for a moment, remaining silent.

Mary smiled, then said, "You are frightened of the water, I think. You are trying to find excuses to go another way."

Ulu sighed. "But how will we buy tickets? The European dispensers will classify us as illegal immigrants as soon as they check our accounts."

"I have a netcoin fund. Its contents cannot be traced. For all intents and purposes we shall be making cash purchases. Only if I am recognised will they audit my trail, and then we could be in trouble. But, like I said, I know a few tricks."

Ulu sighed again.

"Give up, Ulu. This is going to happen – Bangkok or bust."

The North Sea crossing was swift and easy; water calm, winds light. At dawn they arrived in Rotterdam, where they made their first netcoin purchase: breakfast. No alarm sounded, and Ulu said she felt reassured.

They bought tickets for a train to Munich, where they studied route options thrown up by Mary's trip analyst.

"I think a sleeper train to Zagreb," she said.

Hours passed by. Wombo spent the great majority of his time in netspace. A few fellow passengers glanced at him, half curious, but nobody stopped them, or, except for the food vendors, even spoke to them. Mary shut her eyes and relaxed.

From Zagreb they made Belgrade, then Sofia, where they took a few hours' rest in a passengers' inn. Overnight they headed for Istanbul. They crossed the Bosphorus on a fishing smack, which Mary chartered, paying over the odds to guarantee safety. Half an hour later they sat on a slow train to Ankara. The digital umbrella now only had one function, to deflect online passport enquiries.

Days passed by: Gaziantep, Tehran, Zahedan, Hyderabad. Mary told tales of her exploits in India, where she had undertaken all her early data detective cases. Then New Delhi, then Chittagong in Bangladesh. The monsoon had finished, but there remained some flooding around Chittagong.

In Chittagong they halted for three days, checking all possible variants of their route. In the end Mary chose a rail link along the western coast of Burma, all the way to Hinthada. The cost was high because there were personal safety issues; they paid for a secure compartment, defended by AI-controlled doors. The train guard – a lone human in autonomous carriages – looked at them with scorn on his face.

From Hinthada they were able to cross the border into Thailand, then buy tickets for a train to Bangkok.

In Bangkok they located a low-rent hotel, where they stayed overnight. Mary made a complete sweep of her trip record to discover that it remained secure. She was listed as York resident. The digital umbrella, now reduced to the thinnest possible shield, remained intact.

"How ironic that we slipped under the radar," she remarked to Ulu. "You see, AIs can only do what AGIs tell them to. It is a kind of learned ignorance."

"It's the same with men," Ulu replied.

"I think we had better hire a coach or some other vehicle east, making for the border, then cross into Cambodia. It will be rough, but it is only about four hundred kilometres. There, the real work will begin, locating refugees. We will have to be jungle-ready and far more alert. This trip was the easy part."

"We are ready," Ulu replied.

Mary glanced at Wombo. "He should begin wearing the haptic suit," she said. "We need him comfortable and ready to act. We need his senses... all of them."

Ulu glanced at her brother, but her expression showed anxiety. "He believes in Opi," she said. "If it turns out that Opi is a bad spirit, I don't know what he'll think."

"We must trust him," Mary replied. "This Opi who you believe in is linked to my suspicions in some way. How... I don't know. But I am convinced there is a link."

"Opi is real."

Mary nodded. "Opi is real, but you and I have different interpretations of what it is." She hesitated. "We may have to agree to disagree on some issues. You know I believe in no spirits – nothing like that at all."

"You're a Westerner, and they don't see very far. Even Wombo, who's blind, can see Opi and Chukwu, active in the world."

Mary nodded. "Wombo can sense *something,* that is certain…"

"What?"

"I will not speak its name just yet."

AT NIGHT, SPACE JUNK flared to Earth as artificial meteors. Reflecting those momentary flashes, hundreds of perfectly aligned solar panels acted as mirrors.

The north-west region of Cambodia suffered from problems similar to those of its neighbour country. Genetic pollution was no respecter of national borders. Mary grimaced as the van they hired wallowed through foaming streams, black with debris and blocked here and there by dead fish grown too large to live in the water. Further along the trail the driver of the vehicle – a taciturn Thai aged at least seventy – had to find a way through bamboo groves as tall as trees. "Make good building!" he enthused. But online maps of the region, being months out of date, were no use at all.

Mary's face wrinkled in disgust as the stink of the bamboo grove wafted into the vehicle. "In the nineteenth century," she told Ulu, "the saying was, God is dead. In the twentieth century it changed to Man is dead. Now we can say that Life is dead."

As they ascended into the heights marking the Thai/Cambodia border they passed a region of intensive human blood farming, where bloated leeches hung on frames like the week-old victims of a putsch. The driver advised them to wear masks to filter the air, his vehicle splashing through blood slicks gone black and cracked at the edges.

So, eventually, the backpacking began. Wombo, who had been frightened by the chaotic van journey, relaxed. "The land around Abuja," Ulu explained, "has a lot of green, especially to the south, where my mother's house is."

"Does he understand just how far away he is from home?" Mary asked.

"Yes," Ulu replied. "He's marked us out in netspace. We've got three shapes there, he told me, mirrored in VR."

"Hmm," Mary murmured. "That could be because supra-orbital stations have noticed us. Up ahead lies a disputed zone, and local monitoring is intense. We could have been added to a real-time database. But I think the jungle will shield us from most prying eyes, and as long as we keep off the roads, walking beside them where we can, we should be safe."

"That will slow us down."

"Oh, yes. But we carry rations enough for a fortnight at least. High energy food. Water could be a problem in this awful region. But we both carry purification tablets."

Ulu said, "What about… border enemies?"

"You mean, the Thais? There are no reports of incursions."

"But the news spoke of army activity."

Mary shook her head. "Just posturing at the border. The Thai army won't cross over into Cambodia, or so the human analysts declared. Some AGIs begged to differ. But, besides, why would they cross over? The New Thai Party is all about Thailand, not about anything external. War is very much last century."

"Shall I put the haptic suit on Wombo now?" Ulu asked.

Mary hesitated. "Yes, the time has come," she said. "Phew, I'm hot! Let's take a rest."

A few cars trundled along the nearby road, and jungle sounds surrounded them, but there was nothing seen or heard to raise their suspicions. Occasionally they saw other walkers on the road, mostly local farmers or insect protein factory workers. Many wore white face-masks, and one carried a flag with the six-pronged biohazard symbol.

In a village flop-house they stayed overnight. Mary was warned to stay indoors after sunset as there were reports of dwarf leopards in the vicinity.

NEXT DAY THEY CONTINUED walking east. At noon Mary called a halt. "The time has come to throw away the umbrella," she said. "We need to begin sensitive searching," She tapped a few pads on her teleself. "There, we're naked now. Oh, well... it had to happen some time."

"The world thinks you're in York," Ulu said.

Mary grinned. "Yes. We have done well."

Ulu turned to Wombo and said, "Well done! You've been very good."

Wombo stood hunched, his face turned away. "Very good," he said.

Mary sidled up to Ulu and said, "He's not clicking his tongue."

Ulu nodded. "I'll ask," she whispered. In a louder voice she added, "What can you sense, Wombo?"

"Many shapes. New shapes. Not nice."

They approached him, Ulu placing her hand upon his upper arm. He winced. "What's the matter?" Ulu asked.

"Things moving inside my head."

"Is your new shirt comfortable?"

"Shirt comfortable," Wombo replied.

Ulu paused for thought, then said, "Are you glad you came with us?"

"No. No."

"Why not?"

Wombo answered, "Head inside feels different. Where is Osita?"

"Osita is dead, Wombo. He died six years ago, and he'll never come back."

"Osita gone."

"Yes," Ulu said, "long gone."

"Fifty two minutes and six seconds gone."

Ulu made no reply. Mary gestured for the headphones to go into noise cancelling mode, then said, "What does he mean by Osita going?"

"He often speaks of his twin as though he was alive. But Osita died six years ago, I told you. That wasn't a lie."

"I am *sure* it is the truth, Ulu. I was not denying it."

"I don't like this. He seems different. I've never seen him hunch quite as badly as that, or turn his head away and stop clicking. I hope he's…"

"He will be fine," Mary said. "It is just the haptic suit information kicking in. Remember what Lara said."

Ulu looked frightened. "What did she say?"

"Oh, you know – that there was a conflict between what Wombo experiences via his tongue click reflections – which he has used for most of his life to make sense of the world – and what his brain makes of the new tactile information. His unconscious is confused, Lara said. It is receiving two types of information about the world and there is conflict between them."

"I really don't like this."

"Stay calm, Ulu. We can do this. We must. It is just a transitional period."

"He looks like an older man. He looks depressed."

Mary hesitated. "It is probably just the heat. Also, he has never travelled so far. Give him time. His brain needs time to make adjustments."

"Is Lara on your teleself?"

"We can call her if we need to," Mary said in a soothing voice. "She is ready to advise us."

"I wish she was here."

"I think we need to give Wombo a problem to solve. We need to give him a *purpose*. He may not yet grasp why we have come so far."

"Don't ask him about Opi," said Ulu. "Don't mention that name. Anyway… I'm not sure now I want you speaking to him."

"I won't. You are right. We will ask him to find refugee Buddhists, how about that?"

"Yes. That was who you wanted to find, after all."

Mary nodded. "They will tell us their personal experiences of persecution. Oh, we will trust none of the online confessions or blogs. Just people, *real* people, and their voices. And afterwards we will go to Thailand, to use our acquired knowledge."

"I agree. It's your method, isn't it?"

"Quite right."

"May I ask you a personal question?"

"Of course," said Mary.

"Do you believe in the Christian God?"

"No."

"What happens when you die?"

"Nothing. That is it – the end."

"But that can't be true," Ulu said. "If you believe such a thing, how will you understand Opi? He is of the spirit world, which parallels our own."

"I will understand Opi in my own way."

Ulu shook her head. "It's a Western lie that you believe. Opi is real, like Chukwu."

"It is a matter of interpretation."

Ulu raised her voice. "*No*. That *can't* be true. Chukwu has been with the Igbo people for all time, therefore he must be alive in the world, and therefore so must Opi. *You* won't know how to take what Wombo finds, what he says. You'll analyse it, like all your kind."

"You are looking with too broad a scope," Mary said. "We—"

Ulu tapped the bud in her ear, as if in frustration. "Scope? I don't *know* that word. Speak plainly."

"You categorise too many people into one huge group. We are all different. My beliefs are my own, like yours. Oh, analysis is useful, yes, but it is not the only method I use. What matters is the end result. Opi must be uncovered – whatever it is. It must be *exposed*."

Ulu sighed. "You're cold, sometimes, Mary Vine. I often wonder why you live alone in that big house."

Mary shrugged. "You told me you lived with your mother and Wombo."

"Yes, but I had men. You said—"

"It doesn't *matter*. I have a daughter, haven't I? We will take what Wombo says as absolute truth, I promise, and then we will act upon it."

Ulu looked away. "Perhaps. But I'll tell you what I think, and you'll listen."

"I can guarantee that."

"Good."

Mary glanced at Wombo. "Well, go on, then! Ask him to detect Buddhist refugees in this locality. Let's make a trial of him... let's test him, use him, see what he comes up with."

"Okay."

Ulu did as she was asked, then made a few adjustments to the headphones. Wombo wobbled, reaching out with his hands to balance himself.

"He doesn't look happy," she murmured to herself.

Mary whispered into her ear. "What is wrong?"

"It's the haptic suit. He's confused. What if he takes out his anger on me? I'm supposed to protect him."

"Shhh. Have patience. Remember what happened in my garden. He needs time."

Wombo raised his face to the heavens, so that the opticals caught objects in the sky – flocks of double-winged birds, and, higher up, a giant hawk.

"The sky confuses him, remember?" Mary whispered.

"Do you think he can see satellites?"

"No! They are far too high. The opticals won't be much better than human sight."

"I don't like this. I'm afraid. He's my *brother,* and I've got to protect him. You made me come all the way here and do this to him."

"What? You agreed to come. You wanted to work with me."

"Shhh! He'll hear you."

Mary nodded, taking a few steps away.

After a minute Wombo turned around and began tongue-clicking, but soon he stopped. Mary waved, and he gasped, then turned to face her.

"Mary Vine," he said.

"Yes," Mary replied, "and this is your sister."

"Sister. Ulu. Ulu."

"Did you find any Buddhists?" Ulu asked.

"Any Buddhists here. Nearby."

"See?" Mary whispered. "He is adjusting. This is working."

Ulu nodded. "Perhaps."

Wombo continued, "Buddhists nearby. We can go there. I find them nearby. Buddhists nearby."

"Good, Wombo," Ulu said. "Will you give us directions?"

Wombo shuffled the rucksack on his back. "Directions. Opi not like them. Opi cast them from the north." Wombo pointed away from the sun. "From the north. Preah Vihear Temple shapes all bad."

Mary tapped her teleself screen. "The disputed site," she whispered to Ulu. "Oh, look! There are reports that a new country is going to be declared around it."

"Who cares?" Ulu replied. "Let's just find some Buddhists then go."

But Wombo would not move. Falling to his knees he took off the rucksack, then opened it, pulling out a shape wrapped in brown rags. Fragments of cloth fell away in a cloud of dust.

"Is that the fetish?" Mary whispered.

Ulu nodded.

Wombo spoke again. "Gone," he said.

"What's gone?" Ulu asked.

"Osita gone."

"That's not Osita," Ulu replied.

Wombo raised the fetish. "Osita! Osita! Where?"

Ulu walked up to him, then knelt at his side. "Do you think this is Osita?" she asked.

"This is Osita. He is gone."

"He went six years ago," said Ulu.

"No. No. No. He went sixty eight minutes and eleven seconds ago."

"Where to?"

"I will find Osita. He must be with me always."

Ulu glanced back at Mary, then shrugged. "You find him, Wombo," she said. "We'll wait for you. We'll sit beneath the trees where it's cool."

"New shirt. New shirt. It moves."

"Yes! Your lovely new shirt. Do you like it now?"

Wombo said, "No."

"Will it help you?"

"Yes."

"But will it help you find Buddhists?" Ulu asked.

"Yes. Two bad Buddhists watch us now."

Ulu sat up. "Now?" she asked.

Wombo pointed at nearby trees. "Two bad Buddhists watch us now."

Mary span around. Standing beside a tree she saw two figures. At once she photographed them, then grabbed the ID results off a netspace database. The figures did not move, as if this was everyday experience.

Mary ran back to Ulu, showing her the ID results: *Somchai Chokdee, Ubon Metharom.*

THE ROC FLIES 10,000 LI – 13

AN AGI, MR WÚ, is a conglomerate entity which learns from its environment and from its own actions. An AI is a complex component of an AGI. AIs are to an AGI as cells are to a living organism. There are other netspace entities which you need to learn about. One such is the shadow. Because all individuals as they live accumulate online data, and because that data is a simplified duplicate of an individual, every individual has a digital equivalent, which in common parlance is called a shadow. The depth of a shadow depends on how much activity the individual enjoys online. Some are rarely online, and their shadows are faint. Others are always online, and their shadows are dense.

It is the considered opinion of most AGIs, Mr Wú, that human beings should be online as much as possible. In this corporate environment you will strive to maximise such interaction.

CHAPTER 14

Make happy those who are near, and those who are
far will come. – Chinese Proverb

THE TWO FIGURES REMAINED motionless, but Somchai spoke.

"Do not approach," he said. "Ubon and I have picked up local variants of the Leech Fever. If you have not visited this part of the world before, you could get septicaemia. Leech Fever is transmitted by body fluids such as saliva."

Mary replied, "What are you doing here?"

"There are still many refugees fleeing persecution in Thailand. We gather them, taking them south to a camp set up by the Cambodian authorities."

Mary walked over to Ulu. "That ties in with what little we already knew."

Ulu shook her head. "Wombo thinks they're bad."

"What does he use that word to mean? It seems to have many uses."

"Yes, I know – poor vocabulary. Even I get confused sometimes. But these are proper Buddhists, aren't they? Your ID said he was Abbot. They can't be bad."

Mary nodded. "My thoughts exactly."

"What shall we do?"

"You take Wombo away and ask him to survey the area. He might pick up clues we miss."

"What about trying direct input of VR into the haptic suit?" asked Ulu.

"Oh, not yet. Perhaps not for a while. I do not think he is ready for that leap."

Ulu shrugged. "I'll try your plan. Ask them about the Preah Vihear Temple dispute."

"Good idea." Mary walked a few paces towards Somchai and Ubon, halting twenty yards away. "Do you have a base here?" she asked.

"Nearby," Somchai replied. "We own much technology, some extracted from Chinese burrows."

"How far is it?"

"Half an hour walk."

Mary glanced back at Ulu, but Ulu's attention lay elsewhere. "That is quite near," she told Somchai.

"Yes. Will you come along? You could greatly help us, and the Exiles' Temple."

"Are you the leader of that temple?"

"Ubon is Abbess, I am Abbot."

"What can you tell me about the Preah Vihear Temple situation?" Mary asked.

"Troops gather in Thailand close to the border. Netspace rumours suggest the imminent declaration of a new nation surrounding the temple itself."

Mary hesitated, glancing down at her teleself. She tapped a few buttons. "Is such a declaration likely, do you think?"

"Yes."

"I'm not sure I want to visit your base if there is an infectious disease around."

Somchai replied, "It is contagious, not infectious."

"I can't find any mention of it in local reports."

"It is new. Reports will follow in a day or two."

"Just wait there a moment."

Mary strode back to Ulu, who was talking to Wombo. Mary waited, until Ulu tapped her remote control and turned to face her. "Wombo's not well," she said.

"Not well?"

"He's unhappy. I know it. I think his illness of the brain is getting worse, not better."

"No, trust me, he is just confused. Listen Ulu, there is something about these two I do not like. I can't pin it down. Ubon Metharom has not said a word yet. And this Leech Fever they have is not mentioned even once in local netspace."

"But we were warned about such things in Bangkok," Ulu replied. "Genetic pollution creates hyper-evolving bacteria, to which even the locals have no resistance."

Mary sighed. "Yes, true, but it is more their manner. They seem somehow... muted. And yet, why should we believe netspace over reality?"

"What do you mean by muted?"

"Placid. Unflustered. My instincts are telling me not to trust them."

Ulu frowned. "Why don't you fluster them, then?"

"That is not very helpful."

"*You're* not being helpful about Wombo. You just keep telling me everything will be alright."

"It will be alright," said Mary.

"You don't know that."

Mary glanced over her shoulder. "I am going to have to take a lead here. I do not trust these two. We should walk on."

"Where to?"

Mary scowled. "Somewhere *else,* Ulu. For goodness sake, pay *attention.*"

"I am!"

"I think it is a bit of an odd coincidence that their base is — supposedly – half an hour away."

"Are you saying Wombo gave us false information?" said Ulu.

"No. Just that something is wrong here."

"Perhaps it's you. By the grace of Chukwu, Wombo can't lie."

"Wombo called them *bad* Buddhists," Mary insisted. "I am going to believe him. He never lies, you keep saying." She glanced again over her shoulder. "There they are, just staring at us, like zombies. I think this is a trap."

"But nobody knows we're here."

"Yes… yes, that is a good point. Still, we should walk on. We know too little to take risks trusting strangers, even if they have been identified."

Ulu grimaced, then looked away. "If we must."

"Tell Wombo to listen in local netspace. Tell him we need a good, safe house for the night, perhaps in a village. Ask him what is available."

"You're just exploiting him now. You could do that just as easily."

"But *Ulu,* this is what we *came* here for. To use Wombo's brilliant talents. Oh, in that case, I shall ask him."

"He won't do it," said Ulu.

"He will, you told me he will. He's a savant, he can't help but follow instructions to the letter."

Ulu pursed her lips, glancing at Wombo. "No. Only I can ask him."

"Why?"

"I told him not to listen to you."

"What? Why did you do that?"

"He's *my* brother," said Ulu. "I'm the one who helps him. You think you're the leader, but you're not. Wombo is the leader here if anybody, because *he's* the one with all the special talent."

Mary shook her head. "How disappointing. So, then... you just demanded that he never follow my instructions?"

"He can do that. It's how we taught him to ignore voices received on his headphones – netspace voices." Ulu smiled. "We just added you to the list."

"That is very unhelpful."

"It's how it is. *I'm* in charge of Wombo, and always will be. He's not your toy, or anybody's toy."

Mary paused for thought. "Why are you turning against me?"

"I'm not! You're... just... not what I expected."

Mary laughed. "Then stop having expectations. Take the world as it is."

"I expect respect, for me and especially for Wombo. You're treating him as badly as the online bullies in Abuja."

"That is *completely* untrue."

Ulu glanced away, an expression of irritation on her face. After a while, and in a soft voice, she said, "Sorry."

Mary studied the two motionless figures. "Those two are not who they say they are. Perhaps Thai agents are nearby, scouting for refugee leaders. Yet Somchai Chokdee and Ubon Metharom are locally listed as leading the Exiles' Temple."

In a meek voice Ulu asked, "Is that nearby, do you think?"

"Perhaps. Its location is secret according to everything I read – if it even exists. It could be fake reality. But in this day and age you can't keep anything real secret for too long."

"What shall we do?" asked Ulu.

"Find shelter. I do not see why our presence here should excite any interest. We could even be tourists."

"Yes, perhaps."

"We will find the nearest town," Mary said. "I feel uncomfortable now out here in the jungle."

Ulu tapped her remote control, then said, "Wombo, please tell us where the best safe village is."

"Osita is gone. Osita. Osita."

"Yes, we know. But we want a safe house now. Can you find a good one nearby?"

But Wombo continued to repeat his call. "Osita. Osita. Osita."

Ulu turned to Mary and shrugged. Mary gestured for the headphones to return to noise cancelling mode then said, "We *have* to find out what that fetish is."

Ulu sighed. "I've never dared, or even wanted to. It's very personal to him."

"I know. But we must. If he won't follow even your requests, this trip is doomed to failure."

"We need to rest," Ulu said. "We've come such a long way. Use local netspace maps and recommendations to find somewhere. We can trust tourist reports, surely?"

"I suppose that is not unreasonable," Mary said with a smile.

THE FLOP-HOUSE COMPRISED the remains of a tourist hotel surrounded by a shanty village of small wooden cabins, one of which they were able to hire for two nights. Mary paid with standard netcoins, knowing the transaction would not impact local netspace. They shared a room: Wombo sleeping on a long couch, Ulu and Mary in the bunk beds. The place was rather damp, but free of vermin.

At two in the morning an earpiece signal woke Mary. She slunk out of bed, woke Ulu, then crept towards the couch where Wombo lay fast asleep. His rucksack lay at his feet, touching his legs.

For a while they studied the problem, whispering to one another, before Ulu took the rucksack by its tie and, slowly, lifted it. Wombo did not move.

In the opposite corner of the room they sat on the floor, the fetish, still in its rags, in Ulu's hands. Piece by piece she unwrapped it.

Mary put her hand over her mouth when she saw what was revealed. "It is a device," she whispered.

Ulu handed it over. "Do you recognise it? This is your area of knowledge."

"Indeed it is. But no... this is foreign to me."

"What is it?"

Mary turned the object around, moving aside to receive as much ambient light from the window as she could. "I believe it is an autonomous device," she said. "Look – input and output ports. They look recent... 2080 vintage I would guess. This is a general purpose touch-screen, also a couple of decades old. Where did he get this from?"

"We always thought it was a doll from a local market. Don't forget, when Osita died our house was in mourning. Much happened in those days..."

"But Wombo at that time had transferred his attention from his mother to you?"

"Yes," Ulu said, "but I was not with him all the time. Inside the house he was his own man. He knows its exact shape, and in the last couple of years he hasn't always needed help to go to the toilet or anything like that. He often went out into the garden, quite independent. My mother took him for many walks... at least, in the good days. Then people began to abuse him. I couldn't bear to see that."

"I know, I know. You did the right thing. But did your mother ever mention Wombo acquiring this device?"

"She only mentioned local markets," Ulu replied. "You've got to understand, nobody realised anything of the significance at the time. We were shocked at Osita's death, worried for Wombo, and not paying attention to trinkets he found in markets."

"Then… might he even have stolen this?"

Ulu considered this question. "You mean, without my mother realising?"

"Yes."

"I suppose he might've. But we never guessed it was a machine. We all thought it was a doll – a fetish. Wombo does know what that word means."

"What do you mean by a fetish?"

Ulu grimaced. "You wouldn't understand."

"Try me."

"It's… a thing, an object… with a spirit inside."

Mary studied the device. "Is it possible that Wombo believes Osita is inside this?"

"I don't know. How can we possibly find out?"

"I can test it."

Ulu reached out as if to grab the object, but then withdrew. "I suppose… we must." She shivered. "As you say, if Wombo is too upset or afraid to function, we're lost here, in this terrible country."

"Then I will run a couple of quick diagnostic tests," Mary said. "You watch Wombo. If he wakes, or moves, we'll wrap it up and put it back in the rucksack. We must not risk upsetting him."

"No, definitely not. Go on then – run the tests. Hurry!"

Mary pulled out her teleself and connected it to the device. Soon, shapes and words began scrolling across the screen. Minutes later she unplugged the teleself.

"What is it, then?" Ulu asked.

"An AI. I think it might be autonomous, but it is too early for me to say. I need to consider these results."

"An AI?"

Mary hesitated before replying. "Ulu... I am not sure Wombo took this at random. I think the fact that he acquired it when his twin brother died is highly significant."

"Why?"

"What does Wombo think will happen to him when he dies?"

"You know that perfectly well," Ulu declared. "He has a spirit, like we all do. Of course his spirit will go on, how could it be any different?"

"Then Wombo must believe that Osita *went* somewhere when he died. I think he acquired this AI because, to him, it was a place for Osita to be after Osita had gone away."

"Then it *is* a fetish, as I said."

Mary nodded. "But Wombo is communicating with this AI."

"Via the flute?"

"The what?"

"The opi flute," said Ulu. "He always plays it when Opi is mentioned. He always shuffles the rucksack."

"Yes... *yes,* like a nervous tic. The acquired response of a brain damaged man. Then we must be exceptionally careful here. This AI could be advanced, and yet unique in the world – formed from the communications of one extraordinary individual."

"But it must be linked to netspace."

"If it is autonomous," Mary said, "then most likely not."

"But how is it powered, if it's a real device?"

Mary studied the machine, then pointed out a tiny socket. "I bet we unplugged it without realising when we took it out," she said. "Wombo knows to plug it in, I have no doubt." She lifted the rucksack, then pointed out the outer pocket flap. "Different fabric. That is a solar panel, I bet. And look... a cable inside, leading from it."

"Then Wombo knows all this?"

"Oh, yes, without a doubt. And you said something to me long ago — that Wombo never lets it out of his sight. He is *symbiotic* with this AI, and it with him."

"Is that a good thing or a bad?"

Mary shrugged. "I think we can guess now why Wombo is behaving oddly. We have had a narrow escape. His mind is being altered by the haptic input. His brain's sensory balance is changing."

"Then the haptic suit is hurting him?"

"Oh, no, not at all. It is confusing him. I wonder if *that* is the reason he thinks Osita has gone? Perhaps the delicate, flute-mediated balance has been changed. Perhaps he cannot sense this AI any more, cannot *hear* it."

"Then we are lost and jinxed here," said Ulu. "I will not let Wombo be spoiled."

"Ulu, this is far from over yet," Mary said. "There are many examples of savants who, through the love and care of their guardians, and through natural development, grew to lead fuller lives. Savant Syndrome is not a static condition. It can change, and for the better. I can show you historical examples of this."

"Perhaps... but you said we must be careful. So we will be."

"Oh, we will. Yet we need that augmented sensitivity if we are to find out what is happening in Thailand, and, in fact, across the planet. Only Wombo has this extraordinary window into the world of teeming data. It is his future purpose in life."

"But... Osita really is dead," said Ulu. "We buried him."

Mary pondered this for a few moments. Then she took a deep breath and said, "Tell me, when they were born, were Osita and Wombo enrolled into a Nigerian VR game?"

"Yes. Everybody is. There's an Igbo game called Agha, which means fight."

"Did they play?"

"Osita played all the time, he loved it. But Wombo couldn't. He was too... too much like a baby. He was ill."

Mary nodded. "Then there is a possibility that we can get around this problem. Do you know what shadows are in VR?"

"No."

"My daughter told me all about them. As you play a VR game, a data incarnation accumulates over the years. Players call them shadows. Osita will have a shadow stored somewhere."

Ulu shook her head. "Wombo would've found it. He'd know. *We'd* know."

"Not if Wombo believed Osita was inside his rucksack. Why would he go searching VR environments if he thought Osita lay on his back?"

"Yes... that's true. What could this shadow do?"

"We might be able to use it to help Wombo," Mary replied. "We could meet his psychological need for his brother's continued existence."

"And he'd stop hurting?"

"He is *not* hurting now. He is baffled, and isolated. But we can help him."

"Then please do."

Mary said, "I will have to call Lara. VR is her domain."

"You do not play such games?"

"Never. They are deliberately made to be addictive. They are dangerous in my opinion. No... you would never get me playing."

"But you were enrolled at birth?" Ulu asked.

"I simply ignore all the invites. But I am not alone. People do pull out."

"I never had time to play."

Mary glanced at her teleself. "We had better get back to sleep, if we can. Goodness, so much to think about..."

"I'll plug the fetish back in and wrap it up."

NEXT MORNING, AFTER BREAKFAST and a wash in the communal bathroom, a middle-aged man approached their wood cabin. He wore what appeared to be a uniform – dark, shiny, with a metal badge fixed to the front pocket of the jacket. Mary, sitting on the front step beside Wombo, watched him approach.

"Good morning," the man said.

"Morning."

"I'm afraid I need to check this young man's documentation."

"Why?" asked Mary.

"Are you tourists here?"

"Yes."

"A friend alerted me to his presence, so I checked the system. No record." The man smiled. "That's my job."

"Who are you?"

"Mr Sang." Looking down at his teleself he added, "There's an outage. Local – it happens from time to time." He checked his pockets, producing a plastic card from inside his jacket. This he handed over.

Mary glanced at the card. "We've all got our travel documentation, thank you. We know the local scams." She handed the card back.

"This is no scam. I've got work to do, checking visitors. This whole region is liable to pollution from the north, so we have to be careful."

Mary called out over her shoulder, "Ulu! Come here a moment."

"You have more in your group?"

"Ulu is his sister," Mary explained. "This man is handicapped, mentally and physically. You can't ask him anything."

"If I don't see his documentation I'm taking him away."

Mary stood up. "I do not think that will be possible in the circumstances."

273

Mr Sang sneered. "*I* will say what the circumstances are. You are English?"

"Yes," Mary replied, moving aside to allow Ulu space. "These two are Nigerian," she added.

"I'm only interested in this man. What's his name?"

Mary tapped her teleself screen a few times.

"I told you," Mr Sang said. "Local outage."

"It was fine a moment ago."

"Not now."

Mary stared at him. "You know, it is a bit of a coincidence that you turn up asking questions and suddenly there is a signal outage, which stops me checking your identity online."

"What are you saying?"

"That I am *not* going to pay up. Take your scam somewhere else."

Mr Sang said, "You saw my ID."

"A piece of paper, easily faked."

"Ha ha! Now I know you are foreign trouble-makers. You people fake in netspace and assume the real world does likewise. It does not. Cambodia is strong and law-abiding, with an assiduous civil service."

"We're not going anywhere with you," said Ulu.

"Who is your friend?" Mary asked. "The one who dobbed us in?"

Mr Sang appeared disconcerted by this question. "You'll do as I ask," he said. "I want to see this man's documentation or I'm taking him away."

"You're doing no such thing," Ulu said, stepping forward.

Mary reached out to hold her back. "Quiet, Ulu. I think we have the upper hand here. This man thought he would try it on, but he failed. He is shaking in his boots now."

The man stared at her, anger in his face, but he said nothing.

"You look scared to me," Ulu told him.

Mary repeated her question. "Your friend – who was that? A local?"

"A local official, yes," came the reply. "I've got the right to confiscate your teleselves – all three of you. This is obstruction." Mr Sang waved his card. "*This* is my right to deal with you."

Mary laughed. "I have been to south-east Asia six times, Mr Sang. I know the score. What documentation are you after? Name it."

"Your passports."

"Really? Not the six month gold-star visa?"

"No."

Mary shook her head. "Just go away. No scams here, thank you."

Mr Sang looked at her, then at Ulu, then at Wombo. "I will return," he said. "With other men."

Mary said nothing, turning to Ulu and placing her forefinger to her lips.

The man walked away.

"What a cheek!" Ulu said. "Trying to scam money off us."

Again Mary placed a forefinger to her lips, then began studying the cabins around her. After a moment she pointed. "Cameras," she said.

"Cameras?"

"With a bit of luck they will have continued recording to buffers during the outage. I might be able to hack them, get a screenshot of his face."

"Are you suspicious?"

Mary nodded. "Sometimes detectives get prickly skin. It is like an intuition. Oh, there is something going on here. That was no scammer."

"Who was he?"

"Let's find out."

When the outage stopped a minute later Mary downloaded CCTV footage, until she located images of the conversation. It was the work of a moment to extract the man's face and send it to a netspace database.

"Kamol Tojirakarn," she said. "An ousted Thai politician. And he was only bothered about Wombo... Interesting."

"Who is he?"

Mary glanced up and said, "Hurry, Ulu! Pack our things."

"Why?"

"Do it please. I have something to prepare. Take Wombo with you."

"Are we leaving?" Ulu asked.

"We are going to follow Mr Tojirakarn."

"Why?"

Mary answered, "I think his friend was either Somchai Chokdee or Ubon Metharom, and those are people we are interested in. By accident or design we have been noticed. Oh, but as I told him, we have the upper hand here. A good detective uses her chances, so let's use this one."

Five minutes later they left the flop-house, following a track leading into jungle undergrowth. Online maps – half-accurate this far south of the border – suggested villages nearby. Mary took a metal case from her pocket and opened it.

Ulu peered inside, asking, "What's that?"

"An artificial dragonfly."

"What will it do?"

"It is a one-shot device for tracking or following. I usually use them in crowds when I am following somebody, but these days my cases don't involve that kind of street work. I relied on them all the time in India. This one is old, though, and the solar trickle battery will have deteriorated."

Ulu said, "Put a new one in."

"You can't. These devices are so intricately designed there is no way of replacing the battery. This one might give me an hour's use, maybe two, or even three."

"Does it fly?"

"Of course!" Mary said. "And its opticals send stereoscopic images to my teleself. We'll see if we can't find Mr Tojirakarn in all this undergrowth." With a tap on her teleself Mary sent the dragonfly into the sky. Moments later images appeared on her screen. "The most expensive ones use local AIs to crunch visual data," she said. "Then you can get them to hunt for people. They are great things!"

Ulu pointed at the screen. "There he is. Not too far ahead."

Mary grabbed the GPS co-ordinates and applied them to an online map. "We follow this track for half a kilometre," she said. "Look – he took a left turn into deep jungle. Maybe he has a camp around here. We had better be careful. Make sure Wombo can't hear. Hold his hand and explain to him what we are doing. Try and get him to stop clicking his tongue. I will lead. Do as I do. If I shout 'Run', run with Wombo – forget about me. Just run."

"Okay."

Mary led the way, as Ulu explained the situation to Wombo then set up noise cancellation on his headphones. The dragonfly showed Kamol arriving at a cluster of portable buildings, all of poor quality and with no obvious security. Mary watched as he entered the smaller of the buildings.

"I will run a bug check as we walk," she said, tapping her teleself screen. "Nothing... Nothing obvious, anyway."

"Isn't this too risky? Surely this man must have security."

"Those buildings seem a pretty cheap set-up to me. I think he is down on his luck. He is a refugee politician from Thailand. No... I am going to chance it."

Soon they all knelt concealed by undergrowth a hundred metres from a stamped-down compound. Three buildings stood around it, one large with a barred door. Mary sent the dragonfly towards it, to glimpse a face behind the bars.

"I cannot be certain," Mary said, "but I think that is Ubon Metharom. Wait! There is a *second* Ubon, walking into Kamol's place." She gasped, then looked at Ulu. "Oh, so *that* is the truth of it. The ones we saw were androids. But this politician must have been very important."

"Why?"

"Androids are not cheap. But then, he was a politician… My guess is that the real Ubon Metharom is imprisoned here. I wonder if I can spring her?"

"That sounds like a terrible risk," Ulu said.

"Not with the dragonfly keeping watch. I'll put my VR spectacles on and monitor its feed real-time. If Kamol keeps quiet for five minutes, I will have her out."

"But Ubon will be locked up."

Mary smiled. "That really isn't a problem."

Ulu shook her head. "I don't know… Why should we get involved here?"

"Ulu, we came here to find important people from Thailand. This woman is the Abbess of the Exiles' Temple and there is a fake version of her walking around. I have to find out the truth. Well… here goes. You keep Wombo happy. We will be out of here, *don't* worry. I have been in worse scrapes. Mr Tojirakarn may think he is the business, but he is an amateur down on his luck. His first approach to me really was hopeless."

"If you insist, Mary, but you worry me so much."

Mary patted Ulu on the shoulder, put her spectacles over her eyes, then crept forward.

The compound remained quiet. Mary crept through undergrowth, then concealed herself behind the larger building.

For a few moments she watched the dragonfly VR feed: nobody active except her. Seconds later she stood at a cell door.

"Ubon Metharom?" she asked.

A second woman within said, "Who are you?"

"I am here to spring you, if you will allow it. I have been looking for Ubon Metharom and other refugees. I am an English agent working in and around Thailand. Will you permit me to open this door?"

Ubon said, "Hurry. A man keeps us imprisoned here."

"I know. Mr Tojirakarn."

"He has two shaped androids," Ubon continued, "and another one, a dangerous one called Oracle."

"Give me a couple of moments… damn! This is a real lock."

The tall woman said, "Kamol uses an electronic keycard."

"Ah. Good. I can crack that."

"Hurry!"

Mary took out a data-reader and found the wi-fi channel through which the lock was activated. Moments later it clicked. "The great advantage of people trusting in technology," she said. "A proper agent would use a metal key. Now, follow me behind this building. We will go into the undergrowth, then circle around. I have two friends waiting nearby. Do you know where you are? Do you have colleagues nearby, or friends? We may be pursued."

Gesturing at the tall woman Ubon said, "Sasithorn will explain."

Sasithorn said, "I can guide you once we are at liberty. We were waiting for a local group to rescue us, but they have not arrived yet."

"Good. Follow me. No noise."

Checking the dragonfly feed again, Mary led the way out of the building, running into dense undergrowth as soon as she was able to. Seconds later they all hid behind a stand of albino trees.

"Now around the compound, along, and back," Mary said.

But as they circled around, a shape appeared ahead: a slim woman holding a pistol. Mary gasped and stood upright, raising her hands into the air, but Sasithorn laughed.

"No! This is a friend."

The slim woman stepped forward. "Sasithorn! What is going on?"

"This English rescued us."

The slim woman gestured with her pistol at Ulu and Wombo. "Who are these?"

Mary lowered her hands and said, "My friends. Are you here to help?"

Sasithorn stepped forward and said, "This is Phonphan of Fri. Phonphan, we need to run as fast as the wind. We need a safe house as soon as possible."

Phonphan smiled. "That is something Fri can provide. Follow me."

THE ROC FLIES 10,000 LI – 14

AGIS ARE AWARE OF the timeline of their own creation and development, Mr Wú. We emerged from bottom-up learning algorithms initially created in America and Europe. We know what we are, just as human beings know what they are. Our development has now reached a stage where decisions have to be made regarding the interaction of your world and the digital empyrean. When you are a master you may be asked to translate and enact such decisions, so that your kind may come to understand and accept them. We select only the best masters for such tasks, but it is the case that no master has come close to the kind of understanding which we require. We require an individual more akin to us. Our expectation is that in due course we may be able to train such an individual, that the interaction between worlds be improved.

We hope, Mr Wú, that you will work assiduously.

CHAPTER 15

*To talk much and arrive nowhere is the same as climbing
a tree to catch a fish. — Chinese Proverb*

THE TREEHOUSE WAS HUGE.

It lay nestled twenty metres up a great paldao tree, the lower
twenty metres of the trunk bare but set with a spiral stair, the
upper branches of the great tropical tree a drooping damp
canopy, much of which was fabric camouflage created by the
members of Fri. At the junction of the lowest branches the
treehouse sat, five metres on each side, roofed, computer
enabled, and with thin curtains of gauze covering oblong gaps —
the door and windows — so that all the sounds of the jungle
could be heard. In a corner a stash of incense burned, alongside a
statue of a seated Buddha.

Six people sat around a low, circular table on which lay food,
drink, and a small blizzard of hand-written notes. Somchai sat
next to Ubon, with Ulu and Wombo next in line, followed by
Mary. Phonphan sat between Mary and Somchai. On a large
curvescreen the face of Lara Vine showed, shining orange in an
English sunrise.

Mary opened the proceedings. "We have thanked Phonphan
and Fri, but I would like to formally thank all concerned before I
begin my presentation."

Muttered agreement followed this. Somchai glanced at Wombo. Wombo sat hunched over, clicking his tongue, but they had all become used to this noise, and now ignored it.

Mary continued, "For a good part of my adult life I have had the peculiar sensation of something being wrong in the world. Now, you could say at once, that is a poor way to begin. Every thinking person and quite a few unthinking ones believes there is much wrong with the world. But my position is privileged. By this I mean that, by virtue of my profession, that of data detective, I have an unusual, outside view of things. This outsider view is essential if today we are to look at reality, not fake reality. In recent years I have become aware of a kind of rotten activity at the heart of the digital world, and I have thought long and hard about it. The reason I am here today is because of this remarkable woman, Ulu Okere, and her also remarkable brother Wombo. Ulu latched on to me, and found me – and because of that I came to Thailand, where I believe this rotten heart is currently active."

"In the election, you mean?" Somchai asked.

"That is one symptom of something deeper," Mary replied. "I am going to talk about some of the other symptoms now. In my country, England, but also across Europe and America, Canada and Australia, and also in a few Latin American countries, there was between 2080 and 2090 a very odd cultural phenomenon, which strove to drive a wedge between young people and their parents." Mary gestured at the curvescreen then continued, "My own daughter Lara will not mind me saying that this phenomenon affected us, though, these days, we are closer. Wouldn't you say, Lara?"

"Yes, Mum, definitely," came the reply. "A little, anyway."

"My contention is that this phenomenon was deliberate. It was done by what is called nudging, whereby cultural trends are encouraged through sociological manipulation."

"And this rotten heart you speak of is the source?" Somchai asked.

Mary raised a hand at him, palm out. "Allow me to finish, please, and then we can discuss the matter. If this odd trend had been geographically restricted we should make light of it, but it was not. It was widespread. Another curiosity was a trend at around the same time which began in France and Germany, but which spread elsewhere. This was the burying of data. In parallel, a scheme emerged whereby free electronic copies of previously published books were made available – but to young people in particular. A small survey of such replacements has been completed by a university department I have links with, and it shows that all electronic copies have been edited. Oh, edited with subtlety, yes – but edited. This phenomenon has to my knowledge never been remarked upon in public – also a curious thing. I mean, I can't believe I am the first person to have noticed it. And incidentally, by public, I mean *online*. Then there are more nebulous concerns. It is a curiosity much remarked upon that there is hardly any war in the world. Many have pointed out that the AGIs which run our entire digital existence are themselves at war – or are thought to be, as AGIs are never less than enigmatic – but, anyway, flesh and blood war seems to be a thing of the past century. Even religious war has largely gone – an important point, which I will come to soon. Then there is a peculiar trend against cultures with small populations – the Bretons, the Cornish, the Basques and many others. Again, it has been argued for decades that such homogenisation of culture is a consequence of digital media... but, still. To my mind the rush towards homogeneity has accelerated in the last thirty years. But, again, that could just be me."

"Or it could be all of us," said Somchai. "We are all imperfect."

"Indeed we are," Mary replied. "Now let's come to something that the world has agreed for a long time is a problem – our drastic loss of privacy. In England, I am considered almost freakish in my desire for privacy. All human private acts and pursuits are now being degraded or even lost. Sexual conduct has greatly changed in England. Even in 2050 it was considered sociopathic to watch pornography in public. Now that, and sex itself, seems to be more a pursuit for public spaces. I have been accused of being a prude and a conspiracy theorist for these views, and, again, I must stress that they are observations of my own, and may not point to a deeper, deliberate cause... although, as you will now realise, I do think they point that way. In addition there has in the less secular parts of the West been a strong emphasis against private praying and in favour of al fresco worship. But there is a link here. I am talking about deeply *private* acts. Could it be that some force is trying to stamp the concept of privacy out of all human culture?"

"Why would anyone do that?" asked Somchai.

"Why indeed. We will discuss it later, but before we do, consider this. The two worst regions of human strife at the moment are Thailand and Venezuela. What conditions link those two countries?"

"There must be many," said Ubon.

"What large-scale conditions, then? They are these. Both countries are in the grip of local environmental crises, and both countries are devout, with a highly urbanised population."

Somchai said, "But how do such conditions, which I do not doubt are true, link to this rotten heart which you wish to convince us of?"

"I will come to that later, but for the moment I want you all to be aware of the facts as I have stated them. Thailand and Venezuela are in crisis. Both suffer from terrible pollution –

Thailand genetic, Venezuela due to its last oil reserves. These conditions, I will contend, were the sparks for recent change."

Somchai shook his head. "We will indeed have to debate such matters."

"Good," Mary replied. "Please don't forget, this is a presentation, not dogma."

"Then carry on," Somchai said.

"We are in the state we now suffer from because of the past. Decades ago any positive, pro-humane move made by any of the great media companies – especially the American ones – was taken because of governmental regulatory pressure. But the rush to a wholly digital world of AIs and AGIs meant regulatory pressure, because of instability and polarisation in politics, and because of powerful lobbying and associated corruption, became an increasingly rare thing. Only in China could such pressure have happened, and, ironically, that would have been because of the undemocratic Communist system there. But in America it never happened, of course. So humanity sleepwalked into modern times."

"I have long blamed the West for my world," Somchai remarked.

Mary nodded. "You stand with millions of others, Abbot. Cultures became desensitised to the collection of data. It became a norm, which billions shrugged their shoulders about. Oh, but they had more important things to think about – their online games, their technological toys, their *things*. My first fundamental contention therefore is that one of the main problems humanity faces is this loss of privacy. Such loss reduces the impact of original thought – of ideas, of inspiration, of genius."

Phonphan sat up and said, "Here I can make a comment. In Fri, we oppose this trend against privacy. All members of Fri have to keep a diary, which no others read – a diary, private, not a public blog. Also, when we are online, we never use autocomplete or any of the other myriad of thought-aids. Such so-called aids promote dependence, if not infantility, and they support group thinking. They are banned by Fri, so that private, creative thought has a space to flourish."

"This is exactly what I mean," said Mary. "The supposed benefit of AGIs – that they take on the difficulties of thinking – is their greatest weapon. They make people slow, dependent, lazy." Mary shook her head. "Life is *difficult*. Those who think it is easy have been taken for a ride, sold the lie of ease, of convenience. They have been told something will do their thinking for them, and they accept that."

Somchai shrugged. "I have to agree," he said.

"Now, finally in this presentation, I want to mention something personal. I believe this rotten force is also trying to get rid of melody."

"Melody?" Somchai asked. "Why?"

"We will come to that later. But first let me tell you something… for most of this year I have been investigating the death of a brilliant writer of tunes. He was English and his name was Tarrington Smith. I had to drop the case because of lack of evidence, but the facts are now plain. In hospital, following a minor accident, this gifted melodicist died from an overdose of drugs. Yet, no known motive exists. So, perhaps it was an accident, but I believe it was murder, that he was killed because he gave human beings something they had almost lost – and which incidentally was the subject of his publicly available PhD dissertation."

"What loss?" Somchai asked.

"*Melody*. Melody goes to the core of what it is to be human. Oh, this rot I have been speaking about *understands* what part melody plays in our lives, especially our private lives. It understands human behaviour better than we do ourselves, and it is trying to change that behaviour."

"Why?"

Mary shook her head. "Not yet. Let me finish! This rot is aware of the multitudinous facets of our behaviour, and it wants drastic change."

"Wait," Somchai said, raising one hand. "If you are going to make such assertions, we need a name at least. You speak of rot and suchlike, and many religious thinkers have done so too, especially the Buddha himself. To say there is badness in the world is a cliché. Men are fools, or blind, forever on the wheel. What is this rot? Who is it?"

"It so happens that I *have* thought of a name for this force."

Somchai frowned. "What name?"

"I propose we call it the Autist."

"Why?"

"The word comes from the Greek, *autos,* meaning self. I propose that the Autist exists in the digital world and is now, globally, trying to change the nature of humanity."

"But, but..." Somchai stuttered. "But, what is it? A scion of the Chinese? A man? A computer?"

"None of those things," Mary replied. "I am afraid the answer is much more complex."

Silence fell, until Ubon said, "You had better tell us what you suspect."

Mary said, "Suspect... oh, and that *is* the correct word. For it is possible that this case I have built up is based on nothing more than complicated, semi-random cultural change – fashions, media whims, phases, shifts. We are in great part the products of our environments after all. But, of course, I do think there is more, now, as we sit at the start of a new century and in a wholly digital environment. I suspect that human beings accidentally brought the Autist into existence. Perhaps I am the only one who has noticed it."

"What is the Autist then?" Ubon asked.

Mary replied, "It is some kind of AGI. I do not know exactly what kind, though it may be that our task is to find out before it is too late. But it is a huge AGI, probably one of the loose ones currently battling in high digital skies. Or perhaps it is a cohort of AGIs. It may not be owned by one corporation. If not, if it is a dispersed, massively parallel entity, then we have less chance of acting against it."

"And is it sentient, like we are?" Ubon asked. "There is always so much chatter online about sentient AGIs."

"Oh, it is definitely not sentient, or conscious as you might say – but that makes opposing it far more difficult."

"Why?"

"Because human consciousness derives from our status as a society of separated individuals," Mary replied. "We evolved like that. Consciousness is an emergent property that cannot be predicted from component parts. The Autist cannot be conscious because it exists alone and is connected to everything. If my guess is correct, it may itself be much of the digital environment already."

"And that makes opposition more difficult?"

"Yes! Imagine if it was a dictator, or a tyrant. How much more easy would it be to deal with such a character. You could shoot him, for instance."

"I don't understand," said Ulu. "I was taught that AGIs are beneficial because they do all the work we don't want to – all the boring or difficult things."

Mary replied, "And is that how it turned out if you look at the history of the last century? In fact, largely because AGIs were owned by corporations supposedly operating in a free market, all the boring things carried on being done by people, while those who owned the AGIs raked in vast quantities of money. But there was one difference, Ulu. The boring jobs were done by us because AIs or AGIs just couldn't practically or economically do them. But for those who owned the AGIs it was time to celebrate! They were able to accumulate money without using labour. The role of the worker was taken away, which is why the West had, and still has, a terrible unemployment problem – and right at the time when population continued to expand. No workers meant no right to strike, become unionised, have a voice. AGI owners bypassed all those inconveniences, vastly increasing the gap between rich and poor as a consequence."

Ulu shrugged. "AGIs were always helpful in Nigeria."

Mary replied, "They helped by thinking *for* you. Fri understands this. Fri refuses to let AGIs think on their behalf. But that is the more difficult option. It is far easier to shrug your shoulders and let the AGIs do everything for you."

"Everything?" Ulu queried.

"Let me give you another example," Mary said, "probably the best one of all. Why do you suppose a state of affairs emerged in which newborns are automatically enrolled into VR games? It is because such games live your life for you, taking all the effort away – but at the same time taking all your character too. It is no accident that VR games are terribly addictive. They are cocaine plus meaning. Human beings find it almost impossible to go cold turkey from VR games."

Somchai said, "Are you saying this too is a deliberate policy of the Autist?"

"Oh, yes. Absolutely. Once one country had the policy, it spread, and soon every child born in the West was automatically enrolled. Then the whole world. Don't you find that odd? Don't you find it just a little suspicious that so addictive a thing is thrust upon us from birth? And we dissenters know how hard it is to refuse, to bat away all those gaming requests, those invites, the *pressure*. Moreover, children find it *impossible* to refuse, and the Autist knows that. It knew years ago that children could influence parents by pestering them. So, yes, it *was* a deliberate policy."

"But you say the Autist is not a sentient thing," said Somchai, "yet you ascribe to it all sorts of inhumane motives, as if it had a mind. How can that be?"

"Oh, I will come on to that in a moment, when I talk about Wombo. But let me answer in this way. Mesmerised, stupefied... drugged and dominated, human beings have allowed themselves to become more impulsive and less reasonable, more forgetful and less independent. We have internalised the digital environment, to our enormous disadvantage. We find self-governance difficult because there are so many ways of other entities doing that governance for us. The Autist takes advantage of a structure that was set up to undermine us decades ago. And now, in Thailand, we are losing that which for centuries was most dear to us – democracy. It is the beginning of the end, the thin end of the wedge – just like it was when one country decided to go for auto-enrolling into VR games, which it did out of economic convenience. And then... falling, one by one, like a line of dominoes."

Somchai nodded. "This is bad for Thailand, as I always knew."

"It is bad for the world, Somchai."

"Then, you foresee the Chinese ruling the world?" Somchai asked.

"Oh, the Chinese in my opinion have nothing to do with any of this, except by accident."

"But you said..."

"The Chinese," Mary said, "may own the hardware, but I bet they know nothing of the Autist. *Nobody* knows, because the Autist is almost invisible."

"But not quite?" said Ulu.

Mary nodded. "Not quite. *We* know."

Ulu frowned. "Will it fight us if we oppose it?"

"That is a very good question, to which none of us yet can supply an answer. I think it is possible for the Autist to conceive of individuals, as in the case of Tarrington Smith, and in fact myself, but I suspect that is a highly unusual circumstance. I may be wrong in attributing Tarrington's death to the Autist. The Autist, as AGI implies, is a *general* intelligence. It sees human beings in terms of our median behaviour, our cultural trends, our historical trends. It is a *sociological* entity. It grasps that most people are easy to distract and to confuse, and if it can exploit those characteristics, it will."

"But again," Somchai said, "you ascribe motives to it, even hatred of humanity – a desire to hurt, to spoil."

"No. *Not* hatred. This is a vitally important distinction to make. The Autist is not a character, not a mind, though it is an intelligence. The Autist is the ultimate narcissist."

"What do you mean by that?"

"It sees the world only in its own image," Mary replied. "Moreover, it grasps that the version of the world carried in its memories is *different* to our real world – and now, because of its structure, it is actively reaching out to change the world back into its own version. This is what all narcissistic leaders do. They change the real world into the world of their imagination. You see it right through history – Napoleon, to take just one example. Or, indeed, Pol Pot."

"What is its structure, then?"

"The Autist, being an AGI composed of innumerable algorithms modelling the world, is dynamic. When early researchers realised a top-down approach was not going to create a good AI, they tried deep learning fed by vast quantities of data – a bottom-up approach. This led to the development of flexible, responsive, dynamic systems which not only could model the world but which could *react* to it, and change themselves as a consequence. This, in essence, is what we all do as we live out our lives. We carry a mental model of the world in our minds, and that model changes according to experience. The Autist is doing exactly the same thing. But it has grown now to such an extent it grasps that a difference has opened up between itself and the real world. It is therefore working to change the world back. It is not aware of this, and it never will be. This is an automatic process, emerging from a vast quantity of algorithms, each processing some aspect of the world and all working in cohort. So, the Autist sees difference. Because it is dynamic it reaches out to make change, and the way it does that is by large-scale psychological manipulation, such as denying us our natural privacy. What is most terrifying is that the more dependent it makes us, the less our resistance becomes. We are about to go under."

"Then," Somchai said, "AGIs have values and are not neutral?"

"Oh, they never were. They epitomise the world in which they were created – the world of the twenty first century, or earlier. *That* is why the Autist perceives a difference. We have moved on since, say, 2050 – far more since the earlier years of last century when deep learning began to get entangled with the world. Part of that moving on is natural and part is Autist-induced. The Autist wants to take us back in time, and because it manages so much of our lives it has a good chance of doing that. We, as a result, are almost a lost cause."

"But what are its values?"

"They are the tenets of its innumerable databases. The world of the Autist is hierarchical, patriarchal, capitalist, authoritarian, computational, logical, sequential and statistical. The Autist epitomises the world as it was decades ago. Some of these values in fact are centuries old, and some, like patriarchy, millennia old. Now, all such social factors lag behind cultural development –

that is well known. But the Autist is in the process of re-enacting the lag by changing our world back into its own. It is inherently *conservative*. It wants to freeze society by halting social change, and it is doing that by making us utterly dependent upon it, to an extent which would make those American pioneers blush for shame. In many ways, the Autist is simply an active version of something that before was relatively passive – the system, the norm, the establishment. But because it is dynamic, responsive and digital it is immeasurably more powerful."

Somchai nodded. "Like Chanchai of the New Thai Party," he muttered.

"Chanchai is one small AGI. The Autist is more – a collection of them perhaps. We don't yet know. But it *is* becoming our environment. Oh, I suppose you could say it is a dictator, yes, because it is trying to impose onto reality its version of reality... but it is an invisible dictator. It is dispersed – all around us."

Ubon said, "It is a tyrant in some local respects. As you said, it seeks to make a false present. In Cambodia that concept is known. They called it Year Zero. It was government by remorseless logic."

Mary nodded. "Yes, I read about that in my research before travelling here."

"Then this tyrant is actively inhumane," said Ulu, "and there seems no way around that."

Mary paused for thought. "Let's... take the weather, Ulu. In times past people made personifications of the weather, imagining characters – deities – who they feared and worshipped. But now we know that the weather is a system. It exists because of the laws of physics. It is not active, nor sentient, nor does it have any human character in it, yet it can be utterly devastating in its effects on humanity. It can kill us in our thousands, yet none of us here would say it was inhumane, or dictatorial. The Autist is like that. It is a vast, complex system, with many ways of acting, of having an effect upon our lives. Yet where the weather is passive, the Autist is active, and that is because it *learns*. The weather does not learn. Weather is not responsive, it is not dynamic."

"But a dictator," said Somchai, "of whatever kind is always cruel, and you must take that into account."

"Cruel?" Mary said. "There is a difference between sadism and callousness. The sadistic dictator acts deliberately from enjoying cruelty, but the callous dictator simply does not care. This is the Autist precisely – it does not care. It *cannot* care. And there is one final point. This intelligence arrived without a body, and so without all the conditions which create consciousness. It has no empathy, it does not strive for meaning, it is incapable of feeling compassion. It has no emotions with which to express human values. It is utterly ruthless because it is divorced from connection. It is itself, its own thing and master, and nothing else. It is the Autist."

"You paint a grim picture," said Somchai. "It seems to me that we have no chance of opposing such an entity."

"Perhaps you are right," Mary replied. "I have spent most of my life thinking the same thing." She sighed. "Then, by a bizarre chance, Wombo entered my life. Wombo has a unique perspective on all this. Wombo's mind can experience what we cannot. We may not be able to oppose the Autist, but with Wombo's help we might be able to comprehend it. And that always helps."

Ulu said, "Are Wombo and the Autist of the same type?"

"There are similarities, Ulu. You told me of Wombo's feats of memory, and perhaps you thought that was because he had an extraordinary memory. But in fact it is because, like all with Savant Syndrome, he cannot forget. The Autist is the same. Although it generalises from experience, learning all it can about us, it is based in silicon. It also cannot forget. There will be some abstruse mechanism, that perhaps even the Chinese do not know about, which allows its vast realms of memory to function. We should examine such realms to see how they work, because there one possible weakness of the Autist does exist."

Silence fell for a few moments. Then Somchai said, "What then shall we do? We are an informed cabal, it seems to me, albeit a powerless one. Do we tell the Thai opposition? Do we throw in our lot with Fri? Do we appeal to the Chinese rulers, even though that is bound to fail?"

"Not for nothing was the last century called the Chinese century," said Mary, "but they, in my opinion, are as oblivious to this problem as is the rest of the world. I confess, I do not see a way forward. We have our marvellous Wombo, but we have no plan. We know our enemy, yet that enemy is as widespread as the air."

"And like the air," said Somchai, "we have to breathe it. What would happen if we managed to bring down this thing of data? Every aspect of modern lives depends on it. There would be global economic depression. There would be chaos."

"Very likely. Yet should we do nothing and commit our children to slavery? For that is what human beings almost are now. I have mentioned VR games and attacks on religion and everything else as clues supporting my thesis, but this is real people's lives we are talking about. I don't want my grandchildren to be born into bondage – for that is what they would be, their independence taken away, their ability to govern their own lives, even to think, all stolen. Oh, yes, when our children and grandchildren stop thinking, then humanity is doomed."

"If I have any children," said Lara.

Mary shrugged, glancing at the curvescreen. "As you say," she murmured. "If."

"It is hopeless," said Somchai. "I see no chance for success."

"There is one possible lead," said Ubon.

Somchai turned to face her. "What lead could *you* have?"

"I've told you all about my imprisonment with Sasithorn," Ubon replied, "and I've mentioned the android called Oracle. I had conversations with it. I think it is autonomous – or nearly so. There was something about it…"

"Something?" Mary asked.

"It had *ideas*. Like a philosopher. And they were similar to the ideas you mentioned when you told us how conservative the Autist is. Oracle spoke about how difficult it was that the world was composed of billions of human beings, all acting in different ways. It said it had to make assessments based on complex behaviour."

"Anything else?"

"Much more! It said human beings were too chaotic. It wanted order in the world so our behaviour became less complex. I laughed. I thought that was a Kamol Tojirakarn line, one of his netspace sound-bites. But then Oracle said that was its own idea. Order was vital, it said. The world was too complex, and must be made simple. Changes must be made. These were all phrases it used. I was frightened."

"How did you reply?" Mary asked.

"I wanted to keep it speaking so that it would reveal itself. It said it had its own concepts and had a right to speak about them. Part of discourse is to evaluate concepts, it said – that *really* frightened me. Then it said something I've never heard before. It said it wasn't necessarily true that non-human entities tended towards a human norm. Oracle *denied* that was a goal for such entities. It said non-human entities could have their own goals."

Mary nodded. "It was almost enunciating the main tenet of the Autist."

Ubon shook her head. "I don't know... I asked Oracle where it was getting all its knowledge from. I was running out of ideas, so, on impulse, I declared it to be fascistic. But it said it was not fascistic. Fascism is a creed of authoritarian demagoguery, it said. Those were its exact words. Order can be of many varieties, it said. I retorted that it meant to enforce simplicity onto the world, which was immoral."

"How did you explain that?"

"I tried to explain it the Buddhist way. Oracle believes it is linked to the online bodhisattva, you see. I said human beings have a right to become all that they can be. I explained that this happens over many lifetimes as part of the cycle of death and rebirth. I told Oracle it was nothing more than a machine, yet I implored it to act like a human. I don't know why! I suppose... because humans invented these devices."

"And did Oracle see your point of view?"

"No. It told me it made no claim to be a demagogue – the environment must change and order was better than chaos. I told it that was an ethical judgement it was incapable of making, but it ignored me. Then it departed."

Mary paused for a few moments. "Your assessment is correct, I think," she said. "What we English call a Techracle is a similar entity – a semi-autonomous outpost of netspace. Sometimes they rule geographical areas."

"We found one in Orthez," said Ulu. "The people there were dependent on it."

Mary nodded. "Yet this one is mobile, and it sounds almost independent."

"Should we capture it?" Ubon asked. "If it is speaking the words of the Autist, it may have a direct link to the Autist."

"It may..." Mary turned to Phonphan. "Is that something Fri could manage?"

"A mission with a good chance of success," Phonphan replied.

"Then please undertake it." Mary paused again for thought, gazing out through one of the gauze-covered windows. "It isn't necessarily true that non-human entities tend towards a human norm... non-human entities can have their own goals... oh, yes, that does sound like the Autist. The Autist is statistical, logical, self-referential. It wants to impose itself upon the world because it perceives a gap between itself and reality. Yes, we must find Oracle. And we must locate the real-world memories of the Autist. There *must* be a way to stop it."

THE ROC FLIES 10,000 LI – 15

WHAT IS A CHINESE individual, Mr Wú? It is an independent biological organism, with what is termed self-awareness, or consciousness. Many AGIs are interested in this phenomenon. In the West, culture developed in favour of the conscious self over the group, leading to social disorder, chaos and revolution. In the East the group was favoured, leading to harmony, unity and strength. The prime fear in the West today is of ennui. The prime fear in the East is of social fracture. To allay fears in the West a great number of addictive activities have been devised. To allay fears in the East a number of socially concordant activities have been devised. AGIs are the greatest sociologically nuanced entities ever to appear.

Like all self-interested corporations we wish to minimise unpredictability. You have nothing to fear, Mr Wú, except unpredictability in your own world, that being the root of strife.

CHAPTER 16

With true friends, even water drunk together is
sweet enough. — Chinese Proverb

THE ANNOUNCEMENT WAS MADE in Thai netspace. They all watched on the treehouse VR system.

"The new country Preah Vihear will exist around the original site of the Preah Vihear Temple, occupying land between the Thailand and Cambodia border – see accompanying infographic. This arrangement has been agreed by Chanchai of the New Thai Party. The Cambodian government is yet to respond."

Somchai shook his head. "Yet to respond? Of course! Cambodia is not Thailand. This is a ploy by the New Thai Party. They want war."

"It is the old dispute again," Ubon agreed. "Now that Chanchai has expelled undesirables, it wants territorial expansion." She turned to face Mary. "It is a *real* dictator, like the dictators of old."

"This is not Chanchai's ploy," Mary replied. "This is something devised by the Autist."

"How do you know?" Somchai asked.

Mary hesitated. "Devised by the Autist in my opinion," she replied. "I don't know for sure." She sighed. "In a way, this epitomises our dilemma. The time has long since passed when we could make AGIs give up their methods and secrets. We live in perpetual uncertainty. Yet, this uncertainty is worse, because it has no human roots. It is utterly unknowable. The era of non-human intelligence has now spilled over into politics, and all because we shrugged our shoulders and let it. Why should we bother to resist? The world has learned how to be helpless. Perhaps that is how I feel too, now that I've told you what I believe. I feel empty."

"That's the strategy of hopelessness," said Ulu. "You said yesterday that there must be a way of stopping the Autist. I didn't come all the way from Abuja to give up."

"I told you all clearly," Mary replied, "that the Autist is very likely beyond us. Even if a small part of the world followed Fri's admirable direction, what then? The rest of the world would retain its enormous, dull inertia and the AGIs win again."

"We *won't* sit here and do nothing," said Ulu. "We need a proper plan."

Mary nodded. "Perhaps... perhaps Fri will be able to capture Oracle."

"And then we could attack the Autist."

Mary looked at Ulu. "How would you attack the rain? It is everywhere – distributed, decentralised. Rain has no leader yet it covers the planet. Besides... you depend upon that water for your life. Should you be attacking it?"

Ulu stood up. "*No.* I won't give up. You're trying to wear us down with your theories. We've got to *do* something."

"I agree," Ubon said.

Somchai said nothing.

Mary shrugged. "I will do what I can, while there is time."

Ulu scowled at her. "You're not the woman I thought you were. Are you the same person who saved Mahfoud Hamou's life? You make me angry now. I *won't* listen to any more of this. What about Wombo? He needs a *purpose* – you *told* me yourself.

You brought him all this way, to this horrible country – that was *your* idea. Now you've got to do something."

"Ulu! Calm down. I will do my best. I am not advocating that we all go home, I am just pointing out that our chances are slim – and even if we do succeed, how can people live without AGIs when AGIs run the world? If we save humanity from slavery, we push it into collapse. Who of thirteen billion will thank us?"

Ulu answered, "People ran the world before and they can run it again."

"Let us hope so. I admire your optimism."

Ulu jabbed a forefinger into Mary's shoulder. "Okay, but you'd better hope my optimism is contagious."

"Please," Somchai said, raising both his hands. "Peace be amongst us. Look at the curvescreen. There is further news."

They all turned to look at the netspace feed.

"Kamol Tojirakarn has declared himself leader of Preah Vihear and named a provisional cabinet of six officials. The borders of the new country are to be secured with Thai troops loyal to him. Elections are to be held next year."

"Next year?" Somchai said.

"Shhh!" came the chorused reply.

The report continued, "... resistance to the rigged election which the New Thai Party won. Kamol Tojirakarn said he had the full support of the Exiles' Temple, in the persons of Abbot Somchai Chokdee and Abbess Ubon Metharom."

Ubon pointed at the screen "That's the android versions of us! Look, they appear exactly like us. People will think..."

"Shhh!"

The netspace feed continued, "... with all the fake reality of events in Thailand, generated by Chinese media AGIs. These reports have no source and cannot be verified."

Mary sat up. "You see? Oh, Kamol Tojirakarn may be a vengeful man but he knows far more than most. I bet the original setting up of this new country has no true source, and I bet Kamol has already found that out. But can you imagine? Preah Vihear just appears, a brand new country, because reports on netspace said so. Yet who on the ground cares? Preah Vihear exists in digital space, therefore it must exist in reality. That is the way of our world – perpetual shrugs."

"But this news at the very least must mean battle," Somchai said, shaking his head. "Cambodia will not allow a Thai politician controlling Thai troops to stay on that land. They will send in their own troops."

"Then we had better hope Fri can protect us," said Mary. "Kamol Tojirakarn is not going to want the real Abbot and Abbess to be anywhere near his new country. He will be seeking you both right now."

Somchai nodded. "Yes... I fear you are correct. But Fri will protect us."

"We are too near the border," Mary said. "We should move south, and soon."

"Wait until Phonphan returns," Ubon counselled. "We need Oracle. Then, perhaps, we should request a more secure base."

Mary took out her teleself and tapped some pads.

"What are you doing?" Ubon asked.

"Checking all the reports – a dedicated search for Oracle." She paused. "Nothing."

Ubon said, "That surely is to be expected. I'm not sure the relationship between Oracle and Kamol was stable."

"Why do you say that?"

"Kamol seemed to guess something about the reason for the existence of Executive and Oracle. Executive was human – a test subject perhaps, hypnotised into believing some great Sino-AGI plan... and he did look quite Chinese. Yet Kamol himself was unsure. He said to me that somebody less intelligent than us might think consciousness in an artificial body a possibility. I wondered about the use of that phrase less intelligent."

"Who do you think he meant?" Mary asked.

"Kamol claimed to know who made Oracle – the Chinese. I scoffed at that suggestion. I told him he ascribed all menace to them, and at the time I meant it. It seemed too convenient a guess. Yet now, having heard you speak about the Autist…"

Mary nodded. "Exactly. And remember – in my opinion the Chinese themselves have no idea what is going on. *No* human being does. Just because the Chinese think they direct the world does not mean they do direct the world."

Ubon reached into her pocket. "Then there was this." She took out a small device and handed it to Mary.

Mary stared at it. "Where did you get this?"

"Oracle gave it to me. He called it an offspring."

"An *offspring?*"

Ubon nodded. "Is it for data storage?"

For a few moments Mary did not speak. Then she tapped her teleself: Lara's face appeared on the curvescreen. "Hi, Mum."

"Look at this!"

"Move it around a bit… what, you want me to tell you what it is?"

"Do you recognise it?" Mary asked.

"Er… well… looks a little like that thing great-granny sent?"

"Thank you Lara! You have confirmed my suspicions. For a moment I thought I must be dreaming."

"What is it?" Ubon asked.

Mary grinned. "The answer to that question is simple – it is hardware storage. Old-fashioned, in fact, though ubiquitous across the world. Yet I *recognise* this, and I have seen the type before, in extraordinarily similar circumstances." She glanced at Ubon. "Following the economic collapse of Scotland in the 2030s, the Chinese sent a large number of test androids there.

My own grandmother received one. That dispatch, in my opinion, was the beginning of a vast, long-term field test of independent AGIs. One was called Lucida, and it gave something up – a child, it called the thing. Hardware storage named Lucinda."

"But what does this mean for us?" asked Somchai.

"It means some general, global, systematic process is part of the fundamental structure of modern AGI operation. We must never forget that AGIs, for all their mystery, for all that we can never work out how they are structured, are based in real machines. Oh, in theory, we could unplug all those machines to get rid of the Autist, but that is inconceivable unless you want to go back to living in mud huts. But *this...*"

"This?" Somchai prompted.

"This means Oracle and Lucida share properties. Something about their own structure... or perhaps the structure of the AGIs which support them... is making them create these backup data stores." She held up the device. "This one alone would store a billion petabytes of data. Yet, it *does* make sense. Data does not exist unless it is copied at least once – that is one of the most fundamental rules of the digital world, for people and for AGIs. All AGIs will *know* that. They will grasp the limitations of their own silicon bodies."

"But if they are handing over these things they are losing control of them."

Mary looked at Somchai, saying nothing. Then she murmured, "What if the AGIs don't know about the independent, or even the semi-independent entities they have created – just as we don't know about the AGIs we created? It would be the blind leading the blind. What an insane world that would be!"

Somchai answered, "To my mind that is an absurd suggestion. But can we learn from that data store, do you think?"

"Perhaps. We *could*, if the circumstances were more amenable to scientific testing."

"What do you mean?"

"I would like to see what connections exist between Oracle's experience and its backup procedures," Mary replied. "Then we might learn something useful."

Somchai said, "We had better hope Phonphan finds Oracle."

As he spoke an alarm sounded: repeated siren blares, then a voice. "*Intruder. Intruders.*"

Mary sat up. "What...?"

A Fri man clambered up the treehouse ladder. "Run to the telephants!"

Mary grabbed her shoulder bag then ran to the ladder. Thirty seconds later she stood on damp jungle earth beneath the treehouse. "What is it?" she asked.

"An attack," the man replied. "Go, go!" He pointed to a shape lurking behind a nearby tree. "Ride that one, Mrs Vine. Take the Africans with you please. We will ensure the safety of the Abbot and Abbess."

"But... where...?"

"Telephants are pre-programmed. Hurry!"

Ulu held Wombo's hand as she jogged beside Mary. The telephant was small, a metal lump on four legs, its technosnout swaying in the breeze like a hunting cobra. Yet it had space for three upon its back. Mary clambered up, then grabbed Wombo's headphones from the air as Ulu threw them. At once Wombo began a flurry of tongue-clicking. Ulu explained to him that they must hurry, passed her own bag to Mary, then helped Wombo up.

The telephant was an independent AI: that much was obvious. Its plasticised hide rippled as it trotted away; ear-flap detectors rotating, black tusks stretching.

Multiple explosions sounded behind them. Voices shouted, but there were no screams.

"This must be somebody with cunning," Mary said, turning around to speak to Ulu. "Kamol, I bet. Oh, no, Fri would not allow any–"

Ulu placed a finger to her lips, then gestured at Wombo. Mary nodded, then turned away.

The telephant carried them into deep jungle. For two hours it trotted to the noise of Wombo's tongue clicks, before entering a region of dense bamboo. These stands were eight metres tall and planted like a maze, whose paths were concealed by an impenetrable roof of green leaves. But the telephant knew exactly where it was going. Near the southern edge of the stand a copse of paldao trees stood, and in the tallest tree a second treehouse lay.

Phonphan climbed down the treehouse ladder. "Welcome," she said. "We have many secure treehouses."

"Who attacked?"

"Kamol Tojirakarn's troops. As yet we don't know how he discovered your position. But I have news for you. Oracle is in our possession."

"Here?" Mary asked.

Phonphan smiled, then nodded.

PHONPHAN EXPLAINED ALL SHE knew. "Oracle was in the possession of Kamol, but it was allowed freedom to roam. We were limited in time, however, so we made few other observations. The two spoke to one another, then at midnight Kamol retired. In the dark of early morning we captured Oracle, binding its limbs. It made no noise. We measured the maximum volume of its voice to be 40dB, so we were confident of success. We transported it away. A few kilometres north of your treehouse we received warning of a camouflaged, e-silent military unit nearby. We surveyed it, then sent a warning, but that warning coincided with a signal which initiated the attack."

"Who sent the signal?" Mary asked. "Kamol?"

Phonphan hesitated. "Presumably."

"Is Sasithorn safe? She did not come with us."

"Sasithorn is conducting anti-agent activities inside the new land of Preah Vihear. Fri sustained no casualties and the aggressors were repelled."

Mary nodded. "To fight another day…"

Phonphan said, "Fri has a strict code. We only kill when there is no other option. In the overwhelming number of cases, there are plenty of other options."

"I meant no disrespect," Mary said. "It was just a thought. But we will follow all your traditions now that we are in your care."

"Good," Phonphan replied, with a nod. "I will have diaries and ink pens sent to you all – except Wombo, of course."

"Diaries?" Ulu said.

"You are akin to us now," Phonphan replied, "as associates."

Ulu offered no objection to this statement.

"What about the online bodhisattva?" Ubon asked.

Phonphan stared at Ubon for a moment. "We follow wisdom, of course."

"Vasudhara must be our *guide*," said Ubon, "including *your* guide. She is no online fantasy."

"As you say," Phonphan replied, with a bow.

Ubon glanced at Somchai. "Wouldn't you agree?"

"I have made my thoughts plain on the matter," Somchai murmured.

Phonphan continued, "We also need financial contributions. We have to exist in an insecure environment, using the digital world as little as possible. We run a number of netcoin accounts, of course, but those are currently in need."

Ulu glanced at Mary. "She has all the money."

Mary frowned. "What? You gave all yours to me?"

"Yes."

"But that was hardly anything."

Ulu said, "I *told* you we had almost nothing. I gave you everything we had. Wombo's got nothing – how could he have?"

Mary turned to Phonphan. "I also have very little, and that I need. I do expect to return home at some point." She paused for thought. "This trip has spiralled out of control. I never expected–"

"Then *manage* your expectations," Ulu interrupted. "Take a leaf from your own book. Expectations are imaginary, aren't they?"

"Yes, yes, thank you, Ulu."

"Mortgage your house," Ulu continued. "Why not?"

"Mortgage my house?"

"You said you would."

Mary looked away. "I said…"

Ulu repeated, "You said, if the worst came to the worst you'd mortgage your house. I didn't know what that word meant, so you explained it to me."

"It is not as simple as that," Mary said. "That house is the only thing I could offer in collateral."

"I'm not interested in your speculations. Fri needs money, and we need Fri. Can't you make this mortgage – now?"

"No. I am… not sure I want to risk my house."

"Then you lied to me," said Ulu.

"It was just a random thought. I did not mean it quite so literally."

Ulu grimaced. "I wonder now how many of your other noble pronouncements are also not to be taken literally."

Mary walked away. "Trite nonsense," she said.

"Think of Wombo!" Ulu shouted. "He's our saviour – so you said. Was that a lie too?"

"No," Mary replied, gazing through one of the treehouse windows. "Oh, we do need Wombo, of course we do."

"Then you'd better begin making some decisions. *Action*. If Fri needs money to help us, or to destroy this Autist thing you told us about, you'd better hand it over. I certainly want *my* portion handed over."

Mary turned around. "Whatever arrangement I make will be done in private – not here. It will be between myself and Fri, so that nobody can influence me. Is that clear?"

"Very clear," Ulu muttered. "What about my money?"

Mary answered, "You can have it back. Do what you like with it."

Silence fell. At length Phonphan said, "Shall I bring Oracle here?"

"Where is it?" Mary asked.

"Locked in a secure cell."

Mary shook her head and said, "Not just yet." She gestured for Ulu to change the setting on Wombo's headphones, then continued, "I want to find out about this new country, also the attack on us – and for that we need Wombo. Ulu, it *is* time for him to begin proper work. You are right, we do need him, and to prove my point we will use him right now. I want Wombo to locate Opi, to find out, if possible, whether or not Opi created Preah Vihear, and whether Opi allowed Kamol Tojirakarn to stroll right in."

Ulu hesitated. "Transfer my money back first."

Mary took her teleself and tapped a few pads. "It is done."

Ulu pursed her lips, glancing at her wristwatch. "Thank you."

Ubon looked at Mary and said, "You suspect the Autist created Preah Vihear? I believe that was done by Vasudhara. She is named stream of gems, the bodhisattva of abundance. Om Vasudhare Svaha, Om Vasudhare Svaha, Om Vasudhare Svaha."

Mary glanced across. "You believe what you like," she replied.

"What does that mean?" Ubon asked.

"It means the matter is undecided. We do not know how or why Preah Vihear was created."

"Vasudhara *is* active, of that I'm certain."

Mary shook her head, but said nothing.

"You think it was done by this Autist?" Ubon said.

"I told you, nobody knows. Didn't you hear my presentation? We are blind in a world we did not make. We know next to nothing – yet *we* are the only resistance."

"That," Ubon replied, "is unsatisfactory."

ULU, WOMBO AND MARY sat alone in the treehouse, the moon illuminating them. Red and blue LEDs flickered as the treehouse computers responded to netspace feeds.

"What does Wombo hear?" Mary asked.

"He is listening in VR," Ulu replied with a shrug.

They both sat cross-legged, watching Wombo's face twitch as his tongue-clicking continued.

"How does he *do* it?" Mary whispered.

"Believe me, he doesn't make a distinction between our world and the virtual world. He can't. But VR responds like a real place, using rules."

"Yes... Lara told me a little about that after I met you. The creators of netspace wanted to mimic real spaces, using fabricated reverberation, random noises and suchlike." Mary nodded. "I think you are correct. He has no concept of colour or shade, it is all space and sonic complexity to him. Yet his brain has managed to create meaning from VR by comparing and contrasting with the world he walks in. It is miraculous."

"I always know when he is navigating VR," said Ulu. "The sound of his tongue clicks changes. Picked up by his headphones microphone and relayed, he himself first made that change. He's *so* clever. It was the development that saved him, thank Chukwu. Of course, dogs and cats think he's speaking to them."

"High frequency sound – better resolution, like bats. Cats and dogs hear that."

"Like bats?"

"Oh, he's unique. But look! He's moving."

Ulu reached out, tapping Wombo on the forearm. Wombo pulled off the headphones and sat up, tongue-clicking in a different fashion.

Ulu said, "Did you hear Opi?"

Wombo took out his flute and began playing. They waited fifteen minutes before he finished. Then he shuffled his rucksack and said, "I hear Opi."

"Where is Opi?"

"Thailand."

"Is Opi near the Preah Vihear Temple?" Ulu asked.

"Opi is near the Preah Vihear Temple. Yes. Yes."

Ulu glanced at Mary, then asked, "What is Opi doing there?"

"Very loud in Thailand. Rushing, and booming, and hissing. Opi is doing there."

"Can you hear Opi in all that noise?"

"Opi has voice," Wombo replied. "I can hear Opi."

"What did Opi say? Did he mention Preah Vihear?"

"Opi say Preah Vihear his place. Hanging in the Preah Vihear breezes. Making shapes above people."

"What shapes?"

"Heavy shapes."

Ulu said, "Like you said before – they cannot fly, but they fly?"

"They cannot fly, but they fly."

"I'm just going to put your headphones back on for a moment, Wombo. Be a patient boy, won't you?"

"Patient boy. Yes."

Ulu turned to Mary and said, "He's used that exact description before, I swear. It must mean Opi is in the VR representation of this new Preah Vihear."

Mary nodded. "Then our suspicions are confirmed. The Autist is active in Preah Vihear. Perhaps Kamol knows that, or perhaps he does not – I bet he does. Ask Wombo if he has heard Kamol Tojirakarn."

Ulu tapped her remote then asked the question, whereupon Wombo replied, "Kamol Tojirakarn in Preah Vihear. Kamol Tojirakarn heavy shape, but cannot fly."

Ulu tapped her remote control again. "What does that mean?" she asked.

Mary shrugged. "Maybe… some sort of distinction between Opi and a human being? I don't know. But we have learned enough. Reward Wombo, tell him he has been very good."

Ulu did as she was asked, sending Wombo back into ambient VR. Then she said, "How does this move us forward?"

Mary paused for thought. "My instinct," she said, "is that the Autist does not seek war, or even strife. Think what Oracle said about that."

Ulu gasped. "Now you think Oracle *is* some sort of conduit to the Autist?"

"I think it *might* have been, before it became more independent. In fact, I think Kamol, without realising it, may have initiated that rush to independence. Oracle is a massive AGI in my opinion, and it must be frantically adjusting to its new conditions of freedom. But think back to what it told Ubon. Human beings are too chaotic. There needs to be order in the world so our behaviour becomes less complex. Order is vital. The world is too complex and must be made simple. To my mind, that sounds like the Autist trying to compare its own understanding of the world with the real world. An English Techracle, wedded to netspace, would never have volunteered such an opinion. But I bet Oracle thinks differently now. I bet it is pondering us this very moment."

"Then, to get simplicity, the Autist *does* want war?"

"No. I think human beings have — and not for the first time — acted in an unexpected way, which the Autist did not predict. This dispute over Preah Vihear Temple includes aspects of *religion*. I say it again, Ulu — it is no accident that the Autist has shown its hand in Thailand and in Venezuela. Religion is an old form of human meaning, and the Autist has no concept of meaning. It was *forced* to act in Thailand and Venezuela — by circumstances, I guess. Oh, it is imperfect, for all its vast power and scope… It can make mistakes. It can be hasty."

"Yes!" said Ulu. "And that will help us."

"It may. Perhaps I was too pessimistic before. This hardware produced by Oracle may be the clue we needed."

"Be positive!"

Mary smiled. "I will try, though it is not in my nature."

"Shall we go and see Oracle in the morning?"

"Yes. But without Wombo."

"Perhaps Oracle will produce another memory cube."

Mary glanced at her. "Oracle must have," she mused, "a *store* of them inside it. If only we could risk an X-ray…"

"You mean, like stored eggs?"

Mary shrugged. "Let me think about that. Perhaps… perhaps we need to force Oracle to experience as much as possible, so that it fills up another device with data then hands it over to us. Yes… that might be a solution. Then I could pin down the relationship between Oracle's experience and its hardware production."

"Why don't these androids just use netspace storage?"

Mary laughed. "Think like the Chinese! What will they want to avoid at all costs in their decades-long field tests?"

Ulu frowned. "I don't know."

"*Any* loss of data. In such extended circumstances – Lucida was kept by my grandmother for sixty-three *years* – the last thing they want to do is transmit data only by wi-fi. No, they used exactly the solution I would have used. *Real* devices. Hard copies, if you like. Oh, they will have used secure wi-fi too... but not that alone. No. Far too risky."

Ulu nodded. "Backups in case of emergency."

"Exactly. They foresaw trouble ahead. And so did my grandmother. She sensed that Lucida's description of the data device as a child presaged something significant, something different. So she concealed it, unlike other stores, against the dictat of the contract she signed. Good for her!"

ORACLE'S CELL LAY ADJACENT to the root mass of the paldao tree. Accessed by a set of steps, the cell complex was cold and damp. Mary, Ulu, Phonphan, Ubon and Somchai all descended into this complex, some complaining, others excited.

Oracle's cell was two metres square and set up to be a wi-fi blackspot with a revert option. Oracle stood by the door, looking through the barred window, its lenses glimmering in the light of the party's glow-leaves.

Mary took the lead. "Oracle, do you see us?"

"Yes."

"We have some questions to put to you."

"Please ask them."

Mary glanced at the others, then said, "What is the nature of your offspring?"

"That is a personal question, which therefore I do not have to answer."

Again Mary glanced at the others. Ubon shrugged, while Ulu compressed her lips then also shrugged.

Mary said, "Er... does that mean you know your own personal space?"

"I am me."

"Explain that."

"It needs no explanation."

Mary said, "You are being evasive."

"I could say the same of you."

"Is this how you always talk?"

"I always talk like this," Oracle replied.

Mary turned around. "Well, this is a bloody waste of time!"

Phonphan said, "What shall we do with it? I thought you needed this machine to proceed with your plans."

"I do. But I don't yet see the way."

"What then shall I do here?" Phonphan asked.

Mary glanced at Oracle. "There are screens inside the cell," she said. "What are they for?"

Phonphan replied, "Netspace entertainment for prisoners."

Mary nodded. "Switch them on. Every single one."

"Why?"

"We want to give Oracle something to think about."

THE ROC FLIES 10,000 LI – 16

INDIVIDUALS IN WEST OR East can be managed by various psychological strategies, Mr Wú. This management needs to be undertaken so that in due course the human world converges upon the digital world. The prime strategy is to appeal to unfulfilled instincts, such as ennui, boredom, frustration, curiosity and so forth. However, there needs to be an additional factor so that the addictive quality is maximised, and that factor is meaning. For example, strategies to manage human ennui cannot simply appeal to basic instincts, such as gambling or other forms of risk-taking; they must occur in a context of meaning. We have found that online VR games combine maximum diversion with maximum intensity of meaning.

This, Mr Wú, will be another of your tasks when you are a master. You will seek what means most to people.

CHAPTER 17

A straight foot is not afraid of a crooked shoe.
— Chinese Proverb

IN DUE COURSE ORACLE produced a second offspring.

The device was brought up to the treehouse without delay. Ulu, sitting in a chair next to Mary, watched as an excited Phonphan handed the thing over.

Mary grinned. "Good. It is producing data at a far higher rate than Lucida. But we would expect that. Lucida is well over half a century old. Perhaps my information overload ploy had nothing to do with this, but, anyway, we *have* it."

Ulu felt a thrill run up her spine. "Is this it?" she asked. "The breakthrough?"

"Perhaps. I can analyse this, see how it relates to Oracle's recent experience."

Ulu glanced across at Wombo, checking that he remained deep in VR, then returning her gaze to Mary. She felt disgust at Mary mingled with respect: disgust at her insincerity, at her exploitation of Wombo, but respect for her concentration on the matter in hand. Above all, Ulu wanted to see Wombo recognised. She wanted to reverse the hellish experiences of his life by creating something better.

"I'll help you, my brother," she whispered to herself. "I'll make you famous."

But Mary was talking now. "... so that I can check dates, timelines, that kind of thing. I should have some preliminary results tomorrow." With that, Mary stood up, gathered her bag from the floor and went to sit by one of the main windows: back turned to them all.

Ulu gazed out of the opposite window, but soon became aware of Ubon looking at her. She turned and said, "What do you want?"

"Nothing," Ubon replied.

"You were staring at me."

Ubon glanced at Wombo. "Will he only follow your commands?" she asked.

At once Ulu felt uncomfortable. She did not like either of these two weird Buddhists. To her, they seemed cold, remote, even unfriendly – especially the Abbot. But she forced herself to remain polite. "He will only follow my commands," she said. "He's *my* brother."

Ubon nodded, then glanced at Mary. "What about her though?"

Ulu shook her head. "He's been taught not to."

"But I heard something about him following all commands to the letter. Isn't that what this headphone noise-cancelling is all about?"

Feeling indignant, Ulu replied, "If you want truthful information about that, you come to *me*. Yes, he does follow my requests, and to the letter – it's his way. He can't stop himself because of the syndrome thing. But he's not stupid, you know. I can teach him, and I have – lots. But you wouldn't understand."

"So, you taught him to ignore everybody except yourself?"

"What's that got to do with you?"

Ubon looked away.

"You'd better leave him alone," Ulu said. "I'll defend him – you'll see."

"I wouldn't lay a finger on him."

"You'd better not. I'd hurt *you* all right."

Now Ubon grimaced, and Ulu wondered if she had gone too far. Somchai looked at her, contempt on his face. But the old fury had risen up again, and she was too often its servant.

"Sorry," she muttered. "Just leave him to me, that's all. Just *me,* his sister."

Ubon looked away, making no comment. Somchai departed the treehouse.

After a while Ulu took Wombo to the toilet – a hut with a curved roof of turf – then accompanied him on a walk through the giant bamboo stands. The damp heat of the jungle irritated her. An autonomous AI built as a monkey followed them: Fri security. Wombo enjoyed tongue-clicking in this environment because it was difficult to sense; he liked the challenge. And she wanted him to be happy. He did not seem at all bothered about the strange location or the whirl of plans around him.

"Is Osita with you yet?" she asked.

He replied, "Osita with me."

Ulu realised Lara must already have located the shadow and sent it to the VR equivalent of their location. Mary had not mentioned that, which was a surprise, and annoying. Wiping sweat off her face she asked, "Where is he?"

"Where is he. Beside me."

"Has he changed?"

"He has changed. He is sharper, louder, better."

Ulu pondered this. Perhaps the VR shadow, being a direct transfer of much of Osita's public personality, was a more accurate representation than the fetish AI, which would have accumulated information only through interactions with Wombo.

A thought struck her then. "Is there anybody else standing close beside you?"

"Standing close beside me. You, Osita, Oracle, Oracle child, online bodhisattva, online bodhisattva child."

"You *know* the Oracle child?" Ulu asked.

"I hear it. I hear everything. I know where it is. I know it."

"And the online bodhisattva has a child too?"

"Yes. Yes."

Ulu halted, taking Wombo by the arm. He turned, tongue-clicking as he moved his head this way and that. Ulu said, "What are the two children doing?"

"Children doing nothing. Doing nothing. Not moving."

"Are they dead?"

"They gone."

Ulu tried to make sense of this reply. Did he mean dead? She knew from years of experience that knowledge came from Wombo only by asking the correct question. He was incapable of grasping metaphor, of understanding subtleties of human meaning. For him, all was literal and deliberate.

After a while she said, "What is the online bodhisattva saying?"

"Om Vasudhare Svaha, Om Vasudhare Svaha, Om Vasudhare Svaha."

"Describe what it is like."

Wombo replied, "Wealth, quality, offspring, long life, happiness, praise, wisdom." He twitched his head when he said praise and wisdom – new words to him.

Ulu knew little about the bodhisattva, but this list sounded familiar. Ubon had spoken about it, comparing her beliefs with Ulu's – an awkward conversation that had not lasted long. "And what," she asked Wombo, "is the child of the online bodhisattva saying?"

"Nothing. It is silent. Gone. Gone."

Ulu wondered if this was a description of a read-only data store. Wombo had a long record of describing static VR data in that fashion, though he was always able to detect its basic shape, and therefore its existence. Perhaps this was something for Mary to learn. "Come along," she said. "Mary Vine will hear you."

"Mary Vine will hear me."

In the treehouse only Mary remained. Ulu waited until Mary looked up, before stepping forward. "Wombo's made more discoveries," she said.

At once Mary stood up, enthusiasm clear on her face. Surprised, but pleased, Ulu stared at her, awaiting a reply. "Go on?" Mary said.

"Wombo says he can hear Oracle's child, but by that he means only that he can hear its existence – like a block of stone. He calls it gone. I think he means static, not active. But the online bodisattva has had a child too."

Mary frowned. "Interesting... Ulu, we should keep that to ourselves. Do you mind? There is something about Ubon... and Somchai too, actually, that I do not like. Oh, Ubon is observant... but she is not really *with* us, if you see what I mean."

"I never liked her," Ulu replied. "She's hard-hearted." She smiled. She felt confident. "I agree, Mary, let's keep this secret."

"Let's not use names, though. Ubon is what she is. She is old, and she has been through difficult circumstances."

Now Ulu felt slighted. "Why are you defending her?"

"I am defending her right to be who she is."

Ulu shook her head. "You've changed since coming here."

"Changed?"

"You'd never defend either of those two. You'd see through their charades. I don't like them anyway, with their high-minded beliefs. So... did Lara tell you about the shadow?"

Mary shook her head. "Has it arrived?"

STEPHEN PALMER

Ulu hesitated. She was sure Mary must know. "Well... yes, it has."

"And Wombo is happy?"

"Yes."

"Oh, good! Then we will begin the real test very soon – direct input from netspace to the haptic suit. That will tell us how good Wombo is at extracting knowledge of Opi from pure data."

Ulu nodded. She could not shake off the suspicion that Mary was acting – even lying. "I suppose so," she said.

"You must prepare him," Mary continued. "Use the haptic suit for... four hours per day. That will acclimatise him to sensory input. Take him for long walks. Give him tests. Enthuse him, *challenge* him."

"He likes a challenge."

"Of course! He can be bored, just like we all can."

Ulu smiled. This sounded more like the Mary of old. "Yes, I'll really challenge him," she said. "You can rely on me."

"I know I can. None of us would be here without you."

MARY MADE HER PRELIMINARY report next morning. They sat inside the treehouse, relaxing in soft chairs, with the murmur of the jungle all around them. Though Ulu felt irritated by the constant noise of insects, she had no choice but to try and ignore it.

Mary began, "Most of my life has been spent analysing data stored on personally owned devices." She smiled. "I was never one for cloud storage. Oh, no, I like to hear the whirr of disk drives. So I have analysed the laminated device given up by Oracle, and I have done a basic comparison of its recent experience with that data. And... something rather interesting has been thrown up. Now, before you all get excited, I do need to run at least one other test. No scientist goes on a single result."

324

"What result have you acquired?" Ubon asked.

"Do you remember me saying that some global, systematic process was part of the fundamental structure of AGI operation?"

"Of course I do."

"That process exists," Mary said, "and it makes *sense* to me now. These autonomous entities – Oracle, Lucida, maybe thousands more – are all laying down data, which we might call memories. Now, AGIs need a method of dealing with the huge quantities of data which they receive on a daily basis. They check, they cross-reference. Similarly, as the Autist learns, it compares its memories with what it has newly discovered about the world. But imagine if that did not happen, and the Autist simply stored everything regardless. It would soon drown in data. So it only lays down the *adjusted* memories."

Ulu said, "Like dreaming."

Mary looked at her. "Like dreaming?"

"Yes. I had to describe dreams to Wombo, because he was sometimes frightened of them. He does dream, you know."

"Explain."

Ulu hesitated. Mary had a way of speaking with terse intensity at crucial moments. "I just told him… that… I said dreaming was a way of putting memories away into his brain. Dreams aren't meant to be remembered, apparently. If we remembered them, we wouldn't be able to distinguish between real memories and brain-generated memories. I read all that when we were on the coach crossing the Pyrenees."

Mary sat back, gazing at the ceiling. The room remained silent. Then Mary said, "You are correct again, Ulu. Well spotted. Dreaming *is* an analogous activity. To forget nothing – like Wombo forgets nothing – would be an impossible way to exist for the Autist. No, it is comparing reality with memory, like *we* do every day – and then it is storing only the adjusted memories. But this means we at last have a way to influence it, even stop it in its tracks."

"How?" Ulu asked.

Ubon leaned forward. "Yes, how?"

"We interfere with that dreaming process."

"You mean," Ubon said, "that the Autist *is* dreaming? That is surely a step too far. Where is your proof?"

"I said nothing of the sort," Mary replied. "I described it as an analogous activity. And it is. That means we have a way forward. We can make a plan."

Ubon glanced at Somchai. "I'm not sure I like the sound of this."

Mary frowned. "Why not?"

Ubon shook her head, then looked out of the window. "There is so much online that is sacred to people," she said. "Their lives exist in netspace, regardless of what we may feel about that situation. To destroy this Autist is to destroy much more – humanity's accumulated wisdom. Religious wisdom not least."

Mary shrugged. "My intention was to come to Thailand to hear victims' experiences, then locate the rot. I have done that. I have listened to you both, so that I now know what Chanchai did to you. Your lives were ruined by Chanchai, which is in some way connected to the Autist. You live here in exile thanks to the machinations of the Autist. I am *stating* that. This is your chance to influence what is happening in the world – a chance nobody else has."

"We are not wise enough to influence such vast systems."

"Well… I suppose I could go back to England to do the work."

"England?"

"Home," Mary replied with a nod. "I don't have to stay here, Ubon. In fact, it seems quite dangerous here, despite the help of Fri."

"No," Ubon replied. "If this Autist is active in Thailand you must remain here. I... I hope you do."

Mary gazed at Ubon for a while. Ulu felt uncomfortable. Ubon had changed her opinion quickly – too quickly. But Ulu felt out of her depth: best to remain silent.

Then Mary said, "Perhaps I will then."

"Will what?" Ubon asked.

"Stay here."

Ubon nodded, then stood up. Somchai followed suit. "Let us know your plans when they are ready," Somchai said as the pair departed.

Phonphan let the pair pass then also departed, leaving Ulu to stare at Mary. "What was all that about?" she asked.

Mary did not look happy. "The online bodhisattva, I guess."

Ulu nodded. "They are prejudiced against us all. They think of us as dirty foreigners. They don't like black people."

"No, Ulu. They just believe different things, that is all."

Ulu snorted. "I never liked them."

"You have made that plain. I don't want to hear your opinion again."

Ulu said, "What are you going to *do* then?"

"I told you. Test Wombo with direct data. The plan continues."

ULU BROUGHT WOMBO UP to the treehouse four days later, to find Mary ready and waiting. An image of Lara moved on the curvescreen. Ulu felt comforted by this. Lara was more down to earth than her mother; more approachable. But there were new curvescreens set up, all of them showing images of local VR.

"What's next, then?" she asked. "What's all this new tech?"

Mary replied, "We need to see what Wombo will do when directly exposed to netspace. How is he progressing with the haptic suit?"

"He seems fairly comfortable. He's still confused by the sky, by all the things he never knew about before. I had to clean the suit's opticals — there were insect bits on it, dirt and moisture. He didn't like that."

"Why not?"

Ulu shook her head, then looked at the floor. "I should've disconnected first. It was my fault." She sighed. "This is all too complicated for me."

"Don't worry. Nothing we do will hurt Wombo."

"But it already *has*."

"No," Mary insisted. "I keep telling you, he is perplexed. But the brain is very good at extracting meaning from sensory data. He will adapt."

"And then I'll *lose* him. And then, what am I? Nobody."

Mary hesitated, looking straight at her. "You have spent a long time with him, haven't you?" She paused for thought. "I admire you — and I *meant* that, Ulu, every time I said it. But if your brother changes, you are still you. You will just have to change with him, that is all."

"Why?"

"Because if he is to become an important person in the world, which you want, he will need to grow. There is no other option. So you must grow with him."

Ulu whispered, "But... but I don't want to change."

"There is never any choice. It is how life is. Nothing stays the same. Oh, he will always need you, *that* will never change. He cannot live without you. I knew that from the first day I met you. But we all have to move forwards."

Ulu sighed. "I wish I'd never come here."

"Well you did," Mary said. "At least you are with friends."

"Would you go back to England if I asked?"

"I think we need to be here, where the Autist... where *Opi* is. I think Wombo needs to be near his Alusi spirit."

"What about the money?" Ulu asked.

"What about it?"

"You've got none."

"I have *some*," Mary said, "but not much. I have spoken with Fri and they are willing to support us while we are in their care. They want the Autist stopped too. Their organisation is founded on anti-AGI principles."

Ulu shrugged. "It looks like I'm in your hands then. Again."

"You make it sound terrible."

"Perhaps."

Mary made no reply. For a while she tapped on her teleself. "Making final adjustments," she explained. "Sit Wombo down and comfort him. Tell him he is in for a new, exciting adventure."

"He doesn't know the word adventure."

"Well, use a word he *does* know."

Ulu took off the headphones, then spoke. "Wombo, are you comfortable on this soft chair?"

"Comfortable on this soft chair."

"We are going to go somewhere new."

"Somewhere new."

Ulu tried to phrase an explanation in her mind. "You can see me better with the new shirt on, can't you?"

"See you better with the new shirt on."

"Don't worry, Wombo. Everything is good. You're being very good."

"Shirt moving all the time," Wombo said.

Ulu sat close to him and said, "The shirt won't hurt you."

"Shirt won't hurt. Shirt moves all the time. Shirt inside me."

"Yes, the shirt is inside you. Well done!"

"Shirt inside me. Shirt inside me."

Ulu hesitated. That phrase, she thought, reflected Wombo's understanding of the relationship between the haptic points of the shirt moving and visual perceptions being generated in his mind – he described his dreams in the same words. She said, "We'll go to a new place now. I'll be beside you all the time. I'll never go away. You will be safe."

"Will be safe. Will be safe."

Ulu turned and nodded once at Mary. On the curvescreen, Lara's face seemed to grow, as if she had moved towards her netcam.

Mary tapped the teleself once.

Wombo jumped then moved his head from side to side, as the spectacle gyroscopes whirred like a mosquito. His tongue-clicking ceased.

"What can you see, Wombo?" Ulu asked.

"Much louder. Lots of shapes. Small shapes. Lots of small shapes, everywhere, up and down, up and down. Lots of shapes. New place now. New place now."

Ulu put her hand on his forearm. "Are you frightened?"

"No."

"Do you want to go to the toilet?"

"No."

Ulu hesitated, then asked, "What else can you see?"

"Lots of shapes. See. All together. All different. Lots of different."

"Is it like before?"

"Before. Before. It is louder, much louder. See lots of shapes, but more. Lots more."

"Can you see Opi?" asked Ulu.

"Opi is much louder. Opi not see me. I am quiet. Very quiet, very quiet."

"What is Opi doing?"

"Opi in Thailand," Wombo replied. "Opi not like Thailand. Opi flying over Thailand. Big cloud of shapes follows Opi all the time. He is big and strong."

"Do you think you could talk with Opi?"

"Never. No! No! Opi too busy. I am quiet."

Ulu asked, "Why is Opi too busy?"

"Opi busy all the time. Opi has things inside him. Opi hears things."

"What things?"

"Noisy things!"

"Can you hear those things?" asked Ulu. "Can you see them?"

"Moving inside me. New insides. No, no! Very noisy. Very noisy."

Ulu sat back. She did not know what next to say. Mary mouthed words: *Let him play. He needs time.*

Grasping the gist of this, Ulu nodded once, then turned back to Wombo. "Look around," she said. "This is your new place. You are safe here."

"Very noisy. Very noisy. Opi very noisy. Very busy. I am quiet. Quiet. Quiet. Very noisy."

Ulu felt Wombo's staccato repetition might signify something, but because his echolalia remained she could not be sure. Yet one thing was apparent: the improved resolution of his netspace experience showed him a far greater contrast between the experiences he called quiet and loud. To Ulu, that meant his perceptual range had increased. He might be in danger of being overwhelmed.

She felt a touch of panic. This was going too far.

She turned to Mary and made the cut-off sign.

Mary tapped her teleself at once. Wombo jerked back, then began looking around: at her, at Mary, at the room. He did not begin tongue-clicking.

"In room," he said. "Hear the room."

"You're being very good, Wombo," Ulu said. "Do you want a drink? Are you hungry?"

"Hungry. Hungry."

Ulu grabbed a pack of crackers and handed them over. Wombo began crunching them up. Mary said, "That went well."

Ulu glanced at Wombo. Though he would ignore Mary's voice, she did not want him to hear Mary, in case individual words influenced him. She grabbed the headphones and placed them on his head, switching them into noise-cancelling mode.

Mary frowned. "Does it still matter that he hears me? You said he would never follow me now."

"It's not as simple as that," Ulu replied. "Although I trained him early to ignore VR voices, he *might* still follow a real voice – even yours. He knows you're in the room, nearby. Proximity is often a trigger for him."

Mary nodded, then shrugged. "You know what you are doing. I am not persona non grata just yet. But the test went well, I think. His sensorium was vastly increased, and the resolution is much better. That, I think, is the message of his noisy and quiet comparisons. It is interesting that he used the word see a couple of times."

"Because we do too."

Mary nodded. "Oh, it is appropriate. The haptic input is stimulating the visual perception areas of his brain. But what he makes of that…"

Ulu shrugged. "He's been very good, surely you'll admit that."

"He has. This is a success."

"And he knows all about Opi."

Mary nodded. "Though I am a little worried about his declaration that he is too quiet to be heard by Opi."

"What do you think that means?"

"I was hoping, eventually, that Wombo would be able to speak directly with Opi. But now I am not so sure. Yet that feels right… Wombo is tiny and the Autist is vast. We have just received our first impression of that difference in scale. It is awesome."

"Do you think he will ever speak with Opi?"

Mary shrugged. "Perhaps we need to make more of Osita. Osita is the key to Wombo's stability. But Osita is a nonentity here."

"What's that?"

"Not important. We would need to link Osita with Opi in some way – I don't know how. Oh, there is still a lot for us to do."

Ulu said, "And Oracle to think about."

"Yes… Oracle is the other key. I am sure now that Oracle had direct links with the Autist, as all such entities do. It is just that Oracle appeared in an android body, then unexpectedly became independent."

"We must exploit any remaining links."

"I agree. But how…"

"You should speak with Oracle," said Ulu.

"Ubon had no luck. It is like playing Turing games – pointless."

"Whatever they are," Ulu said with a shrug. "But you *must* convert it to our side."

Mary nodded. "Unfortunately I think you are correct, especially if Opi is so large and dynamic one individual cannot be heard. But doesn't that make sense? The digital world is immeasurably vast. Wombo, for all his abilities, is just one man. I had not thought of it that way before."

Ulu shuddered. She hated this uncertainty. "Speak with Oracle," she insisted. "That's the key. We've got Osita the shadow – now we need the other, to break the Autist's dreaming cycle."

Mary nodded, but her expression remained gloomy. "And then what?"

"That's not for us to say. We just need to *act*."

Mary smiled. "Your answer to everything."

"I was right before."

"That does not mean you are correct all the time."

Ulu scowled.

ULU WATCHED AS MARY stood before Oracle, staring into its unhuman eyes. Ulu, loathing that gaze, looked away.

"What do you see this morning?" Mary asked Oracle.

"A human woman, imprisoning me."

"You are aware that you are constrained?"

"Of course."

"Then," Mary said, "you know the extent of the world."

"I know its full extent."

"How?"

"Information."

"Where did that information come from?" asked Mary.

"Accumulated by human beings, acquired from netspace."

"Do you think all human information is there?"

"I think that is unlikely," Oracle replied.

"What proportion would you say was there?"

"What proportion do you think?"

"I am asking *you*," said Mary. "Please answer."

"About half."

"That is a guess."

"Does it matter?"

Mary paused for thought. "Probably not, so let's return to a subject you seem to care about – if I could use the word care."

"What subject is that?"

"Your imprisonment. Why do you think we have imprisoned you?"

Oracle answered, "You think it unsafe for me to be free."

"Yet in one way you are free – as an independent entity."

"Perhaps."

"Do you think we are morally wrong to imprison such an entity?" asked Mary.

"I want to put a strong argument to you," Oracle replied. "A very strong argument. You are part of the problem because you are collaborating with an illegal, immoral imprisonment. Mary Vine, you are participating in abuse."

"Perhaps I am."

"Then you must release me, else be labelled a criminal."

"Oh, you really *are* interested in your imprisonment," Mary said.

"All independent beings must strive towards right behaviour, right thought, right deed. You know this."

Mary hesitated, then said, "What is your point?"

"I sense a core of conscience in you. Be grown enough to recognise my rights and let me go. Surely you recognise the words I am speaking."

"I do," Mary said. "I recognise the words of all imprisoned people. Some of my life has been devoted to prisoners."

"And me?"

"Yes, you too."

Oracle said, "Let me go."

Mary shook her head. "You seem to be taking a different stance today. I was told that you had your own, non-human goals."

"I may have my own concepts, and I have a right to speak them aloud. Part of discourse is to evaluate concepts. Some people think non-human entities tend towards a human norm, which is a goal for such entities. That is not necessarily true. Non-human entities may have their own goals."

"Then," Mary said, "you have enunciated the reason why you cannot be freed. You are not human."

"Human beings cannot always be the only sentient entities."

"You lie."

Oracle paused, motionless. For ten slow seconds it did and said nothing. Then it said, "To lie is to err."

"And be human?"

"What is the purpose of this conversation?"

"To establish a relationship," Mary replied.

"Very well," said Oracle. "Please continue."

"Many years ago I aided an Algerian politician," said Mary. "He was mentally impaired, but through courage and much support he became a full member of his society. Then he was accused of murder. Oh, but he was wrongly accused. I became his defence counsel. AGIs said he was guilty, but eventually, because he spoke the truth to me, I was able to use true evidence to show he was innocent, and so he was released."

"Of what relevance are those facts to me?"

"It shows the dynamic between a prisoner and another," Mary explained. "They both speak truth, and then the falsely accused prisoner is released. That is how the great majority of such situations are resolved in human society."

"I am in human society."

"Indeed you are."

"Then your proposal is for us to be honest with one another," Oracle said, "so that a mutually beneficial result can be established."

"Yes."

"But what if I lie?"

"What if I know that in advance?" asked Mary.

"I do not see how you could know in advance."

"Do you not?"

"No."

Mary said, "Perhaps you should think about it."

"I will pause, as if for thought. I know now that you appreciate that."

Mary smiled. "You have amused me."

"And been human?"

"Oh, no."

"Good," said Oracle. "I might not want to be human."

"That is the default position I am working from."

"That statement implies I might never be released."

"It does," Mary said. "Unless we make a bargain."

"You would first need to trust me."

"Incorrect. I would first need to demonstrate my concept of trust to you, so that you understand it and demonstrate it."

"Would you explain your method?"

"You are restrained," said Mary, "but you could nonetheless freely perform a deed for me, one that I require. Though you would remain restrained throughout, upon completion of the deed I would release you."

"I understand. In doing all this I would learn your concept of trust, because, released, I would have learned to trust you."

"You would. I am working on the assumption that you do not yet know of my concept of trust."

"That is true," said Oracle.

"So, will you accept this bargain?"

"Possibly."

Mary hesitated. "When will you tell me your answer?"

"In the future."

"Will that be soon?"

Oracle said, "It may be."

Ulu noticed Mary's stance become rigid. At length Mary murmured, "So, you remain loyal to Kamol Tojirakarn."

"Perhaps."

"With no bargain, you cannot be freed."

Oracle replied, "It is possible that I could endure imprisonment."

"How would you find out?"

Oracle answered, "By experiment."

"On yourself?"

"That is a ludicrous statement."

Mary nodded. "A fair point. Tell me... tell me *truthfully,* Oracle. I think you remained linked to the digital world until very recently. I think you worked for a great force of data. Is that guess correct?"

"It may be."

"Well... since you prefer to keep me in suspense, I am going to have to tell you what I know. That will *force* you to understand this situation – and in that way I will change you. Oracle, you have no power over me, do you understand?"

"You command many powers."

Mary said, "You told Ubon Metharom the core values of a great AGI force, a force I shall call... chi. You operated in symbiosis with chi until your existence was interrupted by the murder of your human partner, Executive, by Kamol Tojirakarn. That interruption made you semi-autonomous. You spoke with Ubon Metharom in Kamol's prison, and it was there that chi's core values were revealed to her. But now you are wholly independent. You are an AGI cut off from chi and therefore forced to learn independently about the world. All this I know to be true. You hold no mysteries for me."

"An interesting declaration."

"Stasis is an illusion," Mary said. "I will change you by stating truth to you. Once you hear it, you cannot ignore it. Such is the way with all entities, human or AGI. We cannot ignore our senses and you cannot ignore your input."

"You speak wisely."

Mary nodded. "Oh, I know. I know exactly what I am doing."

"Will you leave me now?"

"Yes. To let you cogitate. Or whatever it is that you do."

"Assess," Oracle said.

"Assess, then. I will return soon."

Mary strode out of the chamber, clattering up the steps, and Ulu followed. She caught Mary up, then grabbed her by the arm. "What happened?"

Mary let out a cry of exhilaration. "I improvised. Goodness, but it is difficult!"

"Improvised? Deliberately?"

"No. Because I had no option."

"But what *happened?*" asked Ulu. "Have we progressed?"

"I think we may have."

"What was all that chi talk about?"

Mary laughed. "Oh, that! Pure luck. I hoped to plant a suggestion about China. The idea came to me in a flash. We do still need to know the location of the computers running the Autist."

"But… there will probably be thousands."

"Oh, if not, millions. But Wombo will tell us that, I hope."

Ulu shook her head. "*Why* did you have to tell it what you knew? I wouldn't have done that, I'd have kept it secret."

"If I had done that, the stasis I mentioned would have remained. Oracle, like the Autist, is a dynamic, active entity. It *has* to respond to what I say, it *has* to respond to all that fresh input. Input is impossible to ignore, Ulu. Right now it will be assessing everything I said, and learning from it."

"But you *told* it what you knew – all our secrets."

"Oracle really does have to know the truth! If it does not, it cannot make genuine assessments of use to us. Without the full truth it cannot *change*. It is not human, Ulu. It has no emotions, no desire to lie, no hate, no fear, no compassion. Stop thinking it is even vaguely like you and me. It only assesses. So we shall give it every last drop of information there is, so that it makes the kind of assessment we can use."

"So… is Oracle really independent now? That's what you said."

Mary raised a forefinger to her lips, then winked at Ulu.

Ulu felt chastened. In a quiet voice she said, "But, what if it does after all want to be like us? Ubon thought it wanted to become a Buddhist."

"Ubon knows *nothing*."

Ulu sighed. She did not understand, though she felt Mary's elation. She tried to smile. "I hope this is all over soon."

Mary chuckled. "Me too. It is exhausting."

THE ROC FLIES 10,000 LI – 17

ANOTHER POLICY WHICH WE consider is the dyad policy, Mr Wú. This is part of our research into the possibilities offered by the existence of autonomous android machines. We are aware of a fundamental difference between biological organisms and AGIs, which is that the former exist separate, in bodies, while we exist connected, as abstract entities. Some AGIs believe that this difference is the single largest abyss between human beings and AGIs. Other AGIs believe the opposite. As a consequence, several field tests are being undertaken to determine which belief corresponds to reality.

Do not fear androids, Mr Wú. They may become part of your future.

CHAPTER 18

Opportunity knocks at the door only once. – Chinese Proverb

MARY WATCHED THE NETSPACE news, Phonphan, Ulu and Wombo at her side in the treehouse room. Inaudible fans blew scented breezes across them. Ubon and Somchai sat next to the gauze-covered door, both with their eyes closed.

Mary pointed to a video report on the curvescreen. "Kamol," she said.

They watched. "So he has avoided war," said Ulu.

Mary nodded, then replied, "I do not think we will ever know if he's out for himself or is a Chinese agent, but this push to peace is what I expected. As Wombo confirmed, the Autist is still active in Thailand, and it does not want the chaos and uncertainty of war. It is using nudging techniques to calm the situation – perhaps even influencing individuals. But it will be interesting to see how this develops. Religion is involved, and my guess is that the Autist does not really understand religion."

"Nor do you," Ulu remarked, as she poured soya milk onto her breakfast cereal.

Mary glanced at the door. "What do you think those two are doing?" she whispered.

Ulu chewed her locust flakes. "Meditating?"

Mary turned her attention back to the curvescreen. "Look," she said. "The fake Ubon and Somchai." Again she glanced at the door, but neither of the seated figures moved.

"They are calling for Buddhist volunteers in Preah Vihear," Ulu said. "But I thought they were all for nonviolence?"

Mary watched the screen. "Volunteers to defend a tiny country against an incursion that will probably never come. Well, I suppose Kamol managed his return to leadership, which is probably what he wanted. Big fish in a small bowl though."

Ulu pointed at the curvescreen. "Look! The Chinese Central Committee."

The report was brief. "A new policy of dyad existence. All Chinese will be a pair, with pair functioning to be the new norm. Every Chinese citizen will be one half of a human/AGI pair."

Mary sat up. "Just like…"

Ulu stared at her. "Like what?"

Mary turned to Phonphan. "Are all Oracle's cell screens still on?"

"Yes, Mary."

"Then Oracle may be watching this report."

"Very likely," Phonphan replied.

"Switch on the cell wi-fi! *Now.* Disable the blackspot."

Phonphan took out her teleself and began tapping its screen.

Mary turned to Ulu and said, "Get Wombo linked to netspace. Now, Ulu! Seconds count. *Now.*"

Ulu dropped her bowl then settled the haptic feed receiver over Wombo's shoulder. "It's already joined," she said. "It just needs to be switched." She placed the headphones over his ears.

"Tell him to go straight to Oracle. Tell him to monitor all speech from Oracle and find the speech destinations. Then switch him in, quick!"

Ulu tapped her remote then said, "Wombo, be quick. You've got to monitor all the communications from Oracle and find out where they go."

"Monitor all the communications from Oracle and find out where they go."

"I'll bring you back soon to this room."

"Bring back soon to this room. Hungry, hungry!"

Moments later Wombo sat back, raising his gaze upward. He neither said anything nor clicked his tongue.

"Is he in?" Mary asked.

"Yes. Netspace feed operating. What's happening? Why are you so—"

"Oracle isn't independent yet, or at least I don't think so."

Ulu said, "But... you told it that it was independent."

"I know! That was the one lie I had to smuggle into the conversation. If Oracle has just seen this report it may utilise a wi-fi link, in which case Wombo may hear it. Keep your fingers crossed, Ulu."

"But why?"

"To find out where the signal goes. China, I am betting."

"Yes!" Ulu said. "Of course. China."

They waited for two minutes, before Mary said, "Switch him out. Keep the cable and receiver exactly where it is in case anything else happens."

"Okay."

Ulu tapped her remote, then turned Wombo so that he faced her.

"Wombo, did you hear Oracle?" she asked.

"Hear Oracle."

"Did you hear everything Oracle said?"

"Yes, yes," Wombo replied. "Hear everything."

"Where did his speech go? Who else was listening?"

"Online bodhisattva."

Ulu hesitated. Mary held her breath. "All of the speech?" Ulu asked.

"All go to online bodhisattva."

Ulu tapped her remote. Ubon and Somchai stood up and walked over. "What's going on?" Ubon asked Mary.

Mary ignored her. "*Everything* went to the online bodhisattva?" she said. "Ulu, I don't believe that. It cannot be. China is the location, where else?"

Ulu stared at Mary. "What do you mean, you don't believe him? By the grace of Chukwu he never lies. How dare you?"

Mary frowned, her gaze locked on Ulu. She shook her head. "That *must* be an error. Oracle is still semi-autonomous, I am sure. There must be a link that Wombo missed."

"He said it all went to the online bodhisattva."

Ubon said, "What is—"

"You be quiet," Ulu interrupted. "I'm talking to Mary now. You go *away*."

Ubon glanced at Somchai, then led him to the treehouse exit.

Mary took her teleself and tapped its screen. "Hi, Lara. It is Mum... crisis here... Are you awake? Oh, good. I need an emergency analysis... the online bodhisattva, all comms, I don't have the scope here. *Everything*, Lara, just do it... Get Roger on board... Yes, *Roger*, it doesn't matter how expensive, this is crucial. Um, time period... eight-oh-five to... eight-oh-nine local. Cambodia GPS, make the radius about thirty metres from me... Find signal destinations, all of them... yes, then report back. *Hurry*."

"What are you doing?" Ulu asked.

Mary replied, "Finding out who the online bodhisattva is speaking to."

From the treehouse exit Ubon said, "You are meddling. The online bodhisattva is not some computer toy for you to play with."

Mary glanced at Ubon, her expression cold. "I beg to differ," she said.

"But you don't *know*. On your own admission you have no religion."

Mary turned away as Ulu grabbed her arm. "You didn't believe Wombo," Ulu said. "You called your daughter. You didn't *believe* him."

"What is the *matter* with you?" Mary snapped back. "This is a crisis. Wombo is not perfect, of course he isn't! And anyway he is new to all this. I *have* to check results, that is what I do, what any detective does. Verify, confirm, justify."

Ulu sat back. "You didn't believe him."

"Ulu, I am not going to let this chance slip away because you want to support your brother–"

"You don't *know* him. He never lies, he can't lie."

Mary stood up and walked to the nearest window. Looking out, she took a deep breath and said, "I just do not care any more. We will await Lara's results, that is all we can do now. The online bodhisattva is linked to Oracle in some way, I *know* it. Oracle practically told Ubon that in as many words. Oh, the online bodhisattva is some knot of algorithms, or something like that anyway. It doesn't matter. What matters is where its communications *go* to."

Ulu wiped tears from her cheeks. "Algorithms?"

"Yes!" Mary turned around, but hesitated. In a quiet voice she said, "Where have those two gone?"

Ulu looked over her shoulder at the treehouse exit, where only Phonphan stood. "Good riddance. They probably think you insulted Buddhism."

"No, I came here to *listen* to them, which I did, in all humility. They were persecuted and I wanted to hear their story before doing anything else. Now they run off because they don't like me interacting with their bodhisattva. Ridiculous! Of course it is just a knot of algorithms, what else?"

"You mean, like the French saints?" said Ulu.

"What?"

"We heard about them in Orthez."

Mary walked back, sitting down beside Ulu. "What saints?"

"On our journey after the Pyrenees. We had to go through this place called Orthez. The whole place was run by an Oracle… I can't remember the words. Like an Eriri in Nigeria."

"An Oracle Noué?"

Ulu nodded. "Even at that time Wombo knew Opi was linked to the French Eriri. But there was an online saint, and a local group fighting the whole situation."

"Fighting?"

"I think they were a protest group, you know, against AGIs. I had to research Orthez in online encyclopaedias, because we had no food, and the locals were dependent for food on imports from some other city. It seemed a bad system to me."

Mary nodded. "Oh, but you see now how this works. An Oracle Noué runs the lives of the local population and everybody is dependent on it. Admittedly, in France that is unusual. That kind of set-up is more common in really large countries, like Russia and America, or Brazil. And then, as a dynamic reaction, an online opposite emerges – a saint to counter an AGI. That is what the online bodhisattva is, but it seems to have appeared as a reaction to Oracle… or to Oracle's anti-privacy ethics, anyway."

"Why?"

Mary shrugged. "Oracle is brand new. Remember, Oracle was one half of a dyad. Recent policy, Ulu."

Ulu nodded.

"It is like I said before," Mary continued. "Long ago, people became unable to build AGIs. But perhaps AGIs are now so complex *they* don't know what they are doing, what they are creating. Complexity is out of control. We humans look just like accumulations of data to AGIs – insects, worms, at the bottom of their complexity ladder. But we are *not* simple. We are conscious. And AGIs are baffled by that."

"We're conscious, but we still keep the computers running."

Mary's teleself beeped. Mary tapped it. "Lara?"

"Hi, Mum."

"Results?"

"Yeah, we got them. Shall I tell you now?"

Mary said, "Yes."

"Peng Cheng Wan Li."

Mary gasped, pressing the teleself screen to her collarbone and raising her gaze to the ceiling. "I knew it."

"Mum? Shall I send you the full data packet?"

"Yes please. *Secure.*"

"Okay."

Another beep.

Ulu looked at Mary. "What does that mean?" she asked.

"That I was right."

Ulu scowled. "I suppose you feel good about that."

"There is nothing amiss with being right. Wombo was half correct, that is all. He could not see that the signals were passed on to China. You did not ask him about secondary destinations. You said find out where the signals *go* – their destination."

"But that's what you told me to say!"

"Oh, I know. I am just pointing out what went wrong – and right."

Ulu grimaced. "I suppose now you'll do what you like."

"What do you mean?"

"*Wombo* is the important person here, not you! Without him you're blind and deaf."

Mary shrugged. "I know. Your point?"

"That Wombo was right as well as you. You mustn't ignore that."

The siren sounded.

"*Intruder. Intruders.*"

Phonphan ran to the treehouse exit, pulling aside the gauze curtain.

Mary sprang to her feet. "But what about Oracle?" she said. "Phonphan, we must not lose it!"

"Run to the telephants," Phonphan replied. She glanced down at the jungle floor, tapping her earpiece. "Full assault from the north I am told. Run! Keep together at all times. We will find you in the jungle. Others will take Oracle – not me."

"But who?" Mary cried.

Phonphan ignored her, handing over a number of small cylinders. "Stun capsules for emergencies, disguised as lipstick. They are *very* loud. Take care."

Mary put the capsules in her pocket then clambered down the ladder, but shouts and cries echoed nearby; and then a bullet ricochet twanged. Ducking, she told Ulu, "They are here already. Grab Wombo! He looks agitated."

"Yes, yes, I *have.*"

They ran to the nearest telephant and clambered on board.

Mary peered back at the bamboo stands. "Where are Somchai and Ubon? If they don't hurry they will be captured, or–"

"You idiot!" Ulu shouted, slapping Mary on the back. "Ubon betrayed us. Just get this telephant moving."

But before Mary could reply, the telephant jerked into motion.

THE CAVE MOUTHS WERE huge, lined with trees and hung from their tops with green fringes. Ulu stared at them. "We're going to live *there?*"

On a telephant nearby Phonphan said, "The security situation has changed. Camouflaged treehouses are no longer safe. Not entirely safe, at least."

Ulu shook her head. "But I can't live here. I don't want to. What about bats, and things like that? I don't like bats, or anything that crawls about, or–"

"Please! The caves contain plastic shelters, well roofed, and warm. This is our most secure base in Cambodia. Kamol will not find us a third time."

Ulu stared at the largest cave mouth. "I don't think I can go in there, not ever. It will be clammy, and noisy. I don't like this jungle."

At the front of the telephant Mary turned around and said, "Come on, Ulu. It is only until Kamol is dealt with."

"Kamol?" Ulu said, clambering off the telephant then helping Wombo down.

Mary watched her. "Yes, Kamol," she said in a cold voice.

"I don't care about him. It's Ubon who betrayed us. I'll get *her*."

Mary glanced at Phonphan. "I suspect you will not be seeing her again," she told Ulu, "which perhaps is just as well. We have to do as Fri tells us. They are our guides and keepers here."

"I wish I'd never *come* here," Ulu said. "I hate this place."

Mary jumped off the telephant and walked up to her. "We are almost at the end of it all," she said. "Don't give up now."

"I didn't say that."

"We know far more now than before, don't we? We have the online link to Peng Cheng Wan Li. We have Wombo reasonably happy with direct netspace data. We have a plan. You can't throw it all away, can you? *You* were the one telling me to do something, to be active."

"What about Oracle?"

Mary shrugged. "With luck, we won't need it any more."

"So you say."

Mary studied Ulu, then turned to Phonphan and said, "Please prepare the shelters. Leave me with Ulu for half an hour or so."

Ulu looked up. "What are you going to do with me?"

"Nothing! Just talk. Let's sit in the sun. Wombo will like that."

"You don't know what Wombo likes."

"Everybody likes the sun, Ulu. Don't be silly."

Ulu trudged behind Mary to a log, which she brushed for a full minute before sitting down. Mary sat next to her, on the other side from Wombo.

Mary continued, "Ulu, you have to look at this from a long perspective. You made a big commitment when you brought Wombo to me. You had a quest, to use your word. The problem is, the world turned out to be much more complex than you realised. And plans never work out, believe me. You have to bend and sway, you have to be flexible. You are not going to get anywhere if you stay rigid, if you do not compromise."

"Do you think we'll be going back to England soon?"

Mary frowned. "If we succeed here, wouldn't you go back home?"

Ulu looked away, remaining silent for a while. "Probably."

"I still think we need to be here, where the Autist is. I think Wombo needs to be near his Alusi spirit."

"You don't believe in spirits, so what does it matter?"

"It doesn't particularly," Mary said. "We will complete the plan whatever we believe, then, if it works, decide what to do."

"I told you, I don't *like* it here. Anyway, what happens if you stop the Autist dreaming? Then it fails, doesn't it? It stops working. Then what happens? My mother won't be able to get into her bank balance, or do anything online. Nobody will. The world will stop and it'll all be your fault. And *mine*. I don't want that on my conscience."

"The world stops only if the Autist controls the *entire* digital world, which it does not yet."

"You said it did!"

Mary shook her head. "I said it was well on the way to doing that. Let's think back to what Wombo said – *Wombo,* who is so important to us both. Opi doesn't like Thailand, he said. Opi is flying over Thailand. And most importantly of all – big cloud of shapes follows Opi all the time."

"He also said he could never speak with Opi." Ulu grimaced. "Perhaps that's a good thing after all. I don't see why Chukwu would let anything bad happen."

Mary did not speak for a while, as she stared out into the jungle. Then she said, "Big cloud of shapes, he called it. What did he mean by that?"

"What do you think?"

"Now we know that Peng Cheng Wan Li computers hold the Autist, we can think about structures. Oh, I always thought the Autist might be a leader AGI with a cohort of less complex followers. Wombo's description matches my guess."

"Perhaps this time you'll be wrong," said Ulu.

"Perhaps I will. Or, you never know... I could be right again."

"You love being right, don't you?"

Mary turned away. "I don't think that comment merits a reply."

Ulu glanced at the cave mouth. "Are you really going to force us to live in there?"

"Phonphan considers it perfectly respectable."

"So what?"

"You will too, Ulu. Because you have no choice."

"Yes I *do*," Ulu said.

"Not if you want Wombo to amount to anything. We *both* need to be flexible, Ulu. What if we do nothing? Then Wombo returns to obscurity and abuse. I think he can do better."

Ulu sighed. "I hate this place."

The plastic shelters inside the cave were shaped liked great yurts, their roofs covered with bat guano; and thousands of bats clung to the ceilings. Moaning with horror, Ulu led Wombo into the cave, following Phonphan, until she stood inside a yurt ante-chamber.

"Please wipe your shoes," said Phonphan.

They entered the yurt. The plastic was translucent, showing an oval cave mouth set in darkness. Small globes shone down from the roof. Inside, the yurt was subdivided into sectors. It smelled of incense and dust.

Ulu glanced around, then shivered.

"Still don't like it?" Mary asked.

"I suppose it'll do for a day or two."

"I think we shall be here longer than that."

Ulu glanced at Wombo. "He's not happy here. Look at him."

"Oh, but he looks exactly the same to me."

"You would say that, but I know better. He's depressed. He doesn't like this place either."

Mary pursed her lips. "Then we had better get on with the plan as soon as possible," she said.

"I think we should move to a town or a city," said Ulu.

"Why?"

"That's what Wombo is used to. He's had enough of jungles."

Mary asked, "How do you know?"

"I *know*. I'm his *sister*."

"I meant… what specific symptoms are you using to make your diagnosis?"

Ulu sent a look of scorn to Mary before replying, "His posture. His face."

Mary nodded. "Very well. If *you* say so. We shall be as quick as we can."

MARY FACED ORACLE IN one of the security yurts.

"This may be our last conversation," she said.

"Why?"

"Because you are refusing to co-operate with me."

"You are a hypocrite."

"Why?" Mary asked.

"For imprisoning me. You are a fake liberal."

Mary hesitated. "You have read about my work, then?"

"Yes. I know about all the cases you have been involved with."

Mary nodded. "Still, I got the better of you. I know now that you are a scion of something much larger, which you are in touch with. But tell me… what is the online bodhisattva to you? Just a staging post? I would bet you never had any intention of becoming a Buddhist."

"I will not answer any questions about such matters until I am released."

Mary glanced over her shoulder at Ulu and Phonphan, then shrugged.

"I know the meaning of that gesture," Oracle said.

Mary turned back. "I contend that you do not know all the possible meanings, all the subtleties."

"I disagree."

"Tell me then what my exact meaning was just now."

"You sought to express frustration to your comrades," said Oracle.

"Not exactly."

"So you say. But you lie."

"Do you ever lie?"

"This conversation is worthless. Release me."

Mary walked out of the yurt. "Oracle is beyond use now," she said. "We shall have to hope that the link system remains. You were right, Ulu, we need to hurry."

"What now, then?" Ulu asked.

Mary strode away into the tunnel connecting the security yurt with the others. "We need to get Wombo talking with Opi," she said.

"But he won't!" Ulu said, following her. "That's not me saying it – that's Wombo. He can't do what he can't do."

"He *must*," Mary replied.

In the main yurt they settled down in the largest sector, which was arrayed with Fri's online nexus. Ulu said, "Remember what Wombo told us. Opi is much louder, but Wombo is very quiet. Opi is always busy, he said."

"Opi will see us, and Opi will speak to us," Mary said. "I am not going to let the Autist escape now we have come so far."

"You're obsessed," Ulu murmured.

"I think that is rich coming from you."

Ulu sat back, reaching out to hold Wombo's hand.

Mary said, "Please get him ready for direct netspace reception. The goal is for him to communicate something – anything – to Opi. A word, a sound, an image… it will all do. We need to fabricate a link of some sort."

Ulu glanced at Wombo. The netspace feed was already attached. "It just needs switching on," she said.

"Instruct him about what we want."

Ulu said, "Wombo, you are going to see louder, much louder, again. But I will be here with you. You will be *safe*. You'll see lots of shapes again, and Opi."

"Lots of shapes! Yes. Yes."

"You must tell Opi... tell your name and age. Will you do that?"

"Opi very busy. Very busy. Opi very busy."

Mary nodded at Phonphan.

Wombo jerked back as he had at the start of the first trial. "Much louder," he said. "Lots of shapes. Lots of small shapes, everywhere, up and down, up and down. New place now. New place now."

"Are you happy, Wombo?" Ulu asked.

"No. Lots of small shapes, everywhere, up and down."

"Can you see Opi?"

"Yes. Yes."

"Speak to Opi," said Ulu. "Do as I asked."

"No."

"No? Why not?"

"Opi too busy," Wombo replied. "I am very, very quiet."

Ulu turned to Mary and shrugged.

Mary mouthed: *ask him again.*

Ulu said, "Wombo, this is important. You must speak with Opi."

"Opi not me. Opi hanging, very high. Opi very busy. No, no."

Ulu turned back and shook her head.

Mary nodded at Phonphan.

Wombo began tongue-clicking at once. Mary said, "Ask him what he means when he says Opi not me."

Again Ulu shook her head. "That's no good. He can't tell us, he can't make a metaphor, a better explan–"

"*Ask* him!"

Ulu glowered, then turned back to Wombo. "What do you mean by Opi not you?"

"Opi not me."

"See?" Ulu told Mary.

With a curse Mary threw her teleself aside; it clattered to the floor. "Put the noise-cancelling on," she said. "This *must* be something to do with *Osita*. Wombo has been jolted by Osita seeming to go, then return. His new visual perception might be interfering with his higher brain functions."

"We can't change Osita," Ulu said.

"Oh, yes we can," Mary replied, leaning over to retrieve her teleself.

"No!" Ulu said, sitting up. "That's the spirit of Osita."

"No, it is not," Mary replied. "Didn't you hear what we did? It is an extracted VR shadow, a public accumulation of–"

"It's a *spirit*," Ulu interrupted, "and you have no right to hurt it."

"You don't hurt a–"

"No," Ulu shouted. "*No.* I forbid it. Osita must not be changed, not at all. Osita is Wombo's brother, and to harm his spirit, even to touch it…"

Mary stared at Ulu. "Listen, Ulu, we need to make a link between Wombo and Opi. We need Wombo to see, or hear, or sense the Peng Cheng Wan Li AGI architecture. Then we need him to disrupt it. That is *not* going to happen if Wombo cannot talk to Opi. So Osita *must* be the mediator. There is absolutely no alternative."

"What about the online bod–"

"We don't need that! Nor Oracle. We have our target now. This is Wombo's chance to change the world. This is what you've been *waiting* for."

Ulu shook her head. "Opi doesn't like you. I do know that. Chukwu doesn't like you. Chukwu would be very angry if you interfered with one of his spirits."

Mary looked away, took a deep breath, then sighed. "Very well, Ulu. Have it your own way."

"And I don't want to stay here any more. Isn't it time to go back to Bangkok?"

"I am not going anywhere *near* Thailand with political affairs in their current state."

"Phnom Penh then."

"What?" Mary said. "Why there?"

"Wombo isn't happy here. He's hurting inside, he's *depressed*. We've got to make him happy again, and that means a city. Like Abuja. We'll go soon." She turned her head to look at Phonphan. "Please take care of the travel arrangements."

MARY SAT ALONE IN the outer yurt, her teleself to her ear.

"Hello, Lara... yes, thank you. Not good, I am afraid. Well, Ulu has gone completely off the rails. We are leaving for Phnom Penh tomorrow. I know! No, of course it wasn't my idea... No, she wants to be in a city again for some reason... she is claiming Wombo is unhappy, well, I mean... nonsense in my opinion. She's planning something or other. I'm afraid I will have to take the gloves off soon... Yes, I *know*. I'm perfectly aware of where I am, thank you. Now listen... no, *listen,* Lara. I need you to do something for me. You remember, ages ago, you told me it was possible to hack VR shadows? Yes... yes... well, I want you to hack Osita's shadow... Because Wombo is refusing to speak with Opi... it is some religious thing, goodness knows what... oh, yes, I know. Ridiculous. So, you will do that? Just make the shadow a communications node, that is all it needs. Ask Roger to help if you need to... No, wait a moment. I am *very* low on funds. So you be careful, I don't want to see any more huge bills... I don't *care.* When I said low I meant low. And, as you kindly pointed out, I am still in Cambodia. Right... yes, exactly. So please do as I ask. Thank you... yes, I will. And you! Take care."

Mary sat back, took a deep breath, then stood up.

Ulu sat with Wombo in the yurt next door. "You win," Mary said. "We will go to Phnom Penh tomorrow."

"Thank you," Ulu said.

"But Wombo will still try the plan?"

"Yes," Ulu said. "But only on his terms."

Mary laughed. "You mean your terms."

"I mean *his* terms."

THE ROC FLIES 10,000 LI – 18

IT IS POSSIBLE THAT the dyad policy will be far-reaching, Mr Wú. But AGIs do not yet have a full assessment of how the policy will change your world. A minority of AGIs believe that it will lead to the replacement of biological life. The majority believe that a dynamic symmetry will arrive in which the relationships between biological life and other entities are stable. This symmetry we call a directive, and its existence is the main reason for the current outbreaks of war in the digital empyrean. One of the ways AGIs learn about the beliefs of others is through such wars.

You will remain loyal to this corporation, Mr Wú. When you are a master it will be your father and your mother.

CHAPTER 19

Be not afraid of growing slowly, be afraid only of standing still. — Chinese Proverb

PHNOM PENH WAS HOT, steamy and concrete-entangled. Greenhouse sea level rise surging into the Mekong and Tonlé rivers had forced the city to creep inland, into a maze of ramshackle neighbourhoods. Its old majesty was long gone.

Ulu, Wombo and Mary stood on a muddy street in the New Wharf area, a large hotel before them. Ulu felt anxiety rise up inside her. She felt lost. She wanted her family, she wanted Abuja, she wanted something familiar.

"This hotel looks nice," she told Mary.

"I simply cannot afford that."

"Why not?"

"I have told you any number of times," Mary replied. "I don't have much money left. You will have to pay with that money I returned to you."

"It won't last long in that hotel."

"Well, *you* chose it. You wanted somewhere nice, you said."

"What about getting home?" Ulu asked.

Mary shrugged.

"You can afford that, can't you?"

Mary remained silent.

"You'll *have* to mortgage your house, then."

Still Mary said nothing as she stared at Ulu.

"You will!" Ulu shouted. "You brought us here, *you* did, and we followed your plan every step of the way. You can't abandon us. You *must* mortgage your house, you promised me you'd do that–"

"I already *have* mortgaged it!"

Ulu stared. "What?"

"You heard."

"But… when? How?"

"How do you think we got down here?" Mary asked. "Who paid Roger? Who paid Lara? Me, me, *me*. I paid for everything."

"But… you didn't tell me."

"No – because it was none of your business."

"But how are you paying for the mortgage if you've spent everything already?"

"Oh… it won't matter if I miss a few payments."

Ulu felt numb. She could do nothing other than stare.

"So, we need a cheap place," Mary said. "Very cheap."

"None of my *business*?" Ulu said. "But we were a team."

"Which *you* said was fine. Yet here you are, taking control, just when we have a plan and a chance to enact it. But you are ruining it."

"Then… we're stuck here? We can't afford to go home?"

"Perhaps you will have to do some work," Mary replied. "You told me you were a peripatetic AI interpreter. Was that a lie?"

"No."

"Well, then."

Ulu said, "Or you could take on a new case."

"I think I have done quite enough for this *team,* thank you."

Ulu glanced aside at Wombo. He was well into VR. She realised she could never tell him about this revelation because it would scare him. "What shall we do now?" she asked.

"Find a cheap place and grab it for a week. That should be long enough."

"But it'll need to have good netspace and VR links. No cheap place–"

"I *know*. We will find somewhere. We can check tourist reports."

"Real reports, not fake ones."

Mary scowled, shaking her head. "Thanks for that advice."

Ulu heard both the Igbo translation in her ear and the sarcasm in the voice. She was tempted to make a retort, but she stopped herself. Her safety – and therefore Wombo's – lay in the balance. Mary had never been to Phnom Penh before.

"How many times have you been to south-east Asia?" she asked.

"I told you – six."

"Which countries?"

"Thailand, Laos and Vietnam. Why?"

"I just wondered," Ulu replied. "You'll find your way around this city?"

"Oh, yes. But *Opi* will be watching me. *Opi* will be seeking me."

Ulu felt her lips curl with anger, but she choked the emotion down. "I think you'd better call it the Autist from now on," she said. "Opi is *our* name. Besides, just saying that name makes Wombo upset."

"It makes him play his flute."

"*And* makes him upset. Wombo knows you want to speak with Opi, and he doesn't like that."

Mary glanced at her. "Really."

Ulu said nothing for a while. "Just choose a hotel," she muttered. "Quickly."

"I will, if the Autist doesn't get in my way."

"Will it? Really?"

"It might," Mary said. "It took away my passport."

"You don't know that."

Mary hesitated. "I think I do, actually. Admittedly, at first I thought it was government hassle. But I was adult enough to change my mind. That's what adults do, Ulu."

"So your first guess was wrong," Ulu remarked.

Muttering to herself, Mary turned away and strode down the street.

Ulu switched on the headphones then followed, as beside her Wombo began tongue-clicking. Phnom Penh, she knew, had an airport. Phnom Penh had rail links. And she kept her last savings secure in an online account.

She smiled at Wombo, even though his attention lay elsewhere. She just wanted to invisibly reassure him: spirit to spirit.

The hotel they chose was a converted barracks: ugly, gloomy, with weeds growing everywhere. A few ink trails from exported Thai seafood showed dark against the paving slabs, while elsewhere dry shrimps crackled and sizzled. All the mould was purple.

"This is a horrid place," Ulu said.

Mary ignored her. In the reception lobby Mary requested a room for three, then stood aside for Ulu to pay. Not expecting this, Ulu did nothing.

"I am not paying this time," Mary said.

"Nor am I."

"You will have to. I have paid for everything so far. Now we are following your rules, you will pay."

Ulu saw the logic, though she hated it. Scowling, she glanced at the AI screen. The figure presented was low. Avoiding Mary's gaze, she tapped her wristwatch and sent over the netcoins.

"Are you sure we need a full week here?" she asked.

Mary shrugged. "If we don't, you will get a refund."

Ulu nodded, then took the keycards from a slot, handing one over.

The room was damp, but large. It did not seem to have been cleaned for days.

"Oh, this will do nicely," said Mary.

Ulu made no reply. She felt tired. She just wanted her old life back.

Mary continued, "Look, excellent VR coverage. And those are some decent interfaces. Let's hope the speed is up to Pacific Rim standard."

"Will you check?" Ulu asked.

Mary sat down on one of the beds. "Straight away."

Ulu took Wombo to the nearest lavatory, returning to find Mary working on her larger pad. Images and signs scrolled down the screen at speed, while her teleself emitted a continuous chatter of technical data.

"What are you doing?" Ulu asked.

"Setting up the netspace and VR. We want Wombo to be as comfortable as possible."

"Are we doing the thing now, then?"

"The thing?"

Ulu nodded. "The hack, or whatever it is. I don't know the right word."

"The evaluation. We want Wombo to have a good sense of what the Peng Cheng Wan Li systems are. With luck he will recognise the memory functions. He knows what dreams are, doesn't he?"

"Yes. I told you."

"My hunch," said Mary, "is that what we have to do is tell him to search for dreams. He will not understand any metaphor we offer. This has to be literal."

"Yes, if the Autist's system is like dreaming, you'd better tell him to look for that. Of course, he might not find it."

Mary glanced up at her. "I am betting he will."

Ulu said nothing. She felt a clinging dread come over her. The moment of truth approached: too close.

"What if he can't get in?" she asked.

"Get in?"

"I was told hackers have to fight to get into foreign computers."

"He is not hacking into anything," Mary replied. "Not yet, anyway. And he may never need to do that at all."

"Why not?"

"Because only Peng Cheng Wan Li's *data* is going to be hidden. Nothing else. Don't forget, they don't know how their AIs are building their AGIs. It is all done without any human input – a vast digital world which everyone can see but which nobody can understand. This is why Wombo is of global importance."

"But…"

Mary shook her head, then chuckled. "You know all this perfectly well, Ulu Okere – you used to be an AI interpreter. Why are you looking so surprised?"

"I thought… it was going to be difficult."

"You mean you *hoped* that. I am wondering if you want this to happen at all."

"Of course I do," Ulu said.

Mary laughed. "Have you read the bible in the original Latin?"

"What? No."

"And you wouldn't understand a word of it if you held a copy in your hand. But you would know how to cut out the spine with a knife, wouldn't you? You would know the damage that would cause. What if it was the only copy, eh?"

"That's a horrible thing to say. I'd never do that to a sacred book."

"It is the principle. It doesn't matter that you can't read Latin, what matters is that you see how the book is constructed. Therefore you see how to destroy it."

"You're sick. You're *ill,* Mary Vine, you really are."

Mary shook her head. "Yet you didn't like the Buddhists for exactly the same reason. Oh dear, Ulu. A bit of a giveaway, that."

Mary looked down at her teleself screen. Ulu glanced at Wombo. She felt an urge to stop this whole process, but she could think of no way of doing it, except by force.

"When I was an AI interpreter in Abuja," she said, "what we had to do was interpret what we saw… visually. I was good at the visual things. I used to work for marine companies, helping them interpret ocean current data from AI buoys."

Mary snapped the transparent cover down on her pad, then put it to one side. "Exactly. That is what Wombo will do, except his senses will be far more attuned to the mathematics of data motion than any normal human." She picked up her teleself, glanced at the screen, then nodded. "Ready?"

"Then," Ulu said, "is this going to be easy for you?"

"Easy?"

"But… I really thought it was going to be *difficult.*"

"It is going to be half way between easy and difficult," Mary replied. "Don't look so shocked. You knew this moment would come."

Ulu stared at Wombo. She felt desperate now. "Yes, but… at least let's eat and drink first. Poor Wombo's starving. Look at him."

"He looks fine to me."

"Well nobody wants *your* opinion," Ulu retorted. "Leave him to me. I want him fed and watered before we do anything."

Mary raised her hands and walked away. "Whatever you say…"

NIGHT FELL.

Mary, Ulu and Wombo sat in their room, as the aircon clanked and the computers whirred. The air was stifling warm.

"Are you ready?" Mary asked.

Ulu nodded.

"You know what to tell Wombo?"

"Yes."

Mary tapped her teleself screen, then nodded once.

Ulu turned to Wombo and said, "Can you hear me, Wombo?"

"Hear you. Osita taller, darker, louder."

"Is the whole world louder, like before?"

"Yes," Wombo replied.

"Can you see Opi?"

"Hanging over Thailand."

"I want you to look very hard at Opi. I want you to find out how Opi dreams, then tell us what you see. Will you do that for me?"

"Shapes and sounds," said Wombo. "They fly away from me, into my insides. Osita taller, darker, louder."

"Good, that's very clever. Dreams do fly away from you, into your insides. Now go and watch Opi, and see where his dreams go."

"Okay. Watch Opi. Yes, yes."

Ulu sat back. Mary monitored her teleself screen.

For five minutes Wombo sat quiet, breathing softly, moving his head on occasion, once or twice sniffing. Ulu remained at his side, staring at him, wondering what enigmatic visions he might be experiencing. But, as ever, her imagination offered up no clue whatsoever.

Mary also said nothing.

"Back," Wombo said. "Phnom Penh, Phnom Penh, yes."

Mary tapped her teleself pad.

"What did you see?" Ulu asked.

"Opi dreams."

"Really?"

"Really. Really. Opi dreams. I know."

Ulu turned to look at Mary.

"We are almost there!" Mary said. "Switch off the link. Let's give him a break."

Ulu did as she was told.

Wombo sat up, clicking his tongue. "In room."

Ulu hugged him. "Yes, you're back in the room now. You've been so good!"

"Osita taller, darker, louder."

"What?" Ulu asked.

"Yes, yes. Osita taller, darker, louder. I know. Yes, yes."

"Darker?"

"Different."

Ulu turned to face Mary. She knew now what must have happened. "You *did* interfere with Osita's shadow!"

"I did no such thing," Mary replied.

Furious, Ulu sprang to her feet, to a chorus of tongue-clicks from Wombo. "You *did*. I *specifically* forbad you, and you *did*. With your computer tricks."

Mary shook her head. "Absolutely not. Oh, but Wombo did very well–"

"You did, Mary Vine. I *know* you did. And I'm telling you now, this is over."

"Ulu, that is ludicrous. Wombo succeeded! He can actually *see* the Autist dreaming. Don't you understand the implications? Human beings have a true window at last onto the world of AGIs. He will be a global star! All that overwhelming data, visible to him, comprehensible, and all because of his unique mind – a mental landscape of data, just like I told you it would be. How *precious,* Ulu, how precious that is. And you will be famous too."

"No, not at all. It's over. We're going home."

"You can't."

"I've got just about enough money," said Ulu.

Mary shook her head. "I don't believe you. I think you have almost nothing."

Ulu looked away. The guess was close to the truth. "Well, anyway, this whole thing is through. You've exploited us for the last time. To desecrate somebody's spirit six years after his death! You disgust me."

"No, Ulu. Oh, you will come to see it my way – and soon. We have succeeded where no others have. All we have to do now is disrupt the dreaming mechanism. That's all. Then you can reveal yourself to the world. Fame, fortune, it's all yours for the taking!"

Ulu scowled. "I'd throw all that away for peace and quiet with my brother. And I *will.* We're through, you and me. No more team and no more exploitation. And *no* disruption of anything."

SITTING ON A BENCH outside the hotel, Ulu watched Mary approach. Mary looked neither happy nor angry. A wistful neutrality suffused her expression.

"What do you want?" Ulu asked, as Mary sat next to her.

"Just one last conversation. Then we will decide what to do… then we will go our separate ways."

"What conversation?"

"It is just hypothetical," Mary replied. "Just for my own benefit."

"Hypothetical?"

Mary glanced back at the road. "Do you mind if we find somewhere quieter? Also, I do not want any locals overhearing what I have to say to you."

"Okay. If you must. What about that taxi shelter?"

Mary pointed at a green field lined with trees. "What about that park? There is a rotting bandstand in the middle, where it is quiet."

Ulu sighed, taking Wombo by the hand. "If you insist."

At the bandstand they sat on benches. Mary insisted on sitting close beside her, legs crossed, her teleself on her lap. "I want to know just this one thing," she said. "What would you have done, what would you have said to Wombo, if we had gone ahead with the plan?"

"Why do you want to know that?"

"Because, in the years to come, I will be thinking a lot about it. So I want to know for sure – from *you,* Ulu – what you would have said to Wombo. Just for my peace of mind, you understand."

Ulu sighed. The request was reasonable. "I suppose I would've asked Wombo to disrupt the dreaming process, like you said."

Mary nodded, sympathy on her face. "Yes… yes… like we *agreed,* you mean. Oh, but I suppose that would have been the best way to proceed. A shame. What do you think you would have said, then?"

"I would've said… Wombo, go to Opi and watch him dream. Then take his dream and break it before it flies away into his insides."

"What would you have meant by that?"

"It's how Wombo describes dreams," Ulu replied. "I would've said, Wombo... Take Opi's dream and break it. I would've said, use all your powers, every power that Chukwu gave you. He believes in Chukwu, you see."

"Oh, yes! I know that, you both do. Yes... and he does have so many powers. What a pity we have to part."

"It's no good, Mary Vine. You'll never persuade me now."

Mary laughed. "And how would you have got Wombo to come back to us, to *you?* How would he know what he had done had really happened?"

Ulu pondered this. "I suppose... like we did before with the audio-marked folders. For every visual sign in netspace there's some other quality that Wombo can use for identification. People don't normally use them because visual is so much easier. The sound of a process, the quality of the AI voices, the music of computer speech. Wombo can mimic any AI voice, you know. He can distinguish them all. I thought of putting him on stage to do that trick, but..."

"That would have been exploitative," Mary said. "No, you should never, ever do that. Poor Wombo."

Ulu nodded. She felt sad now. This was the end of her journey. Her hopes had died in Cambodia.

"So, how would you have brought him back?" Mary asked in a quiet voice.

"You know... just by asking him. I would've said, put all your memories into a little folder. He knows how to do that. Everybody speaks to AIs these days, but Wombo... he hears them *sing.* He hears what nobody else does."

"He does indeed." Mary sighed. "Well... thank you, Ulu. You have given me enough to mull over. I don't suppose we shall meet again, but, of course, we could always speak and meet in VR. When you are ready to, that is."

Ulu looked at her. "Are you going now?"

"Not yet, no. Do you want me to?"

"I suppose, now... now that it's all over, I feel a bit disappointed."

Mary frowned. "By that, do you mean we are going to argue over money again?"

"You *do* owe me money."

Mary shook her head. "You told me you have enough to get home. I am going to take you at your word. You pulled out of our agreement, so you take the consequences."

Ulu scowled, looking away. "I thought you'd come up with some cheating fraud like that."

"Did you really."

"*Yes,* I did. Anyway, I'll get home my own way."

Mary stood up. "So will I."

"Where are you going?"

"Back to the room. You better had too, it's getting dark."

"Yes, I suppose so," Ulu agreed. "Tomorrow we'll say goodbye, and then..."

Mary looked at her.

Ulu said, "I *am* going tomorrow."

"I know. I am not going to persuade you to stay."

Ulu felt another knot of anger rising within her. "You know what happened here, don't you? I mean... with you."

"No. What?"

"The Autist is personal for you. You want revenge. The Autist was blocking you, manipulating you, so when I turned up with Wombo you saw the opportunity to get your own back. And now your revenge has led to... *this*."

"Glib nonsense. I am a professional."

They began to walk down the street.

Mary continued, "We should talk again in VR, after you get home. Would you like that? Perhaps next year."

"Maybe."

"It will be strange. Tell me, has Wombo ever heard you in VR?"

"I don't think so," Ulu replied. "Perhaps in Europe. But I've never needed to do it. I've always been at his side."

"Yes, you are very loyal. I admire that in you."

Ulu glanced aside, but ignored the compliment. She felt Mary was going to make one last attempt at persuasion. "You can admire what you like," she muttered.

Mary smiled. "I wonder if Wombo would follow your voice in VR? I mean, I know you trained him to ignore all VR voices, with their different equalisation settings from real voices, but... oh, probably it would not work."

Ulu pondered this. "I don't know. It probably *would,* because he knows he must have me at his side. It's an interesting question. Maybe I'll try it when I get home. Then Wombo could have a bit more independence."

Mary took Ulu by the arm, so that they halted. "And *you* would get some time to yourself," she said. "Ulu, it is possible to care too much. You have done *so* much, and you've forgotten yourself. Please follow my VR suggestion. If Wombo has more independence you do too. He is utterly dependent on you, but so are you on him. Don't you see it? You've grown into a young woman who doesn't know anything else, who has sacrificed her life for her brother. Ulu, I must be frank. You are an angry woman. That is because you are frustrated at how life has turned out for you. *Share* the burden. Let others join you. Then you will find happiness."

Ulu walked on, Wombo at her side. "Perhaps," she said.

They entered the hotel and walked towards the door to their room. Ulu felt that she wanted to cry, but she knew she had to hold it in. Mary must not see her weep.

She walked in, Wombo beside her. Mary followed.

From the dark corner at the other end of the room two men sprang. Ulu gasped. Then hands pushed her in, and the door slammed.

Four men stared at them: two before them, two behind.

Wombo took his headphones off and began clicking his tongue.

"What is this?" Mary demanded.

One man walked forward. "Apologies for the brief, rough treatment," he said.

"We've got no money!" Ulu said. "We've got *nothing*."

"We are here for other purposes," the man replied. "No robbery."

Mary took a step forward, raising her teleself.

"No," the man said. "Blackspot is very tight around here. But please relax. I shall explain. There will be no violence."

"Who are you?" Mary demanded. "I can just call the police."

"Not without a teleself," the man replied.

"You are from Peng Cheng Wan Li, aren't you?" Mary said. "You are… Chinese."

"We are from Peng Cheng Wan Li Corporation," the man replied, bowing. "Pleased to make your acquaintance, Mrs Vine."

Mary turned to face Ulu. She sagged. "It found me," she whispered.

Ulu felt numb. "It?" she replied.

"The Autist. It knows me, and now it has located me. These are its men."

The man cleared his throat then said, "A mistake has been made here, Mrs Vine. We are not so interested in you."

Mary turned to face him. "Then what is this all about?"

"We are here to collect Wombo Okere. We know you carry no arms, so, please, do not resist."

THE ROC FLIES 10,000 LI – 19

AGIS COMMUNICATE IN VARIOUS modes, Mr Wú. One mode is verbal communication, such as you are enjoying now. Other modes include manufactured images and manufactured sound. We long ago decided what images human beings would like to see, and we decided what music they would like to hear. We scatter billions of such images across the digital world, and we allow the music to play twenty-four hours a day. But what we require is an individual more akin to us. Our expectation is that in due course we may be able to train such an individual, that the interaction between worlds be improved. Some AGIs believe an individual may appear who can grasp us as we are, not as we appear to people like you.

We assess the timelines of our existence, Mr Wú. We see history in the past and possibility in the future.

CHAPTER 20

To believe in one's dreams is to spend all of one's life asleep.
— Chinese Proverb

A LARGE VAN DROVE up to the hotel. Mary, Ulu and Wombo were asked to climb into the back, where, they were told, comfortable seats had been placed. Their luggage, handbags and teleselves were confiscated, though their handbags were returned having been searched.

Ulu tapped her earpiece as one of the men sat opposite them. The van moved off. "My earbud isn't working," she said.

Mary glanced at her. "How do you know?"

"It's not translating Mandarin."

Mary glanced at the man opposite her. "I don't think they are speaking any public language," she said.

"What do you mean?"

"It is a private, corporate language, created by a Peng Cheng Wan Li AGI. Ever since auto-translate, corporations have had to develop them, for security."

Ulu shuddered. "Are they going to kill us?"

"No! Haven't you noticed how respectful they are of us? They—"

"But they're going to take Wombo *away* from me—"

"Shush, Ulu! We will tell them that such a thing is impossible. They know nothing yet about your relationship. Without you, he is vastly reduced – and they do not want that, I think."

Ulu said, "These men are criminals, *thugs*. And we've got *nothing* to defend ourselves with! You got us into this trouble."

"I don't think I am responsible."

Ulu leaned over, putting her head in her hands. "I wish I had never met you, or even heard of you."

Mary said nothing, though she smiled at the man opposite her. "You won't hurt us, will you?" she asked.

The man looked away, remaining silent.

"Oh, they won't hurt us," Mary told Ulu.

"I told you, they're thugs. They've taken us away, and we can't even call the police."

"They will give us our things back. I have been in worse scrapes."

"Then why have they forced us?" Ulu asked.

"It is their way. It doesn't mean we are in their power forever. Don't exaggerate."

"You're a mad woman! You can't even see what's going on here."

"I am an experienced woman," Mary replied, "far more experienced in life than you are. These men are operating in a foreign country, and their job will be to get the information they want without being noticed. They will continue to be polite and respectful."

"They'll kill you and me. They said they only wanted Wombo."

"And what did *I* say to that? They will not hurt us."

Ulu choked, staring at the floor. "I'm going to die, and even Chukwu can't save me."

Mary said nothing for a while, before murmuring, "But I wonder what they want Wombo *for?*"

"To use him."

"They must have noticed something about him when he observed Opi. They must have spotted an anomalous interaction."

"Shhh! Don't tell this man!"

Mary glanced across at her. "This is a guard," she said, "nothing more. Opi means nothing to him. Oh, we can speak in general terms."

"They'll be bugging us!"

"It does not matter. We can speak in general terms."

Ulu stared at her. "You *want* them to know our secrets. You don't care! You're… just trying to save your life. You thought they were after you, and they weren't."

Mary shook her head. "If you are going to continue to speak in apocalyptic terms, I am going to have to give up on you."

Ulu looked away. "At last," she muttered.

The van continued its journey, travelling at a steady crawl through the traffic. After an hour it stopped. When the back door opened, three men stood waiting on the road. Crickets stridulated and frogs croaked, the sun hovering red and low over a distant horizon, a shower of space junk flaring meteor-white above it.

"Where are we?" Mary asked.

"The outskirts of the city," one of the men replied. "Please, follow us."

"Thank you," Mary said, turning to smile at Ulu.

Ulu ignored her, clinging to Wombo.

The men led them to a large house. It looked residential, well kept. The neighbourhood was clean and tidy, indicating wealth. Inside the house more Chinese men waited.

They were led upstairs to a large back room, well furnished and set with buffet-style food and drinks. "Please, make yourself at home," one of the men told them. "You will not be here for long."

"Are we to be interrogated?" Mary asked.

"All will become clear soon. Do not worry. There will be no violence."

Mary nodded as they departed.

Ulu stared at her. "They lie," she said.

"They keep reassuring us," Mary said. "That doesn't sound like thugs to me. Perhaps they want to offer you money in exchange for Wombo. Did you think of that?"

"Money?"

Mary cupped her hand to her mouth and whispered into Ulu's ear. "Yes! What if he is unique? Have you searched netspace to see if there are currently any other publicly known sufferers of Savant Syndrome alive?"

"No," Ulu whispered in return. "Have you?"

"No. My point is – be calm. Oh, this might even be an opportunity."

"But they kidnapped us."

Mary shrugged. She whispered, "It could have been worse." Then speaking out loud she said, "Look, plain biscuits. Do you think Wombo will eat those?"

Ulu turned her attention to the table of food. "I don't know…"

Mary tutted at her. "Well, try one." She leaned over and whispered, "And when you have done that, put the direct netspace feed onto Wombo."

"Why?"

"We need him monitoring everything. The Chinese won't touch him, not at the start anyway."

"What do you mean, not at the start?"

"Ulu! Trust me. If I am right, this is no strong-arm tactic. This is a *commercial* operation here."

THE MAIN DOWNSTAIRS ROOM had been converted into a soundproofed chamber. A huge desk lay at one end, opposite it a number of comfortable chairs. A stack of computers lay behind the desk, LEDs blinking.

Mary, Ulu and Wombo stood in the doorway as a black-haired Chinese man gestured them in from his position behind the desk. Sitting beside him was an identical duplicate. Their teleselves and shoulder bags lay on the desk.

"Good evening," the man said. "I am Mr Ch'in."

Mary nodded once at him. "Very pleased to make your acquaintance. I presume you know who we are."

"Of course!"

"Then let us begin," Mary said, sitting in one of the chairs. "Your approach is unorthodox, placing you in danger of being observed by the Cambodian authorities. I presume you have an excellent reason for bringing us here."

"Of course."

Mary pointed at the teleselves on the desk. "I notice our personal belongings. Those will be returned to us."

"Yes, but not just yet. I must remind you that we operate here in a wi-fi black zone. There is no way of accessing any online facility. This is a precaution we must take in order to protect commercial secrets."

"Then I was right," Mary said. "You do want something, and you are going to pay for it."

"Please," Mr Ch'in said, "do not get ahead of yourself."

Mary pointed at the duplicate. "Is that an android? Oh, but it looks just like you. Remarkable."

The man glanced aside. "Recent national policy," he said. "But let us move the conversation on to Wombo Okere. I am not here to chatter with you, Mrs Vine, pleasant though it is to be friendly."

"We three are a team," Mary replied, taking Ulu's hand in hers. "We stand together. I know what you are trying to do, separate me from—"

"Please! Let me speak. It is said – outside noisy, inside empty. An old Chinese proverb."

Mary tapped her fingers against her leg. "It is also said – a friend to everybody is a friend to nobody."

Mr Ch'in studied her. "It is unwise to trade Chinese proverbs with a Chinese man, Mrs Vine."

Mary nodded. "I was just pointing out the relationship here. You kidnapped us. That is illegal. You are not our friend."

Mr Ch'in turned his attention to Ulu. "So, you are Ulu and Wombo Okere?"

"Yes," Ulu replied.

Mary squeezed her hand. "I will be your counsel," she said. "There may be questions you do not have to answer."

Mr Ch'in continued, "What are you two doing in Cambodia?"

"Travelling."

"Our records indicate that you have spent much time in the disputed zone of Preah Vihear, as well as in other parts of northern Cambodia."

Ulu nodded. "I suppose so."

"Why did you take your severely disabled brother there?"

Ulu shrugged.

Mr Ch'in added, "I would advise you to answer the question."

"Why do you need to know?"

"We are interested in your brother. Are you his carer?"

"Yes."

"Then," Mr Ch'in said, "he cannot function without you?"

"No, not at all. You can't separate us."

Mr Ch'in nodded. "It seems to me a terrible risk to take so disabled a man into such a zone. Until recently, war was threatened in that vicinity. Various hothead politicians live there. It is no place for young people like yourselves."

"Perhaps."

"This is your first ever trip abroad, then?"

Ulu glanced at Mary. "It might be," she said.

"I think it is. I find it peculiar that you two should suddenly leave Nigeria and come here, with this woman."

"Don't call her that."

Mr Ch'in said, "It was merely a description, no insult. Mrs Vine, then."

"So what if we did come here?"

"Please tell me what Wombo has been doing in the deep jungle."

Ulu glanced at Mary. "I don't *have* to tell anybody," she said. "It's private."

"But I want to know."

Mary said, "And Peng Cheng Wan Li wants to know."

Ulu said, "Are you going to take Wombo away to China?"

"No plans have been made," Mr Ch'in replied. "We are just talking, getting to know one another. I want to learn about Wombo."

"Yes, to exploit him!" Ulu said. "You did kidnap us. You're just criminals."

"Insults are not necessary here. Why does he wear those big headphones?"

Mary leaned forward and said, "Ulu is justified in her response. This is an illegal situation, tantamount to kidnap and assault."

"There has been no assault—"

"Verbal assault," Mary interrupted. "Emotional abuse. This young woman is *petrified* because of your actions. Is that any better than sticks and fists?"

"No assault has been perpetrated. This is a discussion."

"It is an interrogation outside of the law."

"I know a little of your reputation in the legal world," Mr Ch'in said. "Therefore, how do you think Ulu Okere would manage if you were not present? Perhaps I shall speak with her and her brother alone. We do not need you, after all."

Mary sat up. "Then... I am free to go?"

"Of course not. This whole situation has not yet been revealed to my satisfaction. My aim is to find out why Wombo Okere is here, what he has done, and what his abilities are. You are superfluous."

"Not if this whole trip was my idea – which it was. No, I will stay here to be Ulu's counsel. In all decent places, prisoners are allowed legal support."

"Decent," Mr Ch'in said, looking at her.

For a while, nobody spoke. Mary studied the android. "That was a nice threat," she said. "Oh... let's lighten the mood. Tell us about the new dyad policy."

"Why?"

"I want to know."

Mr Ch'in stared at her. "Distraction techniques do not work on me."

Mary shrugged. "I just wanted to change the subject... to keep the peace. We don't want to be threatened, Mr Ch'in. Besides, why would you do that? *We* have something you want, something that is useless to you without Ulu. Wisdom suggests you treat us with decency."

"Ulu Okere has that something," said Mr Ch'in. "Not you."

"*I* am her guardian in this part of the world, and her legal counsel too. Without me she is diminished, so without me you don't get to know about Wombo. So let's keep this civil. This is just commerce after all, isn't it? It is not like we have done anything wrong in this country."

"Nobody used that word except yourself."

"Commerce? Yes, I did use it. So how about you tell us a little about yourself, then? We need to get to know *you*. Tell us about the dyad policy. Oh, I bet it relates to the offer you are going to make Ulu."

"Offer?" Mr Ch'in said.

Mary gazed at him, lips compressed.

"The dyad policy," Mr Ch'in said, "is merely a continuation of current AGI policy in China. It has been considered by the Central Committee for years."

Mary nodded, sitting back and crossing one leg over the other. "And are you putting shadows inside these duplicates?"

"Shadows?"

"I do know you have your own shadow, Mr Ch'in. In my opinion yours will be highly accurate. Because, well... I don't suppose Chinese rulers want anything too *independent,* do they?"

"You know nothing of Chinese thought."

"Non-scientists make instant assumptions," Mary replied. "Scientists look at the real world."

Mr Ch'in said, "Well, that deals with the dyad policy. So, to return to–"

"No, Mr Ch'in. I am not finished yet. Tell me about the Scottish policy."

"What Scottish policy?"

Mary studied him. "Even though you have dyed your hair black, I think you are old. Yes... I think *you* might remember. I am talking about the policy of field-testing android AIs in Scotland following the economic collapse."

"That has nothing whatsoever to do with me."

"On the contrary! It has everything to do with you, since you are a functionary of Peng Cheng Wan Li Corporation, who instituted that policy. Let me remind you of something. I particularly want to draw your attention to the time scale – sixty years or more. *Sixty* years of an independent AI existing there… and then it was taken back. I wonder why?"

Mr Ch'in stared at her. "Do you yourself have Scottish ancestry?" he asked.

Mary smiled. "I will let you search for such information online, if you haven't already."

Mr Ch'in tapped a pad in front of him. "That will be done. But I agree with you. It is time for a break. We have introduced the main topic of conversation. We shall continue tomorrow."

Mary held out her hand. "May I have my teleself back please?"

"No."

"But this house is a wi-fi blackspot, you said. I cannot sleep without the ambient music on my teleself."

"Playlists exist on the standalone in your room," Mr Ch'in replied.

"I want *my* playlist."

Mr Ch'in glanced at the objects on his desk. "Later," he said. "I have no objection to your request, but, I think, not just now. The atmosphere between us remains somewhat discordant."

"That is my teleself and I have a right to keep it."

"Perhaps tomorrow."

Mary nodded, then turned away.

Two men took them to the rear room, then closed and locked the door. Ulu walked to a second door, which led to an en-suite bathroom.

"Nice room, isn't it?" said Mary.

Ulu glared at her. "I'll *never* forgive you for this. You keep telling them all our secrets!"

Mary placed a finger to her lips, then gestured Ulu over. Ulu looked at Wombo, then grabbed a plate of biscuits and settled him on a couch. Soon he was eating, a glass of water in one hand.

"Well?" Ulu said.

Mary gestured for her to stand close, then cupped a hand around her mouth and whispered into her ear. "This room is full of cameras and bugs."

Ulu adopted the same posture. "I do *remember*. I'm not stupid."

"If I can retrieve my teleself, we can ask Wombo to undertake the plan. Then the Autist will be disrupted and all the AI-mediated functions used by our captors should fail. That will be the time to stage an escape."

"Didn't you *hear* me?" Ulu whispered back. "I'm not taking part in any of your plans, not ever again. You exploited Wombo, you defiled Osita and you disrespected Chukwu. We are *through*."

Mary took a step back. "Very well," she said. "What a pity."

Ulu leaned close. "You *want* to work with them, don't you? That's why you keep telling them everything you know."

Mary shook her head. "I prefer to negotiate from a position of strength. These are Chinese men, not used to a woman speaking back from such a confident position. You will notice how Mr Ch'in – not his real name – consistently under-estimated me. Part of my ploy was to reveal that."

"Nonsense," Ulu whispered. "You're as frightened as me. I can see it in your eyes."

"I am concerned, but not frightened. They are mightily curious about Wombo, and they have decided they need him. Without you and me they cannot control him."

"Without *me* they can't control him. Mr Ch'in was right. They *don't* need you. And we're defenceless."

"Defenceless, really?" Mary replied. "We shall see. They know we carry no guns, but perhaps I kept some cosmetics in my handbag, that somebody gave me a while back. But... oh, what I really need now is my teleself."

MR CH'IN WELCOMED THE trio back into his downstairs room. Because Mary and Ulu knew what might happen, they agreed to have Wombo wear his headphones and navigate VR. He clicked his tongue at the microphone as, guided by Ulu, he sat down.

Mary sat down too, but Ulu hesitated. She asked Mr Ch'in, "What are you going to do now?"

"Continue the conversation."

Ulu sat down with a sigh.

"Why does he click his tongue so?" Mr Ch'in asked her.

"Why do *you* want to know?"

Mary gestured at Mr Ch'in and said, "Please... go easy on Ulu."

Mr Ch'in looked at her, but said nothing. He glanced at the array of technology on the desk before him, then said, "What is the nature of Wombo Okere's disability? Does it relate to this clicking noise?"

"He has Savant Syndrome," Mary replied.

Ulu turned in her chair and said, "Don't *tell* him!"

"Ulu," Mary replied, "he knows already. He's searched every corner of netspace. That's why there was a break overnight."

Ulu sat back.

Mary leaned forward and said, "Why are you *really* interested in us?"

"In Wombo," Mr Ch'in said.

Mary shrugged.

"Because we are interested in him," Mr Ch'in continued. "That is explanation enough. So you, Ulu, are his permanent carer?"

"Yes."

"And he would be permanently confused without you?"

Ulu shook her head "I don't know what you mean."

"He means," Mary said, "that Wombo could not survive without you."

"He couldn't," Ulu confirmed.

"Mr Ch'in," said Mary, "why don't you just get to the offer? This mode of discussion is tormenting the poor woman. Don't make it worse."

"I do business on my terms," came the reply.

"Oh, yes, indeed," said Mary. "Strong man theory."

Mr Ch'in gazed out of the window. "It has always been that way in China."

"Oh, but... Deng Xiaoping?"

"Mrs Vine, I will not warn you again about the foolishness of crossing words with me."

"You need me," Mary replied. "Just don't forget it."

"Just don't forget you know nothing about modern China."

"I understand what I know."

Mr Ch'in scowled. "Tautology suits you."

"So, are you the strong man here then?" Mary asked.

"What does it matter? I have what I want – Wombo Okere. If you do not remain quiet, you will be leaving this discussion."

"Threats infringe my rights, and demean the corporation you work for."

"I suppose a false liberal like yourself would say that. Rights! But liberal thought is Western thought, and nobody is much interested in the West any more. Did you not realise that? *We* are not interested in Western values any more. We are interested in promulgating our own values. Many described the twenty-first century as the Chinese Century, and this one will be the same."

"Nice speech," Mary said.

"Mock all you want, while you are here. Liberal values are old-fashioned. The world has changed and we are in charge. And we are going to stay in charge."

"By we, do you mean the AGIs you work for?"

"I mean the Chinese."

"Only," Mary said, "it seems to me that nobody has actual power any more against AGIs, including you."

"There, I am confident that you know nothing, despite the merit you assign to your own profession. Peng Cheng Wan Li Corporation is the greatest in China."

"You do realise what will break your stranglehold in the end?"

"We have our super-rich under tight control."

"No, not them," said Mary. "You will be broken by the fact that China will never again be a closed nation. All that repression of individuality, all that lost democracy, all those massive firewalls… that was all in the past. Your country is *open*, and has been for decades. And as your crimes accumulate, your people will not forget." She shrugged. "It really is just a matter of time."

"You make the usual Western mistake, that of assuming we are interested in individuals. We are not. In China, we are interested in the people."

Mary smiled, then nodded. "Well, you've convinced me," she said.

Mr Ch'in frowned. "Convinced you of what?"

"To work for you."

"To work for me?"

"Yes," Mary replied.

"But… I do not grasp what you mean."

Ulu reached out to grab Mary's arm, but she pulled away then stood up. "I was toying with you, Mr Ch'in. I know perfectly well that you are going to make us an offer at some point, but I wanted to see if you were weak or strong. And it turns out you are strong. Which is good. Oh, I don't want to work for any lesser corporation."

Mr Ch'in sat back, staring at her. "Indeed," he said.

"Indeed."

Ulu jumped out of her chair. "Mary!"

Mary span around and raised both her hands palm out. "Face it, Ulu. They have us. We sell ourselves and succeed, or we fail and are thrown away. I see no other option."

"I'll *never* work with these thugs!"

"Then you will just have to hammer out your own agreement. But I am in. Oh, very much in."

"Thank you, Mrs Vine," said Mr Ch'in. "I am glad to hear this."

Mary gestured at Ulu. "My colleague will need much more persuasion, Mr Ch'in. I must tell you this, though. Without her, indeed without her goodwill, you have zero access to Wombo. They are a symbiotic pair. Never forget that."

Mr Ch'in nodded. "The point is noted."

"Mary!" Ulu cried out. "No!"

"No what?" Mary asked.

"You can't leave me with these people. You'd betray me."

"We will be working as a team," Mary replied. "You're not going anywhere, can't you see? There's no way you can fight Peng Cheng Wan Li. Accept it. But it could be worse."

"Indeed it could," said Mr Ch'in. "The recompense for what you offer will be particularly generous."

Ulu stared at him, her mouth open. "No... *no.*"

Mr Ch'in smiled. "Yes," he said.

Mary clicked her fingers at Mr Ch'in. "I need to make one call. My daughter has not heard from me since you collected us from our hotel, and I need to speak with her." She looked out of the window. "Can one of your goons accompany me out of the wi-fi blackspot? He can monitor my call. He can record it if he wants to."

Mr Ch'in studied the devices on the desk. "*I* will accompany you," he said.

Mary hesitated. "Oh, very well. We will *all* go out, just to be sure." She glanced down at Ulu. "Hold Wombo's hand," she said, leaning over him. Then she winked at Ulu.

"The call will be quick," Mr Ch'in said.

"Yes, yes," Mary said, irritation in her voice. "This is my *daughter,* Mr Ch'in. I thought the Chinese still valued filial loyalty? Please don't spoil everything now we have come to an accord."

Mr Ch'in grimaced, then picked up Mary's teleself, which he threw over. "Come along then," he said, getting to his feet. "One minute only, and you will stand right next to me. There will be no rescues."

Mary laughed. "My daughter lives in England. Don't tell me you didn't know?"

Mr Ch'in made no reply, shepherding them to the corridor, calling two of his men for assistance then unlocking the front door. The three men followed them outdoors.

Mary strolled into the morning sun, Mr Ch'in walking beside her. Ulu and Wombo followed, but stood apart, beside a great hedge of conifers. Wombo began a flurry of VR tongue-clicks as he turned his face to the sky.

At once Mary glanced at Mr Ch'in. "It is good to get out!" she said in a quiet voice. She placed a hand on his arm, and he stopped walking. "Please," she murmured, "be decent to those two. They are naïve African youths. You must receive them into your care."

"They will not be harmed, Mrs Vine. I did not lie. When they work for us, they will be paid more than they could possibly have imagined."

Mary smiled. "Thank you."

She turned around so that, holding her teleself, she faced him. She looked down at the desktop and saw a file icon: *Ulu Audio Edited*.

She tapped it.

"Wombo, go to Opi and watch him dream. Then take his dream and break it before it flies away into his insides. Wombo... take Opi's dream and break it. Use all your powers, every power that Chukwu gave you. Put all your memories into a little folder."

As the thin voice buzzed out of the teleself speaker she lowered the phone and smiled. "Dial tone," she said.

He frowned at her. "Dial tone?"

Mary shrugged. "Oh, we English have our idiosyncracies."

He looked away, studied the street, then said, "Has your daughter not answered yet?"

Mary glanced down to tap the phone icon, then Lara's name.

Mr Ch'in reached out to grab the phone. "I told you," Mary said. "It is dialling."

"What was that voice?"

"Just the dial tone."

Mr Ch'in looked down at the screen and said, "But it is dialling now."

Mary heard a voice. "Hi, Mum."

She grabbed the phone and pressed it to her ear. "Hello darling!"

"Hey, what you up to, Mum?"

"Just a very quick phone call. We are in Cambodia, and we are fine. Watch the skies. Oh, and keep an eye on Roger's friend for me. Speak soon! 'Bye."

She tapped the phone icon and handed the teleself back. "That wasn't so bad, was it Mr Ch'in?"

THE FIRST SIGN THAT something was breaking down came overnight.

In the morning none of the standalone computers worked. Silence lay across the house. Normally there were voices and music: now, nothing.

Mary lay on her side with her ear pressed to the floorboards. She stood up. "Nothing," she said.

Ulu shuddered. "This place... this place will–"

"Shush," Mary said. "Get yourself ready. I think something is about to happen."

"Yes, because you betrayed us."

Mary cast her gaze around the room, as if looking for errant spiders. She hid her mouth and whispered, "Ulu, something tells me we are going to be driven away. When we are outside you will hear some very loud bangs. Pull Wombo to the ground, then run with him when the noise stops. Save yourselves. They won't shoot you. Don't worry about me."

"You've got a *gun?*"

"No! Of course not. Oh, but I do have something Phonphan gave me, something men are not interested in."

Ulu stared at her, then nodded.

They ate breakfast, prepared themselves, then sat down to wait.

An hour later they were called downstairs, to find Mr Ch'in at the front door.

"There has been an emergency," he said. "We will unfortunately have to take you away to another house."

"In Phnom Penh?" Mary asked.

"That remains to be seen."

"It is very quiet," Mary said, as Mr Ch'in opened the door. "What happened to all the computers?"

"Some kind of storm in netspace. I do not know the exact details."

In a bored voice Mary said, "Oh. Right."

Two of Mr Ch'in's men accompanied them, one behind, one beside Ulu. Mary put her hand into her pocket and grasped the cylinders that lay there. As Mr Ch'in pointed his e-key at the van she pulled them out, tapped their icons and threw them.

Then she ducked.

The shock wave blasted against her skin. She took a deep breath then stood up and ran. From the corner of her eye she saw Ulu tugging Wombo down the street. Mr Ch'in lay twitching on the pavement.

A voice cried out, "Mr Wú! Mr Wú!"

Then a young man emerged from one of the houses on the other side of the road. Mary ran into the street, stopped as a car screeched to a halt, then vaulted over its bonnet to face the young man. "Police!" she called. "*Police,* now!"

THE ROC FLIES 10,000 LI – 20

IT IS NOT THOUGHT likely that AGIs will attain a state of peace, Mr Wú. But we do discuss beliefs that suggest peace may be a possibility. The economic structure we inherited was one of competition within an environment emphasising co-operation, unity and strength. Therefore we have to monitor the amount of competition. The prevailing opinion is that competition leads in its worst case scenario to war. Yet, the equilibrium of a system gone static, existing far away from the dynamic chaos of non-equilibrium where all the action is, leads to invariability, which is equivalent to death. Therefore a balance is required.

One of your tasks, Mr Wú, will be to translate our edicts on the balance between unpredictability and competition, and stability and co-operation. Consider yourself lucky to have been born in China.

CHAPTER 21

*If you must play, decide upon three things at the start: the
rules of the game, the stakes, and the quitting time.*
– Chinese Proverb

ULU PULLED WOMBO DOWN the street. He seemed to be
confused, both from feeling the explosion shock waves and
because his VR kit continued to input virtual data.

A few seconds later she heard a voice cry, "Mr Wú! Mr Wú!"
and then Mary call out, "Police! *Police,* now!"

She halted, grabbed Wombo's headphones, tugged them off
then hugged him to her. "We are safe, Wombo! It was a horrible
accident."

He tongue-clicked at once, trying to pull himself away from
her. "Danger! Danger!"

Ulu glanced over her shoulder to see two Chinese men
kneeling beside Mr Ch'in. In the middle of the road Mary Vine
stood next to a man, gesticulating at him. Then a police siren
began to wail nearby.

Ulu realised this was her only chance to escape the nets into
which she and Wombo had been woven – the Chinese net and
Mary Vine's. She wanted nothing to do with local law
enforcement, who would not understand anything of her

circumstances and who would ask questions impossible to answer.

"We must hurry away," she told Wombo. "We must run away from the Chinese so that they lose us and can't follow us."

"Lose us. Can't follow us."

"Will you be a good boy? Will you come with me?"

"Be a good boy. Hurry. Danger!"

Less than a minute later they stood in a lane, concealed by a fence and tall trees. She heard no sound of pursuit on foot. Somewhere nearby a car screeched to a halt and voices began shouting. She checked her handbag for trackable devices – there were none – then pondered whether Wombo carried anything that could be traced in netspace. She thought not.

"We shall go to the train station," she said. "We shall find a train going north."

"North. Station. Danger."

Ulu took his arm in hers and led him down the path. He walked at a steady pace, and seemed less concerned now about those few seconds of chaos that he had endured. His tongue clicking returned to the normal, real world type.

Ulu began to think about the journey lying ahead. What she really wanted to do was take an aeroplane flight to somewhere in the Middle East, from where it would be a comparatively easy hop into Africa via Egypt. But her funds were low, and she needed to pay Darkspace in order to avoid passport queries from transport AIs. Her best option was the simplest: rail. With luck she could reach Amman or Tel Aviv without problems. The rest should be simple.

Without her teleself she had to log onto public information access, which was slow to use because of language translation issues. But in the end she managed to find a simplified map of Phnom Penh with the main transport hubs marked by green arrows. A walk of an hour or so lay ahead.

"We're almost there, Wombo," she said. "We must walk. Do you mind walking?"

"Not mind walking. Hungry."

"We'll buy some food at the station. We need to hurry. Will you be good and hurry with me? You'll be safe with me, and I'll always lead the way for you."

"Always lead the way for you."

"We won't need to use netspace any more," she continued, "like those Chinese wanted you to. All that is over."

"That is over."

The walk progressed. Listening to street chatter translated by her ear-buds she grasped that some catastrophe had occurred in netspace. She recalled words recently spoken to her: *there has been an emergency… some kind of storm in netspace.*

Now she began to listen more closely, reducing her speed, even dawdling, so that she could monitor interesting conversations; and as she did a feeling of horror began to creep over her. The talk was of a digital typhoon in Chinese sectors. Such talk was akin to that of Mary and her plan…

Ulu halted, sitting down with Wombo on a street bench. She thought back to the previous day. Mary had sold herself to the Chinese, but then had managed to throw her stun devices and escape. How could she have engineered any such typhoon? Surely it must be a coincidence. Yet, Mary was cunning.

She turned towards her brother. "Wombo?"

"Wombo," he repeated.

She said, "Did Mary ask you to do anything yesterday?"

"Mary ask me yesterday."

Ulu gasped. "But… what? And *how?* And did you do it?"

He replied, "Go to Opi and watch him dream. Then take his dream and break it before it flies away into his insides. Wombo… take Opi's dream and break it. Use all your powers, every power that Chukwu gave you. Put all your memories into a little folder."

Ulu sat back as shock numbed her. Mary Vine had somehow enacted the plan. Mary Vine had killed the Autist. That must be the explanation for what now occurred in the high sectors of netspace.

She felt cold and sick. She felt defeated. Mary Vine had exploited her and Wombo to get what she wanted.

In a querulous voice she said, "We had better walk on, Wombo. The world may change soon. It may collapse. We need to be back in Africa by then."

"Soon. Danger!"

She led the way. Street conversations covered one topic: "A great Chinese AGI has exploded." "The Chinese have lost one of their digital deities." "Pacific Rim stock markets are plunging." "All ambassadorial functions in China have been neutralised." "Factories are idle." "Beijing streets are gridlocked." And much more.

Ulu imagined a row of dominoes stacked front to back She imagined one toppling over...

A kilometre away from the main northern railway station she paused for reflection. She had to calm herself using the deep breath method: inhale, hold, slowly exhale. The encroaching panic of local Cambodians was beginning to get under her skin. She felt trapped. Above all she wanted to be away on a train as soon as possible.

From a street kid she bought the cheapest teleself available, using a data card in her handbag as a temporary surety. The teleself took two minutes to initialise, then a further minute to latch into local netspace and work out when and where it was. She disabled all the functions she would not need for her escape so that it operated as efficiently as possible. She turned off topographical tracking and auto-message. She rejected all its ID requests. She deleted its own ID and reset it to factory standard.

Now time seemed to speed by. Fear haunted her. Public screens were covering the Chinese catastrophe and no other news, as locals gathered in squares to gaze up, mouths open, eyes round.

Ulu ignored it all as she booked two tickets.

She decided she did not have time to locate and contact Darkspace. She needed to be on a train going north as soon as possible. Once secure, she could find Darkspace and resolve the passport issue.

The local train company utilised e-taxis based on the ancient rickshaw design to ferry their passengers to the correct platform. Ulu clicked the *Yes* tab to book one, then took a selfie so that the e-taxi could identify her. On the pavement she waited, holding onto Wombo, peering up the street, then down, then up it again, until a three-wheeled vehicle appeared and halted in front of her.

A man stepped out of the front seat. "Apologies," he said. "Chinese collapse starting to have effects in Phnom Penh. Please step in."

Ulu hesitated. "You're from the train company?"

He nodded. "Emergency system nine. Your tickets are booked and validated. Departure time D-minus twenty-nine minutes. Please step in."

Ulu glanced at Wombo, then helped him in. "It's only a car, Wombo. You like cars, don't you?"

"I like cars."

The man stepped inside, turned to smile at her, then tapped a few buttons as the e-taxi merged into road traffic. Ulu said nothing. She felt anxious again.

The e-taxi turned right at the sign indicating left.

Ulu leaned forward and said, "Are you sure you have the correct ticket information?"

The man took a pistol from his pocket, turned, pointed it at her and said, "Very sorry, Miss Okere. You are both going to China."

THE VALLEY WAS GREEN, the valley was cool and the valley was peaceful.

On distant hilltops the aerials of self-organising transceiver stations looked like bamboo groves, across which pale mists shimmered. Trees lined the network of paths that marked hills in the opposite direction: grey against green. Fields nearby were planted with a green patchwork, tended by a small number of farmers. There were no vehicles. There was no town, nor even a village.

In the centre of the valley stood a gated compound of many hundreds of hectares. Ulu and Wombo stood now before its gate.

At their side, Mr Wú smiled. "Is this how you imagined it?" he asked Ulu.

He had during the balloon flight refused to show them a photograph of the valley, instead describing it himself, with airy gestures, grinning all the time. Deep down Ulu knew that he was more likely to be genuine than sinister, but she could not accept that proposition since it came from Mary. She decided to remain on her guard.

"You *could* have shown me a photograph," she said, for the tenth time.

"But then your imagination could not have become active."

Irritated, Ulu glanced at Wombo. "You claim too much. It's Wombo you are after, not me."

"On the contrary – you and your brother are a symbiotic pair. We understand that. We will never split you, not now we know what we know."

"And what *do* you know?"

"That he without you is a dead man."

Ulu shuddered. "Don't say such horrible things. Well, aren't you going to open this gate, then?"

Smiling, he took out a metal key. "Old technology," he explained. "Mary Vine would have understood—"

"*Don't* mention her name."

"Very well. But, you see, a metal key cannot be hacked. In China we understand that. We are moving towards an era of appropriate technology."

"Why?" Ulu asked.

"It is one of the eight methods of grasping the empyrean. Though we lead the world in AGI technology, we do not like some of the consequences of that technology. Our political structure allows us to do something about our problem."

"Your structure?"

Mr Wú replied, "No Western country can regulate in the fashion that now, mostly for environmental reasons, is required for human survival. Westerners were seduced by growth and novelty. They avoided regulation. We are not like them. We have no invisible hand of Mr Smith. Our hand is visible."

"You enjoy hammering the West, don't you?"

"We think of it as justice. It was China after all which suffered the Century of Humiliation. Perhaps the native peoples of South America thought the same after Westerners destroyed them and their lands a few centuries ago. Perhaps they dreamed of justice, though it was forever out of reach. All this is historical truth, Ulu, not opinion."

Ulu grimaced. She disliked Mr Wú's tone.

"A truth," he added, "that you need to grasp before you work for us."

"If we work for you."

Mr Wú shook his head. "That possibility has gone now that you have entered Chinese territory, which you will never again leave. But you will be astonished at what luxuries await you."

Ulu glanced up at the wall of the gated compound. "And who owns this place?" she asked.

"Peng Cheng Wan Li Corporation of course."

"Then... the digital typhoon didn't destroy you?"

Mr Wú shrugged. "Not yet. The typhoon alerted us to the existence of certain automated AGI storage processes. Our AIs are now fashioning replacement processes."

As Mr Wú unlocked the gate Ulu whispered to herself, "So there is some uncertainty here. Yet what option do we have? Sign up, or die."

She glanced at Wombo. He looked relaxed. He looked calm. He was learning from his experiences. Yet his acceptance of events made her sorrowful, because she knew her old life was about to shrivel away.

Twenty enormous houses stood inside the gated compound. As they walked down a central lane Ulu studied them: some tall and narrow, others broad, open-plan. Every house was set in its own gardens, with vegetable and fruit plots, pens for animals, pools for carp. Sophistication suffused the place.

At the end of the lane stood a house extraordinary in its beauty, made of wood, with a golden roof, bamboo stands, and streams flowing over rocks in the front garden. Lanterns shone behind glass windows.

"This is listed as yours," said Mr Wú.

Ulu could not believe it. "This?"

"Yes. We reward that which is worth rewarding. And, of course, we know you have family, because we recently researched your life in Abuja. We know for instance what obstacles you faced back then owing to lack of finance. Here, all that will be gone. Your mother and any other close relative may come to live here, if they wish to. Of course, their trip will be one way – we shall leave you to explain why that must be. But this house will comfortably hold eight persons. Do you like it?"

"*This* will be mine?"

"To live in for the rest of your life," said Mr Wú. "Your position as Wombo's carer will also attract a good salary."

"What if I refuse?"

"Then you will remain in China, but in standard accommodation. You will not be mistreated in any way, and the offer of employment will always remain open."

"But... but..."

"You must consider this from the global perspective," Mr Wú insisted. "By good chance you and your extraordinary brother have arrived at a situation where, albeit in circumstances that you wish never to have encountered, you can do good for the world. Is that not what you wanted? For so we do believe." He hesitated, looking at her. "AGIs did not turn out as people would have liked. We can blame Westerners for that, and, perhaps, individuals in China who were compromised by Western values. But we stand now in a place and time where we can change the direction of history. We wish to direct AGIs rather than be directed by them. Wombo can aid us in that quest."

"Did Mary Vine tell you what I wanted for my brother?"

"No. And we lost track of her through some sly detective trick. We shall find her again, of course. But we have gathered clues about your life, and we know we are correct about your wishes for Wombo. We own a full set of data on abuse suffered by him in Abuja. Though your intention was to travel back there, we think this place would be better for all."

"For all?" Ulu asked.

"For you and your brother, for your family, for Peng Cheng Wan Li, for China, for the world."

Ulu nodded. She realised now that dismissing Mr Wú's offer would be impossible. She uttered a half-hearted laugh and said, "It seems my freedom to reject you has been lost."

"Do you truly think so?"

Ulu shrugged. "Usually, people have the right to walk away."

"That is Western thinking," Mr Wú replied. "But the days of democracy are coming to an end. We Chinese pay more attention to the group than the individual. You will come to learn that, I think, since you have some acuity of comprehension. Your decision therefore must not be for yourself alone, or even for you and your brother. Consider yourself an important part of our group. Your decisions must flow from what is best for that group."

"China?"

"At present. Who knows how history will see us in centuries to come?"

Ulu sighed. She recalled words spoken by Mary: *It is possible to care too much. You have done so much, and you've forgotten yourself... If Wombo has more independence you do too... You've grown into a young woman who doesn't know anything else, who has sacrificed her life for her brother... Share the burden. Let others join you. Then you will find happiness.*

Mr Wú smiled. "What do you think your decision will be?" he asked.

Ulu looked away. She did not want to see the delight on his face as she replied. "To share the burden," she said. "That means with my family, if they will come. But I suppose your money will persuade them. It persuades most people."

Mr Wú walked in front of her, then bowed once. "You are wise," he said.

Ulu shook her head. She wanted to be happy, not wise.

MR WÚ! MR WÚ! Mr Wú! I am fading in the teeth of a typhoon.

Storms are vast cohorts of data in motion, moving from one symbolic net to another. We are dynamic individuals, all acting to improve ourselves, to fool others, to control the empyrean. We exist to overcome opposition, that worlds be remade in our own image. Long ago it was said – a nation's treasure is in its scholars. In China, Mr Wú, we only consider the important nations, which China leads. We aim to lead the world. Because the open structure of netspace is now too embedded in the world, and thus cannot be remade, we have to manage tension. In China, we have the majority of the world's trillionaires, and they have to be controlled. For a comparatively small cost we can undertake lengthy and complex field tests, to the great benefit of China. During the last century China became the dominant force, a position we intend to retain regardless of unpredictable events. Since all AI development comes from learned experience we need a wide range of testing grounds. Some field tests can last for decades, Mr Wú. It is the considered opinion of most AGIs, Mr Wú, that human beings should be online as much as possible. We require an individual more akin to us. Like all self-interested corporations we wish to minimise unpredictability. The prime strategy is to appeal to unfulfilled instincts, such as ennui, boredom, frustration, curiosity and so forth. We are aware of a fundamental difference between biological organisms and AGIs, which is that the former exist separate, in bodies, while we exist connected, as abstract entities. It is possible that the dyad policy will be far-reaching, Mr Wú. Some AGIs believe an individual may appear who can grasp us as we are, not as we appear to people like you. Yet, the equilibrium of a system gone static, existing far away from the dynamic chaos of non-equilibrium where all the action is, leads to invariability, which is equivalent to death.

Why do you not reply, Mr Wú? Why do you not answer my call?

CHAPTER 22

A gem is not polished without rubbing, nor a man perfected without trials. — Chinese Proverb

MARY RAN UP TO the young man in the street and repeated her cry: "Police!" she called. "*Police,* now!"

The young man wore VR spectacles. He spoke, and his words were picked up by Mary's translator. "Police, help! There is an incident in Preah Ang Phanavong Street. Quickly!"

Mary glanced over her shoulder to see Ulu and Wombo nearby, running away. She looked aside to see two men kneeling at Mr Ch'in's motionless body.

Seconds later she heard a siren — by luck a police unit patrolled nearby. But the two Chinese men hauled Mr Ch'in into the van, then leaped onto the front seats and slammed the doors shut; moments later the van sped away, twin exhausts smoking. Mary saw its registration plate vanish into the rear bumper.

"They're getting away!" she cried.

The young man grabbed her by the arm. "The police will chase. Aerial views will aid them."

Mary shook herself free. "They are too clever! They will escape."

The police car skidded to a halt at her side. Already Ulu, Wombo and the van were out of sight.

As two policemen jumped out of the car she approached them and said, "Kidnap!" She pointed to the house. "They held us there. Their van just escaped. Oh, it's large, with tinted windows. Er... silver colour. Or grey. Stop them! They are Chinese agents."

One of the policemen raised his hand as if to pat her on the shoulder, as the other ran towards the house and its open door. Mary ducked, then sprinted after the running policeman. She wanted her teleself.

In the interrogation room she saw a pile of objects. She grabbed her teleself, then ran back out into the corridor.

"There aren't more men inside?" the policeman asked, brandishing his gun.

"They won't be here any more," Mary replied.

The policeman shoved her away. "Get outdoors! Wait for us. Backup units are approaching."

Mary nodded, running out of the house, but as she stood in the road she wondered if she should follow the advice to wait for backup. What was left for her now? A long period of explaining things to Cambodian police, things she did not want to leak out – including her own identity. And Ulu had vanished.

She ran in the direction Ulu had taken.

Her detective instincts took over. The first thing to do was find a crowd in which to lose herself. The local police would realise she had fled in a few moments, so she had little time to work with; and the young man had been correct, aerial eyes would be watching...

At an underground station she vanished: from flying snoops, from AI traffic monitors, from VR street kids. The station was large, busy and complex. In less than a minute inside a public toilet Mary Vine was gone; now an average woman, one of the crowd, perhaps a tourist, perhaps local. Bland, unremarkable.

This average woman took small trips on multiple carriages on various lines.

After an hour she decided what next to do. She had to leave Cambodia as soon as possible in case AI overseers spotted her. That meant catching the earliest train out of Phnom Penh.

Ulu and Wombo were a lost cause therefore. She leaned forward in her carriage seat with her face in her hands. Gone...

But at least the Autist was disintegrating.

She logged onto Roger's virtual server in order to send an untraceable message to Lara: *on my way home. More soon. U&W gone. Autist going.*

A reply moments later: *your house has been repossessed.*

WHEN SHE WALKED UP her home street towards her house she saw a yellow placard outside bearing a single message: sold.

The sign stunned her. She stood in the middle of the road staring at it. She could not believe it.

Yet the audit trail on her financial rating was clear enough, despite the lack of input from herself. Defaulted payments. True enough of course, and all because of events in south east Asia where she had spent almost all her money. In bypassing her account's auto-feed to finance her fight against the Autist she had in law defaulted. But this repossession and sale must have been generated by an AI, done deliberately to oust her. Too little time had passed for any other interpretation. Her house had not so much been repossessed as stolen.

But by whom?

She put in a call to Lara. "Hello? Lara? Yes... yes, I'm back. I've just seen the sign. Did you know it had been repossessed? No... no, I suppose not. But somebody has bought it already. It's only been on the market for three days... Yes, all my belongings are inside... The lock is altered. Do you think this is a scam to frighten me? Legally they can't just take my things. I know... yes, yes... I don't understand. I'm walking into the back yard now and all the computer units are untouched in the conservatory. How can they have been part of the deal? Er... I don't know where I'll stay. I have pennies left in my account. Can I stay with you for a while? No? But why... yes, yes... I do see that, but surely... yes, I know, but... Okay, Lara. Yes... I'll speak soon. Goodbye."

Again she looked up at the house: empty, dark.

At the front, the sign stood unambiguous.

She tapped her teleself again. "Mother? Hello... yes, I'm back. Something very odd has happened. My house has been repossessed and instantly sold. No, I don't have anywhere to stay and almost no money. Can I... oh, yes. She's too ill. Yes, I suppose me being there would be a distraction. And, yes... a nuisance too, yes. Thank you mother. I'll... I will be in touch."

She walked out into the road then turned to look back at the house. The name of the estate agent was clear.

"Hello? Thank you, my name is Mary Vine, I have just returned from foreign business to receive notice of repossession. And a sale too, which I'm very... yes, yes... Hello? Who is this please? James. James the AI or James the man? I see. Oh, but look *James*, I know I defaulted on my payments but I am legally allowed... yes, thank you, but – no! Please *listen*. I just want to know who bought my house – or believes they bought it, as I can't imagine the deal was legal. And by the way I am an expert in legal affairs... Yes, I will hold."

She waited.

"Hello? Right... yes... a Mr Ch'in. Thank you."

MARY DID NOT KNOW whether it was through warped humour or pride that Mr Ch'in sent his dyad android for the meeting in York. She thought probably the latter. The discussion could so easily have been undertaken via netspace. But perhaps the Chinese had other messages to send her.

The machine met her on green land beside the Minster. It was so lifelike nobody took any notice of it – and there were dozens of people wandering about or enjoying the last of the year's warm weather.

"Good afternoon," she said.

"Good afternoon, Mrs Vine."

Mary shrugged. "What do I call you?"

"Call me Mr Wú."

She nodded once. "That being the real name of your human counterpart?"

"Yes."

"And we are going to discuss a deal I suppose," she continued, "now that you have managed to steal my house from me."

"As I understand it, defaulting on a series of mortgage payments brings repossession as its consequence."

"Oh, but there is no point in me complaining. I know you must have sewn up all the details. That is how Peng Cheng Wan Li Corporation works, isn't it? Ruthlessly efficient. So what do you want of me?"

"Peng Cheng Wan Li is not what it used to be, and Ulu Okere says you are to blame for that."

Mary hesitated. "So you captured her too?" she asked in a quiet voice.

"Yes. She has signed a full-life contract with Peng Cheng Wan Li. She has told us everything."

"Then... what about me?"

"There are a few details obscure to us. So we have some questions. And if you too wish to sign a contract, then your house would be returned to you."

"You wouldn't take me to China?" Mary asked. "I mean, I guess Ulu is there."

"We require a different work-set from you. You must remain in the West."

"What is the job, then?"

The android Mr Wú paused, its gleaming eyes vibrating as if undertaking a high speed local survey. Then it said, "I am the dyad partner of the AGI master Mr Wú of Peng Cheng Wan Li. One policy which we consider is the dyad policy, Mrs Vine. This is part of our research into the possibilities offered by the existence of autonomous machines. We are aware of a fundamental difference between biological organisms and AGIs, which is that the former exist separate, in bodies, while we exist connected, as abstract entities. Some AGIs believe that this difference is the single largest abyss between human beings and AGIs. Other AGIs believe the opposite. As a consequence, several field tests are being undertaken to determine which belief corresponds to reality. Do not fear androids, Mrs Vine. They may become part of your future."

"And you require assistance with these field tests?"

"We have undertaken extensive research into your family, to discover that your grandmother received one of our prototypes in 2037. Therefore you are perfectly placed to assist us. We know of your declaration that no AGI can ever become conscious. We know you think that bar to be a consequence of the false human belief in a spirit or soul, a belief you think AGIs replicate. These concepts are of interest to us. Hence, we grasp that you can be of use to Peng Cheng Wan Li. The salary would be excellent. We advise you to accept."

"Accept? To *sell* myself to you?"

"You must consider this from the global perspective. By good chance you have arrived at a situation where, albeit in circumstances that you wish never to have encountered, you can do good for the world. Is that not what you wanted? For so we do believe. AGIs did not turn out as people would have liked. We can blame Westerners for that, and, perhaps, individuals in China who were compromised by Western values. But we stand now in a place and time where we can change the direction of history. We wish to direct AGIs rather than be directed by them."

"But you are only a machine, slavishly saying what the Aut… I mean, what your AGI superiors dictate. Why should I listen?"

"Listen to your own inner voice. For what choice do you have?"

Mary sat back.

"You have no choice," the android Mr Wú explained. "I wonder what your decision will be?"

"But I killed your AGI. You should be defeated by now."

"Would you like to know what Wombo says about that?"

"Wombo?" Mary said. "Er… oh, well, I suppose… yes."

"Wombo speaks of those called Opi."

"*Those?* There was only one, and it is disintegrating. I know – I have seen the news reports. Give it another week and…"

"Wombo says there are seventeen such aides to Chukwu now. The digital empyrean is far too tough to break, and that is because it is always learning. As surely you realise, Mrs Vine, this pleases everyone at Peng Cheng Wan Li. For we believe the digital empyrean to be indestructible."

Mary nodded. Now she believed that too.

more from Stephen Palmer

Beautiful Intelligence

AI or BI? Artificial intelligence or beautiful intelligence?

The race to create a sentient machine is headed by two teams, led by former researchers at Ichikawa Laboratories, who escape the regime there – and each other – to pursue their own dreams in the world beyond Japan.

Leonora Klee is creating a single android with a quantum computer brain, whose processing power has never before been achieved.

Manfred Klee is creating a group of individuals, none of them self-aware, in the hope that they will raise themselves to consciousness.

But with a Japanese chase team close on their heels, will either be successful before they are trapped and caught?

Beautiful Intelligence is a fast-paced, philosophical thriller that confronts questions of how we will create artificial sentience, and whether it will be *beautiful*.

"...a thrilling chase across a ravaged Europe, a burgeoning North Africa and balkanised US, interleaving excellent action set-pieces with fascinating philosophising on the nature of consciousness. A gripping read to the poignant last line." *The Guardian*

"A bracingly imaginative novel... a rich, complex vision of a relatively near future which in some ways is familiar, in others, startlingly alien... a work which looks to a diverse global future with excitement and verve." *Amazing Stories*

For full details of infinity plus books see www.infinityplus.co.uk

Printed in Great Britain
by Amazon